SONG OF THE DAMNED

Recent Titles by Sarah Rayne from Severn House

The Phineas Fox Mysteries

DEATH NOTES
CHORD OF EVIL
SONG OF THE DAMNED

The Nell West and Michael Flint Series

PROPERTY OF A LADY
THE SIN EATER
THE SILENCE
THE WHISPERING
DEADLIGHT HALL
THE BELL TOWER

SONG OF THE DAMNED

Sarah Rayne

severn
House

This first world edition published 2018
in Great Britain and the USA by
SEVERN HOUSE PUBLISHERS LTD of
Eardley House, 4 Uxbridge Street, London W8 7SY
Trade paperback edition first published
in Great Britain and the USA 2018 by
SEVERN HOUSE PUBLISHERS LTD

Copyright © 2018 by Sarah Rayne.

British Library Cataloguing in Publication Data
A CIP catalogue record for this title is available from the British Library.

ISBN-13: 978-0-7278-8814-3 (cased)
ISBN-13: 978-1-84751-944-3 (trade paper)
ISBN-13: 978-1-78010-996-1 (e-book)

All Severn House titles are printed on acid-free paper.

Severn House Publishers support the Forest Stewardship Council™ [FSC™],
the leading international forest certification organisation.
All our titles that are printed on FSC certified paper carry the FSC logo.

Typeset by Palimpsest Book Production Ltd.,
Falkirk, Stirlingshire, Scotland.
Printed and bound in Great Britain by
TJ International, Padstow, Cornwall.

ONE

PRESS RELEASE
SCHOOL'S BICENTENARY CELEBRATIONS TO
HONOUR 200-YEAR-OLD MYSTERY
Celebrations for Cresacre School's bicentenary this
autumn will include a tribute to the 200-year-old mystery
which forms part of its history.

At the end of the eighteenth century, a small group of
nuns vanished from what was then Cresacre Convent.

'Their fate was never known, but their memory has
lived on,' said Bicentenary Events Organizer, Arabella
Tallis. 'We shall be commemorating them in various ways
during the bicentenary of what is now a lively, modern,
co-educational school.'

Further details of the bicentenary and the planned
events are available from Arabella Tallis, or from the
school's headteacher, Miss Harriet Madeley. See below for
contact details.

'It was all going so well,' said Harriet Madeley, crossly re-arranging objects on her desk, as if doing so might restore symmetry to recent events as well. 'And I have to say Arabella Tallis is doing a splendid job. I expect you remember Arabella?' she said to her deputy head.

'I do indeed,' said the deputy head. 'An intelligent girl, although inclined to be somewhat disruptive. Wasn't she the one who caused all that damage to the science lab?'

'It wasn't deliberate. She got the proportions wrong in an experiment,' said Miss Madeley. 'And she was very apologetic about it; in fact she organized the repainting of the wall by her whole class. She did some work for a PR firm in London recently, which is why I got in touch with her.'

'If she's doing such a good job, what's gone wrong?' asked Dilys Davy.

'That annoying girl, Olivia Tulliver, has come scuttling out of the woodwork,' said Harriet. 'That's what's gone wrong.'

'Can't we scuttle her back?'

'I'm not sure. She wants us to stage that opera old Gustav Tulliver wrote when he was headteacher here.'

'It's bound to be terrible,' said Dilys. 'Gustav could no more write an opera than I could.'

'Yes, but Olivia's made the point that her uncle was an eminent man who made the school his life's work and that putting on his opera would be a fitting tribute,' said Harriet. 'She says it's got a great deal of local content – she even says it draws on that old tale about the nuns.'

'Which version of the legend does she say Gustav used?' asked Dilys Davy.

'The one suggesting they sneaked across to France and got mixed up in the French Revolution.'

'Oh, that one. It's one of the more believable theories, of course,' said Dilys. 'Can't we tell Olivia that the programme's already fixed, and we can't change it?'

'The trouble is,' said Harriet, slowly, 'that she's threatening – no, that's too strong a word – she's implying that unless there's this – well, tribute to Gustav – the funds for the Tulliver Scholarship might be reduced.'

'Blackmail.'

'No, she's been clever with her wording.'

'But if the funds are reduced, it could end the scholarship,' said Dilys. 'Which would be a very great pity.'

'Yes. Or at the very least it could cut down the numbers. I don't know how much say Olivia actually has – there's something in the trust deed about one seat on the board always being reserved for someone bearing the family name. When Gustav died, Olivia automatically inherited his seat, aged just twenty-one. I could ask to see the original trust deed, but I don't want to get into a row – or even a difficult discussion – with the trustees. If it got out, it might mean bad publicity for the school.'

'We've weathered worse than that,' said Dilys, briskly. 'There've never been any real scandals here – well, apart from the odd outbreak of smoking cannabis in the bedrooms, and the occasional under-age pregnancy. A bit of porn downloaded onto some of the computers – that's usually the boys. Little groups sneaking out to the Black Boar on Saturday nights.'

'And that girl who disappeared for a couple of long weekends, then came back looking smug,' said Harriet.

'Oh, yes, I'd forgotten about her.'

'But,' said Harriet, 'those are things that happen in most schools nowadays. And I've had an idea for diluting Olivia.'

'Yes?'

'I told Arabella a bit about it last night on the phone – she remembers Olivia – and she knows someone she thinks might be able to help us rule Gustav's opera politely out of court.'

'Arabella always did know all kinds of people. I don't know that I'd automatically trust them.'

'His name's Phineas Fox, and Arabella thinks Olivia might respect his opinion. I looked him up, and he seems to be quite well known in music circles. Rather highly regarded, it seems.'

'I suppose he's a boyfriend of Arabella's, is he? Well, from what I recall of Arabella, he's bound to be. Is he a musician?'

'He's a music historian and researcher. He's worked for the BBC a few times, apparently.'

Dilys observed that this was not necessarily a recommendation.

'No, but he's had a couple of quite scholarly books published – there was one on a famous nineteenth-century Russian violinist that came out earlier this year. I remember reading a very good review in the *Times Literary Supplement*. It said it was masterly and insightful.'

'I don't know about being scholarly and masterly and insightful,' said Dilys, 'but if Phineas Fox can solve this without bloodshed, he'll need to be a cross between Henry Kissinger and King Solomon.'

'If he's going to be Solomon, does that make Arabella Tallis the Queen of Sheba?'

'Hardly,' said Dilys, caustically. 'The Queen of Sheba was fabulously wealthy, wasn't she, and from all I hear, Arabella is permanently on the verge of bankruptcy.'

'Olivia's always wanted that opera to be staged,' said Harriet, thoughtfully.

'It is just about the mysterious nuns, is it?'

'As far as I know. Why?'

'I was just wondering whether Gustav found out something about the Ginevra legend and wrote a few scenes about it.'

Ginevra . . .

It was as if a breath of cold air had gusted softly into the warm, book-lined study.

Then Harriet said: 'I shouldn't think so. I daresay there might once have been someone called Ginevra at Cresacre, but I've never given those tales much credence, and I wouldn't think Gustav did, either. I've always believed the students seized a fragment of an old piece of gossip and embroidered it out of all proportion.'

'Each new intake adding another chapter,' nodded Dilys.

'Well, teenagers do love gothic, all the way back to *Frankenstein* and *The Monk*. And all the way down to the make-up and the clothes.'

'It's the name. That's what got to the artless little grubs in the first place. They think it's romantic,' said Dilys. 'They think of someone called Ginevra as young and beautiful. Soulful eyes and skimpy garments, with her ghost drifting around the west wing on moonless nights, waiting to be whisked away by a sexy hero-villain.'

'Coming from a pragmatic mathematician, that's very nearly lyrical.'

'I don't know about lyrical; it's my belief that if Ginevra existed at all, she was probably some rapacious old harridan who deserved her fate. Whatever that fate was, because it varies depending on which year of students you listen to.'

'What none of them ever get round to explaining, though,' said Harriet, thoughtfully, 'is what Ginevra might have done to deserve that fate.'

Diary entry, 1790s

I wish I knew what I have done to deserve what has happened to me. That is a self-centred way to think, but I am thinking it.

It was, of course, the height of folly to have come here. We all knew – of course we did! – of the brutality taking place in France. But what happened in Cresacre was so huge, so potentially dangerous, that we made the decision to leave. To preserve the secret for as long as possible.

I hear that other prisoners are permitted to walk in what is called the prisoners' gallery during the day, and it is only in the hour before sunset that they are returned to their cells. I hope so much that the others who braved this journey with me are permitted that small indulgence, but it makes me even more fearful for my own situation. I am kept in this room – to call it a dungeon does not overstate the case – and the door is uncompromisingly locked all the time.

There is a sliver of window – with bars, of course – and during the day some light trickles in. But once night falls, it's like being inside John Milton's description of the forlorn Stygian cave. My father used to read short passages from Milton to the servants at home, particularly from *Paradise Lost*, with the aim of reminding them of the likely fate awaiting sinners. If he heard that the scullery maids had stolen out to the local inn, he was apt to dwell on the description of how, when Night darkened the Streets, then wandered forth the sons of Belial, 'flown with insolence and wine'. It was a lively image, but it did not make any difference to the scullery maids, who had no idea who Belial was, let alone his sons, and who carried on visiting the inn anyway.

I would welcome some company in this place; in fact I would welcome Belial's entire family of sons, no matter how wine-flown and insolent they might be. I even think I would willingly barter my soul to them if they would free me . . .

But of course I would not barter my soul to the devil. I have crossed out that last sentence, although I am not sure why I feel the need to do that. It's not as if Belial or any of his offspring are likely to be peering over my shoulder, reading what I am writing, nodding gleefully and rubbing their scaly hands in anticipation.

It's probably the height of folly to be writing all this, but I brought with me the diary I had begun to write at home. I have several of the charcoal sticks I always used for writing, and I'm finding it a comfort to record my thoughts and fears.

Last night I wondered whether I might barter not my soul for my freedom, but my body. With whom, though? There's

certainly no point in considering any of the uniformed officials
who occasionally peer through the grille in the door of this cell.
They never come inside anyway. But what about one of the
turnkeys . . .?

These are shockingly sinful thoughts to have. But I believe
I would do it. Would any of the men be amenable, though? I
am aware that I must look appalling by this time – dirty and
ragged and unkempt.

Even so . . .

Even so, may God forgive me, I believe I may end in trying.
To get out of this place I'd endeavour to barter – a polite word
for a very impolite activity – with one of them; with any of
them; with all of them, if necessary!

TWO

Phineas Fox had been rather pleased to receive a politely friendly letter from Harriet Madeley, which made flattering reference to Phin's work in general and his recent book in particular, and went on to say that the school hoped he might be able to help them with a rather delicate and slightly unusual matter regarding their bicentenary celebrations.

'I believe Arabella Tallis has already mentioned the bicentenary to you,' she said, 'and that you're intending to attend a couple of the events with her. We're very pleased about that and I'm looking forward to meeting you.'

Arabella's invitation had actually been an off-hand question as to whether Phin minded donning a black tie and dinner jacket for a few hours, because if he could manage it she would quite like to appear on his arm for the last night of the celebrations, on account of it being sure to impress people who had previously disapproved of her.

Miss Madeley's letter did not sound disapproving of Arabella at all. She said Arabella was making a great success of everything, but that the school might need Phin's professional expertise. 'A question of your professional opinion on a locally written opera,' she wrote. 'We think it makes use of one of our Cresacre legends, so we don't want to turn it down out of hand. If there's any chance that you could find time to visit us, it would be greatly appreciated.'

A fee had been mentioned at that point, which Phin had initially tried to refuse. However, Miss Madeley said, very firmly, that they would not expect someone of Mr Fox's standing to provide his services free, and Phin had remembered that the quarterly service charge was due on his flat, and had accepted. It was, it appeared, half-term the following week, which would be a good time for a visit.

He was intrigued by the 'delicate and slightly unusual situation',

and as he and Arabella set off for Cresacre, he listened with
enjoyment to Arabella's description of the school's legend.

'Vanished nuns,' she said, gleefully. 'It's beautifully spooky-
sounding, isn't it? We used to have great fun with it. Most
people think the nuns got tangled up in the French Revolution
– it was around that time – but there are wilder versions.
Abduction by aliens, and mass murder by a local madman.
Somebody even once put forward an idea about a plot to assas-
sinate the Pope. Occasionally we'd pick up an unexpected fact,
as if edges of the truth were poking out in places, like bunches
of pilchards' heads glaring up out of the pastry in that Cornish
dish – starry-gaze pie, do I mean?'

'No idea,' said Phin, who was enjoying these images, but
was trying to decide whether to take the turning that would
mean doing battle with the M5 or whether to keep on slower,
but less busy roads.

'And I wrote a one-act play about it for an end-of-term
concert. Very gothic. I used a marvellous old-school legend
about someone called Ginevra – I'll tell you about that later.
But she's supposed to have been part of the mystery of the nuns
and she's always fascinated everyone. In the play, I was the
grey lady, trying to find a fourth to make up a bridge table at
the Old Rectory. One of the boys was a beheaded Cavalier
looking for Oliver Cromwell.'

'I didn't realize the school was mixed sex,' said Phin, who
had decided in favour of the motorway, and had now merged
with the lemming-stream of vehicles. 'And don't raise your
eyebrows like that: you know what I mean by mixed sex.'

'I'm still waiting to find that out,' said Arabella, demurely.
'I don't know much about this delicate situation Hats talked
about, though. Except that it's all to do with a former pupil
called Olivia Tulliver, who's threatening to put a dent in the
Tulliver Scholarship dosh if we don't stage her uncle's opera.'

'Could she do that?'

'No idea. I didn't know her very well – she was a couple of
years below me. She lives in a cottage in the school grounds,
and she doesn't seem to have had much of a life since Gustav
died. I'll show you the cottage – it's very old. The school's old,
as well – there are still bits of the convent in the school grounds,

and even traces of the ancient monastery. We can walk amidst the ruins like drifting figures from somebody's elegy in a churchyard.'

'I'll happily drift around churchyards with you – and, actually, churches are good places to disinter legends anyway—'

'Oh, God, you're such a pragmatist,' said Arabella, tempering this remark by reaching for Phin's left hand, turning it over, and tracing a light pattern on his palm with her fingertip.

Phin resolutely kept his eyes on the road, and managed to continue steering the car reasonably efficiently. After a moment, he said, 'If you start talking about ghosts, I warn you, I'll make you get out and walk the rest of the way.'

'In these shoes? Oh, my dear,' said Arabella, with the grin that made her look like a dishevelled elf. She was wearing a scarlet silk shirt over jeans, which looked very nice indeed, together with a floppy-brimmed hat which looked terrible, and which had turned out to obscure the driving mirror, and had had to be thrown onto the back seat.

'Actually,' she said, 'we've got a really good choral concert on one of the nights – a guest soloist and that conductor who leads youth orchestras. Hats Madeley is secretly hoping you might get a mention of that onto one of those late-night TV arts programmes. The kind you probably get asked to speak on all the time, I expect.'

Phin hastily disclaimed ever having been asked to speak on a late-night TV programme of any kind. 'I'm a lowly researcher. A back-room boy.'

'Even so, it . . . Oh, we're coming up to the exit for Cresacre.'

'This one?'

'No, it's the next one – oh, wait, no, it should have been that one after all. Sorry, Phin. Can you turn round? No, of course you can't, not on a motorway.'

As Phin resigned himself to driving on to the next exit, Arabella said, with what sounded like studied casualness, 'Did you say you booked two rooms at the Black Boar? Not that it matters either way, of course.'

In an expressionless voice, Phin said, 'I booked two rooms, as it happens.'

'Ah.'

She appeared to wait for more, so Phin said, 'I asked if they could be next door to one another, though.'

'Did you really?' said Arabella. Phin could not decide if she was relieved or pleased or amused.

Local people often told Olivia how marvellous it must be to live in a cottage with such ancient associations. Romantic and historic, they said.

Infanger Cottage might be historic, but it was far from romantic. It was damp and dingy. The roof leaked, the plumbing was erratic, woodworm had chewed up half the timbers, and the window frames were so badly fitting that they rattled when you walked across the rooms. It would cost a king's ransom to put the cottage to rights and Olivia did not have a king's ransom. Even if she did, she could never risk anyone coming inside the cottage and uncovering its past.

What she did have, though, was her uncle's opera. *The Martyrs*. The work he had vowed would one day take them out of the narrow confines of Cresacre, and into more exciting worlds. Olivia had believed him. After he died she had vowed that she would do everything to get his opera recognized. And the school bicentenary could have been the very chance she had hoped for. But *The Martyrs* had been ignored. Instead, there was to be a choral concert by the school choir, a murder-mystery evening in the library, and a gala supper on the last night. There were also what were referred to as fun-type auctions, with local celebrities. The only local celebrities Olivia knew of were the mayor, who was a grasping local businessman with a hard-faced wife, Firkin the builder, the DJ from the local radio station who drank like a fish, and the vicar.

Had nobody remembered that Gustav, a former head-teacher at Cresacre School, no less, had taken the Cresacre legend, spent years researching it, and had created an entire opera around it?

Olivia was so angry she had violent indigestion for the whole of one night, and, next morning, she had written to Harriet Madeley. She'd spent a long time composing the letter, but in the end she had got it right. She had found a book called *A Layman's Guide to the Law*, and it had been very useful.

'Dear Miss Madeley', she had written, 'Recently there have been concerns as to whether the present level of funding for the Tulliver Scholarship can continue. This is due largely to the fact that investments no longer yield the profits they once did.'

Olivia did not really understand the financial side of the scholarship, but everyone talked about low interest rates and investments going down. As well as *A Layman's Guide to the Law* she had a book called *Everyman's Accounting*, which she had bought when she started attending trust meetings. It had enabled her to occasionally ask a polite question at the meetings. She thought the board members – most of whom were quite elderly – probably told one another that it was very nice to see young Miss Tulliver taking her board duties so seriously.

But you did not need *Everyman's Accounting* to understand that actually the scholarship's funds were very healthy. Miss Madeley would not know that, though, and the elderly board members would not tell her. Most of them lived quite far away, and the chairman was a solicitor from Worcester. They usually had the meetings at his office; Olivia caught a train there and back, with a taxi to and from the station. She was able to claim travelling expenses. After her first meeting, a man who was the trust's secretary had taken her for a drink at a nearby hotel so that he could explain a bit more about the trust's workings to her. He was staying overnight there, and he had suggested they have their drink in his bedroom, which would be more private. It turned out that he did not want to talk about the trust at all, but after a few drinks Olivia had gone to bed with him because he was the secretary and important, and you never knew where a romantic encounter like this might lead. But he had not phoned her afterwards, and at the next meeting he had ignored her and talked loudly about his wife and two children, which was the first time they had been mentioned. Olivia had felt ashamed and embarrassed, but fortunately the man resigned as secretary afterwards, and she never saw him again.

The real punch of her letter came at the end.

'There is a glimmer of hope for the school, however', Olivia had written. 'It has been suggested that if you could demonstrate its loyalty and commitment, and help perpetuate the Tulliver name, that might go a considerable way towards securing and ensuring future scholarship allotment to the school.

'This could probably be done in several ways, but it would certainly strike a very favourable note with the board if the school were to stage the work written by a member of the Tulliver family – in other words, my late uncle, Gustav Tulliver's, opera, *The Martyrs*, as part of the bicentenary celebrations. As a descendant of the original Tulliver who created the scholarship, and as an eminent man who made the school his life's work, this would be seen as a fitting tribute. The work itself contains considerable local content so it would be of immense interest, and, if a professional company cannot be engaged, there are several excellent amateur opera groups that would surely jump at such an opportunity.

'With kind regards to you and to Miss Davy,

'Olivia Tulliver'.

After she had posted the letter, she sat for a long time in her uncle's study, his books and research notes all around her. The memories scudded through her mind until she could almost see his gaunt figure at the piano, the dim light falling across his face, highlighting the sunken cheekbones. If she listened intently, she could nearly hear his voice.

'*Sing for me . . . Sing as if the music's being torn from your throat and your lungs . . .*' And then, '*Because this is Ginevra's song,*' he had said.

Ginevra. Even now, the name sent a chill through Olivia. Ginevra was at the heart of the Cresacre legend. No one knew for certain what had happened to her – or even if she had ever actually existed. But Olivia knew. She had known for a long time, and she had also known for a long time that she would do anything to keep the truth about Ginevra secret. She would cheat, lie, steal, if necessary. Even commit murder? said a small, sly voice inside her mind.

Murder. The word lingered, and the memories clawed upwards again. *Murder . . .* There was certainly a murder at the heart of all this. A very strange and macabre murder that had its roots in Infanger Cottage.

Diary entry, 1790s

Last night I tried to shut out the fear by playing music in my mind. When I was a child at home, the house would be filled with music – I grew up with it.

I started calmly enough with a Mozart Allegretto, diligently finding every note on an imaginary keyboard, painstakingly trying to get every note right.

It did not work, of course. Because, by some devil-inspired means, a deeper memory slithered inside Mozart's beautiful patterns.

The forbidden music. The ancient plainchant that my grandmother forbade my cousins and I, as children, to play or sing. It was very old, she said, rocking in her chair, looking at us. Really *very* old indeed. It had been handed down within our family over many generations, and it was believed to have macabre associations. No, she did not know exactly what they were – she did not wish to know – but she had been told by her own grandmother, who had been told by hers, that the music had a very dark root.

We would never destroy it, though, said my grandmother firmly, for it was a fragment of history – of religious history – and such shreds of the past should be preserved. 'There may come a time when it can be used for good,' she had said. 'But it must not be allowed into the light. It should be kept in the darkness from which it came.'

To tell a child not to do something is to ignite its curiosity. One afternoon, when I was staying at my grandmother's house, together with the dearest of all my cousins, we stole quietly into the music room. It was a rain-swept afternoon, dark and dismal, and everyone was somewhere else. And we found the music and we played it on grandmother's pianoforte. I did not play it very well or very accurately, but my cousin, who was older and had learned music for longer, achieved what she thought was a fair mastery.

Huddled in this dimness now and writing this, thanking

God's mercy that I am allowed a tallow candle for an hour or so once darkness falls, I am remembering that afternoon, and a tiny part of me is wondering whether on that day my cousin and I disturbed something that would have been better left alone. I cannot dismiss the memory of the music, or the image of my cousin seated at the pianoforte. It's printed on my mind – a small scene; one of those secret, forbidden times that children sometimes share and that the grown-ups never find out about. That small, elfin-faced girl – who my father once said had music in her bones – is long since dead, may God grant her soul rest. But while I have that image of her, she will never really die for me.

The memory of that music will never die, either. I have left traces of it behind – deliberately so. My grandmother wanted it to remain undisturbed in its own darkness, but I think she was wrong.

THREE

Cresacre, 1794

Gina Chandos had enjoyed the evening, but now it was over she was starting to feel nervous about what might lie ahead. It was a pleasant, rather excited nervousness, though.

She had played the pianoforte for her parents' guests. She had worn her lavender gown, and she had played a Mozart Allegretto. She thought it was not being vain to believe that she had played quite well.

He had thought so. He had watched her from across the room, with the smile that made his eyes slant under the dark brows, and that gave him the look of a mischievous devil.

Cesare Chimaera. That was the name by which he had been known to his adoring audiences, to members of the royal houses where he had performed and sung during the glittering years of his fame – to the people who had entertained him in their palazzos and splendid villas. That name had been blazoned across posters outside theatres and opera houses, usually with the words, 'Famous,' and, 'Spectacular,' and, 'Supremely gifted'. Gina knew all this, not only because Chimaera had told her, but also because he had shown her some of the posters which he had brought with him to England.

'Where,' he had said to her, 'I was forced to flee on account of jealous, small-minded enemies. There were people in Rome and in Milan – underlings, footling persons – who were envious.' A sigh. 'And so,' said Chimaera, sorrowfully, 'I am reduced to earning a living as a music master. But I do not give him any thought at all, that person. Instead, you and I shall give our thoughts to Mozart.'

It was clear that neither of Gina's parents had heard any of the rumours about Chimaera. Gina only knew them herself because people who came to Chandos House murmured to one another that they wondered at John Chandos allowing such a man in the house, they did really. Chandos was a justice of the peace, and normally he had an unerring eye for a rogue.

Chimaera was not a rogue, of course, and Gina tried not to listen too much to the spiteful talk. Mother always said eaves-dropping was unladylike and unmannerly, and Father Joachim had preached about that only two Sundays ago, Mother said. *Also take no heed unto all words that are spoken; lest thou hear thy servant curse thee.* Ecclesiastes, said Mother, and Gina would do well to take note of it.

Gina did try to take note of it, and she always tried to follow Father Joachim's teachings, because he was a man of God, and he had known her since she was born; in fact he had been there at the birth. He sometimes talked about that; about how he had waited just outside what he referred to as the birthing chamber, and how it had been a dark, rainy night, and they had feared for Gina's life.

'But I fought to keep your soul safe,' he said, which Gina always found smothering and embarrassing. Still, you had to treat a person who had fought for your soul with respect, so she was always careful to be polite to Father Joachim.

It was impossible to avoid knowing the effect Chimaera had on the servants. Within two days of his arrival, they were giggling and nudging one another, saying he was a one, that Signor Chimaera, you didn't know where to look for some of the things he said, not that you could always understand it all, him being foreign. As for making so bold as to tidy his bedroom alone – well, best not risk that, they said, giggling all over again.

Gina did not understand all the servants' innuendoes, but she understood that Chimaera, who dressed modestly in black, but whose smile was not modest at all, was considered to be what was called a rake. A seducer.

Father would know about rakes and seducers, of course, but Mother would not. To Mother, what happened between men and women within marriage was a distasteful necessity. She had not told Gina precisely what it was, except to say that it was something that had to be endured occasionally. This conver-sation had taken place on Gina's sixteenth birthday, when various social events were being planned, mostly with the aim of securing a good marriage. Most ladies, Mother said, found it possible to politely discourage that side of marriage, and real ladies avoided it as often as was consistent with a happy union. Gina, not entirely following, had felt, vaguely, that this outlook might be a pity for Father.

It was shocking that Chimaera might be a seducer, but what was even more shocking was that after the evening at which she had played the Mozart, he walked lightly along the hall outside her bedroom. She sat up in bed, her heart pounding with a mixture of fear and shameful hope. There was a tap on the door, and he was there. He stood for a moment in the doorway, then came across to the bed and sat down, reaching for her hand. He was wearing a brocade robe, and he said she must not be alarmed or call for help; it was simply that she was the most beautiful, most desirable creature he had ever seen, and he was smitten with a deep and helpless love for her. And since he believed his love might be returned, said Chimaera, he was here tonight so they might explore together how that love could be made into reality.

What was most shocking of all was that Gina had realized she was not going to scream for help, and nor was she going to order him to leave. The fear had completely vanished, and she was tremendously excited and also extremely curious. Ahead of her might be the thing people whispered and giggled and blushed about.

She listened enrapt as he quoted to her from the world's great poets – although he told her that all the poetry in the world could not really convey how passionately he wanted to make her his own love in truth. She was so beautiful, so petite and dainty. A little, perfect, porcelain doll. Somehow, between a Shakespearean speech and a quote from Boccaccio's avowal that an arrow had sped to his heart at first seeing her, he got into bed with her.

At first she was worried in case anyone came in, but Chimaera said there was no cause for concern, because he had locked the door, having stolen a key from the housemaid's cupboard downstairs earlier on. If Gina was still anxious, he would wedge a chair under the door handle, and she had his promise that if

anyone tried to get in he would climb out through the window. 'I
will risk life and limb to preserve your good reputation with
your parents, you see,' he said. Then, his eyes narrowing
with amusement, he said, 'But I do not promise to preserve
your innocence tonight. You will not mind that?'

'I don't know,' said Gina, who had already decided to throw
every trace of innocence out of the window.

'Shall we find out?' he said, and he began to kiss her and
to slide his hands under her nightgown. Until now, Gina had
only had two very mild flirtations with sons of family friends
and had once almost been kissed in the orchard by a good-
looking gardener who had stood so close to her that she could
smell the fresh clean sweat on his body. Chimaera did not taste
of apples or of sweat; he tasted of perfume, as if he might
have dabbed some onto his skin. This ought to have been
pleasant, but at such close quarters Gina found it a bit sickly.
But she was glad that she had not chosen to have her hair
wound in soft rags to curl it tonight, and that it could stream
unchecked over her bare shoulders for Chimaera to bury his
face in.

Between kissing her, he said he understood for the first time
the sentiments of the Renaissance poet, Petrarch, who had
talked of being disarmed by emotion. But when he took off his
brocade robe, even to Gina who had only the sketchiest knowledge of the details of a gentleman's body, it was immediately clear
that he was far from disarmed. It was not immediately apparent,
though, how things would proceed, but Chimaera would know
what to do.

At some point her own nightgown was also discarded, after
which came a series of caresses, starting with gentle ones, then
increasing in intensity and urgency. Chimaera was murmuring
something about crescendos and accelerando, which sounded
romantic and passionate, but which did not tell Gina a great
deal about whether she was doing the right things by way of
response. It was difficult to know what you should touch and
what you should not, and whether you should move or remain
still. Fortunately, Chimaera did not seem to expect her to do
very much at all, and it began to seem that love-making was
a slightly confused and rather frantic activity, involving a good

deal of pushing and encouragement about relaxing from Chimaera, and then a whooshing rush of something giving way which brought a swift, secret pain, and was followed by a pounding thrusting into the most secret part of Gina's body. By this time Chimaera was gasping and crying out, causing Gina to panic again in case anyone heard him shouting things like, '*Mio Dio, io vengo.*' And, '*Sto esplodendo.*' She did not like to ask him to be quieter, however.

Then he suddenly drove frantically against her, which made her wince, gave the loudest cry yet, then pulled back from her, almost as if something had scalded him, and fell against her shoulder. This, it appeared, concluded things. Chimaera lay against her shoulder, panting and gasping, his hair silky against her bare shoulders. This felt good. It also meant he was no longer breathing the scent into her face.

He lifted himself on one elbow and looked down at her, smiling. Gina hoped she might look like a painting of one of those semi-clad ladies reclining on a couch, love-flushed and slumberous, dark hair spread picturesquely over the pillows. There had been one in father's library until mother pronounced it improper and consigned it to somebody's dower house where it would not be seen.

'The cabaletta, it was too sudden, too soon for you?' said Chimaera, a tiny frown creasing his brow. 'But it was because I am so much overwhelmed with the passion, you understand.'

Gina had no idea what he meant, but she vaguely recalled that cabaletta was the concluding, very rapid, part of an operatic aria. Since he seemed anxious, she said, 'Oh no, not in the least.'

He beamed at her. 'You are a delight,' he said. 'And next time we shall do even better.' He got out of the bed, regained the brocade robe, and went from the room. Gina noticed with relief that he paused in the open doorway, looking both ways along the corridor to make sure no one was prowling around before going out.

It was certainly good to know that she had actually done the forbidden bedroom thing – the act about which people wrote magical poetry and composed marvellous music, and in whose name they sometimes even died. Tidying the bed before composing herself for sleep, she was determined not to feel a bit let down, or to think that surely there ought to be more to it than this.

Probably it did not matter that there was an uncomfortable patch of wet stickiness between her thighs, and that it had dripped down onto the sheets. She did not know if it had come from him or from her, and it had seemed rude to try to do anything about it while he was still lying half on top of her. She would try to mop it up with a handkerchief, and hope the housemaid did not notice in the morning.

Chimaera had enjoyed making his stealthy way through the darkened Chandos House to the bedchamber of the *bella* Gina, so dainty and sweet, like a little porcelain doll.

It had been a gratifyingly theatrical thing to do; it pleased his thespian soul, and it made him feel as if he had stepped into a scene from the *commedia dell'arte* – Harlequin making a prancing, goatish way to Columbine's bedchamber, Scaramouche serenading Isabella. Not that Chimaera would be goatish – he had often been described as remarkably graceful, in fact – but he could probably permit himself a brief prance.

He did not intend to live in Chandos House for very long, but while he was here he would make sure he did not risk provoking the ire of Sir John Chandos, who was wealthy and powerful. And a man was entitled to look after an only daughter, he supposed. A priest, also, was entitled to guard the morals of his flock, and Chimaera had already noticed Father Joachim's watchful eye on him. But then Father Joachim was apparently partly French, so allowances would have to be made, what with all the trouble presently going on in that country. Barbaric happenings, which were enough to make a man feel shudderingly ill.

And for the moment Chandos House was pleasant enough, and John Chandos and the whey-faced priest could be kept at bay. Gina was entrancing. A total innocent, of course, and it was very reprehensible to have seduced her, but Chimaera was a passionate man and he could not fight his emotions. The seduction had gone very well, and he had prepared a few odds and ends of poetry to quote to her. It was always a good idea to have such things to hand on these occasions, and it was not necessary to know the entire sonnet or poem, which was fortunate, because Chimaera's memory for such things was not always reliable. Once – he thought it was when he had been with Juliette, unless it had been Renata – he had completely dried halfway through a passionate speech, and had been laughed at with the utmost heartlessness. It had wounded his vanity and made it impossible for him to perform as he would have wished; well, it had made it impossible for him to perform at all that night, in fact. Juliette – yes, it had been Juliette, he was sure of it now – had called him a very hurtful name as a result.

As Chimaera got back into his own bed, he thought it was a pity that there had been that slightly brisk culmination to the very pleasant interlude with Gina Chandos this evening. But he found it was often the case, and a man was at the mercy of his emotions. He would not waste any time worrying about it.

Cresacre might be small and remote, but it was several thousand miles away from footling villainous persons who had chased him from the theatre, brandishing stage daggers, and shouting insults about unprincipled seducers of people's sisters and wives and daughters, and shrieking to the world that Cesare Chimaera was no better than a three-inch fool who often could not fly his flag above half-mast.

Remembering all this, Chimaera was disposed to like Chandos House and Cresacre's rural remoteness. When you lived in cities for so long, you forgot about places like this.

Diary entry, 1790s

When you have lived outside of the world for so long, you forget that places like this exist.

I am trying very hard not to listen to the echoes, though, for in this grim old prison house, they would be terrible things to hear. But I cannot help being aware that this is a place where many people have awaited an inevitable and a brutal death – brave souls, prepared to die fighting for justice and against injustice, speaking out with passion to defend their beliefs. They faced their deaths unflinchingly – or did they? Several times I have wondered whether, if I were to press my ear to the stones of these walls, I would hear the echoes more clearly, and whether they might be cries not of bravery and defiance, but of despair – of people whose courage deserted them at the end, and pleaded for their lives.

What is even stranger, though, is that I believe I am also picking up echoes of my own past. Does that mean I am remembering my grandmother's tales about this place? Might it even mean I am sensing my death – that some instinct is making me look back on my life and bid farewell to it? No. I would rather return to my mad plan of bartering with one of the turnkeys.

The candle is guttering and I cannot write much more tonight. But as the shadows strengthen, so do the doubts as to whether my plan is possible or advisable or, indeed, likely to succeed. There's also the question of whether I can actually remember how to indicate that kind of interest – or invitation – to a man. It has been so long . . .

It feels as if it was in another life – a life I have tried to forget – that I experienced that instant understanding and recognition. The poets write and the music-makers sing and the painters portray love at first sight. Cynics scoff, but it happened to me. From 'our first strange and fatal interview . . .' How does the rest of Donne's poem go? 'By all desires which thereof did ensue . . .'

Those desires ensued in an inevitable culmination very soon after he and I met. It was the sweetest sin I have ever committed. That candlelit night in the large, soft bed . . . That was the first time. There were others, of course. A rainstorm and the two of us sheltering in a deserted cottage, our clothes drenched and clinging to our bodies – both of us clinging to one another . . . And there was a sunlit afternoon in the old orchard . . . If I close my eyes I can see how the dappled sunlight came through the trees that day, and I can taste his mouth – warm and soft and infinitely loving, scented with the apples we had taken from the trees and eaten as we walked between them. After that time there were grass stains on my skirt, and I had to think of a story to explain how they came to be there. Lies on top of that other sin . . . The tally of my sins is really quite high.

It's infinitely sweet to look back on those memories now, though.

This morning I was tempted to tear out the page on which I had set down those shameful, wonderful memories, and burn it in the candle flame tonight. But I shall not. If anyone were to try to read it – if anyone cared enough to do so – it no longer matters who knows what I did all those years ago. But those events that came later – ah, yes, they must remain buried deep for as long as I live.

Now that it is morning, I am facing my fears. I knew – of course I knew – that coming to France would be dangerous. I did not know, though, that we would find such turmoil and intolerance.

I knew about the decadence and the selfish extravagance of the Bourbon royal family, but I did not know the extent to which the Catholic Church was being subordinated and suppressed here – or that much of their land has been confiscated, and that monastic vows have been banned. Members of the clergy– monks and priests and nuns – are being forced to take the oath of allegiance, and if they refuse . . .

If they present me with their oath, what shall I do?

FOUR

'When you live in London,' said Phin, as they drove through villages, and on towards the market town of Cresacre itself, 'you forget about places like this. Villages and farms and fields. I'm glad I came. Is that the school over there?'

'Yes, it's that smudge on the horizon. You can just make out the high gates from here. I don't know if they were left over from when the place was a convent, but they were certainly made use of in my day to keep the wayward maidens safely cloistered. Not that they did,' said Arabella. 'We used to climb over them at weekends, and sneak out to the fleshpots of the Black Boar, and Saturday night discos. You bundled your disco outfit into your gym bag, hoicked it over the wall, and got changed in the bus shelter.'

'All good fifth-form stuff.'

'Well, it was hardly Enid Blyton, but it wasn't too outrageously sinful either, although there was one girl in my year who vanished for at least two long weekends. The police were called in and searches were made, but she turned up each time. After the second time, the police got a bit annoyed.'

'Did Miss Madeley know about the fleshpots of the Black Boar and all the rest of it?'

'I suspect so. She was very severe on the girl who went off on her own – actually I think she ended up under threat of expulsion. On the whole, though, providing nobody came home stoned on booze or drugs, or got pregnant or caught some frightful antisocial disease, Hats was actually quite tolerant. On Sundays we had to troop primly to church, which wasn't as grim as it might have been, on account of being able to eye the sons of local farmers and landowners. You wouldn't believe the assignations that got made in the vestry or the organ loft.'

'Oh, yes I would,' said Phin, grinning.

'It sounds very demure and Jane Austen, doesn't it, but it wasn't so bad.'

'I'll bet you made sure it wasn't. Is this the church of the organ-loft-assignation fame?' said Phin, as a small church with a broach spire and an old lychgate came into view on their right.

'The very one. D'you want to have a quick look round now? We aren't expected at the school until late afternoon, and we said we'd wander amidst gravestones like refugees from an elegy, didn't we?'

'Yes, let's take a look now,' said Phin, pleased at the suggestion, and pulling into the side of the road.

St Chad's Church was cool and dim, and there was a faint scent of old wood, polish, and damp. There were stone floors, rows of pews, several stained-glass windows, dimmed with age, and three or four glum stone effigies that stared with sightless disapproval upon the world.

'That brass plaque is dedicated to the famous Tulliver,' said Arabella.

'The one whose scholarship is causing all this trouble?'

'Yes. He had rather advanced ideas about education for his time. He thought all children should be given the chance to learn. All very worthy. As a matter of fact, I was a Tulliver scholar.' She glanced at him with a hint of defiance, as if she felt it incumbent on her to establish that she had not been a privileged rich pupil of privileged rich parents.

'I'm impressed.'

'Oh, I only got it because I wore very solemn spectacles for the exam and pinned my hair up so I looked scholarly and earnest,' said Arabella. 'You do know I'm not in the least scholarly or earnest, don't you?'

She moved away before Phin could answer, and he continued his journey of exploration. St Chad's was traditional and conventional, exactly what might be expected from an old church on the outskirts of a cluster of villages and market towns, and it all pleased Phin greatly. There was a poster advertising a Bach recital in a couple of days' time, and he thought he would suggest to Arabella that they stay on for that. He walked slowly around, interested in inscriptions on wall panels, many of which commemorated members of a family called Chandos.

As he walked back down the central nave towards the partly open door, sunlight filtered through a stained-glass window, and it was as if the vivid colours had suddenly bled into the mellow golden sunshine. Phin stopped, his eyes on the oak of the door. The blurred crimson and purple and indigo shards lay across the carved figures, making them look eerily alive, and as the carving came into sharp clarity, the old church seemed to blur, its outlines almost shivering. The air seemed to thrum faintly, as if a beseeching echo lingered.

Phin took a deep breath, then went firmly past the glowing reflections of the window. The colours faded, and the door was just a thick slab of carved wood, softly lit by ordinary late-afternoon sunlight. But the carving on its surface . . .

He knelt down to examine the carving more closely. Arabella's voice, seeming to come from a long way off, said, 'Phin? Is something wrong?'

It took a massive effort to pull his mind back to his surroundings, but Phin heard himself saying, in a relatively normal voice, 'No, nothing's wrong at all.' He stood up, brushing down his jeans. All around him the church was quiet and dim. Or was it so quiet?

'It's shockingly dusty in here, isn't it?' said Arabella. Phin glanced at her, and thought she was looking at him a bit quizzically. But she only said, 'Still, as long as it isn't bone-dust remnants from some grisly underground tomb, a few sprinklings don't matter. What's that line about antique footprints in the dust of time – I expect I've got that wrong, though. Let's check in at the Black Boar, shall we, then head out to the groves of academe.'

'Good idea,' said Phin. 'Yes, let's go – it's quite cold in here, isn't it?'

As they walked out into the afternoon sunlight, he pushed away the impression that the faint echo followed him.

Phin liked the Black Boar. It had low ceilings and beams, and bowls of bronze chrysanthemums on the reception desk. The floors all creaked and there was a faint, pleasing scent of old timbers and wood smoke.

'It's very old,' said Arabella, as Phin carried her case into her bedroom and set it down. 'But they haven't chintzed it up too much.' She stepped out of her shoes, leaving them by the door, which was a habit with her. Phin had already twice tripped over a pair of boots left askew inside the front door of her Pimlico flat.

'The car park down there was once the yard they used for mail coaches,' she said, kneeling on the window seat and looking down. 'You can still see the outline of the entrance where the coaches used to drive in. I've been trying to find a link between this place and the school. I couldn't find a link to the convent era, of course, because the nuns wouldn't have been likely to nip down to the taproom to get a jug of beer, or munch pork scratchings while they watched the darts tournament, would they? Still, it's nice to be staying here.' She turned to look at him. Her hair, which she had tied back for the journey, was escaping its clips, and Phin reached out and wound one of the tendrils around his fingers. It felt like silk.

'You have nice hands,' said Arabella, softly. She put up one of her own hands, curving it around Phin's fingers

'Do I?'

'Yes, and—'

'And,' said Phin, regretfully releasing Arabella's hand and the strand of hair, 'there's only half an hour before we're due at the school, and I suppose I should wash off that antique dust from the church beforehand.'

'I suppose you should. Pity.' Arabella considered her reflection in the wardrobe mirror. 'Will I look all right for Hats Madeley in that pinstripe suit I packed? I do want to look businesslike.'

'I shouldn't think you could get much more businesslike than navy pinstripe,' said Phin.

'I don't want to look boring. What are you laughing at?'

'The idea of you ever being boring.'

The sartorial aspect of the forthcoming meeting had not occurred to Phin, but now that it had been mentioned, he thought he could stay in the brown cord jacket he had worn for travelling, but that he had better change the jeans for plain trousers, because it felt wrong to be entering a headteacher's lair wearing denim.

'Exactly right,' said Arabella approvingly, when he rejoined her. 'Suitably academic but not stuffy. I am pleased about you, you know. Did I ever say that?'

'No.'

'Well, I'll say it now. Or is that being shockingly forward?'

'You can be as shocking as you want,' said Phin.

But, even with Arabella's light-hearted company, as they drove to Cresacre School, Phin was unable to entirely shake off the impression of that faint beseeching echo that had brushed across his mind inside the church. It was when you saw the carving, said a small voice. That's when it happened – you know quite well that it was.

Arabella was enthusiastically explaining to him various landmarks along the way.

'That's the road that used to go up to an old mansion, only it was abandoned and left to crumble for years, and nobody ever managed to trace the owner. Then it got bombed to smithereens during World War Two, and not even the National Trust could put it together again. We used to be taken on nature rambles out there – it's rather a sad old place. Overgrown grass and parts of walls where the house used to be. Every few years somebody makes a new effort at tracing the descendants or tries to find deeds or something, because they keep thinking they ought to flatten the ground and build on it. They never do, though.'

'Who did own it?' Phin thought he was finally managing to push aside the strange emotion he had experienced inside the church. 'Some local squire, would it have been?'

'Probably. Whoever he was, I don't think anyone remembers much about him. I expect he was one of those purple-faced eighteenth-century gentlemen who drank too much port and had a habit of smacking village wenches on the rump and making bawdy suggestions to them. I wrote an essay about it once for a local history competition, but they said it was defamatory.'

'Probably the old squire broke his neck while he was out hunting,' said Phin.

'And left a welter of debts and land muddle and scandalous speculations?'

'Along with a sprinkling of bastards,' agreed Phin. 'Might it have been the Chandos family who lived there? The church was peppered with their name on memorial stones and things. Chandos House? Chandos Manor?'

'True, O King. And Chandos House does ring a faint bell, although it sounds somehow respectable and I would have liked a randy old squire rollicking through hayfields, but . . . Oh, this is the turning to the school.'

'Nice old trees,' said Phin, turning into the school's driveway.

'Yes. The stones along the side of the road are from the original monastery. They've been there ever since anyone can remember. When I was here I tried to organize a midnight feast round them to see if the ghosts of the monks could be tempted out. But somebody blew the gaff on us and Hats ordered all the good little prefects to patrol the corridors.'

'You weren't a prefect?' said Phin, already knowing the answer.

'Oh, please,' said Arabella, with a giggle. 'Miss Davy, the deputy head, once said I was the rotten apple in the barrel. That kind of comment could scar a person for life, couldn't it? Oh, and just down there – d'you see? – that windy little track with all the trees that looks as if it might lead to the witch's cottage from *Hansel and Gretel* . . . That leads to Infanger Cottage. It isn't a witch's cottage, of course, and the only witch at Cresacre was Dilys Davy. There's something about the cottage standing on land that was ruled by one of those really ancient laws. Something that goes back to Magna Carta, I think. That's where Olivia Tulliver lives. The story is that it was given to old Gustav as a bribe to get him out of the school. And now,' said Arabella, 'here's the school itself.'

Phin supposed he had expected Cresacre School to be imposing and also slightly awe-inspiring. Imposing it certainly was, but very far from awe-inspiring.

'Not what you were expecting?' said Arabella.

'No. It's friendlier. More welcoming than I thought it would be.'

'That's probably the lingering ghosts. Genevra's ghost, even.'

'I'm becoming increasingly curious about Genevra.'

'It's most likely only the ghosts of these nuns or even the monks.'

There were not, of course, any visible traces of the priory, but it was certainly possible to pick out remnants of the former convent. Within the weathered grey stones of Cresacre School were alcoves and niches, which could once have housed statues. Over the main door, what must be the school crest was carved into the stonework. The windows were tall and wide, so that it was easy to imagine sunlight pouring through, falling across heads diligently, or resignedly, or even rebelliously bent over books. Or to visualize crustings of snow on the glass, but with the warm school scents of radiators and games rooms and energy inside.

Phin said, 'Were you happy here?'

'Actually, I was. It's not the thing to say that, of course.'

'Of course not.'

'You? At your school?'

He hesitated, then said, 'Eventually I was. I didn't fit in for a long time.' He did not say he had escaped from the feeling of isolation into the world of music. 'I was hopeless at games,' he said, 'and I liked English lit and history. You weren't supposed to like things like that. But then—'

'But then?'

'One rainy afternoon, a football match was cancelled and the whole school was incarcerated in the gym. We were supposed to be writing essays about something boring, but there was a piano in the corner . . .' He grinned reminiscently. 'I was still a novice pianist, really – I'm not actually much more than that now – but on that afternoon I bashed out everything from souped-up Beethoven to jazz and then raunchy rock stuff for them. I played partly from memory and partly by ear, and in the end everyone was shouting the choruses of every song we knew, and I don't think anyone noticed all the wrong notes.'

'And they loved it,' said Arabella, delightedly. 'Of course they did. You've never played for me,' she said, suddenly.

'We've never been anywhere where there's a piano.'

'There's one in there,' she said, nodding in the direction of the school. 'Two, in fact. Assembly hall and a rehearsal room. At least, there used to be. And I shouldn't be surprised if there isn't even an organ in a cellar somewhere, with a disfigured hunchback in attendance, bashing out Lloyd Webber chords at midnight. Will you play something for me while we're here? When no one else is around, I mean.'

'Well, I might.' Phin found himself smiling as he considered the possibilities of this. Astonishingly, he could see himself playing one of the slushily romantic songs of the 1930s and 1940s to Arabella. Maybe that all-time great love song, 'The Way You Look Tonight', which Fred Astaire had sung in a film. Astaire had not had the finest voice in the world, but he had sold the song's sentiments brilliantly.

He put the car into gear and drove up to the front of Cresacre School.

More traces of the school's former incarnation were visible inside, as well. Some of the wood panelling might well date back to the nuns' time, although now it formed a background for framed lists of the school's head girls and head boys, and the niches held sports trophies.

There was the vague impression that the school was uneasy with the students all away for half-term, and that it did not quite know what to do with itself. But someone who seemed to be an admin assistant came out to meet them in the hall, and pointed the way to Harriet Madeley's private apartment on the top floor.

'I've never climbed to these dizzy heights,' observed Arabella. 'It's a bit of a breathless ascent, isn't it?'

Miss Madeley's sitting room had views over fields and the tops of trees, and within the trees Phin glimpsed the roofline of a small building that he thought must be Infanger Cottage.

'We're very grateful to you for coming all this way to help us,' said Miss Madeley, shaking hands and studying Phin with interest. Her hair was dark with grey streaks and she had a long upper lip, both of which gave her the appearance of a tabby cat. Phin was not fooled into thinking she had a tabby cat's personality, however.

A gruff-voiced, thin-nosed lady was introduced as Dilys Davy, the deputy head. Arabella's witch, thought Phin. Miss Davy accorded Phin a brisk, dry handshake, but he noticed that the nod she gave Arabella was somewhat perfunctory.

'It's a delicate situation we have here,' said Harriet Madeley, seating herself behind a small leather-topped desk and fixing Phin with a very straight look. 'I gave you a summary of it in my email, didn't I, Mr Fox? Olivia Tulliver wants the school to stage her uncle's opera.'

'And if you don't agree,' said Phin, 'she could cut off funds for your scholarship.' He met the steady regard levelly, and saw a small nod, as if his statement had been accepted. 'I have to ask this, though – is it out of the question to actually stage the opera? Because as something written by a local man and making use of local history—'

'It seems a logical idea?'

'At first look, yes. And there'd be time for a local company to get it together, presumably?'

'Oh, yes.'

'Have either of you read Tulliver's opera?' asked Phin. 'Sorry, that sounds like a misprint of *Gulliver's Travels*.'

'No, we haven't. But we do know that it's been turned down by more theatrical agents and music directors than you can imagine,' said Harriet.

'The word is that the rejections were pretty scathing,' said Dilys Davy. 'Even then, we might have considered it more seriously, except—'

'Except that we believe a number of those rejections more or less said it was a straight steal from another opera. Something called *Dialogues of the Carmelites* by Francis Poulenc. D'you know it?'

'Yes. Not well, but I do know it. It's the story of a group of Carmelite nuns who were beheaded during the French Revolution. It's very dark – very moving, though. Has *The Martyrs* got French Revolution content?'

'We think so.'

'We think Gustav depicts it as the reason for the Cresacre nuns' disappearance. The solution to the old mystery. And,' said Harriet, fairly, 'it is a reasonable theory.'

'Yes, I see. Are you worried about copyright infringement if you put it on?'

'A bit,' said Miss Davy. 'I looked up copyright law, and it lasts for seventy years from the death of the author – that's correct, isn't it?'

'In a general way, yes. And Poulenc died in 1963,' said Phin, thoughtfully. 'Which means his work would still be within copyright.' He frowned, then said, 'But if you did put it on, even if it's a blatant copy, it would be a small audience – a semi-private event.' Dilys was handing round cups of tea from a tray on a side table, and as Phin accepted a cup, he said, thoughtfully, 'On the other hand, it wouldn't be the first time that *Dialogues des Carmélites* attracted a copyright squabble. Poulenc wrote it from an unfilmed screenplay, and I think there were some arguments about who owned what. I'd have to look it up, but I think it was all amicably resolved. Poulenc did make a good many acknowledgements to his sources, though.'

'Which means copyright on that particular opera could still be a bit sensitive.'

'It might. What would you like me to do? Read the opera to see if it's worth staging? Compare it with Poulenc's work to see if it's a copy? If it is, you could use the copyright concern for declining it politely.'

'Exactly,' said Harriet. 'But I'm not going to enter into any arguments about Gustav's opera without being very sure of my ground.'

Phin thought it would be a brave person indeed who engaged in battle with Miss Madeley. He reminded himself that he did not need to be in the least bit intimidated by academic tabby cats, and that he was here by her explicit invitation.

'Tell me about Olivia Tulliver,' he said. 'Does she have a job of any kind?'

'Not in any conventional sense,' said Harriet. 'I believe Gustav left a bit of money.'

'She got tangled up with one or two men who made inroads into it, though,' put in Dilys.

'I heard that,' said Arabella. 'Didn't she do an Open University course at some stage?'

'Yes, and I think she managed to get on to the panel for marking exam papers for them. I shouldn't think that would bring much money in, but presumably it'd bring a bit. She'll get a small fee from the Tulliver Scholarship trust.'

'I suppose,' said Phin, 'that she'll let me see her uncle's opera?'

'Mr Fox, Olivia Tulliver would walk across burning coals barefoot to get someone like you interested in that opera. I'll give you her phone number – she won't answer the phone to me.'

Phin took the number. 'I'm assuming the opera will be in the form of the book – that's the actual storyline of the opera,' he said, in case they were not familiar with the term, 'and that there'll be a music score with it.'

'I should think so. Whatever else Gustav Tulliver was or wasn't, he was a musician, and he actually did quite a lot of good work here on that side of things. He was the one who created the school choir, in fact.'

'Would it be all right if I played some of the music here? I'd only need a piano for an hour or two. To get an idea of the music.'

'Of course you can use the piano,' said Harriet. 'There's one in the assembly hall, and another in the small rehearsal room. Arabella can show you.'

Phin resolutely quenched images of Fred Astaire and 'The Way You Look Tonight', and set down his teacup with determination. What he was about to say next might be greeted with incredulity and even hostility. But he could not quench the memory of that small, disturbing echo he had sensed in the church. So, despite being aware of a jab of apprehension, he said, 'Miss Madeley – Miss Davy – I don't know how relevant this is going to be, but I believe there might be a strand to your legend that no one has picked up. I don't know if it links up to the vanished nuns or Ginevra – Arabella's told me a bit about Ginevra,' he said, as the two women looked up sharply. 'Or if it's something else altogether, but—'

'Go on.'

'This afternoon, on the way here, I found a carving in St Chad's Church that depicts something very macabre – something that's also very rarely found in this country,' said Phin. He was aware of Arabella looking at him quizzically. 'I'm almost certain that it depicts an extremely old ritual – a musical ritual, in fact, that was banned by the church several hundred years ago.'

'What kind of ritual? I hope,' said Harriet, rather severely, 'that you aren't about to present us with evidence of satanic goings-on at St Chad's.'

'No, although heaven knows how a carving of it found its

way to Cresacre. But possibly the present vicar and his predecessors wouldn't have recognized it for what it is—'

'What is it?'

Phin said, 'It's a ritual that was followed in twelfth- and thirteenth-century France – occasionally in parts of this country as well. It was known as the Lemurrer – from the French *l'emmurer.*'

Harriet Madeley said, '*L'emmurer*? To immure?'

'Yes. Specifically,' said Phin, 'to wall up. That's what the Lemurrer was. The walling up of someone.'

There was a brief silence.

'Walled up *alive*?' said Miss Madeley, at last.

'I'm afraid so. While it was being done, the Lemurrer would be sung – complete with gestures – while the bricks were being laid in place.'

The three women stared at him in horror. 'That's one of the grisliest things I've ever heard,' said Harriet.

'Yes. But,' said Phin, 'it looks as if it was done in Cresacre. Has there ever been any suggestion that the nuns from Cresacre Convent – or that anyone local – might have been—'

'Walled up? I've never heard of it,' said Harriet, slowly. 'And I've been here for a fair number of years now, and it's the kind of place where memories are long, as the novelists like to say. Dilys?'

'I've definitely never heard of it,' said Dilys, managing to convey disapproval.

Harriet turned back to Phin. 'I'll have a look at the carving as soon as I can,' she said. 'But it's in the church. Why are you connecting it to the legend?'

'Because,' said Phin, 'this school – these buildings – used to be the convent of those vanished nuns.' He paused, and then said, slowly, 'And because you've got the same carving here. There's an image of the Lemurrer in this room. It's over the fireplace. I'm looking straight at it now.'

FIVE

A second round of tea had been organized, and a couple of table lamps had been carried across and tilted, so that their light shone directly onto the fireplace carving. 'It's smaller than the one in the church, of course,' said Phin. 'But it's perfectly clear.'

'I've never paid it much attention,' said Harriet. 'Except to occasionally think it collects dust. I thought it was simply a series of figures for decoration.'

'They sort of cavort all the way along the mantelpiece, don't they?' said Arabella, kneeling in front of the fire, occasionally putting out the tip of a finger to trace the carved figures.

'I've seen illustrations of medieval woodcuts of the Lemurrer,' said Phin, 'and the hand gestures are unmistakable – very distinctive. I'll see if I can find any of them online while I'm here and compare them, but I'm sure these – and the one in St Chad's – are the same. The liturgy itself is long since lost, of course.' He knelt down by Arabella. 'Here and also here,' he said, 'you can see that the actions of the figures is almost like modern bricklayers.'

'No hard hats, but I do see it,' said Arabella.

'The movements progress, don't they?' said Harriet. 'Like the figures in Egyptian tomb carvings. The bricklaying starts here – on the left . . .' She indicated.

'And as you go along the row of figures,' said Phin, 'you see the wall's a little higher with each figure. Until at the end there's just the blank wall.'

'Wasn't walling up a fate reserved for ladies found screwing where they shouldn't?'

It had probably been inevitable that if this question was going to be asked, it would be Arabella who would ask it. Phin waited with interest for the response.

Harriet Madeley said, deadpan, 'Clearly we never did teach you how to turn an elegant phrase, did we, Arabella?'

Arabella grinned and Miss Davy said, 'I believe you're right, though, Arabella. And I think it's correct to say it was especially licentious nuns who received that particular punishment.' Her tone suggested she considered it had probably served the culprits right. 'I've never heard of the Lemurrer, though,' she said. 'I don't mean I'm questioning your judgement or your knowledge, Mr Fox.'

'It's quite an obscure ritual,' said Phin, annoyed to hear the slight placatory note in his voice. 'And it's so far back, a lot of the details are lost. It was mostly practised in France, but it does seem to have trickled into this country here and there – I'd hazard a guess that it was brought over by the various migrations and invasions.'

'The Norman Conquest wasn't all good for everyone,' observed Miss Davy.

'Well, no. In the end,' said Phin, 'the early Church banned the Lemurrer, of course. I don't know that they exactly objected to punishing wayward nuns, but they didn't like the fact that the Lemurrer had so many elements of pre-Christian and pagan ritual. That figure there . . .' He indicated the carving. 'He looks as if he might be making the Sign of the Cross.'

Miss Madeley said, 'You're saying the Lemurrer might once have been celebrated – is that the right word? – in Cresacre? That someone might have been walled up alive? In the church? In this building?'

'I don't know. But it's unusual to find a carving portraying it,' said Phin. 'Especially in a church, and then repeated here.'

'There's never been any record or any suggestion of that kind of ritual being performed here,' said Dilys. 'Although I suppose that doesn't mean it didn't happen. Only that it was never found out.'

'But somebody did find out,' pointed out Phin. 'Or somebody already knew about it. And whoever it was, blazoned it across the church door, and had the carving repeated in this room.'

'Maybe the waller-upper did the blazoning,' said Arabella, eagerly. 'As a bizarre kind of confession. People flaunt the most astonishing things, don't they? You've only got to think about the stuff that's posted on social media – or Jack the Ripper sending letters saying how much he enjoyed eating his victims' kidneys. And they say murderers are usually massively vain and they want to tell the world what they've done; although, of course, the waller-upper might have been mortified with guilt afterwards, and spent the rest of his life trying to wash off the mortar and brick dust in nightmares, like Lady Macbeth, wailing that all the perfumes of Arabia could never—'

'You really should have taken to writing gothic horror, Arabella,' said Miss Davy, repressively.

Phin said, 'I wonder if we could find out who commissioned the church carving. Miss Davy, you said you'd made a study of local history. Would you know local people, and church authorities?'

'Well, it's only a very amateurish study, but I could ask around.' She looked pleased to be asked.

'The Chandos family is mentioned a few times in the church,' said Phin. 'Could they have been involved? Who were they?'

'They've long since died out,' said Dilys. 'I don't think they contributed much to the area, and they aren't really part of any local lore.'

'Always a pity when that happens,' said Harriet. 'But there it is; the old order changes, giving way to the new. More tea, Mr Fox?'

Olivia had watched the post every morning since sending her letter to Harriet Madeley. Harriet might not write, of course. She might phone or she might even call at the cottage. So after posting the letter, Olivia cleaned the cottage as thoroughly as its decrepit condition would allow, checking the phone after vacuuming the rooms, in case it had rung and she had not heard it.

Then, on the third morning, a letter in a thick white envelope came through the door, and Olivia seized it eagerly. This would be it – she might have known that Harriet Madeley would stick to the old-fashioned methods. She tore the envelope open, and drew out the contents.

It was not from Harriet Madeley. It was from the local county council – the planning department – and it was an offer of purchase for Infanger Cottage by them. Olivia read the letter with incredulity and mounting fear. The fear threatened to swamp her, making it difficult to take the letter's contents in, but she forced herself to read the letter again, because clearly she had misunderstood.

She had not misunderstood at all. The council said they would be widening the road that ran alongside the school's eastern boundaries, and a slip road would have to be created. That slip road would slice right across the patch of land on which the cottage stood, hence the request to buy the cottage and the land. Miss Tulliver was pleased to dial the contact number provided on the letter to arrange a convenient time for a surveyor to call to make an appraisal of the property. After that, a fair and honest offer would be made.

Olivia was shaking violently, as if she was about to have flu. It had never occurred to her that anything like this would ever happen – all those sayings about an Englishman's home being his castle. Now, it seemed, council departments could arrogantly demand you sold your house to them.

She was not, of course, going to agree to sell the cottage, because she would never sell it to anyone, and this was something that could be dealt with. All she had to do was phone the writer of the letter, saying she was not prepared to sell. She would make the phone call saying this, and she would send a letter confirming it. She began to feel better. Then she read the second page of the letter.

'We hereby give notice that if a reasonable and fair purchase cannot be agreed, it may be necessary to invoke a Compulsory Purchase Order, in accordance with the Acquisition of Land Act of 1981. Under such circumstances, please be assured that a fair market value would be paid for the property and compensation would be arranged to cover moving, legal, and other related expenses.

'Notes regarding CPO procedure are enclosed for your guidance, together with the description of the property that has been prepared, and a map delineating the course the new road and slip road will take.'

Olivia unfolded the enclosed notes, horror sweeping over her. The CPO notes were full of phrases about subordinate legislation and Highways Acts and something called a 'compelling case in the public interest'. This was utter nonsense. There was nothing compelling about any of this, and it was not in anybody's interest to buy and tear down this cottage.

For a wild moment or two she actually wondered if she could accept. To be given money – money that might include compensation – that would enable her to buy a house somewhere else . . . To find a normal life away from Cresacre and all the smothering memories . . .

But even as the thoughts were forming, a sly soft voice in her mind was saying, Stupid! Of course you can't sell this cottage! You can't ever sell it and you can't ever leave it – you know that, you've known it for ten years. You can't leave because of Ginevra.

She reached for the phone to tell the officious, snooping, meddling council that Infanger Cottage was not, and never would be, available for purchase, not if they threatened her with fifty compulsory purchase orders.

It was a week – a whole week! – before Olivia heard from the school about *The Martyrs*.

Miss Madeley did not phone or call, she sent a polite letter, thanking Olivia for writing to her, and saying they had a music researcher and critic visiting the school during half-term week. She was going to talk to him about Olivia's suggestion of staging *The Martyrs*, and she would be in touch again as soon as possible. The music researcher, whose name was Phineas Fox, might also want to talk to Olivia himself, so Miss Madeley hoped that could be arranged.

She added that they were also hoping Mr Fox could stir up some publicity for them – for the choral concert in particular. She signed her letter with kindest regards, which Olivia thought they both knew was a lie.

The letter was an insult. Olivia did not need the opinion of some pretentious music expert on *The Martyrs*. She knew everything there was to know about it, and if either Harriet Madeley or this Phineas Fox phoned her, she would not answer the phone.

She was, in fact, starting to be very nervous of answering the phone or the door, because she did not trust the council planning people not to sneak their way inside, brandishing legal notices.

The woman she had spoken to at the planning office had seemed to find it difficult to believe that anyone would actually want to continue living in a damp, mouldering cottage in the woods, and asked whether she had seen the new houses being built on what had been Cresacre Marsh out near Little Minching. Beautiful little semis, they were – ever so smart. Two bedrooms, and a garage and central heating. A shopping precinct within walking distance – a school, as well . . . Oh, Miss Tulliver did not have children? Still, you never knew, did you? As an apparent afterthought, she said, of course, it must be marvellous to live in such an historic old place as Miss Tulliver did.

Olivia did not say that the cottage's age was a nuisance. It even caused people to take advantage of you. The previous year she had been taken out to dinner by the local radio presenter. She had been flattered and excited at the thought of going out with somebody who worked in radio – she had even thought he might know people who could help with getting her uncle's opera staged.

But it transpired that he had only taken her out because he was compiling a programme about curious local buildings, and he thought he might use Infanger Cottage. He attempted to have sex with her in the taxi on the way home, failed embarrassingly, and was sick all over the back seat and Olivia's best coat. The taxi driver sent Olivia the bill for the cleaning, and said he knew all about the kind of females who screwed drunken men in taxis, and please not to use his taxi service again. The coat was declared by the dry-cleaner's to be beyond redemption.

Olivia had been almost fifteen when she and Gustav had gone to live at Infanger Cottage.

It stood on the edge of the Cresacre grounds, quite near to where the old Chandos mansion had once been, although nobody nowadays was sure about the exact boundaries, because the Chandos family had left things in a shocking muddle, and there were pieces of ground for which the ownership was uncertain. Infanger Cottage stood on one of those pieces of ground.

But after a great deal of correspondence, and a number of explorations of shelves and forgotten corners of solicitors' offices, it was agreed that the cottage and its bit of garden could be regarded as falling within the school's environs. This was a decision that suited the school, because it meant Infanger was in their gift. It meant they could add it to the bribe they had put together to get rid of Gustav Tulliver. It also meant anyone who had had the smallest claim on the place no longer needed to worry about maintaining it.

A wodge of papers tied with green tape was handed over. Gustav frowned over them for a while, then said he was now the owner of Infanger Cottage. He had been the victim of a conspiracy, though, he said, but it did not matter because he was going to compose a marvellous opera. He had had the idea in his mind for a very long time, and now he had the time to actually write the story – the libretto, it was called; Olivia might as well learn the right term. His eyes had burned with fervour, and patches of colour showed on his usually sallow cheeks.

After living in the headteacher's large apartment at the top of the school, Infanger seemed small and dingy. Gustav said it might be a bit run-down, but the governors had at least put in a workable bathroom and kitchen. He and Olivia had souls above crumbling plasterwork and scarred floorboards, and oil stoves that smelt like stale chip-fat when they got hot. As for Olivia's schooling, she could become a day-girl at Cresacre and return to the cottage each evening to cook supper. He would be able to get a reduction in the fees.

The Martyrs ate into those years. Gustav bought a second-hand upright piano, which he said did not have a very good tone, but which was all they could afford because of the pittance of a pension grudgingly awarded by the miserly governors.

Infanger Cottage was surrounded by trees, and the rooms were quite dark, even in the daytime. Olivia thought they could put a light over the door – a lantern-type, which would be welcoming and warm, but Gustav said they had not the money to be spending on such things, and it would be a drain on the electricity, and they did not especially want to welcome people, because they did not want folk tramping in and out. He needed quiet and solitude for his work. He refused to have high-wattage light bulbs anywhere; it would create too much light, which would cause the past to shy away into obscurity, and he could not have that, not when he was trying to create scenes set in the 1790s. You had to immerse yourself in the time you were writing about, and dimness and shadows helped. Soon after they moved in, he ordered the local builder, B. Firkin & Sons, *est. 1790*, to put up shelves in his study, so that he could have all his books and his research notes around him. This made that room even darker.

After the move, she heard people in the village saying it was a bit of a comedown for the Tulliver family to end up in a cottage. A strange old place it was, as well. Dark and gloomy, and you could not get a car along the narrow footpath that was its only means of access. It was a mite eerie, as well.

Trimming trees was a costly exercise, but Olivia got used to the dim footpath each evening. She did not find the cottage particularly eerie, and Gustav was so deeply immersed in *The Martyrs* he would not have noticed if half a dozen ghosts clanked along the path every night and gibbered at all the windows.

Not that there were ghosts, of course. At least, not at the beginning.

Olivia had helped with the research for *The Martyrs*. She was not especially knowledgeable about music, but she liked being in the school choir, and last December they had sung Handel's 'Hallelujah Chorus' from *The Messiah* as part of their end-of-term festivities, and the church's Advent services. The entire school choir had joined forces with the church's own choir; everyone had thought it had gone very well, and Miss Madeley had been very pleased indeed. It had been a bit of a let-down when Gustav said he had found most of the singing a bit shrill, and the alto very nearly tinny. He also said he considered it irreverent that one of the girls had had a sneezing fit halfway through. Sneezes could be suppressed, he said severely, and the sneezer had even seemed to deliberately time the sneezes so that they punctuated the most energetic of *Hallelujah, Hallelujah, Hall-e-lu-jah*. Olivia did not say the sneezer had been Arabella Tallis, who had been hoping the recital would end early because she had a date with the organist's son afterwards. She did not think that even Arabella could time sneezes quite so precisely, either.

But she liked helping with *The Martyrs*. She had even

visualized Gustav dedicating it to her. 'To my dear niece, Olivia, for her invaluable and devoted help'. Something like that, anyway, because it was the kind of thing people did write as a dedication. If so, she would be immortalized. In years to come, people might even refer to her as 'Tulliver's Muse', in the way they talked about Shakespeare's Dark Lady.

So when, one night after supper, Gustav suddenly said, 'I need to hear a particular aria from *The Martyrs* sung aloud by a young soprano voice,' Olivia's heart jumped with delight. He would be remembering her successes in the school choir, of course (always allowing for the sneezing episode during *The Messiah*), and he wanted her to sing part of his work now.

Then he said, 'I thought about that girl who was in the Advent performance with you. I marked her particularly. I don't remember her from my time, but she was in the front row of the choir, at the centre. Long brown hair.'

Sick disappointment swept over Olivia, and it was a moment before she could identify the girl. Then she said, 'I think it was Imogen Amberton. She's new since your time.'

'Imogen, is it? Ah. Is she by way of being a friend of yours?'

Olivia did not really have friends, and since becoming a day-girl she was not part of the evening life of the school – the little get-togethers in bedrooms, or in the TV room, or the giggling discussions in the girls' common room, where home-work was supposed to be done, but where it was more likely to hear discussions about boyfriends or make-up, and which often ended up spilling over into the boys' common room anyway. Segregation at Cresacre was a fluid affair, except for the bedroom floors, where it was strictly enforced – although not always as strictly as Miss Madeley thought.

But she said, 'Imogen's two or three years older than me, so I don't know her very well. I think this is her last term.' She did not, in fact, like Imogen very much, but she did not say so. She would like her even less if she was going to sing part of her uncle's opera. She said, 'She was under threat of expulsion last term.'

'Why?'

'Well, um, she went off by herself for a few days. Actually, she did the same thing just after Christmas. That was almost a

week. The police were called both times.' The police and Miss
Madeley had been furious when on both occasions Imogen
had turned up of her own accord. The rumour was that she had
spent the time with a boyfriend, and that nightclubs had been
involved. Olivia had never heard the truth, but Imogen's own
year had listened with delight to the tales she had brought back.

'In my day there was no such thing as being under threat of
expulsion,' said Gustav. 'She'd have been out there and then.
But that's not relevant for this. What sort of a girl is she?'

'She's a goth,' said Olivia. 'Outside school uniform everything she wears is black. She has a tattoo of a raven perched
on a skull.'

'Dear God. Still . . . Do you know her well enough to invite
her here?'

'I suppose so.' There was, in fact, no reason why Olivia could
not ask Imogen – or anyone else – to the cottage. Within certain
restrictions, and subject to a few rules, the boarders could go
out and about. Nobody would think twice about Imogen
Amberton coming to Infanger Cottage, perhaps on a Saturday
or Sunday afternoon, as a friend of Olivia's. Gustav would know
this, of course, but Olivia said it anyway.

'Yes, but I don't want anyone else to know about it,' said Gustav.

'Why not?'

'Because I don't want people knowing about the opera – not
until I'm ready,' he said impatiently.

'Oh, I see. It might have to be late at night, then. She could
slip out through the downstairs cloakroom window.'

'That happens, does it? In my day it certainly wouldn't have
been permitted. Still . . .' He frowned, then said, 'Yes, all right.
Do it. And as soon as possible. Until I hear this aria sung
properly, I can't finish *The Martyrs*.'

SIX

'I suppose,' said Imogen Amberton, suspiciously, 'that this is for real, is it? I mean, your uncle isn't some weirdo trying to get off with me?'

Imogen always thought people were trying to get off with her, and she usually tried to claim prior involvement with other girls' boyfriends, as well. Olivia remembered her telling everyone that the organist's son had only asked Arabella Tallis out last Christmas because Imogen had turned him down. Nobody had known if this was true. Nobody knew if the stories she had spread about where she had been and what she had been doing when she absconded on those other occasions were true, either. One of her year had said, crossly, that Imogen had been holed up in a seedy flat in Peckham with a drop-out from a rock group, which most people thought was as near the truth as they were likely to get.

When Imogen said this about Gustav wanting to get off with her, Olivia could not think what to say, because it seemed to her utterly bizarre to allot any kind of sexual behaviour to him.

'Oh, no,' she said, after a moment, 'nothing like that. He's composing this really great opera, only he needs to hear some of it properly sung.'

'Why can't you properly sing it for him?'

'I haven't got a good enough voice.' It was necessary to bite down the angry jealousy, and Olivia said, 'He heard you at the Advent recital, and he wants you. It'll only mean an hour or so, I think. He'll make tapes to send to – um – agents and music people when it's all finished.' Imogen was displaying a spark of interest now, so she said, 'He'd put your name on it, of course. And . . . and when it's performed, they might even ask you to be in it.'

She had no idea if that was remotely likely, but Imogen clearly thought it was. She tossed her hair back from her face, and said, 'Yes, I'd be up for that. I'm exploring all the avenues, you know. I'm applying to go on *The X Factor* next year. And that other one that's coming here from America.'

'Really?'

'Yes, really. And there's another one starting up – that's only a radio thing, but I saw details online, and they want photos, so I'm sending some to them.'

'Should you do that kind of thing? I mean it could be anyone—'

'Oh, it's perfectly legit,' said Imogen. 'In any case, I'm seventeen now, which is practically adult. It was my birthday last week, did you know that?'

Olivia did not say most of the school had known it, because Imogen had told everyone.

'I did know,' she said.

'I had a party,' said Imogen. 'Midnight feast – like those old schoolgirl stories, only we had better food. Arabella Tallis sneaked in a few bottles of vino. And everyone's really envious of the TV things, of course. Mad Hats and Davy Lamp don't know about it yet, though, and if you dare tell them—'

'Of course I won't.'

'Right. Good. But this opera thing – that'd be a different league altogether, wouldn't it? That'd be really classy.'

'Very classy indeed. Royal Opera House. The Met. Paris and Milan,' said Olivia, snatching at the names and the places almost at random from things Gustav had said. It seemed to be having the right impact. Imogen's expression was avid. She really is greedy and vain and self-centred, thought Olivia.

'So can you come to the cottage?' she said. 'Could you come tonight?'

'Don't see why not. But listen, any hint of groping or dicking around, and I'll raise such a fuss Gustav Tulliver won't know what's hit him. You tell him that. And,' she said, 'tell him I'll be wearing my Phillip Lim's, so one kick and he wouldn't be interested in groping anyone again.'

'It isn't about that. I *told* you.'

'I've only seen him in the distance, but he doesn't look as if he could grope anything anyway,' said Imogen, dismissively. 'OK, I'll get out about half eleven, and be with you by midnight. I can't do it any earlier, because Hats and the Lamp prowl the

corridors like SS officers in one of those old films. *Colditz* and
stuff like that.'

'Midnight's fine,' said Olivia. 'I'll leave lights on for you so
you can see the way.'

'Bit of an adventure,' said Imogen. 'Creeping along the woodland path at midnight. And if it really might mean a bit of fame
and fortune at the end of it—'

'It's a marvellous work,' said Olivia, earnestly. 'Once it's
finished, it'll be snapped up for the West End. You'd be part of
that.' And I'll hate you if you are, she thought.

But when midnight came there was no sign of Imogen, and
Olivia began to wonder if she might have had second thoughts.
Or if one of the teachers had found out and stopped her getting
out. Or even whether Imogen had told people about it, after all,
mocking and sneering. 'Can you imagine,' she might have said,
'that they believed I'd go to that horrible cottage at midnight
just to sing bloody opera. *Opera*, for heaven's sake! Fat women
screeching and wailing, and people warbling – probably in
Italian.' And the others would have laughed with her, and said
what a stupid thing to expect of anyone, and Gustav Tulliver
had always been a bit mad anyway. Some of them might even
have added, 'And so is that weird niece.'

It was ten past midnight. She had stayed in the sitting room,
half reading, half watching television. It helped to blot out the
sounds of the piano from the music room. They were quite
faint, because the cottage walls were thick, but she could hear
Gustav playing the same few bars over and over again, occasionally trying out different chords and runs, or transposing to
another key. At intervals he came into the sitting room and
peered frowningly out of the window, each time asking Olivia
if she was sure she had made the arrangements properly. Imogen
had definitely said midnight, had she? Then he went back to
the piano.

Olivia was starting to slip down into sleep – the TV voices
were blurring into a single drone – when she heard the sound
of the door being unlatched. She sat up abruptly. Imogen must
have come along so quietly Olivia had not heard her. She hastily
smoothed her hair in the mirror that hung on the chimney breast,
because Imogen was the kind of person who looked down her

nose at you if your hair was a mess. The mirror was a bit foggy from the years of smoke from the fire, and it always made her look like a worried brown dormouse, but it could not be helped. She went through to the music room.

Imogen was standing by the piano, studying a music score. She was wearing a black leather jacket, very slim-fit, deliberately ripped jeans, a good deal of goth-type black eye make-up, and the threatened Phillip Lim boots. Seeing the height of the boots' heels, Olivia was not surprised Imogen had been a bit late; in fact she was surprised Imogen had managed the woodland path without breaking her ankle. It looked as if she had straightened her hair before coming out, because it had the drenched-in-the-rain look that Olivia had frequently tried to achieve, but never managed.

Gustav was playing the music, and Imogen was following it on the score. She looked up when Olivia came in, and Olivia said, 'You got out all right then?'

'No trouble. I told the other two in my room that I had a date.'

'Won't they want to know about it when you get back?'

'Yes, but I've already told them I'm meeting someone who's working with that new TV show. I told you about that, didn't I, Livvy? And I'll spin them a good story, anyway. Trust me to do that. Wouldn't be the first time, not that I often have to make anything up.' She smiled suggestively, then glanced at Gustav and returned to studying the music score. At least she seemed to be taking the music seriously.

'So,' said Gustav, removing his hands from the keys and not appearing to have heard this exchange, 'you've heard it and you can understand what's wanted. I'll play it for you again, but you can follow it, can you?'

'I think so.'

'It doesn't matter if you hit some wrong notes the first time round. The important thing is that the singing needs to be filled with fear – with pain, even. It's that I want to record. This character is a young girl, probably not much older than you are, who's in torment. I want you to sing as if the music is scalding its way out of you.'

It sounded a bit peculiar, said baldly like that, and Olivia expected Imogen to make some derisory remark. But Imogen said, 'Yeah, OK, I've got it. It's Ginevra's song, right? That's what you said, isn't it? Ginevra's song.'

Ginevra . . .

To Olivia, who had curled up unobtrusively in the corner chair, it was as if the name had wrenched at something deep within the very roots of the cottage.

Gustav said, 'Yes. In the opera, Ginevra is a young girl who's left Cresacre to help the Revolution in France. But she's been imprisoned, and in the scene I want you to sing, she knows she's going to her death. She can hear the executioners coming to her dungeon. I need to hear her fear in the music.'

Olivia knew she could have sung this quite as well as Imogen. She beat down the resentment, and said, 'Shall I make us some coffee?', not waiting for them to accept before going out to the kitchen.

She tried to blot out the sounds of the piano by clattering cups loudly onto a tray, but she could still hear the piano and Imogen's voice, but when she went back with the coffee, Imogen was saying, 'I can't do it.' She sounded angry. 'I can read the music and I can follow when you play it,' she said, 'but I can't do any of that crap about pain and fear and stuff. Singing isn't about that stuff, anyway.'

'Of course it is. Your generation has it in all of your music,' said Gustav, at once. 'Loss of love, despair at life. For pity's sake, girl, it's the cry of every teenage generation. Surely you can link up to a girl of your own age who was frightened of dying.'

Imogen gave a petulant shrug and picked up the mug of coffee.

Gustav said, 'This scene – this solo – is the pinnacle of the opera. Terror has to explode into the music. It's the moment when Ginevra knows her death is approaching. And it's a very bad death.' He got up from the piano and went to the door. 'If you're going to do this properly, and if I'm to write it convincingly, I need to hear Ginevra's emotions. So come with me now—'

'Oh no.' Imogen put up both her hands in a gesture of defence and denial. 'I'm not going anywhere with you,' she said. 'I only came here at all 'cos Livvy said I could end up famous if we did this. West End. Opera Houses. That's what you said.' She glared accusingly at Olivia.

'Yes. And you said you thought it'd be better than *The X Factor*,' said Olivia.

Gustav said, 'Ah, celebrity. The double-faced, double-mouthed fame of Milton's Dalila. It's what all your generation wants, isn't it? Still, with this you could get it. Your name will be on the recordings and I'll refer to it in the submissions.'

'My name's going on it as well,' said Olivia, eagerly, but he did not seem to hear.

He said, 'I can't finish the opera until I can hear Ginevra's voice. Imogen, I need you to *be* Ginevra.'

He went out to the hall. Imogen looked at Olivia, then shrugged, and said, 'Oh, what the hell,' shook back her hair, and followed him.

There was not much light in the hall, but there was enough to see Gustav go into the small side hall, and reach for the latch of the low door set into the wall. Imogen took a curious step forward, but Olivia hung back. The cellar, she thought. I don't want to go down there. Whatever's down there is dark and secret and it shouldn't be disturbed.

The door scraped slightly against the frame and, as Gustav pulled it back, a faint stench reached her, as if something cold and dead had huffed out its earthy breath.

Imogen said, 'Jesus, that's a disgusting smell down there. What is it?'

'Damp. Mould. And don't blaspheme, at least not in my hearing.'

'Ginevra would have blasphemed. If she was going to be executed she'd have effed and blinded like mad. There's a cellar down there, right?'

'Yes. It's part of the cottage's original foundations. Probably part of the old monastery.'

'Bloody monks and sodding nuns. This gets weirder by the minute.'

'West End and Royal Opera House, remember?' said Olivia.

'Oh, all right. You want me to go down there? And pretend I'm Ginevra in a dungeon, having hysterics and stuff like that?'

'Yes, I do. Ginevra's alone in the dark when she dies.'

'And shut in a cellar I'd be alone and in the dark. This is method acting, isn't it?' said Imogen. 'What did your character have for breakfast, and how many times did you shag last week, and all that. Still, it's the start of the fame, right? And I'm up for that. Fear, that's what you want?'

'Yes.'

'Make a good story later, I suppose,' said Imogen. '"What was your strangest experience as a performer?" they'll ask. And I'll say, "The night I was forced to sing in a cellar." That'd make a good line, wouldn't it? Make the shit hit the fan.'

She looked at Gustav and then at Olivia, as if expecting an approving response, and when neither of them said anything – Olivia had no idea what to say anyway – Imogen sighed, and said, 'Give me that music again. It'll be *a cappella*, right?' It came out with a kind of smug insistence, as if she wanted to show she knew the term.

'Unaccompanied singing. Yes, it's *a cappella*,' said Gustav.

'Won't it be too dark to read the score? Can I have a torch?'

'I'll leave this door slightly open. Olivia and I will wait here at the top of the stairs.'

'No light at all?' she said. 'Let Livvy come down there with me, then.'

'No.'

'Just let her sit halfway down the stairs. Otherwise I won't do it.'

Olivia would have let herself be shut in the cellar to sing Ginevra's song for as long as it took, but she said, 'I could sit just inside the door – at the top of the steps. Imogen would be very nearly on her own.'

Gustav seemed to hesitate, and Imogen said, 'It's either that, or no deal.'

She went back into the music room and shrugged on the discarded leather jacket, as if preparing to leave. Gustav made an impatient gesture, then said, 'All right. But Olivia, you're to go no further down than just inside the door, and you're to stay on the top step, and be absolutely still and silent. Imogen, here's the recorder. It'll be on battery, but it'll run for long enough. Make sure you sing as close to the speaker as you can.'

'God, what an antique,' said Imogen, examining it disparagingly. 'Haven't you heard of the digital age? I'd've brought my Sony recorder with me if I'd known. Oh, there's an app on the phone, though, and you can record stuff with that—'

'I want this machine used,' said Gustav, stubbornly, and Imogen shrugged, thrust the recorder into the pocket of her jacket, put the music score in the other pocket, and went through the cellar door.

Olivia followed her, and the minute she stepped onto the top stair she knew that she had been right to think that this was where that dark distorted feeling came from. Something bad had once happened in here. Something connected to Ginevra?

But she sat on the top step, hugging her knees and trying not to shiver. She supposed she must have been into the cellar before – she had explored the cottage when they moved in – but the cellar was larger than she remembered. She had forgotten there were arches and brick alcoves. Some of the alcoves had been bricked up – it was possible to see the line of the later bricks – but two had not. The walls and the bricks were different from the cottage itself – Gustav was probably right to believe this was a remnant of the original monastery's foundations. At the far end was a kind of shallow semi-arch just under the roof. It looked as if it had once been a shallow window, just about at ground level from outside, that had been bricked up.

Imogen went cautiously down the steps, swearing because it was so dark and the steps were steep.

'If I twist my ankle or damage these boots, you'll be in big trouble, is that clear?'

Gustav only said, 'Can you see to read the music?'

'Tell you when I get all the way down. It's bloody spooky here, and – oh Jesus, something's rustling in a corner. It's like somebody whispering. Mice, I s'pose.'

Olivia's heart lurched again, and for a moment she thought she, too, could hear the strange whispering echoes.

Gustav was closing the door, doing so very slowly, and Olivia was aware of panic again. Supposing he was able to shut them in – barricading the door in some way – and that he left them? You heard of men becoming mad and imprisoning girls for years. She looked up at the door. It was still open by about a foot, and through that gap, Gustav was staring in, one hand grasping the edge of the door. His eyes looked strange in the dim light. And then he looked down to Olivia and nodded and there was uncharacteristic reassurance in the small gesture.

He left the door slightly open, and Olivia saw with relief that a sliver of light from the hall fell across the top of the steps. It did not reach the dark well down in the cellar itself, though, and after a moment, in defiance of her uncle's orders, she crept down a few more steps.

She could see Imogen, but only as a dark, formless outline. She looked smaller in this dimness, or was she simply hunched over the music? No, she looked different, almost as if—

Olivia shut this thought off, but it was too late, because it had already formed. It was as if it was not Imogen she was seeing at all. She heard her swear, and then there was a faint click. A tiny oblong of bluish light sprang up, and Olivia realized Imogen had switched on her mobile phone. It must have been in her jacket pocket. Was there a torch on it? Was she going to cheat and switch the torch on?

But Imogen simply left the phone on and directed the glow onto the music. The small illumination lit her face from below. Her hair had fallen over her face again.

For a moment, behind Imogen's shoulder, the darkness around one of the alcoves seemed to thin. And there, so faint it was like a pencil scribble on the darkness, Olivia thought she saw the outline of a second face, as if someone was standing behind Imogen, looking over her shoulder. It was a small, heart-shaped face, framed by dark hair. A hand came out, as if reaching for the faint radiance on the phone's screen . . .

Olivia gasped and half stood up, and the small movement and the scrape of her shoes made Imogen look up.

'Livvy?' she said. 'Is that you?'

It was all right. The shadows had folded themselves away, and the impression of someone peering over Imogen's shoulder vanished. Olivia realized it had been one of those double images you sometimes get with a digital light. Like waking up at three a.m. and looking at the alarm clock and seeing the figures twinned.

She said, 'Of course it's me.'

'Just checking.'

Imogen reached into her pocket for the recorder, but she did not immediately start singing. She's absorbing the atmosphere, thought Olivia, and she shivered, because it was creepy enough to sit up here on the stairs, within touching distance of the door. But to be down there in that black well of darkness with the strange whispering shadows, with elusive silhouettes on the darkness, must be very eerie indeed.

It was eerie and terrifying . . . You can have no idea how eerie and how terrifying . . .

The words brushed against Olivia's mind and she pushed them away. Stupid imagination again.

The silence stretched out, and Olivia was just thinking she could not bear this any longer, when Imogen began to sing.

SEVEN

The minute the singing began, Olivia knew that, no matter what it had sounded like in the normality of the rooms upstairs, down here something extraordinary had happened to it. Because although this was undoubtedly Imogen's voice, familiar from school concerts and choir recitals and even impromptu rock-band sessions in the common room, now it was somehow the voice of a terrified girl. A girl who was facing death, and who was singing her way into that death. A bad death, Gustav had said.

'*Step by measured step the murderers came to me . . .*
Inch by measured inch, the light is being shut out from me . . .
Breath by measured breath, my life is being cut off from me . . .
Heartbeat by measured and precious heartbeat, my life is ending . . .'

The words were macabre and menacing, and Olivia wanted to press her hands over her ears to shut them out. But she did not. What she did was to creep down another step to listen more intently.

The music bordered on being ugly and discordant. But it was the most disturbing music Olivia had ever heard. It really was as if she was listening to the long-ago Ginevra – the girl who might never even have existed – singing her way into death.

This was not music anyone would associate with the prim, dry – even miserly – man who was Gustav Tulliver. This was music that scraped into your emotions and dredged up your darkest fears. It was filled with dread and despair, and it was the nightmare side of all the fairy stories. It was Tolkien's Dark Middle Earth with the repulsive Gollum creeping gulpingly along the underground caves of Mordor. Or it was the fateful beckoning of the Pied Piper, or the siren song of the Rhinemaidens who lured unwary sailors to their doom. The images spiked jaggedly through Olivia's mind, and for a moment she was surprised to find herself knowing about such things. So this was what Gustav had been struggling to bring into existence all these months. The dying voice of the mysterious Ginevra. It had an extraordinary effect on Olivia. Like the whispering voice, it seemed to be soaking into her mind.

'*Inch by measured inch, the light is being shut out from me . . . Breath by measured breath, my life is being cut off from me . . .*'

The words and the unusual pattern of the music thrummed through her senses, and they churned up thoughts and emotions Olivia hardly recognized. There had been jealousy of Imogen, certainly, and it was still there, but now there was a bitter hatred as well. She looked at this stupid pretentious girl who was doing what she, Olivia, should have been asked to do – who was being sulky and childish about it – and deep loathing and anger coursed through her. If Imogen were not here – if she could not sing . . .

Then Imogen stopped. The recorder clicked off and silence closed down.

It seemed a long time before Gustav's voice said, 'That was very satisfactory.' He stood in the doorway, a tall, slightly stooped figure, outlined against the dim hall, then came down the cellar steps, brushing past Olivia as if he had forgotten she was there. The door swung slightly inwards, shutting off some of the light from the hall, but the tiny oblong of radiance from Imogen's phone was still visible. It suddenly erupted into a bright, cold light, and Olivia realized Imogen had switched on the phone's torch. It was like a small spotlight cutting through the blackness, and she directed it straight at Gustav. He flinched, and put up a hand to shield his eyes.

But he said, 'No need for so much light. We'll go back upstairs now. I'll take the recording. You can go back to the school – you'll be all right getting back on your own, will you?'

Imogen said, 'It sounds as if I'll have to be.' She moved away from him, one hand in her pocket. She's put the recorder in there, thought Olivia. She's not going to give it to him.

'I hear it's not the first time you've gone slinking back after a few nights away.'

'No, it isn't. But this recording—' Gustav took a step closer to her, and she moved back to stand against the brick wall now.

'It's good, isn't it?' said Imogen. 'It's unusual.'

'Yes.'

'Just the kind of thing that might get me noticed in all kinds of useful areas. Recording studios. Agents. Record producers. It's something they won't have heard before. I think record producers would sit up and take notice of this.'

'Don't be stupid,' said Gustav, at once. 'This isn't a shoddy bit of modern music you can play for three minutes to get onto some trashy talent contest.'

'No, and that's the point. So listen, I'll make another deal with you. I'll copy this onto my recorder and we'll both have one. And we can each do what we want with our own copy.'

'No!' It came out sharply and the word rebounded off the old bricks. 'Give me that recording this minute,' said Gustav, and Olivia heard the authority in his voice.

'I won't. Not until I've copied it.'

Olivia had been trying to beat the hatred down, but now she felt it well up again. She had been prepared – just about – to accept that Imogen should sing and help Gustav to finish *The Martyrs* rather than Olivia. She was not prepared, though, for this silly, vain creature, greedy for stardom at any price, to spoil *The Martyrs'* chances. To spoil Olivia's own chances of reaching that marvellous life her uncle had so often described. The hatred bubbled up again, blurring everything, so that she felt as if she was seeing the cellar through a mist, or under water. It scalded through her, sending her down the stairs, not noticing the uneven steep steps. She snatched the phone from Imogen, and Imogen kicked out in instinctive defence. There was a crunch as the toe of one boot made contact, and Gustav gasped and reeled back. Olivia turned the phone directly onto Imogen, and saw that she was making her way along the wall towards the stairs. The perilously high heels of the boots were hampering her, and it was easy for Olivia to bound up the steps ahead of her and to stand against the door, barring Imogen's way.

'Move, you bitch!' yelled Imogen. 'Open the fucking door!'

'No,' said Olivia. 'Give me the recording. You can go then.' A small part of her could scarcely believe she was actually speaking like this – and to Imogen Amberton, who was so confident and so disparaging of people like Olivia, and who would probably sneer and spread all kinds of horrid things about her at school tomorrow.

Gustav's voice from below, cried, 'Stop it! Both of you, stop it! Come back down here! Imogen, give me that recording!'

Imogen ignored him. Instead, she lunged forward, her fist raised, and brought it smashing across Olivia's face. 'Get out of my way,' she yelled.

The blow knocked the phone from Olivia's hand, and the light cut off as it hit the ground. Pain exploded across her cheekbone, and her eyes were streaming, but she pushed Imogen back against the stone wall and there was a sickening crack as Imogen's head hit the wall. *Good!* thought Olivia, viciously. *Serve her right.* Imogen made a groping movement with one hand, clearly dazed. Below them, Olivia could hear Gustav fumbling through the darkness. Could he see her? No. With all her strength she pushed Imogen towards the steps. Imogen cried out, and tried to resist, and Olivia pushed her again.

Imogen flailed frantically at the air to stop herself from falling, then tumbled forwards, going down the steps in a series of jolting bumps, all the way to the foot. The sounds seemed to go on for ever, then Gustav was calling out.

'Olivia? Are you all right?'

'I . . . yes. But Imogen fell. I think she's at the bottom of the steps.'

'We need light. Push the door all the way back.'

Olivia was shaking violently, but she managed to do so. Light came in from the hall, and she saw that Imogen was lying at the foot of the steps, half against the brick wall. One leg was stuck out at an impossible angle, and there was something wrong about her head – something dreadfully, grotesquely wrong, because no head should lie at that ugly angle to its body . . .

The sounds of the fall were still echoing around the cellar – the sudden shout of fear, the scrambling fall . . . For a moment it seemed to Olivia that there was a sly, knowing voice inside the echoes . . . A voice that came from a long way off, and that was fuzzy and uncertain, like not being quite tuned in to the station on a radio. But she could hear what the echo was saying. '*This is how it was before . . . This is exactly how it was before . . .*'

Olivia crammed her fist into her mouth, fighting panic. Most of the feeling seemed to have gone from her legs, but she clung to the rail and managed to get down the steps.

'Is she—?'

She flinched from the word, but Gustav said, 'Dead? No, I don't think so. I think she's badly injured, though.' He stood up. 'I'll get a torch,' he said. 'Don't move her.'

He went quickly up the steps, and Olivia knelt down at Imogen's side. A trickle of dark blood had spilled from Imogen's mouth. Like dark lipstick. As if somebody had kissed her vigorously and smeared the lipstick all over her mouth. She looked like a broken statue. She looked as if death was about to overtake her.

Breath by measured breath, my life is being cut off from me . . .

Heartbeat by measured and precious heartbeat, my life is ending . . .

Almost of their own volition, Olivia's hands reached down. Her fingers curled around Imogen's throat. It would not take much – not with Imogen so near to death. Just a little bit tighter . . . There was a faint tremor of movement beneath the skin – a pulse? – and she tightened her hold. The tremor came again, and then the slight movement died away. Olivia kept her hands in place. She had no idea how long it was before she realized her uncle was standing at the top of the steps, and her heart jumped, because she did not know how long he had been there.

She moved back from Imogen's body, and watched him. He thrust a hand beneath the leather jacket, then bent lower to listen for signs of breathing.

Olivia said, falteringly, 'She's dead now, isn't she?' and her uncle sat back on his heels and looked at her.

'Oh yes,' he said. 'She's dead now.' He walked across to the steps, and sat down on the lowest one. His face was gaunt and, speaking slowly, as if he might be testing each word, he said, 'This has to be carefully handled.'

'Are you sure she's dead?'

'There's no heartbeat – she's not breathing. She's unquestionably dead,' said Gustav, impatiently. 'Even if I hadn't taught science and physics all those years, I'd know.'

'What do we do? Shall I . . . call for an ambulance or something?'

'No,' he said, quietly. 'No, I don't think we can do that, do you? Don't worry, though. I can work something out.'

'We could explain that it was an accident,' said Olivia, and stopped. It had not been an accident at all. There had been that coursing, burning hatred. There had been that violent push down the stairs and then the pressure of her hands around Imogen's throat. But no one knew that. Gustav did not know. He had been upstairs, finding a torch.

He took her hand, which surprised her, because he normally shied away from all physical contact, even a birthday or a Christmas kiss. 'You pushed her down the stairs,' he said.

'Yes, but—'

'As for my part in it,' he said, 'I'm in a cellar with two young girls, and it's one o'clock in the morning.' He made an abrupt gesture, indicating the cellar. 'How will that sound to an outsider?'

'But . . . there was nothing, um, wrong about that.' Olivia was horribly embarrassed at the implication in his words. 'It was to record the music,' she said. 'OK, Imogen shouldn't have sneaked out of school, but that wouldn't be such a big deal. She's done it before. And she wouldn't have fallen down the stairs if she hadn't been wearing high-heeled boots. I can say all that.'

'For pity's sake, don't you understand? It wouldn't matter if you swore a hundred times on the Bible that it was an accident. Some people might believe you, but most wouldn't. And even if they decided it was an accidental death, it would still look suspicious. People would whisper that something odd – something sick and warped – was going on.' The deep-set eyes were blazing with fervour now. 'Even if you were exonerated, I could be ruined,' said Gustav. 'I could be charged with any number of offences. God knows what would happen to us then. If I were imprisoned, they'd put you in care – you're only fifteen. Do you really want that?'

'Oh no,' said Olivia, in a whisper.

'And if any of that were to happen,' he said, his voice suddenly quieter, 'we'd certainly have lost any chance of getting away

from this poky cottage and from this introverted place. Because
The Martyrs would be stillborn. It would never have a chance.'
   The Martyrs. That's all he really cares about, thought Olivia.
And then, with surprise, But I care about it as well, she thought.
It's that pathway to a different life. He's right.
   Gustav said, 'So, let's think carefully. Imogen said no one
knew she was coming here. Can we trust that?'
   Olivia considered, then said, 'Yes, I think so. She told the
others – the girls in her room – that she was meeting somebody
important. It sounded as if she hinted to them that it was something to do with singing – maybe with the TV show.'
   'A new TV show, she said,' put in Gustav, almost eagerly.
'That's what she told us, wasn't it? Does it actually exist, that
show, do you suppose?'
   Olivia had no idea. 'Imogen said it was something she found
online.' Reluctantly, she added, 'There probably was something,
but she was . . . well, she was the kind of girl who'd always
make a lot out of anything. That's a terrible thing to say about
her, isn't it, with her . . . um . . . lying there like that.'
   This sounded good. It sounded as if she was still in shock
from what had happened, and deeply distressed. She even
managed to put a tremor into her voice at the end and to shiver,
as if she might be trying not to cry.
   'But,' Gustav was saying, 'would anyone at the school –
the other girls, I mean – would they believe she was meeting
someone at midnight?'
   'Oh, yes.' Olivia was glad she could answer this truthfully.
'She'd make it sound really believable. She'd spin some
tale about someone fancying her and wanting to make secret
arrangements.'
   'And she's done it before,' he said, thoughtfully. And then,
'Would anyone make a connection to this cottage? Or to you?'
   'I don't think so. No.' Olivia did not say most of the students
regarded Infanger Cottage and Gustav himself as things to avoid.
   'Good.' He got up, and gestured impatiently to her to hand
him the torch. 'Olivia, you'll have to trust me from now
on.' He looked at her very directly. 'I do want to protect you
– remember that, won't you? But you'll have to do exactly as
I tell you.'

'All right.' The strengthening hatred and anger was starting to recede – not all at once, but in little trickles, like the sea going out. Olivia was beginning to understand that this was a massively terrible situation. She would get out of it, of course. Nobody would try to send Gustav to prison or Olivia to some horrible foster home.

Gustav walked round the cellar, pausing at intervals to shine the torch onto the walls, as if he was examining the bricks closely. Several times he tapped against the bricks, dislodging sprinklings of dust.

He stood at the centre, looking around with a small frown, then he went back to one of the bricked-over alcoves, and shone the torch closely onto the surface again. He rapped at the bricks again with his knuckles, then nodded, as if satisfied.

Olivia said, in a small, frightened voice, 'What are you going to do?'

Gustav turned to look at her. 'I'm going to open up one of the alcoves and put her inside,' he said.

As Olivia stared, he said, 'And then I'm going to seal up the alcove.'

He was unexpectedly practical, which surprised Olivia, because normally he could scarcely even change a light bulb.

But he found hammers and trowels and what Olivia thought was a pickaxe from one of the cottage's outbuildings. There was also a tub of some kind of cement or putty in one of them, which he said had been left behind by Firkin's, the builders, when the cottage had had its rough-and-ready sprucing up before they moved in. It was a bit gloopy because it had been mixed for a long time, but it would stick the bricks together perfectly well.

'I should think it'll take two or three days to actually set firm, but it'll be perfectly safe and secure.'

Safe and secure. So she won't be able to get out, thought Olivia, and then wondered with horror where such a thought had come from, because Imogen was undoubtedly dead.

At Gustav's request she fetched candles and matches from kitchen cupboards. 'And there's an oil lamp somewhere. Oh, and another torch if there is one.'

By the time Olivia had found the candles and the oil lamps and the torch, Gustav had been up to the airing cupboard and taken a sheet, which he had thrown over what lay by the steps. He had dragged it to the centre of the cellar so that they could move up and down the steps without having to step over it.

'Don't switch on any lights upstairs,' he said. 'It isn't very likely that anyone will be around at this hour, but you never know. A poacher, a young couple up to no good.'

Olivia did not know if he visualized people using the forest for love-making, or illicit smoking, or even for dealing drugs.

She sat on the bottom step, watching him, and she thought the candlelit cellar with its shadowy alcoves was starting to seem like something from a nightmare or a horror film. The candlelight flickered over the blanketed shape, so that at times it seemed to be moving slightly. The lamps were old and tarnished and Olivia had brought olive oil for them, not knowing what else to use. It took Gustav a little while to fire them, but eventually he managed it, and a coppery light burned up. As the lamps became warm, the metal glowed, and sent out a peculiar smell. It was partly the olive oil, but there was another scent with it – the scent of age and of secrets, as if the lamps had stored up all the images they had ever illuminated. Olivia found herself wondering what their light might last have shown up. The lamps created shadows in the two alcoves on the other side of the cellar, and she tried not to look at them, because shadows could be sly and deceptive and these shadows were very sly and deceptive indeed.

When Gustav swung the pickaxe onto the bricks for the first time, the sound reverberated around the cellar, and clouds of dust billowed upwards. He stepped back, coughing, one hand flung up to shield his eyes. Olivia flinched, feeling the gritty dryness against her eyes and her throat.

But Gustav wiped his face and pushed back his hair, and swung the axe again. 'Once I've broken a small area open I can chip out more of the bricks fairly easily,' he said. 'It isn't necessary to remove all the bricks – just enough to—'

'I understand,' said Olivia, quickly.

'Goodness knows when these alcoves were bricked over, or why,' he said. 'It might have been done to strengthen the foundations. I suppose. I can't think of any other reason – it isn't as if there are any pipes or electricity cables down here. This cellar dates to well before electricity and modern plumbing.'

The pickaxe whooshed through the air a second time. It took two more attempts before any of the bricks loosened, but suddenly several fell away, three or four on the outside, but a couple toppling backwards, into the alcove. Gustav frowned at that, but reached for the trowel and began to chip at the other bricks, being careful that no more fell down inside the alcove. As more of them came free, a stench of something old and dry and sad gusted out. Then he stepped back, and Olivia saw that he had opened up the alcove at eye-level – about four feet up from the ground. The hole he had made was roughly two feet across, and beyond it was a dark, shallow recess.

She was about to ask if this was large enough, when, within the dark recess, something moved.

Her heart gave a great leap. There's something in there, she thought. Something that's moved . . . But it'll only be a trapped animal – even just a bird. At any minute it'll come pelting out, terrified and frantic, and we'll let it out and it will be all right.

But Gustav was staring into the alcove, his face sheet-white, his eyes horrified. One hand went to his chest in a convulsive movement. He's clutching at the left side, thought Olivia – heart attack? Oh God, what will I do if he has a heart attack down here? What is it he's seen that's made him look like that? She scrambled up from the steps and went over to him. His hand came out to her, cold and shaking, pushing her away.

'No . . . Stay back . . .'

But it was already too late, because the glow from the oil lamp fell directly into the alcove, and there, within the shallow dimness, was a mummified body, festooned with thick cobwebs. Empty eye sockets stared out of a face from which the flesh had long since shrivelled, and whoever this was must have been there for years. Decades. Centuries.

The movement came again, and with it a sound like dry old sticks scraping against one another. One hand, nothing more than finger bones and knuckles, loosely attached to thin wrist bones, fell forward, as if reaching out for help.

Olivia screamed – or at least somebody screamed, because

she could hear the sound echoing all round the cellar. She wanted to run up the stairs and pretend she had not seen anything. Her legs were giving way, but she got as far as the steps before she fell. She bent over, shuddering, and when finally she managed to sit up, Gustav was still staring at what was inside the bricked-up alcove. Then he seemed to recall himself to his surroundings, and he came to sit by her on the steps.

For some moments he did not speak; his hands were shaking, and when he finally did say something, Olivia could hear how he was struggling for normality.

'I think that by law we're supposed to report this,' he said, speaking slowly and carefully. 'The finding of any dead body, no matter how old . . . But that would mean explaining what we were doing down here.' He frowned, then said, 'We'll have to stay with the original plan.'

He got up slowly and with obvious reluctance, but went back to chiselling at the bricks, opening up the wall a little more. Olivia tried not to look into it; she tried not to see the sad, terrible thing in there.

At last Gustav laid down the chisel. 'I think that's large enough,' he said, 'but I'll have to try reaching those bricks that fell down inside. We need to replace them all as exactly as we can.'

Olivia waited, watching him, and after a few moments he straightened up.

'I've got them,' he said. 'And now . . .' He hesitated, then said, 'Olivia, this next part . . . I'd spare you if I could, but I can't – I can't lift Imogen on my own. And we need to get her more or less upright so we can tip her over the edge of the hole. There isn't much room – it's shallower than I thought – but between us we could do it.'

Olivia said, 'She'll be in there – with . . . with that other—'

'Yes,' he said, quickly. 'But once we've done that, and once we've put the bricks back, it will be all over. No one will ever know what happened tonight. They'll look for Imogen, but they won't find her. And we can forget the whole thing. All right?'

Olivia was not all right, and she would never forget any of this, but she took a deep breath and said, 'Yes. Yes, all right.'

'Good girl.'

As they lifted the body, the sheet slipped back, and Imogen's head fell bonelessly all the way across onto the other shoulder. Gustav snatched the sheet back into place at once, but Olivia had already seen the eyes that stared blindly at nothing – or did they stare accusingly at Olivia? Did the whispers come suddenly nearer, and hiss the word, *murderess*, with Imogen's voice . . .?

Between them they manoeuvred the body onto the edge of the aperture, and then forced it through and down into the alcove. It fell in a slow, awkward tumble, and wedged against the back of the alcove, just touching the sad, shrivelled remains. There was another of the dry-stick movements, and the head seemed to incline slightly to its left, as if looking round curiously. This was a ridiculous way to think, though. What Olivia did think was how Imogen would have hated lying in such a messy, squashed-up way. But a tiny voice, deep in her mind, said, gleefully, *Serve her right, the stupid vain bitch.*

'Now for her things – her bag and her phone,' said Gustav. 'Where are they?'

'The bag's upstairs. The phone's at the top of the stairs. I think it's broken.'

'We won't take any chances,' said Gustav. 'Do those phones send out a signal even if they're switched off or damaged? You see those police reports on television of missing girls and police tracing their calls and where they've been—'

Olivia did not know. 'We could take the batteries out,' she said. 'No, that wouldn't be any good – if anyone found it, it would look odd, and anyway, I think they could just put new batteries in and charge it again.'

'The best thing,' said Gustav, 'is probably for me to take it with me when I go to Worcester the day after tomorrow – you remember about that? It's to let that opera company see a treatment of *The Martyrs*.'

Olivia knew what he meant by 'treatment'. It meant printed extracts from the whole work – parts of the dialogue and print-outs of the lyrics – together with parts of the music which Gustav had played into the small recorder. They were not being allowed to see the whole opera, he had said, his lips puckered tightly together like an old-fashioned drawstring purse. He was not revealing his ideas for other people to steal.

Olivia said, 'Of course I remember about Worcester, but you surely aren't still going—'

'I'll have to,' he said. 'We can't do anything that's out of pattern. So I'll take the phone with me on the train, and throw it away somewhere. Then if it is tracked it'll be tracked to somewhere a long way from here.'

'I could see what numbers she's got on her phone,' began Olivia.

'And phone people up? No, of course you can't do that.'

'I meant I could send one or two texts,' she said. 'It's the kind of thing Imogen would have done if she was going off on one of her adventures again. Bragging.'

'Who would you send messages to?' Gustav sounded suspicious, but then he was not familiar with the practice of texting.

'Well, to the aunt in Scotland – that's her guardian. Her parents are dead and I don't think there's any other family. I could text one or two of the girls in her class, as well.'

'You'd have to keep it brief,' he said. 'Not give any details that might be checked.'

'Texts are brief. I could say something like, "Met someone fab. Off to the bright lights again". Or, "Brill opportunity – grabbing it with both hands. Watch this space".'

'All right. Yes, it might dilute suspicion. Do it, will you? Oh, and get her bag, and make sure she didn't leave anything upstairs.'

Olivia went up the stone steps again. She collected Imogen's bag, and checked the other rooms, although Imogen had not gone into any of them. Nothing anywhere. She took the coffee mugs into the kitchen and washed them up.

When she went back to the cellar, Gustav was sorting the bricks. While he did so, Olivia switched Imogen's phone on again. There were a lot of names and numbers in the contacts list, but after careful thought she sent three texts. One to Imogen's aunt, sending love, and saying she would be in touch soon – exciting things were about to happen. Two to girls in Imogen's class. In those, she said, 'Brill opportunity came up – grabbing it before too late'. Did that sound convincing? Did it sound like Imogen? Olivia flipped through several of the *Sent* texts, and saw that Imogen signed them all as LIMOX. LIMOX? Oh, it would be LIMO – love from Imogen – and X for a kiss. She added this to the texts, pressed *Send*, then switched off the phone and went to help Gustav with the bricks.

'Once they're cemented in,' said Gustav, 'we'll smear dust over the wall, so if anyone does make enquiries here – if anyone does come down here – it will look like an old, neglected, underground room. But pray God no major work's ever needed to these foundations, because we can't risk anyone needing to get through this wall.

As he began to lay the bricks in place, cementing them with the mortar, Olivia gradually became aware of a soft sound. At first she thought it was coming from outside – an animal or a distant car or motorbike engine – but then she realized it was coming from her uncle.

She glanced at him, thinking it was a nervous humming – in the way a man might whistle softly to himself for company or reassurance. But after a moment she recognized the faint, soft harmony and the words.

'Step by measured step the murderers came to me . . .
Inch by measured inch, the light is being shut out from me . . .
Breath by measured breath, my life is being cut off from me . . .
Heartbeat by measured and precious heartbeat, my life is ending . . .'

It was the song Imogen had sung for him. The death chant he had written for the girl who had probably never existed outside of the legend. Ginevra.

They had breakfast in the cottage's kitchen around six a.m. A dull light was showing outside, and it felt peculiar to be doing something so ordinary as scrambling eggs and grilling bacon and making toast. Gustav made a pot of strong coffee. He did not normally do anything domestic, and he was a bit clumsy and could not find things in cupboards, but Olivia was grateful to him for trying to help.

After breakfast she asked if she could stay at home for the rest of the day. They could phone the school and say she had flu or something, couldn't they? But Gustav said they must not do anything out of their usual routine. It would be discovered today that Imogen was missing – it might have been discovered already. Olivia could not be missing, as well. She must behave as normally as she could today, and she could catch up on sleep tonight.

Olivia had already had the hottest bath she could bear, and had shampooed her hair over and over again to get rid of the smell and the feel of the old dust they had disturbed. She could still smell it on her hands, though. And the smell of murder? Would she ever be free of that?

EIGHT

mogen's disappearance had been reported to the police by the time Olivia reached the school. Officers came out to question everyone. There was a sense of concern, but there was also a sense of Imogen doing something she had done before. The two girls showed the police the texts they had received; they said Imogen had been talking about going on a TV talent show. The police said they would be checking Imogen's social media profile – she was on Facebook and she had just signed up for that new thing, Twitter, although she did not seem to have used it much. As for the phone, they would be getting records from the provider, and would be following up leads from that. Olivia felt a jab of apprehension at this last, but she thought even if the police could tell that the texts had been sent from Cresacre, that would seem perfectly innocent; it would mean Imogen had sent them before she left.

Olivia herself was questioned along with the others, and when she got home later in the afternoon, she found that the police had been to the cottage as well. Gustav did not seem very worried about it. He told Olivia he had simply said he had not known the missing girl, and he was very sorry that he could not be of any help. He shut himself in his study to get everything ready for his trip to Worcester, where he would be showing the new opera company parts of the opera, and letting them hear extracts of the music. They were currently performing Mozart's *Magic Flute*, he said, and new companies were always looking for different things that might attract the public's attention. He would be meeting their director – he had written to the theatre, and the man had replied with a very courteous letter, suggesting a meeting. As an afterthought, Gustav told Olivia that they were an amateur company, but they were very well thought of, and you had to start somewhere. He thought it very likely that they would be extremely interested in *The Martyrs*.

That night, he said, 'Olivia – that recording of Imogen singing.'
'Yes?'
'We should destroy it. Can you do that while I'm away
tomorrow?'
'Yes,' said Olivia. 'Yes, I can do that.' She held out her hand
for the cassette, and he handed it to her.

Throughout the day the police came and went. Searches
were made for Imogen, fields and woodland areas were scoured,
and appeals were made for information. There was talk of a
local radio or TV appeal. But in the absence of any apparent
struggle, or any other evidence, there seemed to be a feeling
that Imogen Amberton had done what she had done twice
before. Run off with – or to – a boyfriend. There was no real
reflection on the school – although security around the bedrooms
might have been a bit tighter. But teenagers were notoriously
rebellious and also notoriously inventive.

The students said, a bit defiantly and with unexpected
loyalty, that the security was quite good, although one or two
of them – including Arabella Tallis – admitted that it was not
the most difficult thing in the world to get out at night if you
really wanted to.

Olivia supposed that if there had been conventional parents
and a conventional family there might have been a bit more
fuss. But most people seemed to think Imogen had seized some
chance to become a celebrity. A check of her laptop showed
she had been on several celebrity-competition TV sites. A check
of her phone records showed she had not made a call since
the night she had vanished. But it was a throwaway society,
and phones could be bought over the counter these days. If
she had gone away to start a new life, she would probably
have bought herself a brand-new, state-of-the-art phone. Or
had it bought for her. They did not say whether they would be
making any more detailed checks on the phone's possible
whereabouts, and Olivia was relieved to think that by tomorrow
the phone would be discarded many miles away, and she was
glad, after all, about Gustav's Worcester expedition.

A rumour circulated that the police were considering down-
grading what they called the risk assessment. There were three
levels, it seemed: low, medium and high. In light of Imogen's

past behaviour and the fact that no struggle seemed to have taken place anywhere, it was likely that this would soon be a low-risk case. Somebody even said it would probably be put in the time-waster class, and that Imogen Amberton would next be heard of flaunting herself on some glitzy TV programme, scantily clad and heading for stardom.

The next day Gustav set off for Worcester, catching an afternoon train. He did not have a car, because he did not approve of the internal combustion engine, although this did not stop him from travelling in other people's cars. But there was a through train to Worcester, and he would get taxis to and from his meeting, he said.

He had told Olivia he was likely to be home very late – probably on the eleven p.m. train. Theatre people were apt to be convivial – even amateurs; maybe especially amateurs. There might be the offer of a drink in some local pub, or even a late supper somewhere, which he would accept, of course, said Gustav. Olivia tried to visualize her uncle as part of a lively pub group, or partaking of a late Indian or Chinese meal, and could not.

Rain was sheeting down when she left her final class that afternoon. It dripped from the trees and the woodland path was muddy. Olivia was relieved to reach the cottage, and dry her hair, and get into warm, dry clothes.

Infanger Cottage always felt different when she was here on her own. It was not exactly eerie, but there was a vague feeling that if you opened the door of a room a bit too quickly you might glimpse something whisking itself out of sight. But this might simply be because she was not used to being here on her own. Her uncle did not often go out for any length of time as he had done today. He did not often go out at all, in fact.

With the rain rippling against the windows, the rooms were bathed in an eerie greenish light, almost as if Infanger Cottage had sunk to the bottom of a deep old ocean. Olivia shivered, pulled on a thick sweater, and was about to go into the kitchen to make something to eat, when she heard the tapping.

At first she thought it was the rain beating on the roof. Then she thought it was a branch blowing against a window. It might even be something in the plumbing. Mr Firkin, the local builder, who could turn his hand to a blocked drain or a leaky stop-tap if required, had said the plumbing at Infanger Cottage was a law unto itself. When Olivia and her uncle moved in, he had told them that there was a bad case of water hammer in Infanger. Airlock in the pipes, that was what it was, he said, and it meant the pipes sometimes juddered against floor joists or rafters. Difficult to get rid of without major upheaval, but not impossible, he added, hopefully. Gustav had said that if he wanted Mr Firkin's help, he knew where to find him, and after Mr Firkin had left, Gustav had said he would not trust Firkin's Builders from here to that door, and he did not care if they had been established for two hundred years, he was not paying good money for somebody to rip up floors and tighten a few joints.

Olivia, remembering this conversation, felt a bit better, and when she went back downstairs the tapping seemed to have stopped. But as she was looking in the fridge the sounds came again. And it really did sound as if it was coming from below. From the cellar.

A lurch of fear twisted her stomach, but she made herself go into the hall and open the cellar door. Silence, apart from the rain beating against the windows. It had been her imagination then. Or it had been water hammer after all—

No, there it was again. A tapping, coming at intervals, sometimes strong, sometimes weak. It might be a trapped bird somewhere. Might it even be an intruder? This was a shivery thought, although an intruder would not tap on walls. What it really sounded like – Olivia faced it – was someone trying to attract attention. Someone wanting help, and someone whose strength was failing, and whose hands were weak. The fear gripped her more tightly, and she sat down on the hall chair, and reminded herself that it was nearly two days since Imogen had died.

But supposing Imogen had not been dead? Supposing Gustav had been wrong, and Imogen had been knocked into a coma? And supposing she had come out of the coma and found herself trapped in that dreadful dark space, and was hammering to get out?

Olivia forced herself to consider the situation sensibly. Could she wait for her uncle to get home and ask what they should do?

But he would not be back until at least midnight, and Olivia did not think she could wait all that time, constantly hearing the sounds, wondering . . .

Wondering whether Imogen was still alive.

Moving slowly, she took the torch from the kitchen drawer. Then she took a deep breath, and forced herself to open the cellar door and to go down the steps. A smeary rain-light came from the narrow window near the ceiling, and from here it was impossible to tell that the alcove on the right-hand side had been disturbed. Olivia switched on the torch, grateful for the sharp modern light that cut through the dimness, and went over to it. She placed her ear close against it, listening. There was nothing.

'Imogen?' Olivia had not realized she had been going to call out, and the sound of her own voice startled her. 'Imogen? Can you hear me?'

Still nothing. But suppose Imogen had cried for help for the last two days – shouted over and over again until her voice gave out? Suppose she was swimming in and out of consciousness, and not able to answer now? If she were alive, that would mean that – after all – Olivia was not a murderess. But it would also mean she would be able to tell people Olivia had tried to kill her.

Olivia rapped against the brickwork, grazing her knuckles on the harsh surface. Still nothing. She sat on the stone steps, and waited. If the sounds came again, if they were definitely from behind the brickwork, she would have to do something. Or would she? If Imogen were to be rescued, she would tell people what had been done. Olivia could not risk that.

But the minutes ticked away and nothing happened. It must have been a bird after all, or that thing in the plumbing. She was about to go back up the stairs when she saw a small glint within the bricks she and her uncle had put in place almost two days earlier. Something there was catching the strong torchlight.

She shone the light more closely on the bricks. Partly wedged into the mortar was a ring, tarnished, but with the glint of silver. What looked like a small black stone was set into it. Had this been here last night? If so, surely she or her uncle would have seen it? But they had only had candles and the old oil lamps, and the flickering light from those might not have picked this up.

Olivia reached for the ring and tried to pull it free. At first she thought the mortar was already set, but when she tugged a bit more forcefully, the ring came away. She went back up to the kitchen and carefully wiped the ring clean. It certainly looked like silver, although she did not really have any knowledge about that kind of thing. She had no idea what the black stone might be. Could it have been Imogen's? But when, almost automatically, she slid it onto her own finger, it was far too small; in fact it was too small for any of her fingers. Olivia thought she had quite small hands and quite slim fingers, but this ring would not go past the first knuckle of any of them. It couldn't have been Imogen's. It might have been a child's ring, though. Or the ring of someone who was very small and very fine-boned.

She took ring up to her bedroom and put it at the back of a drawer where it would not be found.

Gustav arrived home shortly after ten o'clock, having caught a much earlier train than he had planned.

He was in a bad mood, because he said the trip had been a waste of time and money – the cost of train tickets and taxis was shocking these days. The amateur company had been very amateur indeed, and all they wanted was to prance around a stage in nice costumes, singing *The Merry Widow* or choruses from Gilbert & Sullivan. Gustav had not even bothered to show them *The Martyrs* because it had been clear that it would be completely out of their class.

Olivia said, 'Did you remember about Imogen's phone?'

'Yes, I did. I left it on the train,' he said, looking pleased with himself. 'I pushed it down behind a seat. It could be days before it's found. Weeks, even.'

'Would anyone connect you with the train?'

'I bought tickets at the station, and I paid cash,' said Gustav. 'It was very busy – I don't think the ticket person even glanced up. And the train was crowded – it was going on to . . . Carlisle, I think. Dozens of people were getting on and off. There couldn't possibly be any connection back to me. And even if it was noticed that I went to Worcester the day after Imogen vanished, it was a perfectly innocent journey, and it had been fixed up a couple of weeks ago.'

This sounded all right, and Olivia relaxed.

'Has anything happened about the police search?' said Gustav.

'No.'

'Good.'

But as he was going up to bed, he called to her.

'What is it?' Olivia had been finishing some homework, but she went out to the hall.

Gustav pointed to the cellar door. 'It's open,' he said.

Olivia's heart lurched. I left it open, she thought. I must have done. It's the only way it could be open like that. She said, 'It doesn't fit very well. Maybe the wind blew it open. It was very windy earlier on.'

He frowned, then pushed the door wide, and went down the stone steps. Olivia waited, her heart bumping against her ribs. But there would be nothing wrong. There would not be anything to show she had been down there earlier.

Gustav came back, and closed the door firmly. 'I think you're right about the door not fitting properly,' he said, examining it. 'I believe it's warped or the frame's slipped, or something. I'll see if I can fit a bolt or something to it tomorrow. We can keep the bolt across, and that will keep it shut.'

'Will you be able to do that yourself? We can't call anyone in, can we?'

'Can you get a bolt from one of the DIY places?'

'I suppose so. Yes, I could do it on Saturday.'

'Then I'll fit the bolt myself,' he said. 'And we'll keep the door shut.'

After she got into bed, Olivia looked at the silver ring again. Definitely it was too small to have been Imogen's. It looked very old, and there was an initial inside it. Olivia looked at it closely. It was worn and it took a while to make it out, but in the end she was sure that the initial was *G*. G for Ginevra?

Could it be Ginevra whose body was down there? Was that the truth of the legend? That she had been walled up alive?

Diary entry, 1790s

This isn't how I expected to die. Not like this – with brutality and hatred and misunderstanding. And with fear that almost chokes me.

My death will happen in four days, so they tell me.

This morning, the turnkey brought in two men from what I took to be either the National Guard or perhaps officials from the Republic. They wore the distinctive red and blue uniforms, with the tricolour cockade. I suppose it looks striking and smart.

The minute they came in I felt as if something had driven a fist into my very guts, but I forced myself to be calm, and sat with my back very straight and my hands folded in my lap.

I knew what they would say before they spoke. They would demand that I take the oath of allegiance to France, just as they were demanding it from all professed *religieuses*. Because even though I was born and had lived most of my life in England, they would know of my French ancestry, and it would weigh in the scales against me.

When we made our decision to come to France, we had thought of ourselves as English – women who would not be in danger from the Revolution. We had thought – foolishly as it turned out – that our vows would protect us. If I had given my French grandmother a thought, it was simply to be grateful that I had grown up able to speak French nearly as well as I could speak English.

It was not the oath of allegiance these two men were demanding, though. They stood in the centre of the cell, their faces hard and their expressions implacable, and the younger one said, 'We shall be presenting the nuns who accompanied you with the oath of allegiance.'

'Yes?'

'But we shall not be presenting you with it,' said the other man. 'We shan't waste time doing that.'

I said, as coldly as I could, 'Why not?'

'Because we already know you to be guilty of a very grave crime,' said the younger man.

'A crime,' said the other one, 'which is punishable by death. You are to be taken to the guillotine, Sister.'

The fear almost engulfed me completely then, but somehow – with God's help, I believe – I managed to say, 'What is this grave crime supposed to be?'

'It's a crime that has not been encountered in France – or any other country, I think – for several centuries,' said the younger one, coming closer. His skin had an unpleasant resemblance to badly cooked porridge. 'We know who you are, Sister Cecilia. We know your family, and we know about the music that has been in their possession for several centuries. When you entered the English convent, you took that music with you.'

'You preserved it,' said the other one. 'And now you have brought it back to France.' He paused, then said, 'You are here, Sister, to revive the custom of the Lemurrer.'

The Lemurrer. The word fell into the room like a heavy stone.

After what felt like a very long time, I managed to say, 'I have no idea what you mean.' Thus adding the sin of lying to the tally, because of course I knew what they meant. I knew all about the dark, forbidden chant, handed down in my family through the generations, and never destroyed. My grandmother's words came to me. 'It should be kept in the darkness from which it came,' she had said. 'But it should never be destroyed. There may come a time when it can be used for good.'

'Of course you know what we mean,' said the younger man, impatiently. 'Your family has possessed the Lemurrer chant and its music for several hundred years. Your ancestors were among those who carried out the ritual – who put to death the sinners who committed fornication.'

'I am hardly responsible for the sins of my ancestors,' I said, coldly.

'The Bible suggests otherwise, of course. And your eyes filled up with a memory when I mentioned committing fornication. Is it a guilty memory, Sister Cecilia?'

I said, coldly, 'Fornication is a mortal sin.' But even as I said it, I was thinking: forgive me, my dear, lost love for speaking of you as a sin – you were never that to me.

'We aren't concerned with your mortal sins,' said the man. 'We don't really care who you've fornicated with, or how many times.'

(He did not, in fact, actually use the word 'fornicate', but another word – one which I have certainly heard before, but which I find repugnant to write down.)

'We are concerned with the fact that you have brought the Lemurrer to France,' said the older man. 'Because you have done it with the intention of using it against our Church.'

'How?'

'You came here to call together your own kind in secrecy—'

'My "own kind"?' I said, sharply.

'Catholics,' he said, with a sneer. 'You brought the Lemurrer back to the place of its birth in order to use it to rally Catholics. To ignite hatred against the Revolution and the Republic. The Republic is suppressing your religion, Sister – and you hate that, don't you? Your crime is the crime of incitement against people you see suppressing your religion. And incitement is punishable by death.'

'I have no music of any kind with me,' I said, meeting their eyes without flinching. 'You must know I brought almost nothing on the journey. We – my sisters in God and I – came to France to give support to some Carmelite nuns who were imprisoned for refusing to obey your constitution.' It sounded convincing. It sounded true.

'We were travelling to Compiègne to be as near to them as we could,' I said. 'Our mother house is in Compiègne – we knew we would be given shelter there.'

'The Lemurrer does not need to be written down,' he said, ignoring the last part of my words. 'It's handed down by word of mouth. You grew up knowing it. It's stored in your head.' He tapped his own forehead significantly. 'If you had reached Compiègne, if we had allowed you to reach it, you would have reached out to Catholics – you would have gathered them to you.'

'But our people are loyal and alert,' said the other one. 'And all members of religious communities are taken for investigation at the moment. That's why you were taken when you reached Calais. And then when we realized who you were—'

They feared us because of the music, my grandmother used to say. *They watched us, because they were afraid we might start to use it again . . .*

'What will happen to the others who were brought here with me?' I said, abruptly.

'I've already told you what will happen to them. We shall offer them the chance to take the oath of allegiance. If they refuse, they will join you on the guillotine. But for you it will not be offered. You are too dangerous, Sister Cecilia. An enemy of France. As such, you have already been sentenced to death.' He paused, then said, 'You have four days to make your peace with God.'

Before I could say anything – although I have no idea what I would have said – they had left, and there was the sound of the lock being turned in the door.

NINE

Cresacre, 1794

Gina had heard people imply that sin was very pleasurable during the actual committing of it. Satan knew how to spike his barbs, they said, slyly. Certainly, nobody had ever suggested that sin might be boring. But during the committing of Gina's sin with Chimaera – there had been four occasions in all – on two of them she had been thinking about her spring wardrobe, wondering whether green watered silk would be more becoming than blue, and whether last year's hat with ostrich feathers could be dyed to match.

On that final, fateful, afternoon, she had been lying beneath the panting, thrusting Chimaera, staring up at the ceiling, and wishing he had not once again drenched himself in lavender hair oil because the smell was making her feel slightly sick. She had also been hoping that he would hurry up and give the sudden cry of triumph that signified that the bouncing and writhing and gasping were over.

He had already cried out, '*Dio mio*, I am to die, oh, I am to die,' and Gina had been feeling rather guiltily grateful to hear this, when the bedroom door banged open and her father stood there. It was the most embarrassing thing that had ever happened, because Gina and Chimaera were intertwined in a way that could not possibly be misinterpreted. Chimaera was wearing only the skimpiest of shirts, and Gina was wearing nothing at all. Father took all this in instantly, and Gina flinched, waiting for the explosion of anger.

But for a strange, never-to-be-forgotten moment, there was no anger. Instead, Father looked at her, and Gina saw something in his face she had never seen before. Sadness?

Then he clenched his fists, and shouted that Chimaera was a black-hearted whoremonger, and that he would deprive him of his manhood there and then. He plunged across the room to where Chimaera had half fallen out of bed, and was scrabbling across the floor, in an ungainly attempt to escape.

Gina huddled against the pillows, trying to pull the sheets around her, waiting for Chimaera to stand up and courageously defy Father – to fling back his head and declare that he loved Gina and he was prepared to take the consequences of loving her. But he did not. He stood against the wall, clasping his hands in an attitude of prayer, and casting his eyes to the ceiling, either in entreaty for divine intervention or from a wish that the ceiling might collapse and put an end to his plight.

Mother came into the room with a quick, impatient tread, demanding to know what was going on – did John not *realize* all the servants could hear him? And Father Joachim was in the house, conducting some scholarly research in the library, and what on earth must he be thinking at hearing the noise . . .? Then she saw Chimaera, let out a horrified cry, turned scarlet with embarrassment, and ordered Gina to put on some clothes.

Father was still shouting that he would mete out to Chimaera a fate that would render him entirely useless in any woman's bed, and he had seized Chimaera's arms and was dragging him away from the wall, to the centre of the room.

Mother sat down on the nearest chair, talking about mortal sin and virginity lost for ever. 'And in the middle of the afternoon, in broad daylight; oh, Gina, how could you? Disgusting. I feel sick to even think about it. What will people say if it ever becomes known.'

It was a relief to hear footsteps running towards the room at that point, but it was disconcerting to realize that the person who had answered the shouts for help was the gardener who had almost kissed Gina in the orchard. He was wearing moleskin breeches with a leather belt, and a thin shirt open at the neck. He brought into the room the scents of grass and apples and fresh masculine sweat, and he paused in the doorway, looking towards the bed where Gina was trying to scramble back into her nightgown. There was a moment when the entire wild scene seemed to stand absolutely still, and the gardener stood there, staring at her. Gina stared back. His eyes were green, flecked with gold – she had not noticed that in the orchard that day. In that unreal moment, she had the impression that he might be wishing he had been the culprit in her bed, and she also had a brief conviction that he would have been equal to any number of punishments from an outraged father. For a really shocking moment, she wondered what the bed bouncing and writhing would be like with him. No, it would be just as tedious.

Father was still fighting with Chimaera, and Mother said very sharply that somebody had better do something about it or murder would be committed here, at which the gardener seized father by both arms and dragged him away from Chimaera. Father cursed the gardener, who listened politely. His name turned out to be Dan and, despite the outward show of humility, Gina thought there was a glint of amusement in his eyes at the sight of Chimaera, who was still trying to tug down his shirt over his upper thighs.

Father, regaining his temper, brushed back his hair, which had flopped over his forehead, and said in his sternest voice that Chimaera was to leave the house at once – *now*, was that understood? – and to think himself lucky he would be escaping with his cock robin intact.

He instantly apologized to Gina's mother for this last remark, which Gina did not think mother had entirely understood anyway, but said he could not have Gina at the mercy of whore-mongers and unprincipled seducers.

'There's only one thing to be done,' said Mother. 'The girl must be sent to Cresacre Convent.' Gina was used to Mother effectively disowning her as a daughter when she was annoyed, but this afternoon it stung.

She said, 'I don't want to go into the convent.'

'You will not have any choice, madam,' said her mother. 'You will go to the nuns, and they will help to absolve your sin. To drive out the . . . the lust.' She could scarcely bring herself to say the word.

'We don't need to go as far as that.' Gina had never heard her father use such placatory tones before.

'I insist,' said Gina's mother, her lips a thin line. 'She must be cleansed of the mortal sin – the revolting, sickening sin she committed in this very room. She can stay in the convent's retreat house. Father Joachim can see to it, I should think.' She looked at Dan. 'Fetch Father Joachim here.'

Gina said, pleadingly, 'I don't think I was very lustful, Mamma.' She wondered whether to say she had not actually found it especially enjoyable, but this would be hurtful to Chimaera, who had subsided in anxious silence against a wall.

Father Joachim, ushered up the stairs and into the room by Dan moments later, was deeply shocked to hear what had happened. He looked with distaste at Chimaera, but said eagerly that most certainly he could arrange for Gina to go to Cresacre Convent.

'This very night, if you wish it, Lady Chandos.'

'I do wish it. I can't even look at her. She has behaved like a slut.'

'The mother superior will help,' said Father Joachim. 'You are right, of course, Lady Chandos, that this sin must be cast out. The Bible tells us that a harlot is an abomination to the Lord.'

'My daughter is not a harlot,' said father coldly. 'Or,' he said, looking at his wife, 'a slut.' He turned back to Dan. 'Why are you still here? Your place is outside. You will not, of course, speak of what you saw here today. You understand me?'

Dan said, gravely, 'I shall say nothing. You have the word of a gentleman on that, Sir John.' He went swiftly out of the room without looking at Gina again.

'Insolence,' said mother. '"Word of a gentleman" indeed. You had better turn him off tomorrow, John.'

'So that he can talk spitefully about us in the village?' said Father, crossly.

'Perhaps that's true. I suppose it would be charitable to allow him to stay.'

Father Joachim observed that the Bible taught that all people should be trusted.

Mother said charity was all very well in its place, and went out.

Father said, a bit helplessly, 'Gina . . . your mother—'

'It doesn't matter. I understand. Don't let's talk about it.'

Gina's mother made preparations to visit her cousins. She said this would seem a perfectly natural thing for her to do. Also, if they were both away at the same time, it might prevent gossip. She did not look at Gina while she said this, and she did not address her directly. She still seemed to think the worst part of Gina's sin was that it had been committed in the middle of the afternoon.

Father Joachim sat next to Gina in the carriage on the journey to St Cecilia's. Gina tried not to notice that he smelt musty. When he turned to speak to her, she tried not to flinch from his breath, which was sour.

'It is hard for you to leave your home, Gina,' he said. 'But remember it's for your soul's sake.'

Gina thought: please don't let him say he fought for my soul the night I was born. But he did say it, of course.

'I fought to save your soul the night you were born,' he said, as solemnly as if he had not said it at least a hundred times before. 'I wrestled with heaven to keep you in the world, Gina. So tiny and helpless and fragile you were that night. But God heard my pleas. He let you stay. And we were so glad I succeeded, weren't we, Sir John? So very glad.'

Gina's father looked at Joachim for a moment as if he did not much like him, then gave a brief, impatient nod. Father Joachim smiled and leaned his head back on the padded squab of the carriage, and Gina went back to looking out of the window. Here was the Black Boar, where the men of the village congregated in the taproom, and where some of the livelier village girls went to eye the men. It had recently become one of the new coaching inns, and Alberic Firkin, who obliged in the way of small building jobs, had had to create a large yard to allow the stage coaches and mail coaches to come in. Dan, the gardener at Chandos House, had been called in to help with some of the work. Lights burned in the window of the Black Boar and, at the sight of them, Father Joachim sat up straighter.

'A place of sin,' he said.

'The local people like to relax a little after the day's work,' said Gina's father, tolerantly. 'They enjoy the company.'

'Sir John, the Bible tells us how gluttony will be punished with the force-feeding of rats, toads and snakes, and as for the sin of lust—'

'It's hardly gluttony to down a few tankards of ale and one of Mistress Firkin's steak pies,' said Father.

'Well, perhaps not.'

They went past the straggle of cottages in the little square, and past the blacksmith's forge at the far end. It was strange to be seeing these familiar places by night; Gina had hardly ever been out after dark. They turned off the main road, and started along the narrower, tree-lined track that led to the convent. Here and there were massive old stones, which were all that was left of the priory that had once stood here. Finally, the driver reined in the horses, and there ahead of them was the convent.

'This is the convent's retreat house where you will sleep, and this is your room,' said the nun who had opened the door to them. She was rather tall, with strongly marked cheekbones, and she looked at Gina very closely.

The room was small, but there was a narrow bed with a crucifix hanging above it, a small writing desk and a chair. There was a small window with lead strips.

'We lock all the rooms each night after the Great Silence begins,' said the nun, indicating the lock on the outside of the door. 'It started an hour ago, but I am allowed to break it for long enough to welcome you, and make sure you have all you need. I am Sister Cecilia. Have you had supper?'

Gina said she did not think so. She could not remember when she had last eaten.

'Fasting has its purposes, but this will not be a good time for you to fast,' said Sister Cecilia. 'Your father would wish you to have proper sustenance – of the body as well as the soul.' She spoke as if she knew Gina's father, and Gina remembered that he had some sort of involvement with the convent – something to do with helping to administer their money.

Sister Cecilia went out, reappearing a few moments later with a tray, on which was a wing of chicken, together with a twist of fresh bread and a pat of butter. There was also an apple, a sliver of cheese, and a small flagon of milk. It was hardly a feast, but it was perfectly adequate, and at least it did not seem as if they were going to give her bread and water, or starve her into penitence.

Sister Cecilia went out, and Gina heard a key turn in the

door, then the sound of footsteps going away. She suddenly felt very lonely and dismal, but she sat down to eat the food, then wrapped herself in her cloak and lay down on the bed.

She did not really think that what she had done with Chimaera could have imperilled her soul very much, but she understood that her parents wanted her to find repentance and be given forgiveness. Her last thought before falling asleep was to wonder if her mother had left Cresacre as she had said, and gone to stay with her prim, humourless cousins. She usually fled to them to avoid facing any unpleasantness.

Chimaera had been cross about being caught with the *bella* Gina, and being ordered to leave Chandos House.

He had only gone as far as the local inn, which the English, with their curious way with a name, called the Black Boar. It was all he could afford until he saw where his fortunes might next lie, and a man could not spend the night sleeping in a ditch.

In the attic room assigned to him, he contemplated his situation. He considered it all very unfair. He was a man of many passions. When he performed on a stage, his singing was infused with such ardour that ladies swooned, and members of ancient royal houses flocked to his dressing room to beg he would come to their palaces. It was inevitable that such ardour should also inform and infuse his private life, which was why there had been so many affairs of the heart, and also, of course, of the loins, because the two usually went together.

The afternoon with Gina should have been a charming, sweetly satisfying interlude – one of a series of such interludes. Chimaera had set the scene as he always did, doing so as carefully as if it were a stage being dressed for a public performance – not that he had ever given this kind of intimate performance before an audience, of course, although it had occasionally been suggested. Juliette, that naughty girl, had once proposed it as a very amusing diversion, even offering to bring along a friend to form a trio – even two friends, if Chimaera felt inclined towards a quartet? Chimaera would, of course, have been more than equal to satisfying two women in the same bed, or even three, but he was very glad he had declined, because if

Juliette's brother, Fredo, had heard about it, he would have scoured the world and trawled the oceans to mete out revenge.

This afternoon, Chimaera had described to Gina how he would one day return to the theatres where he had been so adored, and how Gina would go with him.

'It will happen, my *bella signora*. But until then, we shall do this – oh, and this – and you will do this to me – I guide your hand down, you see . . . Ah, yes . . . *Yes* . . .'

It was very unfortunate indeed that the series of caresses had progressed to the ultimate intimacy when Gina's father burst into the room. He was furious. He threatened Chimaera with a castrato's fate, and called him a common deceiver and a vulgar, lowborn debaucher. These were great insults. Chimaera's admirers, of whom there had been many, said he was undoubtedly of the nobility. People writing of his triumphs hinted that he was a *visconte*, perhaps even a *marchese* – a renegade from his class, a rogue member of the aristocracy who had turned vagabond, strolling player, for the love of music.

And now he had been called lowborn and vulgar by a provincial English squire, and he had been glared at by a fish-eyed English lady and regarded with cold disapproval by a jowly, pig-eyed priest.

Still, there were not many gentlemen who could have made such a sweeping and impressive exit from such a chaotic situation, clad only in a silk shirt and one stocking. Chimaera was glad to remember that he had managed it with considerable dignity. He could don any role.

Any role . . . An idea that had been germinating in a corner of his mind took on a little more substance. Could he now don the role of the heroic lover, and rescue his beloved from her convent prison? It was an entrancing prospect. Gina – so lovely, so tremblingly innocent and so grateful to be shown real love: surely he owed it to her to try to reach her. He also owed it to his own current impoverished state to try to ally himself with a wealthy family, although this was not the main point.

He remembered he had a velvet jerkin in his carpetbag (a maroon colour and extremely dashing), and a lawn shirt with wide, full sleeves, in which he had played the womanizing Macheath in *The Beggar's Opera*. The garments would be exactly right for the rescue of Gina, and Chimaera would add leather boots and a swaggering walk.

The more he considered this, the better he liked it. He would be the hero, the princely lover bracing all dangers for his lady and finally galloping away with her. The fact that he did not have a horse did not matter. He would borrow the cloak of night so richly described by one of the poets (he thought it would be Shakespeare, because it usually was), and he would carry his Gina away to the glittering life he had enjoyed – providing access could be gained to her father's money. Then Chimaera would again perform to adoring audiences, and Gina would be in the stage box each night, swooning with admiration.

TEN

Cresacre, 1794 (cont'd)

On Gina's first morning in Cresacre Convent, she was sent to the refectory to help the kitchen nuns with the peeling of potatoes and the chopping of onions. Sister Agnes, who was in charge of the kitchens, was shocked to find that Gina had no idea how to peel a potato, and that she had not previously realized that potatoes needed peeling anyway. She had thought they were just part of a dish that appeared on the table, she said, and Sister Agnes pursed her lips and did not know what the world was coming to when young girls were so ignorant. She furnished Gina with a selection of knives and gave severe instructions that everything was to be ready for the cooking pot in an hour.

If potato peeling and onion chopping were the nuns' method of driving out the sin of lust, it was likely to be effective. Gina thought you would not have much opportunity of being lustful with anyone when your hair and your hands smelled of onions, and your entire body was wrapped in a sackcloth apron.

But Sister Agnes, questioned as to whether Gina could take a bath and wash her hair, said, tartly, that she supposed Gina could rinse her hair tomorrow or the next day under the pump outside the kitchen. Washing took place at a deep stone sink, where there was only cold water and what appeared to be a communal bar of lye soap. Gina reminded herself that she would not be here for ever, and that once she was at Chandos House again she would bathe in blissful hot water every day with scented soap, and sinfully vain and expensive oils and creams to rub into her skin.

There was not much conversation between the nuns, even outside the Great Silence, but Mother Superior sought Gina out and asked if she had settled in.

'Yes. Thank you.'

'We all of us take a wrong turning at times, Gina, and we all need to be helped back.' She nodded, and went on her way, leaving Gina feeling rather unexpectedly comforted, although it sounded as if Mother Superior had been told about her sinful exploits with Chimaera. If so, it was likely to have been Father Joachim who had told her.

On the second day, during the midday meal, there was some discussion about the unrest in France, where monasteries and convents were being suppressed by the revolutionaries.

'I hear that some Carmelite nuns from a convent at Compiègne were imprisoned last month,' said Mother Superior.

'That's near to our own mother house,' murmured one of the nuns.

'Indeed, it is. And all for defying the revolutionary government and refusing to obey the new civil constitution of the clergy,' said Mother Superior. She glanced at Gina, who was listening with interest, and said, 'You see, Gina, that we are not so far away from the world that we do not know what happens in it.'

'Mother Superior,' said Sister Agnes, with pride, 'often sends Dan – your own gardener at Chandos House – to procure a copy of the *London Gazette*.'

'I do. And I don't mind in the least that the *Gazette* comes by way of the Black Boar,' said Mother Superior, serenely.

'How could you tell that, Mother?'

'Its pages have a strong smell of ale.'

'Oh, I see.'

Sister Agnes, passing the vegetable dish down the table, remarked that the man, Robespierre, was nothing but the spawn of Satan. 'I don't care who hears me say it,' she added, belligerently, 'and nor do I make apology for using such a term at the dinner table. Cabbage, Sister Gabrielle?'

'We shall include the Carmelite sisters in our prayers,' said Mother Superior, and made a knot in the woollen cincture around her waist by way of an *aide-mémoire*. Gina found this small, homely action unexpectedly endearing.

From her place at the end of the table, the young novice, Anne-Marie, asked, hesitantly, what would happen to the imprisoned nuns.

'They're regarded as traitors because they defied the revolutionaries so persistently,' said Mother Superior.

'And because they refused to take the oath of allegiance to France,' put in Sister Cecilia. 'I'm afraid that very few people come out of the revolutionaries' prisons alive.'

'They would execute professed nuns?' said Anne-Marie.

'I'm afraid they would. They are doing.'

'The martyr's death,' whispered Anne-Marie, her eyes huge with horror.

Sister Agnes, still spooning out vegetables, said that martyrdom was very admirable, but Anne-Marie would do better to pay attention to saying her daily office rather than dwelling on macabre events. And, said Sister Agnes, while she thought about it, Gina might kindly make sure tomorrow's serving of potato did not contain bits of peel and the eyes.

Gina did her best to enter into the life of the convent, because if she had to be here for a time, she would try to behave as well as possible.

She attended the various services that took up so much of the convent's day, liking the chapel, which was small but imbued with serenity and with the music the nuns made such a part of their lives. It appeared that Sister Cecilia, who was the convent's bursar, had a particular interest in music. 'One day,' said little Anne-Marie, sounding awed, 'she intends to write a treatise about the pathways of religious music – about how people used it for worship over the centuries.'

Gina told Sister Cecilia, a bit hesitantly, that she had herself been studying music.

'Only in a very small way, of course.'

'I'm pleased to hear it, though. Would you like to play the organ while you are here?'

'I don't know if I could manage it. I'd like to try. I was studying a Mozart piece,' said Gina.

'I'm not sure how much Mozart we have. There's a good deal of Bach, of course.' She got up to look along the carefully stacked rows of music at the side of the organ, then stopped suddenly, frowning.

Gina said, 'Is there something wrong?'

'It's just that . . . it looks as if this section has been disturbed.
As if someone has been looking for something.' She frowned,
then said, 'It's unusual – this is regarded as my province. But
it's of no importance. And I've found some Mozart for you.'

It was on the fourth night of Gina's stay that she was woken
by sounds outside her window. A kind of scraping, and then a
faint, rythmic squeaking. Wheels on some kind of cart? But
Gina could not think why a cart would be coming up to the
convent in the middle of the night, and the window was too
high for her to look out, even standing on tiptoe.

There was probably a perfectly ordinary explanation, but after
a moment she slid her legs out of bed, and reached for the robe
she had brought from Chandos House. The door of her room
had been locked when the Great Silence commenced, but Gina
had no idea if the key was left in the lock outside any of the
rooms. She could not get out. But it was possible that someone
could get in.

The scraping sounds had stopped, but other sounds had
replaced them, and now the sounds were not coming from
outside, they were coming from within. Footsteps. Firm, rather
heavy footsteps were coming towards this room. There was no
reason why anyone would come to her room at this hour, unless
there had been word of something wrong at home. One of her
parents taken ill, perhaps? But her mother would be at the dreary
cousins' house, which was a day's journey away, and her father
would not have wanted her woken in the middle of the night.
Could it conceivably be Chimaera? Breaking into the convent
by night and stealing along to her room was the kind of risky,
romantic thing he might do. Gina hoped it was not Chimaera,
because if he got into her room he would certainly expect to
make love to her there and then. He would find the secrecy and
the surroundings exciting, and the danger of discovery would
add to it for him. Gina did not think it would be exciting at all;
on the contrary she thought it would be a bit sordid, quite apart
from worrying about one of the nuns finding them. The prospect
of Mother Superior or Sister Cecilia coming in and seeing her
with Chimaera was unthinkable.

The steps came all the way along the stone corridor, then
stopped. No light showed through the small grille at the top,

but Gina sensed someone's presence. Did that mean that whoever it was had not wanted – not dared? – to bring a lantern or even a candle to see the way?

A voice said, in a hoarse whisper, '*Gina? Gina – are you in there?*'

Gina's unease spiralled into outright fear. She shrank back against the wall, clutching the thin robe around her and, as she did so, there was the sound of the lock being turned from the other side of the door. It was pushed slowly open, and a shadow fell across the floor.

Father Joachim said, 'Don't scream, Gina. Even if you do, no one will hear you.'

He closed the door, and came towards her.

Chimaera thought rescuing Gina from the convent, and carrying her off to Italy, would make a splendidly dramatic adventure. It might even form the basis for a new and exciting opera – an opera in which Chimaera himself would play the leading role. This was an alluring prospect, and the only problem was how the staging could be afforded. The idea of Gina's father came into his mind again. Was it possible that John Chandos might be prepared to hand over a suitable sum of money, to ensure that his wanton daughter was out of reach of gossip and scandal? Chimaera would not really have spread scurrilous stories about his beloved Gina, but Sir John would not know that. Lady Chandos would certainly not know it. And the result would be that Chimaera would have enough money to return to Italy, taking Gina with him, and stage his opera. The world would get a new and marvellous musical work and Chimaera himself would regain his former glittering life.

Careful thought would have to be given to the creation of such an opera. Since Mozart's death there was no one who could be trusted to compose something so important. Could Chimaera turn his own hand to it, perhaps? He did not see why not. The plot was already there – the heroine yielding to the persuasions of the hero in her bedchamber . . . Then the ill-starred lovers discovered *in flagrante delicto* by the enraged papa. Chimaera might add one or two underlings at that point; they could wring their hands and wail in the manner of a Greek chorus. Then would come the spiriting away of the hapless heroine into captivity, from which the hero would rescue her. All very good. *Supremamente buono*, in fact.

As for the music – it should not be so difficult to compose some uplifting arias and to write the libretto. It would stage very well at Teatro alla Scala, for example. And his own career would take a new, and even more glittering direction than before.

The following morning, after a robust breakfast, Chimaera set off to explore the general area more fully than he had yet done. 'Reconnoitring the terrain', army officers called it. He was rather hoping he might meet Sir John Chandos during this foray. He did not dare go up to Chandos House, but if he could contrive a meeting with Sir John, he would not flinch from making his request for an appropriate sum of money to allow him to leave the area, taking Gina away from any incipient scandal and gossip. Sir John had threatened him with several undignified fates, but Chimaera was not very worried, because he thought John Chandos was a man of quick temper and that he would have cooled down now. Also, he thought Sir John was very fond indeed of his daughter.

But there was no sign of John Chandos anywhere, so Chimaera returned to his room at the Black Boar, and consoled himself by drafting out an opening scene (with full chorus) for his opera. This task occupied him for most of the next day, after which he felt he could spend a convivial evening in the taproom. You did not know what bits of useful information you might pick up, and also there was a serving wench who had cast several come-hither looks his way. Chimaera would be faithful to Gina, of course; well, he would be faithful in spirit. But a man had needs.

In the event, the beckoning-eyed lady was nowhere to be seen, and Chimaera found himself in conversation with several local people, including Cresacre's builder, a person by the name of Alberic Firkin. Master Firkin was disgruntled with his lot, and did not scruple to say so to anyone who would listen, which meant most of the assembled company.

'Cresacre Convent expecting me to do work for next to nothing yet again,' said Alberic, puff-cheeked with indignation.

'They've got the roof of that rubbishing old retreat house practically falling in, and Mother Superior saying they haven't the money to pay large bills, and wanting me to reduce my charges. Me, a master builder, that has served my apprenticeship, and knowing exactly what needs doing and what building materials cost. Never mind finding a load of bricks and a tub of mortar going missing, which I did only this morning.

Several people said you could not trust anyone any longer.

'It's Sir John Chandos as'll be at the root of the convent's miserliness, you mark my words,' observed an elderly carter from the chimney corner. 'They call him a trustee or some such. I call him a pinchpenny.'

'If you ask me,' said Alberic, 'it's not so much Sir John as his lady. Mighty watchful of the money, that one.'

The landlord, who happened to be in the taproom mopping up spilt ale, said warningly that Sir John and Lady Chandos were very well respected. Very respectable.

'Respected she might be, and so might he,' said the carter. 'As for respectable – well, Sir John might be respectable *now*, but it wasn't always so. Very fond of the ladies in his youth was Sir John, so I always heard. Bit different now. Repented his sins, that's what he'd have you believe.'

He made a disgusted noise, and the landlord told him to hush, and reminded him that Sir John was a justice of the peace and a trustee of St Chad's as well as the convent, and he was not a man anyone wanted to cross.

'Well,' said the carter, who had attained venerable years and did not give a tinker's curse about justices of the peace or trustees, 'in my opinion, it's the repented ones as are the worst when it comes to a bit of forbidden rogering.' He glared round the bar, and was hastily provided with a tankard of cider by the landlord, with the hope that he might drink himself into insensibility and have to be taken home in Alberic Firkin's wheelbarrow.

'There's no prude so great as a reformed rake,' said Alberic. 'Look how Sir John bundled that girl of his into the nuns' hands. Faster than a rat up a drainpipe.'

'Ask me, it was his lady at the back of that,' put in someone. 'Cold as charity, that one. And I'll be bound all the little wench

was about was a bit of mischief with a young man. Nothing
wrong in that. What maiden of seventeen don't enjoy a bit of
a kiss and cuddle with a young man?'

Chimaera, listening closely, was immensely relieved that no
one seemed to know any more on that topic. He remained
unobtrusively in his seat, and his patience was rewarded a
moment later when Alberic Firkin said that Gina Chandos had
been taken along to the convent's retreat house.

'That very place where folk go for peace and serenity,' he
said. 'Fat chance of that with the roof threatening to fall in and
bury anyone unfortunate enough as to be beneath it.'

Chimaera had no interest in disintegrating roofs, but he
had the information he had wanted, so he nodded a goodnight
to the company, and went out.

In the small room in the retreat house, Gina tried to force down
the rising panic, and to think that it was not so very unusual
for Father Joachim to be here in the convent. Her heart was
thudding, but she said, in as ordinary a voice as she could
manage, 'What are you doing here, Father? It must be midnight
at least – I was asleep. How did you get in? I thought everywhere was locked up after Compline.'

'I can come and go as I wish in this place,' he said. His eyes
flickered on her body, thinly covered by the silk robe. 'The
mother superior herself gave me a key to the side door that
opens directly into the retreat house,' he said. 'I daresay she
hasn't made that known, though. She keeps her secrets, that
one. You would be surprised at some of the secrets that she
keeps.'

Gina said firmly, 'Father, if you don't mind, I don't really
want you here in my room in the middle of the night.'

'I have no sinful intent towards you,' he said, at once. 'That's
not how I think of you, Gina – even seeing you that day with
that man, that Italian fornicator . . . Both of you naked in a
bed . . . That caused me great pain, you know. You had been
so pure, so innocent, untouched; I wanted you to remain that
way.' He came closer, and said, 'But with such a parent, perhaps
it was to be expected.'

'I don't know what you mean,' said Gina.

'Don't you? Were you never told who you really are, Gina?' Without warning, he seized her wrist, and pushed her back onto the bed. Gina cried out, and resisted, but the girdle of her robe had come loose, and Joachim snatched it up and wound it tightly around her wrists, binding them together.

Gina kicked out at him for all she was worth, but her feet were bare and she landed only the lightest of blows. If she screamed would she really not be heard? As if this thought had reached him, Father Joachim took a large, folded handkerchief from a pocket. A sickly sweet smell rose up and Gina flinched, but he was already pressing the handkerchief over her lips, holding it firmly in place. The cloying scent smacked into her senses and the room began to spin around her. She tried to claw the smothering cloth away, but Joachim had knotted the handkerchief too tightly.

Through the dizzying waves, Gina was aware of being lifted and carried from the room into the stone corridor beyond. There was the sound of the door of her room being shut, and the key turning in the lock. That meant no one would realize she was missing until Matins. Five, six hours away?

Then came the sensation of cool night air on her face, and she thought they had come through the side door into the kitchen garden. A handcart was propped against the wall, and Father Joachim laid her in it, then reached for the long handle at the front and began to pull it away from the convent. It bumped over the uneven ground, and it was difficult to see where they were going, but they did not seem to be going very far, because before they reached the highway, he turned onto a narrow track. Low-branched trees thrust into Gina's face, and the cart jolted and bounced even more wildly on the uneven surface. Once Joachim stumbled, and Gina felt a surge of hope because, if he fell, would that give her an opportunity to run away? But she was still so light-headed from whatever had been on the handkerchief that she did not think she could even stand up, let alone run anywhere.

Mist lay patchily on the ground, as if something just under the surface was smouldering.

The rotting-sweetness taste was still in Gina's mouth, and the stench of whatever Joachim had given her was still in her nostrils. She was starting to think it might be laudanum, which her mother occasionally took. It would have been easy for Joachim, who was a frequent visitor to Chandos House, to take some from the bottle in her mother's cupboard, especially since her mother would have left to visit the prim cousins. But why? What was the reason for this wild behaviour?

The trees thinned and she managed to twist her head around to look about her. The handcart had been brought to a small clearing, with a cottage directly ahead.

Joachim wedged the cart against one of the walls, and walked round to look down at her.

'You'll recognize that place, I expect,' he said. 'It's Infanger Cottage. It's on convent land – we aren't far from the convent itself, of course. Sir John tries to insist it's on the Chandos estate, but the convent insist it's theirs. No one has ever been able to establish the truth, so it often stands empty for years at a time.'

Gina knew in a general way about Infanger Cottage and its tangled ownership. Father had once said it was a battle as to whether the convent paid Firkin's account for work to stop the place falling down, or whether he did so himself. He said Mother Superior was a tartar to deal with, and Sister Cecilia, the bursar, was nearly as bad in her own quiet way.

Joachim reached down to lift Gina out of the cart. 'Don't struggle,' he said. 'You won't get free anyway – I have the strength of ten men because my heart is pure, and my soul is unflawed and safe. But you – repentance won't be enough to save your soul, Gina.'

As he pushed open the cottage's door with a foot, he said, in a voice of such menace that spikes of cold terror went through Gina's body, 'And now here we are. This is your place of execution, Gina.'

ELEVEN

G ina had often seen Infanger Cottage from the windows of Chandos House, and had thought it rather picturesque, a tumbledown witch's cottage, something she might one day try to sketch. But seeing it like this, crouching in the darkness with the trees framing it like curving claws, it was not picturesque at all. It was sinister and menacing.

As Father Joachim carried her inside, the cottage's atmosphere seemed to rear up to hit Gina like a physical blow, reaching her even through the laudanum. *This is your place of execution . . .* There was a smell of damp and neglect, but there was also the impression of sadness, and of loneliness. Gina had the sudden thought that in the past people had been deeply unhappy here. Then she thought: and people who live here in the future will be deeply unhappy, as well.

The hall was bare except for an oak chest standing against a wall. At the far end a door was open; the room beyond it was wreathed in shadows, but Gina glimpsed windows with narrow strips of lead, and a view of the dark forest beyond them. There was no furniture except for a couple of wooden chairs and a rag rug on the floor. She had not often been inside this kind of house, although she sometimes accompanied her mother who visited Chandos tenants, and liked to distribute gifts of food to the poor of Cresacre. But it was clear that this cottage had been empty for a very long time – which meant no one was likely to come here, and that Gina was wholly at Father Joachim's mercy.

Beneath stairs that must lead to the upstairs rooms was a heavy-looking door, the oak worn and dark with age. It had been propped open, and it was possible to see a flight of stone steps, wreathed in shadows, leading down. As Joachim began slowly to carry Gina down these steps, she thought: we're going down into the past. We're going down through the layers of this cottage's history. What will he do to me when we get down to that past? He's mad, of course. How strange that I never realized it before – that no one realized it. But he must be mad – all that talk about repentance not saving my soul and about knowing who I really am.

Joachim reached the bottom of the steps and set Gina down on the floor. It was partly stone flagged and partly hard-packed earth and it was dreadfully uncomfortable, but lying flat helped steady the dizziness a bit. Joachim made sure that her wrists were still securely tied, then went to one of the corners; Gina, twisting her head round to see what he was doing, realized there were two oil lamps, and that he was firing them.

The laudanum-soaked cloth had loosened and fallen around her neck. She was able to take several deep breaths, which helped, and then to partly sit up. As the lamplight flared up, she saw that the stories about the foundations of Infanger Cottage being older than the present house must be true. Alberic Firkin had always maintained that its foundations were medieval, although most people said you could not trust Alberic's judgement, especially after a night at the Black Boar. But the cellar must be considerably larger than the house standing above it. And it was old – oh, God, it was so *old*. The walls were crusted with dirt, and cobwebs dripped from the ceiling like tattered grey cloth. Halfway along was a brick archway. It looked as if it might once have supported a massive structure directly overhead.

There were several shallow alcoves in the walls; they had straight sides and rounded tops, like niches in churches, fashioned for statues. These alcoves were man-sized, though, and two – no, three – of them were very wide. It looked as if someone had been working down here, because piled high against one of the alcoves were what looked like the bricks Alberic Firkin had used to build an extra wall at one side of the Black Boar so that the mail coaches could drive in and out. Gina and her mother had driven past while this work was in progress, although mother had ordered their driver to whip up the horses to a faster pace, so that brick-dust did not blow into the carriage. With the bricks was a bucket containing grey, wet-looking paste, and next to it was what looked like gardening tools. Trowels?

Set high up on one wall was a long window. It was barely a foot deep, and Gina saw that it was level with the ground outside. The glass was smeared with dirt, but it was possible to see thick grass growing up to the cottage's walls and the stunted roots of trees. In this light they looked like diseased hands thrusting up out of the ground.

Father Joachim set the oil lamps down in the centre of the cellar. He moved slowly and deliberately, the radiance from the lamps all around him, faint curls of smoke spiralling up. Gina suddenly realized that he was singing, very softly. She could not make out the words, but the impression that Joachim was preparing to preside over some macabre religious ceremony – that it was not greasy smoke that came from the lamps, but incense – was impossible to miss. His face blazed with all the fervour that the old prophets – Ahab and Elisha and their ilk – might have displayed.

Then he turned to look at her, and the eerie chanting ceased. 'The Bible commands us to root out evil,' he said. 'And for certain sins there was once a very particular punishment. A very old punishment. It used to be known as sacred murder, and it was a punishment that was meted out hundreds of years ago. It fits your own sin now, Gina.'

Gina said, 'What were you singing?' She thought this was probably the most supremely irrelevant thing she could have said, but Joachim nodded, as if he did not find the question strange.

'It's a form of plainchant,' he said. 'I found it in the convent quite recently.'

A memory stirred, of Sister Cecilia saying something about her music being disturbed. She had sounded upset – had she known this music was there? Had Father Joachim stolen it?

'It was hidden inside a stack of plainchant,' he said. 'They're so sly, those nuns, with their secrets. But I know those secrets, and because of it they don't dare refuse me anything I ask. That's why I had a key to the retreat house tonight. The words of the chant were written in French,' he said, 'but it wasn't difficult to translate them. And once I did that, the music soaked deep into my mind. It was a very long time before I recognized what it was, though.'

'What is it?' I'll keep him talking, thought Gina. Then I might get a chance to escape. Or people will realize I'm missing and start a search. He's mad, of course. But perhaps he's only trying to frighten me with all that talk about sacred murder and punishment. Probably he won't actually do anything.

Father Joachim said, 'It's called the murderer's chant.' He reached for the handkerchief again, and from his pocket took a small bottle, tipping its contents onto the cloth. Before Gina could do anything to stop him, he had pressed it over her mouth. The sickly stench invaded her senses for a second time, and the cellar spun wildly around her, the dimness shot with crimson flashes. Through it she felt Joachim pulling her to her feet, and dragging her over to the alcove.

He did not bother to tie the handkerchief in place this time, and in any case the laudanum was spinning a web across Gina's vision and her hearing. She tried to beg him to let her go, but her voice came out so weakly it was likely he had not heard. He pushed her into the shallow recess of the alcove, so that she was standing against the bricks at the back. Moving swiftly, he untied the silk belt from around her wrists, and wound one end around her left hand. He tied the other end to a protruding brick or a jutting bit of brickwork, level with her shoulder. Then he did the same with her right hand, this time using the handkerchief that had been soaked in the laudanum.

'Why are you doing this?' whispered Gina, struggling against the bonds. Surely she could tear a bit of silk and a piece of cotton? But her whole body felt as if all the bones had been pulled out of it. 'Please let me go.'

'Don't you know why?' He sounded surprised. 'It's because you have the taint. I didn't think it had been passed to you,' he said. 'I watched you all these years, and I believed you had escaped it. That you were perfect. My dear, lovely girl – that was how I thought of you. But then that afternoon, when I saw you with that man, I knew I had been wrong. I knew you had the taint after all. I knew you must have had it from the moment of your birth. It was a bitter discovery.'

He turned away, reaching for the tub with the thick paste, and for one of the tools near to it. Through the thick waves of the laudanum, Gina heard him start to sing again. And this time the words came clearly to her.

'*Step by measured step with murderer's tread . . .*
Inch by measured inch with murderer's brain . . .
Brick by careful brick with murderer's hands . . .
I make the layers of death . . .'

The chant echoed around the cellar as Joachim began to lay the bricks across the shallow recess. As he reached the end of each row, he covered the bricks with the paste, then started a new row on top. He's building a wall, thought Gina, with horror. He's going to wall me up in this place.

On and on, he went, layer after layer. The alcove was narrow, and it was not going to take him very long. This was a nightmare – it could not be happening. But it was happening – the height of the bricks was rising. *Brick by brick . . .* Gina fought with the puny strength she had left, but the silk belt and the handkerchief held firm. She tried to cry out, even though she knew no one could hear her, and she heard herself weeping with frustration and fear. It was hateful to let Joachim see her like this, but she could no longer help it. She was going to die, here, in this dark and dreadful place; she was going to die alone, and there was no escape.

The sound of the wet paste and the grating of the bricks being set in place was starting to form a terrible rhythm. It was mingling eerily with the sound of the chanting, and the bricks were up to her shoulders now; the glow from the oil lamps was already partly hidden.

'Father Joachim – please let me go . . .' Gina pulled again at the cloth bonds, but they did not tear and, at last, she let the laudanum pull her into the dark, bottomless well.

As she fell down into it, she could no longer see Joachim very clearly.

But the uncanny singing of the murderer's chant followed her into the blackness.

Coming out of the laudanum's darkness was like fighting up through thick, clogging water that swirled at your eyes and tasted sour in your mouth, threatening to choke you. Gina's arms were starting to ache from being strung up against the wall; she dragged at the silk belt and the handkerchief again, praying for one of them to rip, but neither did. I'll try again in a little while, Gina promised. I'll let the laudanum wear off a bit more, then I'll have more strength.

The macabre singing had stopped. Had Joachim gone away? Gina listened, but could not hear anything. Or could she? The sounds were so faint that it was impossible to be sure. They might simply be echoes of this cottage's past – of the long-ago monks whose priory had stood on this land, centuries earlier.

Were they peering at her across the years, those monks, chattering their rosary beads together, telling each other that this was the wanton, wicked Gina Chandos, the girl who had done the forbidden things with a man, and who deserved to be the victim of a sacred murder?

But Gina would never believe she deserved this, not if a hundred dead monks hissed and gibbered at her, and not if a thousand rosaries chattered and rattled and swung to and fro like cracked bones.

She moved slightly in the small, cramped space and, as she did so, something moved with her – something that was on her right-hand side, something that was impossibly close to her.

A hand came out of the dark, enclosed space and cold fingers closed around hers.

Gina's screams echoed and reverberated in the tiny space, and her mind felt as if it was exploding with panic, because there was someone in here with her – someone in this brick tomb and, whoever it was, was clutching her hand with icy fingers . . . She must get out; she must find a way to get away from this dreadful clutching hand . . . She fought against the thin bonds all over again, but to no avail.

And then a voice close to her said, 'Gina,' and, incredibly, it was a voice she knew.

The pulsating waves of panic receded slightly, and Gina stopped screaming and stopped struggling, and turned her head towards the sound.

On a note of disbelief, she said, 'Father?'

It would not be, of course; it could not possibly be: this was a nightmare and soon she would wake up safe and secure. Or was she going mad and imagining the voice?

But her father's voice said, 'Yes – yes, it's me, Gina. It really is. I'm here with you. I'm not a nightmare.'

He had often been able to understand – to hear – her thoughts in a way her mother had never done. The fact that he had heard her thoughts now made it possible to believe he was real.

But his voice was wrong – it was a struggling voice, as if he had been running hard or as if he did not have enough breath to speak.

Gina said, in a frightened whisper, 'What's happening? Why are you here? Did Father Joachim put you here?'

'Yes. He's mad, I'm afraid. Genuinely mad. I should have realized, but I trusted him . . . Oh, God, I trusted him with so much . . . But today he attacked me . . .' The words broke off, and there was a dreadful sound of indrawn breath bubbling wetly. But then he said, 'I fought him and shouted for help – but no servants around when you need them, not even that rascal Dan . . .'

Dan. The man who had almost kissed her and who had stared at her in her bedroom that afternoon, and who had gold-flecked green eyes . . . There was a faint, far-off comfort in that memory.

'Joachim planned it that way – he waited until no one would be there. And he swung a blow at me – didn't see what it was, but something heavy; it smashed into my ribs . . . Then there was something that sent me spinning into a darkness – laudanum, I think. I couldn't stop him . . .' Again he broke off, and the wet, struggling breaths came again.

Gina wanted to ask again why Joachim had brought her father here to die with her, but she only said, 'Don't talk. Preserve your strength. We'll get out – between us, we'll manage it.'

'I can't help you.' The voice was not just thready now; it was becoming slurred, as if the speaker could barely summon the strength to form words. 'I'm dying, Gina . . .'

'No! I won't let you die. Keep holding my hand.'

'I'm trying to.' Even as he said it, the clasp of his hand was loosening. 'Such pain,' he said. 'So difficult to breathe. Blood in my mouth . . . Keeps welling up . . . The blow that evil creature dealt me – I think it damaged something inside me . . .'

'I won't let you die,' said Gina. 'I'll keep hold of you. We'll get out somehow. Someone will miss us and start searching.'

Again there was the glimmering memory of Dan – this time with an absurd touch of guilt because, if she had been clinging to the idea of a rescuer, it ought to be the idea of Chimaera.

But even as the thoughts and the spark of hope were still forming, Gina knew that even if the entire community of Cresacre turned out to search for them – even if they came to this very cottage – no one would think of breaking down a wall in the cellar. Not until long after it was too late.

John said, 'My poor, dear girl – oh, Gina, I never dreamed he'd bring you here as well. Did he give you laudanum, too?'

'Yes. I thought he had probably stolen mother's.'

'Your mother is . . .' He stopped, gasping, the painful breathing quickening again.

'Don't talk,' said Gina, at once.

'Let me talk while I can.' The clasp of his fingers tightened briefly. 'You don't deserve to be here,' he said. 'Perhaps I do, though – I'm the real sinner.' With a new note of urgency, he said, 'Gina – you must get out – you must find a way to get out.'

'I will. But it will be to get both of us out. I'm tied up, but it's only a piece of silk on one hand and a handkerchief on the other, and if I keep pulling at them, one of them will tear.' She did not say her shoulders were already aching with trying to do this. She said, 'And the stuff sticking these bricks together—'

'Mortar.'

'Mortar. It'll still be wet, won't it? For a while yet, at least. So the bricks won't be fixed in place.'

'I think so.'

'Then once I've got my hands free, I can push the bricks out.'

'Yes. And you'll do it,' he said. 'You must . . .'

The voice trailed off again, and with the idea of keeping his mind awake, Gina said, 'That chant Father Joachim was singing – do you know what it was? He called it the murderer's chant.'

'It's a form of a death chant,' he said, and she heard that his voice sounded a bit stronger. 'An old French custom. Medieval – perhaps even older. It was used when a sinner was being put to death. Immured behind a wall. It's called the Lemurrer, and it's a dreadful thing, Gina. A twisted version of prayer. Pre-Christian. There's the other part of it too. The victim's chant.'

In the failing voice, he said,

'*Step by measured step the murderers came to me . . .*
Inch by measured inch, the light is being shut out from me . . .
Breath by measured breath, my life is being cut off from me . . .
Heartbeat by measured and precious heartbeat, my life is ending . . .'

'That's the victim's chant, Gina. I never knew the murderer's chant – until tonight, I didn't think it existed.'

'Joachim said he found it in the convent,' said Gina.

'Yes. That's where I know it from.'

'How do you know about it? How would such a thing come to be in a convent? They have such beautiful music—'

'They do, don't they?' he said, with almost a note of gratitude. 'I know about it, because . . .' His voice faded into the wet blur again, and Gina could not tell what he said. She could feel that his fragile strength was draining fast, and she wanted to keep gripping his hand, as if by doing so she could keep him alive.

She thought he said, 'I'm so sorry. My dearest love, I'm so very sorry.' And then she thought, he said, in a voice of extreme longing, 'Oh, Ginevra, I've loved you so very much . . .' But the words were threadbare and she could not be sure, and calling her Ginevra was not something he had ever done . . .

There was a flicker of something within the flesh and the bones of the hand clasping hers – almost as if all movement and all feeling was being gradually inverted. There was the curious feeling of something being wrenched out of her grasp, and of something fighting and resisting, but finally, quietly, yielding to the inevitable. Slowly, the hand slid away from her. There was a sighing-out of breath, followed by something that was not quite a choke but more than a gasp.

John Chandos's dead body fell sideways against Gina, the head resting on her shoulder.

Diary entry, 1790s

This morning I woke to a thin light trickling between the bars of my cell, and to the sound of loud hammering and the rattle of wheels outside my cell window.

I went to the window, and stood on tiptoe, grasping the

bars with both hands, and pulled myself up so that I could peer outside.

I knew what I would see, of course, and I did see it. It was only a quarter completed, but it was recognizable.

My window looks out onto a small, enclosed courtyard, with the walls of The Conciergerie rising up around it on three sides. At the far end is a low stone archway leading, I suppose, to other parts of the prison.

Men were working and they had arranged several rows of seats around the courtyard. The seats rose up in a semi-circle, as if people would be coming to watch a theatrical performance. On the ground in front of them were a few wooden stools.

The focus of it all – the place to which the eyes of those people who took seats in the semi-circle and who squatted on the stools on the very ground – was not yet there, but its skeleton was. A raised platform, and above it a terrible shape that was stark and black against the sky. A thick, ugly oblong with a mechanism at the top that could be operated from below.

The guillotine.

As I stared, a tilt-cart was brought in, heaped with straw, and armfuls of the straw were spread over the ground immediately beneath the dreadful outline.

I stayed there, clinging to the bars, watching it all, until the strength in my fingers gave way, and I dropped back to the floor.

And now I am sitting on the narrow pallet bed in the corner of the cell, reaching for prayers that are slithering away from me, trying to calm my panic.

It is only two days since the men came to my cell. I am writing it all down, because it feels as if I am telling a friend.

I thought I had four days in all. Have they brought my death forward? If so, how many hours of life do I have left?

If only I had made that attempt to barter with the turnkey – to barter my body for freedom. Probably it wouldn't have worked . . . And yet . . .

Is it too late to do it, even now?

TWELVE

Harriet Madeley's assertion that Olivia Tulliver would walk barefoot across burning coals to get Phineas Fox to read his father's opera had stuck in Phin's mind. Driving back to the Black Boar, Arabella happily disinterring the details of the discussion in Harriet Madeley's study, he suddenly said, 'Would you object if I phone Olivia Tulliver, and see if I can go back to Infanger Cottage to see her before we have dinner?'

'To get a copy of *The Martyrs*?'

'Yes. This might be quite a good time to catch her – just on six.'

He waited to see if she would suggest accompanying him, but she only said, 'That's a good idea. And you're here to sort out that opera, anyway. I'll have a long hot bath while you're out, and we can have dinner when you get back.'

Phin, who had not been able to decide if he wanted Arabella to accompany him to Infanger Cottage, said this sounded fine.

'I feel as if I'm imbued with church dust and grisly old legends,' said Arabella, as they went up to their respective rooms. 'And also with the moral rectitude of Cresacre School in general and Dilys Davy in particular.' She unlocked the door of her room, and Phin followed her in. 'Dilys has never liked me since I organized a ghost-hunt one term. It's a daunting feeling to be disapproved of so thoroughly, you have no idea.'

'You didn't sound especially daunted.'

'I'm good at pretending.'

'That's what worries me.'

She swung round to face him, and put her hand up to trace the lines of his face with a fingertip. 'You'd know if I pretended with you, Phin.'

'Yes,' said Phin, who had no idea if he would know or not.

He sat down on the bed to make the phone call to Olivia Tulliver. It was annoying when the call went straight to voicemail, but Phin left a message saying he was in the immediate area, and that he would call at the cottage anyway – in about twenty minutes or so – in the hope of catching Miss Tulliver in. He added that he wanted to talk about *The Martyrs.*

'She's probably there anyway,' said Arabella, who was hunting through her suitcase. 'She never used to go out much, as far as I can remember. She was never part of anything at all social.'

'Was she – is she – attractive?'

'I don't remember her as very attractive. Boiled gooseberry eyes and hair like shredded wheat. But, of course, she might have masses of WAG-style blonde locks now, and turquoise contact lenses. Anyhow, that mention you made of old Gustav's opera will get her. She'll welcome you with open arms, gooseberry eyes or not.'

'I hope she won't think I can get the opera onto a stage,' said Phin, slightly alarmed.

'She probably will.' Arabella was still burrowing in her case. 'D'you know, Phin, I have the horrible suspicion that I didn't pack a dressing gown—'

'You can borrow mine if you want.'

'Well, I will, if you don't mind.'

Phin had a sudden alluring image of Arabella wearing his dressing gown, which would certainly be too large for her, and with her hair tumbling untidily around her shoulders, slightly damp from the shower. She would have used the scented bath stuff she always used . . . He began to wish he had delayed the meeting with Olivia Tulliver until tomorrow.

But he fetched the dressing gown from his room, remembering to pick up a notebook as well. 'Enjoy your bath,' he said. 'I'll be back in time for dinner.'

She kissed him. It was quite an explicit kiss. Phin thought the meeting with Miss Tulliver did not need to take very long at all.

'Bring an appetite back with you,' said Arabella, and her eyes slanted mischievously.

'Oh yes,' said Phin. 'I will.'

It was important to quench thoughts of the evening ahead with Arabella, and to focus on Olivia Tulliver and her threats about old, dark scandals, and also on her uncle's troublesome opera. Phin, driving back to the school, already aware of a pleasant air of familiarity about the surrounding countryside, could not decide if he was intrigued or annoyed by the prospect of reading *The Martyrs*.

He assumed it would be all right to leave his car on the sweep of gravel at the front of the building, so he parked and locked it, then set off along the drive, to the little track that Arabella had pointed out.

It was very narrow indeed – certainly too narrow for a car. Trees overhung the path and thick shrubbery crouched on the edges, shutting out the light. There was a scent of leaf mould and rain, and it was not difficult to see why Arabella had called this the path to the *Hansel and Gretel* witch's cottage. It was astonishingly easy to imagine that a witch, 'old as stone', lived at the end of this track. Phin thought he would look out that particular section of Humperdinck's opera to show Arabella the lyrics. He might even take her to a performance of it, if one happened to be running anywhere at the moment. He had a sudden vision of the two of them in seats in the Royal Opera's grand tier, and having supper afterwards in the famous Crush Room. Arabella would wear something noticeable, if not necessarily appropriate, and if she did not lose a scarf or an earring halfway through the performance, she would probably dislodge a contact lens, and the entire row would end up crawling around on the floor to find it. Phin was trying to decide if this would be endearing or maddening, when the track widened slightly, and directly ahead was Infanger Cottage.

And of course it was not the grim gingerbread house, although neither was it exactly benevolent-looking. It was built of dark red brick, crusted here and there with lichen and ivy. The windows were small and some of them were set slightly askew, giving the house a squinting look. It was impossible to estimate its age, but Phin had the impression that bits might have been added over the years, and without much aesthetic consideration.

No lights showed, but it was not yet dark enough for lights to be necessary, so he went up to the front door and reached for the knocker. The door was opened almost immediately – so quickly that he could almost have believed the house's occupant had been standing on the other side, watching his approach. This was disconcerting, but what was even more disconcerting was that the door was only opened by about four inches, and a security chain was visibly kept in place.

A portion of a face appeared, and a suspicious voice said, 'Yes?'

'Miss Tulliver? Olivia Tulliver? I'm Phineas Fox. I left a voicemail message for you about half an hour ago.'

'Oh, yes, you did, didn't you? And I got your message. But I don't often answer the phone. People can be very intrusive at times.'

'If this isn't a good time, I could come back tomorrow—'

'No, it's fine.' There was the sound of the security chain being unfastened, then the door opened more fully.

Arabella's description of Olivia Tulliver had been a good one, although she had not mentioned the nervous air, or the habit of peering closely at everything. Perhaps this was not permanent, or perhaps she was simply short-sighted.

'I'm sorry to seem suspicious, but I'm always careful about who I let in,' said Miss Tulliver, closing the door. 'It's a bit isolated here, you see.'

With the closing – and then the locking – of the door, Phin suddenly felt as if he had been shut in with something that might be unfriendly. But he said, 'I think you're very sensible to be cautious.'

The hall was small and dimly lit, and the house smelt of stale food. The room into which Olivia Tulliver took Phin was at the far end and it was clearly a study. Phin normally found studies interesting, and he usually liked seeing where people worked, but he did not like this one. It was untidy, but it was not a comfortable, books-and-work-in-progress kind of untidiness. There were bundles of papers and notebooks, as if things were seldom thrown away, and alongside the stale smell was a faint impression of burned oil from an old-fashioned stove. Through the window was a rather dismal view of a yard, with weeds thrusting up through the cracks, and several ramshackle outbuildings beyond.

And for a moment Phin thought he was hearing again the faint echo he had picked up twice already in Cresacre – in the church and later in the school as if hands were beating against bricks, and terrified cries for help were gradually becoming weaker . . . But he was letting his imagination run riot, and it was largely Arabella's fault for conjuring up images of crones with macabre appetites, and assorted dark fairy stories as their backgrounds.

Olivia was looking at him. She said, 'I'm sorry about the clutter in here. I'm normally a very neat and tidy person, but I'm currently fighting a battle with the local authority. They want to buy this cottage to make a wider road. They insist they have a right to do that. Now that's never right, is it?'

'Well, I . . . It must be very worrying for you.'

'It is, Mr Fox. Very worrying indeed. Compulsory purchase order, they call it. I told them in no uncertain terms that I wouldn't sell,' said Olivia, tightening her lips. 'This is my land, and I have the title deeds and land registration documents to prove it. My uncle left me the cottage in his will. I've told the council that, and I've told them not to phone me or call at the cottage. So I don't answer the phone or the door – that's why I kept the chain on when you came. They can be sneaky, those council officials, you see. They trap you by pretending they're someone else.'

'That sounds dreadful.' Phin had never actually owned land as such, although the ground rent of his current flat seemed to imply that the ground on which it stood might be paved with the gold of Dick Whittington's pavements.

'Oh, it is. I could never sell this cottage. I would never dare.'

As Phin looked slightly startled, she said, a bit too quickly, 'I would never dare go against my uncle's wishes. That's what I meant. The wording of his will was very explicit. He wanted me to have this as my home. For always.'

'Yes, I understand,' said Phin. 'He wanted to be sure you would be safe. Perhaps a solicitor could advise you.'

'I don't trust solicitors any more than I trust council officials,' said Olivia at once. 'There was a solicitor who said he could help me once with some investments, but he was very unscrupulous.' Her lips tightened and she frowned, as if at an unwelcome memory. 'So I'm dealing with everything myself. My uncle kept all the paperwork – it was at the back of his desk. Correspondence and odd documents going a long way back. That's why there's a bit of a muddle in here.'

'I always work in a bit of a muddle,' said Phin, hoping to strike a friendly note.

'Oh, I don't like muddle. Not in the normal way.'

Phin switched tack. 'Miss Tulliver, about your father's opera—'

'The title is *The Martyrs.*' It was almost a rebuke, as if Phin had committed a solecism by not referring to the work by its title.

'Yes. I've been asked to take a general look at it—'

'Have you?' It came out suspiciously, and she came closer. Phin tried not to take a step back. 'It's brilliant, Mr Fox. And I've . . . well, you could say I've dedicated my life to getting it recognized.'

This was so extreme a statement that Phin could not think how to answer it. Instead, he said, 'Would you be happy to lend me a copy of it? The book and the score, if that's possible. It'd only be for a day or two. I'd take great care of it, of course, and I'm staying at the Black Boar, so I could look through it there and let you have it back by the weekend. Miss Madeley will let me play some of it on the school's piano, so I'll get a good idea of the main arias and the general mood of it all.'

'So you're a musician, too.'

She said this half accusingly, half disparagingly, and Phin said, 'Not exactly,' then was angry with himself for sounding defensive.

Olivia considered him for a moment, then looked back at his card, which she was still holding. 'I'll lend you a copy,' she said. 'I don't allow the original out of my possession.'

'A copy would be very—'

'I'll get one for you now. I have several.' Her mood altered suddenly, and disconcertingly she became eager. 'I'll give you permission for you to show it to any colleagues or contacts you've got in the music world, as well. I own the rights, you know. I'll put the permission in writing.'

'I wasn't exactly intending—'

'I like to be businesslike about these things,' said Olivia, and this time it was definitely a rebuke. 'And while I'm getting the copy, I'll put the kettle on. I'm sure you'd like a cup of tea, and I can show you the most effective scenes while you drink it. No, it's no trouble at all. I always make a cup of tea for my friends when they call. I have a number of friends, of course.'

'I'm sure you do.'

By this time Phin wanted nothing more than to get out of this sad, stale place – with its air of harbouring uneasy unhappinesses – and to be back with Arabella. She would have been liberal with her expensively scented shower gel, and she was probably even now getting ready to sit opposite him over dinner in the Black Boar's oak-beamed dining room. He remembered that there had been moussaka on the menu. He also remembered that Arabella had said, 'Bring an appetite back with you,' and that they had both known she did not mean for the moussaka.

But he could hear Olivia Tulliver opening cupboard doors, and then turning on a tap. There was a faint clanking, as if elderly pipes had been forced into reluctant life. He would have to stay to drink the tea and be shown some of the scenes of Gustav Tulliver's work.

He looked about him, curious, but trying not to be intrusive. It was difficult not to home in on the papers on the desk, of course. There were what looked like surveyors' plans, presumably delineating Infanger Cottage's boundaries, several legal-looking documents, some of them tied with fraying green legal tape, and a few faded and discoloured papers. But you do not furtively rifle someone else's private papers while that someone is making you a cup of tea and looking out the score and book of an unperformed opera. Phin was not going to do so.

Instead, he went to study the rows of books; there were a good many that were clearly from Gustav's teaching days, but ranged beneath the window were books on opera and on the French Revolution. Phin bent down to see these, noticing the names of one or two authors who had scholarly reputations within the music world. Whatever Gustav Tulliver's other faults, he seemed to have been able to recognize good research in others.

Phin stood up, and went across to the piano standing against the far wall, to see if there might be any music on top of it. But there was nothing. He glanced up at a framed photograph on the wall immediately above the piano. It was of a man with deep-set eyes, an elongated jawbone, and a rather humourless mouth. A silver chain with what looked like a small, silver, pearl-studded ring hung over the photograph. Gustav Tulliver? A memorial? Almost certainly, yes. Phin studied it with interest. The silver ring seemed a curious memorial, but perhaps it had belonged to his mother or his grandmother.

He turned back to the desk, and this time a name on one of the papers on the top of the untidy pile leapt out at him. The writing was the graceful slanting hand of at least a century ago. It would not be easy to read the writing of the main body of the page, but a few lines down was a name that leapt out at Phin.

Sir John Chandos.

He looked away almost at once, but the name had already printed itself on his mind, like sun-dazzle. John Chandos. *Chandos.* The vanished manor house of Cresacre, and the almost-forgotten family whose name now only lingered in the dim stones of the church. The church that had those disturbing illustrations of the Lemurrer. It was still unthinkable to read this document. Phin reminded himself that he was here to provide an opinion about *The Martyrs* and not delve into the disappearance of a band of nuns over two centuries earlier, or an elusive legend about someone called Ginevra, never mind wood carvings depicting an old ritual.

But he had the impression of whirling jigsaw fragments trying to slot together in his mind – here and there fitting, but not making any real picture or any real sense, because too many of the pieces were still missing. Might it be just about accept-able if he took a very quick glance at the document to see if there was a date on it? If there was, and if it was during the late 1700s – the time the nuns vanished and the Ginevra legend began – then Phin would ask Olivia openly if he could read it. Part of his research, he would say.

The room was growing darker, but when he looked across at the desk again he was able to read parts of the graceful writing, and to see that it looked like a letter. At the top was written the name of Master Alberic Firkin, Builder. Firkin was not a name you would easily forget; it was practically Dickensian.

Just beneath this name was a date. June 1794. By this time, Phin had taken in the closing sentence as well. This might have been because it seemed to have been written with considerable force – as if the writer might have pressed his or her pen determinedly into the page to add weight to the words. Even after two centuries, they stood out black and thick.

'I thank you for your letter, but must stress, Master Firkin, that no work of any kind whatsoever or wheresoever is to be carried out on Infanger Cottage or within its immediate environs. Nor is the cottage ever to be sold, but is to remain in its present state of ownership.'

And not ten minutes earlier, Olivia Tulliver had said, 'I could never sell this cottage. I would never dare.'

She had instantly tried to counter this rather strange statement by saying she did not want to go against the wishes of her uncle who had bequeathed her the cottage, but taken in conjunction with the emphatic tone of that sentence penned more than two hundred years ago, it was still a very curious thing to have said.

Phin cast politeness and the social niceties to the winds, picked up the letter and began to read it.

THIRTEEN

Master Firkin,
It was the act of a good neighbour to draw attention to
the fact that the roof of Infanger Cottage requires some
attention. I thank you for this, although I have no doubt
you had an eye to a little business on your own account.

Phin could not decide if this was a jibe or a note of dry humour.
He read on.

As for your other enquiry, as to whether the cottage might
be available for you to purchase, as you know – indeed,
I believe as everyone in Cresacre knows – the cottage's
exact ownership has long since been in question. It stands
partly on the land belonging to Sir John Chandos's family,
and partly on land owned by this convent – or, more
specifically, by the convent's mother house, which is near
to Compiègne in France. No deeds as to the cottage's
precise boundaries have ever been found and I believe its
foundations date back to the original monastery. There-
fore, with the approval and knowledge of the legal
advisers both to the Chandos family and to our own house,
decisions as to its maintenance and occupancy have been
jointly made by ourselves and Sir John Chandos.

In my capacity as bursar, I am therefore able to advise
you that Infanger Cottage will not, and indeed can not,
become available for a purchase. Sir John wishes, unequiv-
ocally, for privacy for that piece of land. To that end, I
believe he recently gave his gardener – you will know Dan,
I am sure – clear orders to post signs warning that any
acts of trespass on the land will be summarily dealt with.

I appreciate that you think the cottage could be, as you
term it, renovated and restored, and again, clearly this
would be to your advantage, since you would most likely

*then sell it at a considerable profit to yourself. However,
the decision can not and will not be altered, so I must
ask that you do not approach me or the Chandos family
again on this matter.*

*I thank you for your letter, but must stress, Master
Firkin, that no work of any kind whatsoever or wheresoever is to be carried out on Infanger Cottage or within
its immediate environs. Nor is the cottage ever to be sold,
but is to remain in its present state of ownership.*

*I send you God's blessings, and I am, good sir, yours
very truly,*

The signature at the foot was in the same firm, clear hand.
'Sister Cecilia, Bursar, Cresacre Convent.'

Phin laid down the letter thoughtfully. It was strongly
worded, and the refusal to sell the cottage or even to allow
repair work to be done to it was a curious precursor of Olivia
Tulliver's words earlier.

'I would never dare sell this cottage,' she had said.

Surely that was not an unreasonable statement, though,
given that she seemed to have lived here for a very long time.
As for John Chandos, he had probably been nothing more
than an eighteenth-century squire protecting his interests –
although Phin found it slightly odd that the letter appeared
to have come from the convent's bursar, rather than from Sir
John himself, or a solicitor. Perhaps Sir John had simply been
away from home at the time. It sounded as if the convent had
power to act on his behalf.

Phin was just wondering if he was falling into the classic
researcher's trap of linking two, if not three, unrelated pieces of
information, when Olivia came back into the room. She was
carrying a sheaf of manuscript swathed in bubble-wrap, and she
placed it on the desk with what might almost have been rever-
ence. Then she went back to the kitchen for the promised cup
of tea, after which she moved a chair alongside Phin's, unwrapped
the manuscript, and began to turn over pages and point out
scenes which Mr Fox must read with particular attention.

'It's based on the premise that the Cresacre nuns were involved
in part of the French Revolution,' she said. 'A stirring story.'

'It looks,' said Phin, glancing through several pages and trying to bring critical and objective judgement to bear, 'as if the structure is what's usually known as *tragédie en musique*. Short arias contrasting with recitative – snatches of dialogue.'

'The music itself is only composed for a piano,' said Olivia, 'but my uncle always said it wouldn't be much of a task for someone with sufficient musical knowledge to transpose it into full orchestral.'

'Did he really?' said Phin, expressionlessly.

'This scene here is a very strong one. The condemned cells. The guillotine is in the courtyard outside.'

'It sounds very moving,' said Phin, politely, and forbore to mention that the lyrics beginning, '*Alas, for pity's sake, spare the final blow . . .*' although perfectly appropriate for the scene, were lifted wholesale from Donizetti's opera *Maria Stuarda*, shortly before the doomed Queen of Scots ascended the scaffold.

'You could play any of the music now,' said Olivia, suddenly. She indicated the piano. 'It was my uncle's piano, you know – it was what he used for all his composing. It's out of tune, of course, but even so—'

'Well, I won't at the moment,' said Phin. 'I'll read it all through first.' He folded the bubble-wrap around the manuscript and stood up.

'You are taking the manuscript straight back to the Black Boar, aren't you?' said Olivia, following him out to the hall. 'You won't be calling anywhere else on the way and leaving the manuscript unattended in the car?'

'No, I won't be doing that. I'll collect my car from the school, and go straight back to the pub. I have a meeting later, so I'd better get away now—'

'It's just that there are people who would give a good deal to get their hands on this – even though it's only a copy. There was a journalist once – I thought I could trust him, but he turned out to be a real snake.'

Phin remembered the earlier comment about an unscrupulous solicitor, and he remembered that Arabella had said something about Olivia getting mixed up with a couple of unfortunate men. He felt an unexpected twist of sympathy. 'I'll look after it very carefully,' he said. 'And I'll phone you tomorrow or the day after, and arrange to return it.'

He beat a swift retreat along the woodland path, reached his car with relief, and placed the manuscript in the boot. Driving down the wide carriageway, and turning towards the Black Boar, his mind went back to the letter. How much could be deduced from it? Either John Chandos or the mother superior or Sister Cecilia – or even all three of them – certainly sounded as if they had been hell-bent on keeping people away from the cottage. But there might be any number of relatively respectable reasons behind that letter. There might have been a quarrel between Chandos and the builder, or between the builder and the convent. Or Chandos might have been using the cottage for some secret purpose of his own. It would not be the first time a wealthy landowner had installed a mistress on his doorstep, although Phin could not see Sister Cecilia writing that letter under those circumstances.

Perhaps the cottage had been a secret meeting place for plotters against some high-up figure in the government or even a member of royalty. How about the Terror in France? The favoured theory for the nuns' disappearance seemed to be involvement in the Revolution, and the letter was dated 1794, which Phin thought was a time when the French Revolution had been at its height.

As he neared the Black Boar, he smiled, thinking how much all this would please Arabella, and how she would immediately start spinning a whole new fantasy about the lustful manorial overlord. It was at this point that the Black Boar came into view, and he saw with a lurch of apprehension that standing outside were two fire engines and a paramedic's car.

Phin slammed the accelerator down hard, and rocketed the car forward, swerving into the pub's car park, then leaping out and bounding towards the main doors.

He was halted by a fireman who was just coming out, and who did not seem either fazed by a dire emergency or to be smoke- or soot-smeared.

'I'm staying here,' said Phin without preamble. 'What's happened?'

'Oh, minor thing really. Flood on the top floor, but they

called us out because of diverting the water from the electrics. They called a paramedic because one of the staff skidded on a wet patch of floor and they thought she'd broken her ankle.'

Phin started to say, 'How on earth—?' and stopped, already suspecting the answer.

'A scatter-brained female somehow dismantled a bath tap and water cascaded everywhere. It's pretty much sorted out now, although the first floor's still sopping wet. You might have to find somewhere else to spend the night.'

'It was the kind of thing that could have happened to anyone,' said Arabella. She was standing in about two inches of soapy water, which was not so very much, but which seemed to have washed across the entire upper floor of the Black Boar. The bedroom, as well as the small bathroom, smelled expensively of Arabella's bath essence, and firemen were pumping out the overspill. The pub's staff were scurrying around with mops and buckets and cloths.

Phin could not decide whether to laugh or be exasperated, except that it was usually difficult to be exasperated with Arabella for very long.

'What happened?'

'Well, you see – oh, wait, I'd better help them, because that poor girl skidded and sprained her ankle and that was mostly my fault on account of I knocked over an entire bottle of bath cream in all the flurry, which is why everywhere smells like a Turkish bordello.' Arabella seized a passing mop and bucket from a uniformed maid, and began energetically to mop up some of the water.

'But how—' began Phin.

'I had a bath – well, I told you I was going to do that,' said Arabella, mopping water with enthusiasm. 'And there I was, lying in it with Classic FM on the radio – Schubert, as a matter of the fact the 'Unfinished', and I was just wondering whether it would make a good background for . . . well, for after dinner for the two of us.'

'Not Schubert,' said Phin, before he had realized what he was saying.

'No?'

'He's too good a melodist. It'd be distracting, and . . . Arabella, will you for pity's sake tell me how you managed to flood this entire floor!'

'Schubert was just starting the second movement,' said Arabella, 'when I suddenly discovered that the tap had stuck in the *on* position – fortunately it was the cold tap. I couldn't turn it off, so I leapt out of the bath, and I reached in to pull out the plug – well, yes, of course I pulled out the plug, Phin! – and I tried to unjam the tap, but that was when it snapped off altogether. And water started spurting out like a firework display, and it was going everywhere. Walls, ceiling, windows. Me. It absolutely drenched me. I switched Schubert off at that point, though.'

'Oh, good,' said Phin, rather helplessly.

'I didn't want the water to ruin the radio. I grabbed your dressing gown, because there wasn't time to worry about getting properly dressed – and I'm eternally grateful you lent it to me, although I think it will have to be severely dry-cleaned, but I'll foot the bill, of course, in fact I'll buy you a whole new one, and it can even be from somewhere extravagant like Harrods.' She indicated the hem of the dressing gown which, being too long for her, had trailed its hem in the water. 'And I ran downstairs like one of the Four Furies to get help. I was perfectly respectable because of the dressing gown, so I think it was extremely rude of several men from the bar to wolf-whistle. I paid them no attention,' said Arabella, with uncharacteristic dignity. 'I said to the receptionist that the mains water needed turning off absolutely immediately because the first floor was about to succumb to a flood of Biblical proportions. That might have been an exaggeration, but it got them fired up to take action. Somebody found the stop-tap thing in a basement somewhere, although it took them ages, and when they did find it, it had rusted into its moorings, which isn't surprising, because people *never* use stop-taps, do they? By then the water was all over the floor of the bedroom, and trickling out into the hall, so that was when we had to call the firefighters, in case it reached the electrics. Firefighters aren't just for fires; they deal with floods and disasters as well, did you know that? I didn't.'

'I did know, as a matter of fact,' said Phin, with a sudden vivid memory of Arabella's ebullient cousin, Toby Tallis, who had an extraordinary facility for creating disasters and had twice caused devastation in Phin's flat. It had been Toby who had introduced him to Arabella, which, on balance, Phin was still inclined to view as a good thing. 'I do see how it all happened,' he said. 'And, Arabella, I hesitate to ask this, but—'

'Where are we going to spend the night?'

'Yes. Because it doesn't look as if any of the rooms up here will be habitable.'

'No, they won't. Thankfully the other two rooms checked out earlier, so there would only have been the two of us up here. Which would have been nice, wouldn't it?' said Arabella, rather wistfully. 'You, me and Schubert – oh, no, you said not Schubert. But what I did, I phoned Hats Madeley, and because it's half-term and everything, we can be put up at the school.'

Phin said, in an expressionless voice, 'So our first night together – our first night actually sleeping under the same roof – is going to be in a boarding school?'

'Yes, it will be.' Arabella had abandoned the mop and bucket, and was making a disorganized attempt at packing a suitcase. 'I know it's a bit off-the-wall, but it'll be perfectly comfortable, and Hats says she'll put supper back so we can join her and Dilys Davy. The kitchen staff's on half-strength because of half-term, and the temporary cook's on a vegetarian mission. So supper is lentil soup and fishcakes.'

'I can hardly wait,' said Phin.

In fact, the lentil soup was unexpectedly palatable and there were fresh wholemeal rolls with it. The fishcakes reminded Phin of his own schooldays, but at least here there was parsley sauce with them.

Over a wedge of sharp Cheddar, which was served with celery and crisp apples, he was asked about his visit to Infanger Cottage. He said, guardedly, that he had met Olivia, who had seemed a bit over-focused on *The Martyrs*, and that he had been loaned a copy of it, which he would read over the next day or so. Yes, he added, it did appear to lean heavily on the theory of the French Revolution as a solution to the mystery.

'How did you get on with Olivia?' asked Harriet. 'She was

always rather an odd girl. A very poor judge of character, as far as I remember.'

'She was a bit anxious about the cottage,' said Phin. 'Apparently she's going to be served with a compulsory purchase order.'

'Oh, that's for the road-widening thing,' said Dilys Davy. 'I heard about that.'

'The planners say it's inevitable,' put in Harriet. 'It won't affect the school, because it'll only slice a corner off on that bit of land, but it'll certainly affect Infangers. A pity, I think.'

Arabella said, 'But isn't Infangers too old to be bulldozed? Isn't it listed or something?'

'It's such a confusion of styles, it's difficult to know what it is,' said Miss Davy, and rather unexpectedly produced a bottle of port and another of brandy which she set down on the table, together with four balloon glasses.

'Good for the digestion,' she said. 'My grandmother used to say that cheese digests a meal, but what, then, digests the cheese? So port and brandy is the answer.'

'In the same glass?' said Phin, slightly startled.

'Purely medicinal, of course,' said Miss Davy, pouring a hefty measure for Phin, and then, having appeared to consider the matter, a somewhat smaller one for Arabella.

Harriet said, 'I daresay you never expected to be glugging down port and brandy on these premises, did you, Arabella? We won't mention the time when a dozen bottles of Pinot Grigio were smuggled in for somebody's birthday.'

'You didn't miss much, did you?' said Arabella with a rueful grin.

'I didn't miss anything. I still don't.'

'Imagine Hats knowing about the Pinot Grigio that time,' said Arabella, as she and Phin walked across the main hall. 'Sorry about tonight. The meal wasn't exactly *haute cuisine*, was it?'

'It was perfectly acceptable, though,' said Phin, as they went up the wide staircase. 'Pity about the moussaka, of course.'

'Yes, it was. But I think everything will be dried out at the pub by tomorrow,' said Arabella. 'Hats has put me in my old room tonight,' she said, as they reached the top landing.

Phin said, 'I think I'm along the corridor.' He paused, then said, 'I'd like to suggest I tiptoe along the corridor to your room—'

'Like a character from a French farce.'

'Only to have a goodnight drink, you understand,' said Phin, gravely.

'Which would be perfectly innocent,' agreed Arabella.

'But,' said Phin, 'with your former headteacher sleeping just one floor up from us—'

'It might kill the romance?'

'Exactly. So I think I'll go to bed with *The Martyrs*.'

'You do realize how peculiar that sounds?'

'This is a peculiar situation,' said Phin. He looked up and then down the corridor, and being sure that no eagle-eyed teachers were lurking, pulled Arabella to him and kissed her.

When they parted, Arabella, looking up at him, said, a bit breathlessly, 'It really is a pity about that moussaka, isn't it?'

'Yes, but I'll work up an appetite for it again.'

'Good. And – not Schubert, you said?'

'Not Schubert.'

'Who then? Because I expect you'd quite like a music background for – um – atmosphere.'

'Providing it was the right background,' said Phin, with a sudden disconcerting memory of the red-haired Canadian editor who had flitted briefly through his life just before he met Arabella, and who had been a jazz enthusiast.

With one of her flashes of unnerving percipience, Arabella said, thoughtfully, 'You wouldn't want jazz, of course, would you? All that bounce and energy in the wrong place.'

The Canadian editor had been a devotee of blues jazz, and had once insisted on playing several tracks of what Phin had thought inappropriate music at an even more inappropriate time.

He smiled at Arabella, and said, 'I'll look out some well-paced Bach.'

After Phineas Fox left, Olivia had some supper then went round the cottage closing curtains, and making sure doors and windows were all securely locked. She did this every night, of course, because you could not be too careful. She still sometimes had dreams about the night Imogen had died. Sometimes, in the dreams, she thought she could hear Imogen tapping on the wall, or calling to be let out, and on those nights she had to force herself to get out of bed and go down the stone steps to listen. There was never anything, of course. The sounds were in her nightmares and in her memory.

The meeting with Phineas Fox had gone well. He had been very interested in everything Olivia had told him about *The Martyrs*, and he had been keen to take a copy of it to read; it was a good thing there had been a copy ready to hand. It was a pleasant feeling to fall asleep knowing that he would be in his bedroom at the Black Boar, reading the opera. Or would he? Mightn't he be spending the night with Arabella Tallis? Arabella had always been able to collect all kinds of men, of course, although Olivia had never understood how, because Arabella was nothing special to look at. She would not have thought Phineas Fox would have been Arabella's type, but you could never tell, and probably they would be in bed together tonight. But Olivia would not think about that, because it would remind her of her own attempts at relationships, which had been disastrous.

Arabella would not have disastrous relationships; she was a person for whom sex would be successful, and it would never be complicated by things like the other person being too drunk to be effective or turning out to be married, or being sick in a taxi. Or, indeed, by someone slyly dazzling you with his legal qualifications within weeks of your uncle's death – making respectful love to you after two dinner dates, and promising that he could invest your inheritance to bring massive returns. That man had decamped a week later to some unpronounceable country, and it had emerged that not only had he deposited Olivia's money in an inaccessible account, but the money of a number of other gullible ladies as well.

It was impossible to think of Phineas Fox behaving so appallingly; in fact, Olivia realized she was wondering what it might be like to be in bed with him. He might be quite gentle at first – he was what used to be called a gentleman, although it was not a term that you heard very much nowadays, but it could be used for Phineas – and then later he might be excitingly assertive and masculine.

Olivia went to bed feeling optimistic about the future. She managed not to think very much about Phineas and Arabella together in a deep, soft double bed at the Black Boar.

FOURTEEN

Even with the generous measure of Dilys Davy's port and brandy to mellow his outlook, Phin found that *The Martyrs* palled after the first few pages. There were several scenes in an area called Cresacre Woodland, which Tulliver, with unexpected whimsy, described as a 'sylvan setting', but which Phin suspected did not actually exist. There was much focus on the inhabitants of the convent, many of whose lines Phin thought were lifted from Puccini's convent-set *Suor Angelica* of circa 1918.

But something that did stand out was that one of Tulliver's characters was called Ginevra. Was that simply a nod to the local legend, or was Tulliver going to unfold some curious theory about Ginevra? Had he even found something out about her and woven it into the plot? So far, though, 'Ginevra' did not seem to play a particularly significant role in the story. Tulliver had, however, allotted her a solo, which attracted Phin's attention.

'Step by measured step the murderers came to me . . .
Inch by measured inch, the light is being shut out from me . . .
Breath by measured breath, my life is being cut off from me . . .
Heartbeat by measured and precious heartbeat, my life is ending . . .'

Phin read this several times, partly because the line about the light being shut off 'inch by measured inch' was eerily evocative, but also because he could not help wondering if it came from the Lemurrer. Could Gustav have known about it? It was unlikely, but it was not impossible – Phin thought it could be argued either way. But he would certainly try playing it tomorrow from the score to see what kind of harmony Tulliver had created for such lyrics.

A few stage directions were peppered through the scenes, one of which called for 'upwards of fifty men and women, in the garb of the *sans-culottes*' to march on the Bastille and storm its walls, while singing rousing rebel choruses. Grappling hooks were an integral part of this scene, which also involved the tipping of vats of boiling oil onto the marauders from the Bastille's battlements. Phin wondered how Gustav had thought the pouring of boiling oil could be stage-managed, and whether he had appreciated how much space fifty singers would take up. The Royal Opera House or the Met might manage it, but the majority of stages would struggle. He also wondered if Tulliver had checked his dates, because as far as he could recall from general history, not only was the use of boiling oil a medieval ploy, the real storming of the Bastille had taken place five years before this opera seemed to be set. Then he wondered whether Olivia Tulliver had considered how those scenes could be performed on the modest sweep of lawns outside the school.

There was, however, a touch of light relief in the form of a duet between two of the Bastille gaolers or turnkeys, during which they drunkenly divided up the clothes of recently executed prisoners, and capered around the stage wearing some of them. This was so lively and so enjoyably comedic that Phin wondered, for a startled moment, whether someone other than Gustav Tulliver had written it.

But, so far, *The Martyrs* seemed to him to be a pallid and clunkily written copy of *Dialogues des Carmélites*. He thought Harriet Madeley's concerns about infringement of copyright were fairly valid, and he also thought the boiling-oil scenes could be pointed out as being entirely impractical for the surroundings. Still, he would reserve judgement until he had read the whole thing and tried some of the music on the school piano.

It was approaching midnight, and the school was wrapped in silence. Harriet Madeley and Miss Davy would be sleeping blamelessly in their beds, and Arabella – Phin smiled thinking of Arabella – curled up in bed, her hair tumbled over the pillow.

He put the manuscript on the bedside table, switched off the light, and lay back on the pillows, staring up at the ceiling, his mind still filled with *The Martyrs* and whether there really was a tenuous link in it to the Lemurrer.

'*Inch by measured inch, the light is being shut out from me . . .*'
The words went back and forth across his mind, and sleep

had never seemed so impossible. Phin sighed, rearranged his pillows, wondered if port and brandy were ever responsible for insomnia, and finally sat up and switched on the light. Normally if he could not sleep he reached for a book – something light and undemanding – but he had not packed any books and he had not brought his Kindle, either. But this was a school, for goodness' sake, and schools had libraries. Since his dressing gown was temporarily out of action, he pulled a sweater over his pyjamas, slipped his feet into shoes, and went quietly down the stairs.

The school was not entirely dark. No lights were actually on, but there was a faint overspill from outside – possibly from a security light. Phin reached the foot of the stairs and paused, trying to remember if anyone had actually pointed out a library to him. He had a memory of Arabella indicating a window on the building's right as they drove up. That was the library, she had said. Vellum and leather, and large tables. In her time they had held debating evenings in it, and there had sometimes been a guest speaker.

It was a curious experience to walk through this building, knowing that two hundred years ago a community of nuns had lived and worked and prayed here. Including Sister Cecilia who had written that letter to Master Firkin? Yes, she must have been here.

The library, when he found it, was a rather endearing blend of country house library and modern school equipment. Rows of leather and calf-bound books lined the upper shelves – there was even an old-fashioned library ladder that could be wheeled back and forth to reach them. There was a modicum of order to the arrangement of the books, which seemed to be ordered more or less by date: Charles Dickens rubbed shoulders with Mrs Henry Wood and Elizabeth Gaskell, and Laurence Sterne and Henry Fielding shared a shelf with Samuel Richardson.

But there were also computer terminals, and the lower shelves held set books – school editions of Shakespeare's plays and nineteenth-century novelists. There were also, Phin was pleased to see, a good many of the acclaimed modern writers.

He switched on a desk lamp, and wandered along the shelves, taking down a book here and there at random, then climbing cautiously up the wheeled ladder to reach the upper shelves. There were a good many bound sermons by vicars and rectors who had served Cresacre, and who had lived here during the eighteenth and nineteenth centuries. These were not very likely to yield any useful information, though, and Phin was about to abandon the search when his eye was caught by the name of Cresacre Convent on one of the older volumes. This was probably no likelier to contain anything relevant than the books of sermons, but he reached up to take it down anyway, and perched on the bottom rung of the ladder to open it.

The book's title page announced it, in an ornate script, as being the reminiscences of an eighteenth-century religious, who had lived and worked within the convent's community. Lower down the page, in slightly less florid print, the reader was advised that the reminiscences had been privately printed in 1798, and had been edited and annotated before publication. 'Annotated' probably meant tedious lists of local references. 'Edited' might mean anything from a few corrections to re-sequencing and re-writing entire chunks.

As Phin turned over the title page, the scent of old paper and the breath of the past brushed against his mind. He smiled. There was no denying that the internet was a marvellous instrument – providing you checked all sources and made sure to discern between genuine facts based on primary sources, and the flights of fantasy or misunderstandings, or even outright fake news. But there was nothing like holding a piece of the past in your hands – of touching the leaves of a book written and printed centuries earlier, of hearing the indisputable voice of someone speaking to you from a vanished century.

He turned over the preliminary pages, hoping to find some clue to the author's identity, or even to the fate of the vanished nuns, but prepared for the book to be nothing more than the laborious meanderings of a nun who had lived a cloistered life in these surroundings. Solitude and serenity, thought Phin. Incense and plainchant, and a quiet, ordered life.

But the foxed pages contained more than religious treatises or tracts, or theological philosophies.

The first sentence might have been penned by one of the masters or mistresses of literature – the men and women who had known the value of grabbing their readers' attention in the very first line of their book.

The book began with this statement:

'I had not expected, when I entered our Order, that I would find myself treading dangerous and tragic paths, or that I and my group of sisters would become helpless strands in such a violent and bloody part of history's tapestry.'

Phin climbed down the ladder, switched off the desk lamp, and carried the anonymous nun up to his bedroom.

Propping up the pillows, he began to read.

'Embarking on the hazardous journey which faces us in three days' time, I am endeavouring to hold fast to my courage. I am also endeavouring to quench my astonishment at the company in which I find myself. Our Lord frequently dined and supped with all levels of society, and I have whiled away part of the journey by trying to imagine what Jesus would have thought of an Italian opera performer, who hints that he was the toast of most European capitals and the darling of theatre audiences. He also hinted that he is the scion of ancient Italian nobility, although this, I feel, is questionable.

'Chimaera – he assures us that this is his name – was a music tutor to Sir John and Lady Chandos's young daughter. I believe he was quite efficient and conscientious, and was also required to sing for their guests at evening parties. I have no idea how such a man comes to be in a fairly menial capacity in a quiet backwater like Cresacre, but honesty compels me to admit that – for all his faults – he can be a charming and entertaining companion. I suspect there have been a good many ladies in his life (our young novice, Anne-Marie, stares at him with wide-eyed admiration) but, to his credit, Chimaera keeps any reminiscences of his bedchamber exploits to himself.

'His experience of travelling is proving very useful to us, and his knowledge of languages even more so. I am moderately fluent in French, and most of the nuns have Latin, of course, but, as Mother Superior confided, it is more of an ecclesiastical Latin, and outside of the confessional box and the Mass, not likely to be of much help in such places as wayside inns or finding our way to our eventual destination.

'We had also considered taking with us the gardener from

Chandos House – his ancestry might be anything at all, and he has the prosaic name of Dan. However, it has been decided that this would not be practical for several reasons.

'Tonight, he looked at me very directly – he has the most extraordinary green eyes, flecked with gold – and he said, "The secret will be kept, Sister Cecilia. No matter the cost, it will never be known."

'And, despite his air of caring for no man, Mother Superior and I are agreed that Dan can unquestionably be trusted.'

This image of a group of professed nuns preparing to travel to some foreign destination, and of being involved with two such disparate-sounding gentlemen was so astonishing that Phin re-read the whole section in case he had missed some vital fact, or misunderstood. But he had not missed anything, nor did he think he had misunderstood anything. He rather liked the sound of Chimaera, who had apparently charmed the nuns, and clearly Dan was the gardener referred to in the letter found in Infanger Cottage. There had been something about a gardener by the name of Dan being instructed to post 'No Trespassing' signs.

He read on.

'We are all unhappy about leaving the convent buildings empty and untenanted, and there has been some discussion as to whether we should admit Master Firkin, the local builder, into the full truth. It's doubtful, though, if he could be entirely trusted, for he is very fond of taking a drink in the Black Boar, which could lead to indiscretions.

'Yet, as ill luck would have it, going through my desk to make sure I was leaving no clues behind, I came upon a letter from Master Firkin. It had been sent several days ago, and I had not yet answered it – which was remiss of me. It had to be answered there and then, of course, for Alberic had pointed out some dilapidations at Infanger Cottage, for which he thought we might wish to engage his services. He had ever an eye to the main chance.

'Master Firkin closed his letter with an apparently casual question as to whether the cottage might be available for him to buy for, if so, he would be very interested to discuss the matter.

'Thankfully, there was time to draft and then to dispatch a letter to Alberic (by way of the invaluable Dan again, who

promised to deliver it into Alberic's very hands). I wrote that
no repairs were required, and that instructions are that the cottage
is to remain in the joint ownership of the Chandos family and
this convent, and never to pass from that ownership.

'I fear it was not an entirely satisfactory response, but it was
the best that I could manage in the short time available. Dan
will see to it that signs warning trespassers away are posted
around the land at strategic points as soon as possible.

'Mother Superior and I have charged Dan with the task of
caretaking the convent for us. In my capacity as bursar, I have
been able to place a sum of money at his disposal, for the
undertaking of any repairs to the convent's fabric. He will engage
the services of Master Alberic Firkin as and when necessary.

'After Mother Superior had gone away, I laid upon Dan
another task.

'"A memorial, d'you mean, Sister?" he said, having listened
carefully to my request. "D'you mean like a statue or a stone
tablet?"

'"Not exactly a memorial, Dan. A memory. Something I want
to preserve in the event that . . . In the event of my not returning."
I handed him the page I had carefully cut from the old book. I
had done this in the privacy of my room, cutting the paper close
to the centre binding of the book so that it would be virtually
impossible for the page's removal to be noticed.

'"I want these images to be created in some form," I said.
"And for it to be placed in the church. Can you arrange for that?"

'Dan was studying the illustration. It is a reproduction (I think
this is the right word) of an old engraving, and extremely clear.

'"It doesn't matter what form is used," I said. "Stone, marble,
glasswork – whatever seems most suitable."

'"I'm no expert, but I'd think wood carving'd be best," he
said at length. "What they call alto-relief."

'For a gardener, he has a remarkable amount of knowledge. I
said, pleased, "Yes, alto-relief. I think that would be exactly right."

'"It's the kind of thing you see in churches," he said.
"On rood screens and suchlike. You could have a screen – or
even panels. A panel inside the main door, maybe."

'"That sounds very suitable. Would you know of a workman
who could do that kind of work?"

'"There's a chap over to Little Minching I could have a word with," said Dan. "He'd charge a fair amount, but I'd argue the convent's cause for you." He folded the illustration away carefully and gave me another of his direct looks. "I'm hoping it won't be necessary to do any of this, Sister."

'I said, "It won't be, Dan. We intend to come back."

'I hope that work – that carving – will never have to be commissioned. But if I do have to face death, it will feel good to know that I may have dispersed the darkness of those images; not by destroying the music, because I don't believe music is something that can ever be destroyed. It lingers in people's memories – it gets passed on, generation to generation. But by placing those images in a church – perhaps it is not fanciful to say by *trapping* them in a holy place, a place consecrated to God – the dark essence of it may be diluted.'

It's the Lemurrer, thought Phin, laying down the small book for a moment. That's what she's talking about. She went to France, although she doesn't make it clear why – maybe she will later. And she never came back. None of them did. But Dan faithfully carried out her request. He had the engraving she gave him copied – carved in wood – and he had it placed in the church. Then, to make sure he had done what she wanted, he had another one made for the convent itself – this building I'm in now. Did he know what the images actually represented, I wonder? It doesn't sound as if he did. She knew, though. Sister Cecilia. I'm glad I've got a name for her.

It was after one o'clock by this time, but sleep was the furthest thing from his mind. He re-arranged his pillows, wished he had another slug of Dilys Davy's port and brandy, and turned to the next section.

It looked as if this had been written immediately before the nuns had left Cresacre. It was vaguely annoying that Sister Cecilia had not dated any of the entries – there was only the information on the title page that the book had been printed in 1798. But it would not have been written with an eye to publication. It seemed likely that it had been edited and printed after her death.

It was intriguing to wonder who had done that editing, and who had arranged for the publication.

FIFTEEN

'Earlier this evening we held a small service in our chapel. I believe Mother Superior thought we should draw strength and comfort from the familiar surroundings and the atmosphere of prayer and serenity.

'We prayed for strength and guidance during our journey, and Chimaera and Dan both attended the service; in fact Chimaera insisted on taking part in it. He said he had sung in an Italian choir as a boy; he was very fond of sacred music, and he would like to sing as part of the service this evening. He rendered for us "Joy to the World", and I was able to accompany him on the organ. With all his faults, it must be said that Chimaera's voice is beautiful, and also his disposition is extremely amiable. He did not in the least mind Sister Agnes telling him afterwards that "Joy to the World" was a Christmas carol. He simply said, very courteously, that it had turned out to be the only piece that he and I both knew, and added that he thought the lines about heaven and nature singing were applicable in any season.

'He and Dan took supper with us after the service (Dan very irreverently referred to it as the last supper), and the two of them shared a flagon of wine. I have no idea where the wine came from and I cannot think either of them would have plundered the little stock of communion wine, which is kept in the sacristy. Mother Superior once offered a glass of it to Sir John Chandos, and when she told him that it was obtained for us by the Black Boar, and that she believed it was what was termed "off the wood", Sir John said, "Oh, dear God", and politely declined.

'While we ate, Chimaera suggested that we might infuse our journey with a modicum of adventure by thinking of it as a quest. He embarked on a description of some of the great quests of literature – he speaks fluently and vividly, and his accent makes his speech attractive. Everyone was very interested, especially Anne-Marie (I do hope we are not heading for a difficult situation there). Chimaera waxed lyrical on the voyages of Sinbad and also of Jason and the Argonauts. I suspect Mother Superior and Sister Agnes both wished he had not gone on to relate the tale of Odysseus, though, which is full of violence, and that Dan had not then contributed the legend of Scheherazade, which has certain questionable aspects.

'I would not have expected a gardener to be familiar with Persian legend, but Dan constantly surprises. And it has to be said that he was quite restrained in his description of the thousand and one nights, and that he fielded Anne-Marie's innocent questions afterwards very tactfully.

'Finally, and at last, we are ready to set off.

'At first light we shall make our quiet and unobtrusive way down to the highway, and wait at the appointed place. We shall wear our dark cloaks, and we do not think we will attract any attention.

'Chimaera will join us there. He has already painted for us a vivid and very amusing picture of how he intends to steal along the lanes, his cape folded across his face, constantly looking over his shoulder to be sure no one is following him. He will wait beneath a particular tree, he insists, with obvious relish in the adventurous romance of this. I hope he will pay his reckoning at the Black Boar before he leaves.

'Dan will be there as well, to help us into the coaches and make sure the arrangements are all reliable. I believe two mail coaches have somehow been commandeered, but no one has wanted to enquire too closely into Chimaera and Dan's methods, and we are all hoping that nothing actually criminal has taken place.

'Our modest possessions are ready in the hall. They do not take up much space, even though Sister Agnes has insisted on packing various foods for us to take, saying there is no knowing when we shall be able to procure meals for ourselves. I pointed out that we will have money with us to buy what we need as we travel, and Chimaera reminded her that France is said by many to be the centre of gastronomic excellence. He also mentioned my knowledge of the French tongue and his own native Italian. We should fare very well, he said.

'Sister Agnes sniffed dismissively, and said that was all very fine and good, but there was no use pretending we were not going into foreign lands, nor was there any knowing what currency or strange food we might have to grapple with. She makes it sound as if we shall be fording the River Styx and bargaining with Charon himself, or venturing into such uncharted lands as are believed to be populated by cannibals. But then dear Agnes has never travelled far beyond Cresacre, apart from when she accompanied Sister Gabrielle to visit her dying mother, and that was only on the other side of Little Minching.

'It feels as if we have packed up our lives and are leaving an emptiness in this convent – an emptiness that once was filled with prayer and work and study. Will those things remain, I wonder? Will the secrets remain as well? Please God they will – please God I have hidden them sufficiently.'

There it was again, that glancing reference to secrets inside that long-ago convent. *Could* it be the Lemurrer that Cecilia was referring to? But if so, why had she left those instructions with Dan for the carvings? Phin turned the page and read on.

'I feel it is better to draw a polite veil over the actual crossing of the English Channel, which was a sore trial to several of us. Poor little Anne-Marie was shockingly indisposed, and as for Chimaera, he retired with some haste to a discreet corner of the ship's deck, carrying a basin, wrapped himself in a blanket, and quaveringly ordered us not to approach him until the storm was over. The sea was perfectly calm, it seemed to me, so I assumed he referred to his own inner tempests. Sister Agnes observed that it was fortuitous that she had thought to bring along a flagon of her peppermint and ginger infusion, which was sovereign for such indisposition. Mother Superior, meanwhile, had by some means or other procured a bottle of brandy, and she and Agnes spent most of the journey administering these two remedies to anyone who might be in need of them. Nobody has dared ask how the brandy was come by.

'A short while ago I saw a smudge on the horizon that can only be the coastline of France. Calais. I stood watching it approach with eagerness, because this is a great adventure.

'And yet . . .

'And yet I am conscious of a growing apprehension – almost

as if a darkness is gathering just out of sight. Adventure this may be, but it is a dangerous adventure, because France is a dangerous place in these times. I have to remind myself, though, that Cresacre had become a dangerous place for us. We could not have remained there. God willing, though, we shall one day be able to return.

'As we prepare to step onto French soil, I find myself remembering Chimaera's light-hearted comparison of this journey to the quests of fiction, and I can't help thinking that the analogy of Jason and the Argonauts might turn out to be closer to reality than any of us thought. We shall not, of course, be likely to encounter harpies or sleepless dragons, but on the other hand we might be confronted by *sans-culottes* and revolutionaries. Of the two, I am not sure which I prefer.

'I shall place this diary in a corner of my own small travelling bag. By keeping it close at hand, I feel I have a friend I can talk to. I can't imagine that anyone will ever read it – I can't imagine I shall ever permit anyone to read it! – but it provides a comfort.'

Phin saw that he was three-quarters of the way through Sister Cecilia's reminiscences. He resisted the temptation to turn to the ending. He would take the journey Cecilia had taken, and see it unfold. But it puzzled him how – if she had taken the diary with her to France – the diary had got itself back to England and into print. And since Dan had arranged for the carvings to be carried out, that must mean she had not returned.

Or had she returned in such secrecy that no one had known?

It was two a.m., but by this time Phin had given up the idea of sleeping. He turned to the next page.

'I write this in a jolting and hideously uncomfortable carriage which is rattling over cobblestones and through ill-smelling streets with huddles of wizened houses. I can only write with considerable difficulty, but am persevering because it is better than looking at the soldiers who are riding with us outside the carriage. I cannot ignore them completely, though – they are keeping very close to us, peering through the windows at intervals. They have rifles and they wear the tricolour. Their eyes are cold and their lips set in implacable lines.

'Our small group is crammed into several coaches – I am with

Chimaera, Sister Agnes, and Anne-Marie. A guard travels with us. He has a rifle, with a bayonet.

'The soldiers surrounded us almost as soon as we arrived – there were too many of them to resist, and even though I sought to explain that we were here only to seek out our imprisoned French sisters and give them what comfort we could, it was to no avail. Chimaera demanded to be set free, using a mixture of French and Italian and much hand-waving, but that was to even less avail, and he was told, very sharply, to hold his tongue if he did not want to find it ripped from his mouth.

'He has spent the last few miles earnestly describing to us (in a low voice), what he will do to the soldiers when the coach finally stops. I do not think there is much substance behind his words, but it is reassuring to have him with us.

'On a more prosaic note (and perhaps to keep me from wondering what lies ahead), at least no one has been unwell from the jolting of the coach. This is fortunate, because there is nothing left of Sister Agnes's peppermint cordial, and the brandy is in one of the other coaches with Mother Superior.

'It is growing dark, and the coach drivers have lit flares which flicker wildly and make it seem as if strange creatures prance alongside us, rather than soldiers on ordinary horses.

'I have lost all sense of time, and I think I have drifted in and out of an uneasy sleep, so that I have no clear idea of how long we have been travelling, or how far we might have come. It feels as if it might have been quite a long journey.

'As far as I can see, we have left the smaller districts behind us, and we are passing through a more prosperous quarter. Several times it's possible to see the glint of a river, with crimson lights reflecting in it from the buildings along the banks. The River Seine? I think it must be.

'A few moments ago I leaned forward to look again, and this time I saw, directly ahead of us, a sprawling grey building, crouching on the banks of that darkly glinting river. Turrets rose into the night sky, and as we drew closer I saw that there were rows upon rows of windows. Most were in darkness, like sightless eyes, but lights burned in others. A prison house? Cold dread began to clutch at my chest, and I leaned forward to ask the guard where we were.

'"Paris, of course," he said, with a kind of pitying surprise, as if there was nowhere else it could be.

'"That building—"

'He looked at me then he said, "That's the old Palais de la Cité."

'I was still staring at the monstrous building. "The City Palace," I said, half to myself.

'"Yes. They call it The Conciergerie now,' said the guard. "That's where you – and the others – are being taken. It's the place where—"

'"Where Marie Antoinette was held before she was beheaded," I said.

'"Yes. But our orders are to take you, Sister, to the Bonbec Tower. It contains a place you will not have heard of, but it used to be known as—"

'"The Salle de la Question," I said. "The torture room. Yes, I have heard of it." Within my mind, I whispered the other name I knew for the place.

'It was my grandmother who called the Bonbec Tower the place of darkness.

'"A medieval palace," she used to say to my cousins and me. "It is the royal palace of the medieval kings of France – all the way back to the old Merovingian rulers." She would tell us of the Sainte-Chapelle that housed the crown of thorns – the thorns placed on Christ's head during the crucifixion – and of the Silver Tower, used as a storehouse for royal treasures. They were tales to enchant any child, and Grandmamma had the gift that so frequently comes to the elderly: the art of tale-spinning.

'But as she aged, her mind would sometimes slip, and she would forget her audience. "In that palace is the Bonbec Tower," she would say at those times, her eyes fearful and inward-looking, as if at some black memory we could not see. "It was named from the French word, *bec*, for mouth. So-called, because the poor souls taken there always ended in confessing whatever was wanted. They were the damned. Always they confessed." She rocked herself to and fro, slightly, until the one who was the dearest to me of all my cousins got silently out of her chair, and put her arms around Grandmamma.

"'Always, the confession, and then the punishment," said Grandmamma, softly to herself. "And always this family watched. They knew we possessed the ancient forbidden music, and they were fearful that we might use it against them. Perhaps some of our ancestors did use it – I don't know. Stories handed down over so many centuries become frayed . . . distorted. But I know for myself that one of the Bourbon line took my grandfather to the Bonbec Tower – the place of darkness – and imprisoned him."

"'Because of the music?" I whispered.

"'Yes. They believed he had tried to revive the Lemurrer ritual. I was a small girl, but I remember it happening. I saw him dragged from the house – I saw my grandmother sobbing, begging the soldiers to let him go. They did not, and we never saw my grandfather again. We knew where he had been taken, though. We knew we would not see him again."

'She would shiver then and her eyes would cloud over, and my cousin would nod to me to go to the pianoforte and play something that would chase Grandmamma's devils away. I always did so, of course. I usually played Scarlatti, in which there are patterns like delicate lace, or something by one of the family of Bach. And the images of the Bonbec Tower with its dread torture room would gradually recede.

'And now I am inside that tower myself. I am in the place of Grandmamma's stories. It cannot be because of the music, in the way it was for my ancestors. Not after so many generations. Do I even believe those stories my grandmother used to tell?

'But supposing it is all true – what will they do to me . . .?

'There is a further anguish in having been separated from the others. I have no idea where they are – my last glimpse of them was of terrified, tear-streaked faces, and of their hands reaching out to me, trying to keep me with them . . . And of voices imploring the guards not to separate us.

'Of Chimaera there was no sign at all.'

Phin leaned back on the pillows, considering this last section. He was inclined to think a degree of embroidering might have gone on over the attitude of the French royal houses towards Cecilia's family and towards the Lemurrer, but he thought it could be forgiven. While it would be shocking to know that your ancestors had practised such a brutal ritual, it must have been tempting to gloss over the facts by creating a culture of romantic danger – to let it be quietly believed that your family was regarded as a potential threat to the royal houses of France, or to the established religions.

There were only a few pages left; Phin read on.

Cecilia's description of her imprisonment in The Conciergerie cell, and of how she had tried to play music in her mind to shut out the darkness of her prison moved him very much.

And later was again the reference to the forbidden music; to how Cecilia and her cousin had played it in their grandparents' house. The images were vivid; Phin could see a firelit room, a glossy piano, and the two young girls bent absorbedly over the music.

But Cecilia had written, *A tiny part of me is wondering whether on that day my cousin and I disturbed something that would have been better left alone.*

He thought the accusation that Cecilia had come to France to revive the Lemurrer and use it to rally French Catholics against the Republic was a bit extreme. Still, some fanatical high-ranking official of the Republic could have known about the Lemurrer and about Cecilia's family, and made use of it for his own ends. It was not difficult to imagine an ambitious man – or woman – realizing who Cecilia was after she had been captured. And for that person to then present the whole concept of a subversive Catholic plot to someone like Robespierre or Danton, as a way to gain kudos.

He turned to the final page, and the description of hearing the guillotine being built outside the cell window.

'I thought I had four days in all. Have they brought my death forward? If so, how many hours of life do I have left?

'This knowledge brings the memories of my life flooding back, and I am seeing, as vividly as if I am looking through a window into a brightly lit room, those dear cousins and my grandparents' house.

'My cousins are long since dead, may God grant their souls rest, but while I have those memories they will never die for me.

'The man I loved better than life is dead as well. That is
difficult to bear. It was a sin, but I never thought of you as a
sin, my dear, lost love. I ache to see your face again – to see
your eyes smile at me – to hear your voice . . . But I have the
memory of those candlelit nights and those sunlit afternoons.
Memories do not die.

'But what of the music? Will that die when I die? I trust Dan
to arrange those wood carvings for me, and I fervently hope
doing that will in some way act as an exorcism of the music.
And with the thought comes another. The Church teaches that
in order to exorcize a demon, one must first name it. I'm not
sure if I believe in the power of exorcism, just as I'm not sure
if I believe in demons.

'But supposing I were to follow that belief now, and name
that ritual and that music by setting down the words here. Those
words that in essence form a plainchant, but that are infused
with menace and brutality. Would doing that disperse the darkness? Will the creation of those carvings in Cresacre do that?

'I don't think dying holds any fear for me now, although
knowing the form that my death will take is difficult to bear.
Beheading. Is the guillotine efficient? There are whispered tales
of how it does not always slice through the neck at the first
attempt . . . Even of how it is sometimes rigged to descend
slowly if a particularly hated prisoner is to die.

'But I shall not think that. Instead, I shall think that my dying
act shall be to set down the old chant. It would be an act filled
with passion and pathos, and it's just such a grand gesture as
the great dramatists would love. As I wrote that last sentence,
I suddenly had the thought that it's an act that would appeal to
Chimaera. That has made me smile.'

Phin almost did not dare to turn the page to read what Cecilia
had set down. He thought he did not really need to do so,
because he knew what he would see.

And so it was.

'Step by measured step the murderers came to me . . .

Inch by measured inch, the light is being shut out from me . . .

Breath by measured breath, my life is being cut off from me . . .

Heartbeat by measured and precious heartbeat, my life is
ending . . .'

There it was, exactly as in Gustav Tulliver's opera. But what Phin had not expected was a second verse.

'Step by measured step with murderer's tread . . .
Inch by measured inch with murderer's brain . . .
Brick by careful brick with murderer's hands . . .
I make the layers of death . . .
Quenching the light . . . stopping the heart . . .
Murderer's hands making the layers of death . . .'

She didn't – perhaps couldn't – reproduce the actual music in her journal, thought Phin, staring at the page. Gustav Tulliver must have written his own. But this is the victim's song. It's the song of the poor damned creature being put to death. And not just that – it's the song of the murderers, as well. *Brick by careful brick with murderer's hands . . . Making the layers of death . . .*

It's verse and chorus, he thought, and it's what was sung, hundreds of years ago, when some wretched captured sinner was bricked up alive. Gustav Tulliver found this account while he was headteacher here – he must have done – and he used it in his opera.

Phin looked back at the page, and it was then that he saw that something was written in the margin at the very foot of the page, beneath the last line of the verses. It was very faint – age had dimmed the ink – but when Phin tilted the bedside light so that it fell directly onto the page, the words were readable.

'A marvellous discovery! I know that one day I shall use this.'

Gustav, thought Phin. Who else? He turned to the last page of Cecilia's memoirs. It was very brief; she had simply written:

'If only I had made that attempt to barter with the turnkey – to barter my body for freedom. Probably it wouldn't have worked . . . And yet . . .

'Is it too late to do it, even now?

'I think it is. I shall commend my soul to God.'

The memoirs ended there, and Phin was aware of a sense of loss. What happened to her? he thought, putting the book on the bedside table. Was it indeed the guillotine in the end? For her and for those other nuns?

He feared it must have been, even though he would prefer to think it had not. He had rather liked the sound of all the nuns: the brisk, down-to-earth Sister Agnes; the timid, romantically inclined Anne-Marie; and Mother Superior, who had somehow got hold of a bottle of brandy to help counteract seasickness.

Phin had the strongest feeling that there was more to be uncovered – what were the secrets they kept left hidden? – but he had no idea how he could uncover it. Out of all those people in Sister Cecilia's story, was there one who might have left some mark – something he could find and follow?

Even before the question had finished forming, he realized the answer was there.

Tracing Sister Cecilia or any of the other nuns was likely to be difficult, if not outright impossible. Quite apart from all other considerations, they might well have followed the religious practice of taking other names on entering the convent. Dan, remaining behind in Cresacre, and probably ending in marrying some nice local girl, would not have left any traces of his life, either.

But what about that other one? What about the Italian music tutor in the Chandos household – the excitable gentleman who had hinted to the nuns that not only was he the toast of most European capitals and the darling of theatre audiences, he was also the scion of nobility?

Chimaera. If only half the claims he had made to the nuns could be believed, it might be possible to pick up details about him, and his eventual fate. How successful had he been? What traces of his career might remain? He had stayed at the Black Boar – how far back did their records go?

As Phin finally allowed sleep to overcome him, he was smiling. Whatever Chimaera had been or done – whether he had been lunatic, lover or poet, whether he had been hero or villain, saviour or murderer – trying to trace his life and discover what had happened to him could be very interesting.

SIXTEEN

Cresacre, 1794

Chimaera had begun to doubt whether rescuing Gina and carrying her off to London, and then to Italy, was really such a good idea after all.

But he went about his careful preparations, and he established that a post coach was expected at the Black Boar in two days' time, and that there would most likely be a seat which he could book. Well, no, there was no guarantee that the seat would be actually inside the coach, but one would certainly be available on the outside. Chimaera, who had been made free of the conveyances of the nobility in his time, and whose adoring admirers had once unharnessed the horses of a carriage in which he was travelling so that they could pull their idol from La Scala to the Teatro alla Canobbiana, shuddered. Still, it was not a time to be worrying about dignity or prestige, and he would make the journey comfortable for his beloved Gina by swathing her in furs. He had not yet thought how to procure the furs or, indeed, how to pay for the coach, but he was still determined to prove himself a hero, so, that same night, he donned a velvet jerkin which he thought struck a suitably dashing note, and wrapped himself in his cloak. In his carpetbag was a sword, which had been part of a stage costume. It was not a real sword, but a stage prop, fashioned from thin wood, studded with paste jewels and pinchbeck. Chimaera had no intention of using it and it would not inflict much damage if he did, but he could make a few dramatic lunges and parries to impress Gina.

The dark lanes should have provided him with atmosphere for the part of his opera where the hero steals up to the grim fortress to reach his love. The reality was that it was so dark Chimaera could scarcely see where he was going, and a thin mist obscured the moon, and clung to the trees. You could say what you liked about the delights of the countryside; Chimaera would not give you a thank-you for it, and he would take the properly laid pavements and sensibly built roads of a city any day. But he went doggedly on, because Gina would be delighted when he appeared, and the form of her gratitude was likely to be extremely gratifying. This last thought caused a stir of desire, which would have been extremely pleasurable if the sword had not developed the uncomfortable habit of twisting itself around and jabbing him between his legs when he least expected it.

As he approached the stone pillars marking the entrance to the convent's carriageway, the night was filling up with sinister sounds. Owls hooted and creatures scurried in and out of the undergrowth. Also, Chimaera was starting to suspect that someone was tiptoeing along behind him. Several times he stopped and wheeled sharply round, and the third time he did this one of the shadows detached itself from the darkness, and walked towards him.

'Well now, Signor Chimaera,' said a voice he recognized. 'What the devil are you doing out here? Because it looks remarkably as if you're prowling up to the doors of a convent. Are you after pilfering the Mass vessels or getting drunk on communion wine? Or is this the classic rescue of the damsel in distress?'

It was Dan, the Chandos House gardener, and it was an awkward moment. Chimaera tried to think of an innocent – or even an acceptable – reason why he would be prowling towards the convent in the pitch dark, and could not.

Dan said, 'If it is a rescue, are you sure the lady will want to be rescued? You have taken into account that she might have decided to take the veil and renounce the world and all its pomps, have you?'

'That is extremely unlikely,' said Chimaera at once, and Dan smiled.

'It is, isn't it? Particularly since that remarkable incident that afternoon in her bedroom— I do hope you were able to get your torn shirt mended,' he said, politely.

'It was of no account,' said Chimaera, annoyed at this reminder that Dan had seen that undignified scene.

Dan looked towards the dark bulk of the convent. 'There are no lights showing anywhere,' he said. 'They'll all be tucked

virtuously up in their cells. Listen, though, if you really are
staging a midnight rescue, you'd be as well to go along
the forest path, past Infanger Cottage. You'll be less likely to
be seen, and it will bring you to the retreat house. I dare say
that's where the lady will be.'

'It is where she will be. I know that. I had not known about
any forest path, though.'

'It's just here on the left. If you like I can show you, so
that—'

Dan broke off, and one hand came down painfully on
Chimaera's wrist. Chimaera gasped and started to say, 'What—'

'Be quiet.'

'But what—'

'Be *quiet*! There's someone there.' He pulled Chimaera into
the shelter of a thick patch of bushes.

When Chimaera had regained his breath, he said, 'It might
be someone with a perfect right to be walking along the path.
Or a poacher, or a pair of lovers.'

'No one walks out here at this hour,' said Dan.

'You're here,' pointed out Chimaera.

'I followed you. I was in the Black Boar and I saw you.
Frankly, signor, you looked suspicious.'

'I am not suspicious,' began Chimaera, hotly.

'Do hush, will you? The footsteps are getting closer.'

The footsteps were indeed coming closer, and there was a
furtive, creeping sound to them. Chimaera was glad that the
bushes screened himself and Dan, and, as the steps approached,
he tried to think that after all it would only be someone after
illicit game or resolved on illicit love-making. He was about to
say this, when he realized that whoever was coming through
the trees was singing. It was the strangest, most disturbing sound
Chimaera had ever heard, and the harmony was the strangest
he had ever heard as well. He glanced at his companion and
saw that Dan was looking towards the path, and although he
was very still and quiet, Chimaera felt a tension in him.

As the singer came nearer, it was possible to discern snatches
of the words.

'*Step by measured step with murderer's tread* . . .
Inch by measured inch with murderer's brain . . .

Brick by careful brick with murderer's hands . . .
I make the layers of death . . .
Quenching the light . . . stopping the heart . . .
Murderer's hands making the layers of death . . .'

Then the figure appeared, and for a moment Chimaera thought it was a complete stranger. The shoulders were hunched in a curiously predatory fashion, putting him briefly in mind of a massive bird of prey, shuffling between the trees. The head was bent low, as if wanting to avoid any light, but as the figure went past, he saw with a jolt of surprise that it was the priest who acted partly as house chaplain to Sir John and Lady Chandos, and partly as the convent's chaplain. Father Joachim.

Chimaera had the sudden impression that the chilling music was not part of Father Joachim, but that it trailed after him, like a black snail's trail that could not be shaken off. He shivered, then looked at his companion, expecting this gardener, who did not act like a gardener, to seize the opportunity to make good their escape.

But Dan said, very softly, 'I don't like the look of that man, do you? Let's follow him and see what he's up to.'

'He might be going up to the convent.'

'At this hour?'

'One of the nuns could be ill,' said Chimaera. 'Dying. In need of the Last Sacrament.'

'If the nuns had sent for Joachim, someone would have had to fetch him, and that someone would be with him now.'

'You are right. And,' said Chimaera, 'he would not be singing about murderer's hands making layers of death.'

His instinct was, in fact, to retreat and abandon Gina's rescue until tomorrow. But he was damned if he was going to display cowardice in front of this upstart English gardener, and he reminded himself that a great many operatic heroes had servants, lesser characters who played useful roles in the plot. *Comprimarios.* Dan the gardener should be cast as a *comprimario*. He could be a Don Curzio or a Bartolo from *Le Nozze di Figaro* and appear in Chimaera's opera in that guise.

So he squared his shoulders, and said, firmly, 'I am with you, my friend,' and followed Dan through the dim trees, glancing over his shoulder several times to be sure no one was following them. This had a pleasing echo of the more comedic aspects of Harlequin, although it really required an exaggeratedly tiptoeing walk, which Chimaera was not prepared to try tonight, partly because his companion might think it was peculiar behaviour, but also because he might slip on the wet ground and receive another jab from the sword.

'He's vanished,' he said, suddenly.

'No, he's just stepped off the main carriageway,' said Dan. 'He's taking the forest path – the one I told you about. There he is now – can you see? It looks as if he's going to Infanger Cottage.'

'Do we follow him there?'

'Yes. That cottage is on land that's half owned by the convent and half by Sir John Chandos,' said Dan. 'They've argued over its ownership for years, and they more or less share the responsibility for it. I don't think either the mother superior or John Chandos would like to have a wild-eyed priest wandering around, muttering about murderer's tread and murderer's brain, do you?'

'Put in such a way as that—'

'Good,' said Dan, and set off again in pursuit.

Gina was exhausted from screaming for help, and her wrists were raw and bleeding from trying to pull them free of the cloth that Joachim had used to tie her to the wall. Her father's head was still heavy against her shoulder. His hair had flopped forward and it was brushing her upper arm. There was a faint scent of the pomade he used on it – it brought memories of him sharply and poignantly to her.

At first his head felt warm, but as time slid by she began to realize it was cooling. This was dreadful. Gina was aware that she was sobbing – it was a terrible sound in this enclosed space; she forced herself to stop and instead tried to think of all the things waiting for her when she got out of this cellar. Her home – her own bedroom. She would not let herself think she was going to die in this dreadful place, with her father's body cooling at her side, with the dark stifling silence pressing down . . .

But the darkness was like a thick curtain, and the silence was the silence of the grave – no, she would not think that.

With this last thought came an awareness that the darkness was no longer completely silent. Gina's heart bounded with hope. Was someone out there? She began to shout.

'Help! Help me! I'm here – in the cellar – please help me!'

Please let the next sounds be made by someone tapping on the wall, and then by hammers smashing into the bricks, and people calling that she was being rescued.

The sounds had stopped, but Gina shouted again, and after a few moments she heard the door of the cellar opening, then heavy footsteps coming down the stone steps. She renewed her shouts, but she was suddenly and sickeningly aware of a single voice reaching her. She pressed her face against the bricks, trying to hear more clearly, but a cold dread was forming in her, because she had already recognized the words. They came to her in broken fragments, like shards of splintered glass.

'Step by measured step with murderer's tread'

Joachim. He must be only a few inches away from her. And he was singing the dreadful chant her father had said was called the Lemurrer. The murderer's chant.

But why was he singing it again?

SEVENTEEN

Second role players – *comprimario* – were not supposed to take over and rush the hero forward into the waiting danger. But before Chimaera knew it, Dan had swept him along a muddy, tree-lined path, and they were standing in front of a remarkably ugly cottage. It looked as if it had been put together out of random fragments of stones and bricks. Old, wizened ivy covered several of the windows, and trees pressed in on the cottage. The mist that had clung to the ground earlier seemed to have dispersed, but in its place were thick shadows like crouching figures.

'Infanger Cottage,' said Dan, softly. 'And look there.' He pointed to the muddy ground. 'Footsteps – freshly made.'

'They go up to the door,' said Chimaera, staring at the prints. 'And then they go inside.'

'You're right. And look there – that's a handcart. Probably one of Alberic Firkin's for transporting building materials. That's a very strange thing to find out here at this hour, wouldn't you agree?'

Chimaera said, 'Master Firkin was in the Black Boar, saying – complaining – that some of his things had been stolen.'

'Then it's probably his. But what in the wide world is it doing out here?'

As Dan said this, the cottage door opened and Father Joachim came out. He looked about him, almost as if he might be making sure no one was watching, then he took the handles of the cart and pushed it around the side of the cottage, into the concealment of some bushes. He seemed to take considerable care to hide the handcart, then he went back inside. There was the sound of the latch being dropped.

'That's a strange thing for a man to do,' said Dan, and went forward again. Chimaera, mindful of his own role as main hero, followed. The door of Infanger Cottage, which was set back between two jutting windows, was uncompromisingly shut, and when Dan cautiously tried it, the latch held firm.

'He's locked himself in,' he said, very softly.

'It surprises me that there is such a thing as a lock in this tumbledown house.' Chimaera stepped back, looking up at all the windows. 'Do we go in?' he said.

'I think so. But we'll need to be soft and wary. Polite, even. We can't very well batter the door down. He might even have a lawful reason for being in there.'

'We could find a window and look in.'

'That's a very good idea. Let's go around to the back. In fact, I think there's a cellar window there – low down, right at ground level. We might be able to lever it open and squeeze through.'

The basement window, when found, was barely two feet deep, and Chimaera thought it would take a very agile person indeed to squeeze through it. He was about to say this, when he realized that a smeary light was glowing from beyond the window.

'And,' said Dan, who had also seen the light, 'can you hear him still singing that hellish song?'

'*Step by measured step with murderer's tread . . .*

Inch by measured inch with murderer's brain . . .'

'Yes, I do hear it,' said Chimaera, repressing a shudder.

Dan dropped flat to the ground and began to work his way towards the window. He did not seem to mind the mud and he seemed to expect Chimaera to join him, so Chimaera, remembering to be careful of the sword, followed. He was trying not to wish he had stayed in the safety of the Black Boar, and he was reminding himself that this was a splendid adventure which would make a marvellous scene for his opera.

The uncertain light from the window had seeped across the ground like watery blood oozing from a wound. Once, a shadow moved across the light, as if someone had walked across the underground room. It might only be the flickering of a candle flame or an oil light, of course . . . But who would have lit candles or a lamp down there at this hour of the night?

Dan reached the window first, and there was a moment when his head and shoulders were outlined against the sullen glow from within. Then he recoiled and flattened himself on the ground again.

'What have you seen?' demanded Chimaera, when Dan returned.

'I'm not sure. But I think we need to go in there. I don't know what he's doing, but I think he's mad. We'll have to break down the door after all.'

He led the way to the cottage's front, and kicked at the door. The sound was like an explosion in the quiet forest and Chimaera glanced worriedly about him, but nothing stirred. There was no movement from inside the cottage.

Dan redoubled his efforts and Chimaera joined in. At the fourth, joint kick, the latch snapped. They pushed wide the door and went in.

The inside of Infanger Cottage was a terrible place. The walls were crusted with mould and moss, and there was a thick, smothering stench of damp and dirt.

And at the heart of this bad-smelling dereliction, the singing was still going on.

Dan paused, looking about him, then advanced several cautious steps along the hall until he reached a flight of wooden stairs going up to the bedrooms. Set back, close to the stairs, was a low door. 'Cellar door,' said Dan, very softly.

'Yes.'

Dan reached for the door's handle and pulled it back. It came open easily, revealing a flight of stone steps, leading down. The dull lamplight lay across the steps.

With the opening of the door, the singing stopped abruptly, as if something had slammed down on it, and a voice – Father Joachim's voice – said, 'Is someone there?' Chimaera thought that this voice coming up from the lamplit depths of the cellar was the eeriest thing yet.

'It's Dan from Chandos House,' said Dan. 'Signor Chimaera is with me.'

For a moment there was no response, then Joachim's voice said, 'Chimaera. Indeed? Won't you come down here, Signor Chimaera?'

This soft invitation added another layer of eeriness, but Dan had already started down the stairs, so there was nothing for Chimaera to do but follow.

The cellar was larger than he had been expecting, and it looked very old indeed. It was all far too elaborate for a small woodland cottage, but Chimaera remembered that the convent was said to have been built on the site of an old monastery. There were arched alcoves within the walls – three, no, four of them – but they were little more than ghost outlines. Heaped in a corner was what looked like a tumble of bricks and a tub of a paste-like substance.

Two oil lamps stood at the centre of the cellar, and in the glow from them, Father Joachim was holding up a crucifix. It was impossible to know if his stance was defiance or defence, and although the crucifix was probably silver or wood, the lamplight turned it to fiery copper.

Chimaera had not known he was going to speak, but he heard himself say, 'Father Joachim – we heard your singing earlier, and we were curious about it – I was especially interested.' Dan sent him an appreciative look and, encouraged, he said, 'I would like to hear more about it.'

'It's very old, that chant,' said Joachim. 'It's called the murderers' chant.' His voice was low and furtive, like a child confiding a secret. 'It used to be sung centuries ago,' he said. 'Part of a ritual – the Lemurrer, it was called. It was used in sacred murder.'

Dan said, 'Sacred murder. I've never heard of that.' His voice was soft and Chimaera knew he was trying to calm down the priest. So that they could pounce on him? But then what would they do?

'The music's been hidden away,' said Joachim, 'but I found it. And once I had found it, it took hold of my mind – it wouldn't let go. And then, that day, when I saw you in her bedroom—' He turned to Chimaera. 'I saw the arousal of your body and it was an abomination. But it was not altogether your fault. She had the taint, you see. Despite everything I had done, it was part of her.' He stepped nearer, and the dreadful confiding note came back into his voice. 'Until then she had been my dear, perfect girl,' he said. 'The soul I snatched from death at her birth. But since that afternoon . . . She's come to me in dreams,' he said, his eyes dark and staring. 'Shameful dreams – I wake from them wet with my own lust, there in the bed.' He broke off, with a shuddering sob. 'That's when I began to know she must be punished,' he said. 'And then the music came to me, and I understood what the punishment must be.'

With the words, there was the faintest movement from the shadows, and Chimaera felt something clutch at his heart. He turned his head, and now, because his eyes had adjusted to the light down here, he saw that although the first two alcoves were empty, a figure stood in the farthest one; a figure that must be tied up – tethered – to the bricks in some way, because it was upright, as a statue might stand. But statues did not huddle helplessly against the wall like this. They did not have a pale coif framing a face with high cheekbones, and nor did they have a thick cloth tied over the lower part of their faces to prevent them from crying for help . . .

It's one of the nuns imprisoned there, thought Chimaera in horror. This madman has tied her up. He started forward and, as he did so, he was aware of Dan going towards Joachim. As Dan grabbed Joachim's arm, Joachim lashed out with the crucifix, landing a blow on Dan's shoulder. Madness was blazing from his eyes, and Dan instinctively recoiled, throwing up his hand. Joachim lifted the crucifix again, and this time it fell on the side of Dan's head. Dan stumbled back, clearly rendered dizzy from the blow, and Joachim gave a cry of triumph, threw the crucifix aside, and fell on him. His hands closed around Dan's neck, the fingers tightening, and Chimaera darted forward and seized Joachim's shoulders, trying to pull him away. The strength and the resistance of the man shocked him, but he persisted because, if he did not, Dan would be throttled there on the ground.

Joachim was screaming. 'You don't understand,' he shouted. 'She must die. They both must die. They must see the light cut off, inch by inch. I want them to die.' The sob came again, and Chimaera darted forward and grabbed him again. This time he managed to drag him clear of Dan, and push him onto the floor. Joachim crouched there, sobbing and thrusting a clenched fist into his mouth, as if to force back the sounds. It was terrible but it was also pitiable.

Dan, although he was gasping and coughing, seemed to be recovering. He nodded to Chimaera, as if to say he could deal with Joachim now, and Chimaera judged it safe to get to the figure trapped in the alcove. But as soon as he moved, Joachim sprang to his feet, and ran at Chimaera with an eldritch shriek of fury.

'You shan't stop me,' he cried, and as he reached for Chimaera's throat, Chimaera hit out instinctively, his fist landing hard in the centre of the priest's chest, catching Joachim unawares. He staggered back, tried to regain his balance, but fell against the wall, his head smashing against the bricks with a sickening crunch. He fell to the ground and his eyes rolled up so that only the whites showed.

As Chimaera stared in utter horror, Dan said, in a raw, painful-sounding voice, 'My God, is he dead?'

'I don't know.' Chimaera was shaking violently, but he forced himself to bend over Joachim's still form, to feel for a heartbeat, to see if breath came from the lips. After a moment, he said, 'There is . . . no heart beating. No breath coming from his lips. I think he is dead.' He straightened up, staring at Dan. 'What do I do? *Dio mio*, I have killed a man – I was only defending myself, but I have committed—'

He could not bring himself to utter the word, but it was exploding inside his mind. Murder.

Murder . . . And, as if seizing on the word, something seemed to whisper through the old cellar. *Yes, yes, it has been murder tonight, and it will be murder again in a time to come . . .*

Chimaera looked round, startled, momentarily distracted, because the whisper had seemed so real he thought someone must have crept unseen into the cellar, then realized it was only the faint hissing from the old lamp he had heard.

But there was still the shadowy figure in the alcove, and as Dan went towards it, Chimaera reached for the oil lamp and followed, setting the lamp where its light fell across the alcove.

Dan was tearing aside the scarf tied over the prisoner's face. 'Everything is all right now, Sister,' he said. 'You're quite safe, and we'll get you back to the convent. It's—' A pause, then he said, 'It's Sister Cecilia, isn't it?'

She was gasping and shuddering, and trembling violently, but after a moment she managed to say, 'Yes. Thank you . . . God sent you, I think—'

'Let's hope God helps us untie these ropes,' said Dan. 'Chimaera, see if you can find something in the house to cut them. Take that other lamp with you to see the way. It's as dark as the pit of hell up there. Sorry, Sister.'

'No need – you're quite right, anyway.'

Chimaera reached for the lamp, and went quickly up the stairs. Opening cupboards with half-rotting doors, and pulling out drawers festooned with dust and cobwebs helped to keep his mind away from what had happened to Father Joachim. The man had been in the grip of a madness, of course, but that did not justify . . .

It did not justify murder. *Murder.* It was a word that gibbered at you in huge, distorted letters, scarlet and crimson, the edges dripping gorily. But there was no getting away from it. He had committed murder. He thrust these thoughts from him, and found a large, wooden-handled knife, and a pair of what he thought were called pliers. He ran back down to the cellar, where Dan was still trying to loosen the ropes that held Sister Cecilia prisoner.

'Father Joachim was going to kill you, wasn't he?' said Dan, taking the knife that Chimaera held out, and sawing at the ropes that bound Cecilia's wrists. Chimaera saw now that they were looped around to two thick nails jutting out of the brickwork behind.

Sister Cecilia's face was white and her eyes were huge in the coif-framed face. Chimaera caught himself thinking that – even like this – she was a very striking-looking lady. Once, she must have been a real beauty. She was no longer so very young, of course, but she was not all that old.

Cecilia said, 'Yes, Joachim – for I *cannot* call him "Father" any longer – was going to kill me. He was going to wall me up. That's what the music is about, the music he was chanting. It's called the Lemurrer, and it's an old ritual – the walling-up, the immuring, of . . . of those found committing the sin of—' A glint of humour showed. 'Of fornication,' said Cecilia, and, as they both looked startled, she said, 'I've shocked you.'

'Nothing shocks me,' said Dan. 'I've never heard of the Lemurrer, though.'

'Nor I,' said Chimaera. 'But Joachim said something about it taking hold of his mind.'

'To the pure of heart it is harmless. At least,' said Cecilia, with a slightly crooked smile, 'that was always the belief in my family who had the music for generations—' She suddenly turned her heard, staring across the dim cellar.

'What's wrong?' Chimaera sent an anxious glance to where Joachim lay, half expecting to see him crawling across the floor towards them.

Cecilia held up the one hand that Dan had freed. 'Listen.'

With the word, the two men heard, faintly but unmistakably, a cry close by.

'Help . . . me . . . Please . . .'

The voice was cracked and faint, but it was recognizable. Gina Chandos.

EIGHTEEN

Dan hurled himself at the wall before Chimaera could move, clawing at the bricks, then cursing with a fluency Chimaera had not heard in this country, and using a good many words he had not previously encountered.

He seized the knife they had used to cut Sister Cecilia free moments earlier and dug it into the mortar between the bricks.

'No use,' he said, angrily after a moment. 'Chimaera – find me something to break these bricks down. Hammer – axe – anything.' Leaning his face against the wall, he shouted, 'Gina? Gina, can you hear me? It's Dan. I'm here and so is Chimaera, and we'll get you out as quickly as we can.'

At first Chimaera thought there was not going to be a reply, and he beat against the bricks with his fists.

'Gina? Can you hear? I am here with Dan. We are going to get hammers and axes to break down the wall. It will not take very long.'

They waited, and then, faintly, but blessedly, the cry came again.

'Help me . . . Get me out . . . Oh, please . . .'

'We'll get you out,' said Dan. 'I promise we will.'

'Dan . . .?'

'Yes. I'm here. It's all right.' He laid the flat of both hands against the bricks; almost, thought Chimaera, as if he might be trying to touch the person trapped on the other side. He had the unnerving feeling that Gina Chandos had done the same thing at the exact same moment. Like two people pressing their hands together. Handfast, it was called in some places. It did not matter for the moment, and he snatched up the oil lamp and plunged up the stairs again, taking them two at a time, and then frantically ransacked the cupboards for the second time. He had no idea where people kept such things as hammers and he was not entirely sure what a pickaxe looked like, but he would find something – anything – that would enable them to reach Gina. Eventually, in a noisome building adjoining the cottage, which might be a washhouse, he found a large hammer with one section shaped to a point, an axe with a stout wooden stave, and two thin-edged chisels. He scooped them up, and ran pantingly back across the cobbled yard and into the house. The light from the oil lamp flickered wildly as he went, and shadows leapt up and ran with him.

Back in the cellar, Dan snatched the hammer and began to attack the bricks and, as Chimaera joined him, Cecilia said, 'You will be able to reach her, won't you?' She was sitting on the ground, wrapped in Dan's jacket, massaging her wrists and ankles, but her eyes were watching their efforts to break into the bricks. Chimaera thought he had never seen such anguish in anyone's face.

'Yes, we'll reach her,' said Dan. 'Can you still hear me, Gina? Are you still all right?'

'Yes.' The word came weakly as if it hurt her to speak, but then she said, 'Oh – I can see . . . tiny threads of light—'

'That's us. That means we're nearly with you. This mortar hasn't fully set, so . . . Oh, here it goes now! Try to keep clear of it if you can.'

With the words a large section of the brickwork gave way, and bricks began to tumble out – at first in ones and twos, then showering onto the ground, some of them smashing as they fell. Brick-dust and the cellar's own grey dust billowed out, and both Dan and Chimaera recoiled, flinging up their hands to shield their eyes.

'But we've done it,' said Dan, exultantly. 'Gina, where are you? Chimaera, for Christ's sake tilt the light so I can see . . . Oh, God, I'm sorry, Sister, I'm doing nothing but swear and blaspheme.'

'I feel like swearing and blaspheming with you,' said Cecilia, and Chimaera realized she had come to stand with them. Her eyes were on the gaping, jagged-edged hole that Dan had made and that they were now widening by chiselling at the bricks.

As Dan knocked out more bricks, the dust swirled up again, gritty and dry, but this time there was a movement from within the clouded alcove.

'Gina?' Dan seized the lamp and held it aloft, reaching out with his other hand.

As the light fell across the enclosed space, showing what was within it, there was a dreadful moment when Chimaera thought they had got it completely wrong – that the sounds of Gina's voice had been some kind of trick – something within their own imaginations. Because what they were seeing could not be Gina, his Gina, his *bella* porcelain doll.

This was a wild-eyed, tousled little creature, with hair that streamed in tangles, and whose cheeks were smeared with dust and tears. Then the moment of shock passed, and of course this was Gina, and of course she would look wild-eyed and the porcelain skin would be grimed and marked with terror and despair. Dan had grasped her hand, but before Chimaera could take her other hand, Sister Cecilia stepped forward, and as Gina half fell out, she caught her and held her in her arms, her head bent over the tousled hair, her eyes half shut. She clung to her as if she would never let her go, and then she released her and stepped back, almost with an air of submission.

Dan took one of Gina's hands and Chimaera took the other, and Gina said, in a voice that sounded as if it might be drawing on the last reserves of strength, 'Please – he's still in there . . . You must get him out.'

Dan started to say, 'Who . . .?' and Chimaera said, 'What do you mean . . .?' and then they both stopped, because the light fell more strongly into the alcove now and they could see that crammed into the alcove was a second figure. The space was so narrow that he and Gina must have been standing in a macabre embrace.

John Chandos. His eyes were wide and staring – dead eyes – and his lips were drawn back in the rictus of death.

Sister Cecilia gasped, and her hand came down on Chimaera's arm, as if to stop herself from falling. Before he could steady her, she fell forward in a swoon.

Gina was not sure if she would ever be able to shut out the memory of herself and her father together in that cramped space. Certainly she would never manage to shut out the feel of his hand clinging to hers as he died. It was important to hold on to the thought that he had not been alone when he died, though. As I nearly was, thought Gina. No, I won't think that. I'll only remember that Dan and Chimaera got me out.

Dan and Chimaera.

Chimaera had picked her up in his arms and carried her out of Infanger Cottage, through the trees and into the convent. Gina had been fighting to remain conscious by that time, but she had heard the door knocker fall on the massive old door, echoing inside the building, and then there had been running feet and cries of shock, and shouted orders for the lighting of ranges and the boiling of kettles and heating of soup. A scared-faced Anne-Marie had brought a novice's robe for Gina to put on after she had washed away the dust and dirt of the cellar. It had been too big, but it was clean and it held a comforting scent of lavender from the sprigs that Sister Gabrielle liked to place in the cupboards.

And now she was in a deep chair in a corner of Mother Superior's study. A rug was over her knees, and there was a blazing fire at her feet. A small table held four bowls of hot soup, together with a large pot of coffee and some wedges of bread and butter. There was also a small flagon of brandy – Gina could not imagine where that had come from.

The soup, which was Sister Agnes's best chicken broth, was wonderfully reviving, and Mother Superior poured coffee for Gina and Sister Cecilia, and for Chimaera and Dan. Before she handed them their cups, she added a dash of brandy to each one, observing that brandy was warming and also good for shock.

Sister Cecilia said, 'And we should remember that St Paul believed in a little wine for the stomach's sake.'

Hearing the light, ironic voice, Gina was suddenly glad to have Cecilia there. She said, 'Sister Cecilia, when did he – Father Joachim – bring you into the cellar?'

'About an hour before Dan and Signor Chimaera rescued us, I think,' said Cecilia. 'I lost all real sense of time, but my ordeal did not last very long.'

'I lost all sense of time as well,' said Gina, instantly understanding.

'Joachim simply walked into my room here, and used . . . I believe it was laudanum.'

'He used laudanum for me, too,' said Gina. 'And he took me to the cottage in a handcart.'

A faint smile showed. 'It was very undignified, wasn't it?' said Cecilia. 'Although all I really remember is discovering that I was in that loathsome cellar, with Joachim tying me up, and telling me I would be immured there. And then he began the chant. Mother Superior, I am deeply sorry I brought that music with me when I entered the Order.'

'None of us can be held to account for the sins of others – and it's even verging on the sin of pride to do so. You are not accountable for Joachim Bouton's actions,' said Mother Superior, crisply. 'For now, there are other matters to discuss. I would have preferred to wait until you're both recovered, but we can't do so.' She frowned, then said, 'Put bluntly, we have two bodies on our hands – a murderer and his victim. In the ordinary way we would call the local justice of the peace, but—'

'But the local justice of the peace is Sir John Chandos himself,' said Dan.

'Yes.'

Chimaera said, 'You also have a second murderer on your hands, Mother Superior, and he is here in this room now.' He made an expressive gesture with both hands. 'I am guilty of the death of Father Joachim,' he said. 'I do not seek to hide the fact. It is the truth and I am devastated and distraught at the knowledge of what I have done.' He paused to pinch the bridge of his nose with his forefinger and thumb. Gina tried not to think he had deliberately imported a trace of a sob into his voice at this point. Then he sat up a little straighter, and, squaring his shoulders, said, 'If I must face justice for my action, I shall do so.' He looked at Gina. 'I shall walk bravely to the gallows with my head high,' he said. 'There will be no breath of scandal, for I shall not allow your name to pass my lips, Gina.'

'Gina must be kept out of it at all costs,' said Sister Cecilia at once. 'For her name to be linked with the murder of a priest is unthinkable.'

'She would not come under suspicion,' said Chimaera. 'Because I should confess.'

'But then the whole story would come out,' said Mother Superior. 'And for it to become known that Joachim Bouton committed a murder and would have committed two more if Dan and Chimaera had not stopped him, would cause a great scandal.'

'In Cresacre?' asked Dan.

'Oh, far wider than Cresacre. Priest turned murderer. That priest chanting an ancient barbaric ritual while killing.'

'*Dio mio*, that would send shock waves through the churches of the land and probably as far as the Vatican.'

'It would,' said Dan. He looked at Mother Superior. 'I think you're trying to think of a way to cover it all up,' he said. 'Am I right?'

'Regrettably, Dan, you are.'

'I daresay your Church has covered up worse things over the centuries, Mother Superior?'

'Is that a criticism?'

'An observation. A question. Because I believe that there might be a way of covering this up.'

'Tell me.'

Speaking as if he was thinking aloud, Dan said, 'There's a saying that the best way to hide a leaf is in a forest. You'd agree with that?'

'Yes.'

'Then, working on that premise, the best way to hide a scandal and a mystery would be to hide it beneath another scandal and mystery,' said Dan.

Sister Cecilia said, 'Dan, you are the most unusual gardener I have ever met.'

'Am I? Good. My thought is that we create another scandal and a mystery – something that will push into second place any speculation about John Chandos's sudden death and about Joachim's disappearance. A scandal – a mystery – that would cause such an upheaval in Cresacre that no one would talk about – or think about – anything else for weeks. Months. No one would ask any awkward questions. Gina would be safe, and you would all be safe,' said Dan. 'And the Catholic Church could continue unscathed.'

'What kind of scandal and mystery did you have in mind?' asked Chimaera, sounding suspicious.

'It's a very large proposition, but supposing the nuns – all of you – were to disappear from Cresacre,' said Dan. 'To vanish in the dead of night, quietly and secretly, the convent abandoned – empty – and no one knowing why it had happened. That would be such a massive event hereabouts that no one would have any interest in very much else for a very long time. "Dear me, Sir John Chandos has died suddenly," they'd say. "How sad." They'd attend a memorial service for him, of course, and they'd be genuinely sorrowful. But afterwards they'd repair to the Black Boar and return to their speculation about this convent. That would be of far more interest to them. After a while, perhaps, it would even get about that the convent was becoming haunted. Strange stories usually do grow up around buildings that remain empty for a long time.'

'Especially,' said Chimaera, 'if there is someone to carefully start those stories.'

'Exactly. And with all of that happening, Sir John and his family would take second place in people's minds. As for Father Joachim's disappearance—'

Sister Cecilia said, slowly, 'If this entire community here had vanished, it would be assumed Joachim had accompanied us to . . . to wherever people thought we had gone. But where would we have gone? Unless . . .' She stopped, staring at him.

'You're keeping pace with me, Sister, aren't you,' said Dan. 'In fact I think you're ahead of me.'

Cecilia said, 'Unless we let it be believed that we had travelled to France.'

'But why would we do that—? Oh!' said Mother Superior. 'Yes, of course.'

'To give support to the imprisoned Carmelites in Compiègne, of course,' said Cecilia. 'We'd go to our mother house, which is only a few miles outside Compiègne. We would be welcome there, wouldn't we, Mother?'

'Unquestionably. And I believe this is a fiction that could be made fact, because we might indeed be able to help those imprisoned nuns.'

Sister Cecilia said, eagerly, 'I'm fairly fluent in French. I could shepherd us through quite a lot of the practicalities of the journey. But I am not at all an experienced traveller. There were holidays with my French grandmother when I was a child, but my parents always took charge of everything then. I would be nervous of arranging the Channel crossing and the journey across France.'

Chimaera said, eagerly, 'But I . . . I have travelled. And such a journey would serve all our purposes – mine, also. I will be honest about that, because if I came with you and escorted you—'

'You'd be out of reach of the law if the truth about Joachim's death were discovered,' said Dan, dryly.

'It is a consideration. I admit it.'

'But there are ten of us, signor,' said Mother Superior, and Gina saw that, to his credit, Chimaera did not flinch.

He said, 'That is a good, round number. To escort ten ladies – twenty ladies, even – would be my privilege.'

From her corner, Sister Cecilia said, 'And what shall we do about Sir John's death?' She looked at Gina as she said this, and Gina stared at her, the pain of her father's death clawing into her mind all over again.

Dan said slowly, 'Could his body simply be found near Chandos House? As if he had suffered a . . . a heart seizure or something of the kind while walking his land. Would that be credible? Would his injuries be visible?'

'We could conceal them. They were inward injuries, anyway. We could let it be thought that a physician had examined him – as Dan said, people will be too interested in our own disappearance to ask many questions,' said Cecilia. 'Chimaera, you're frowning.'

'We are smudging over too many important facts,' said Chimaera. 'The question of a physician, for instance. Would the church accept him for burial without a physician being involved? I do not know the laws here, you see, but . . .' He frowned, then said, 'I am trying to think of a better solution to that.'

'There's Lady Chandos to be thought of as well,' said Mother Superior. 'Gina, I don't see how we could hide the truth from her.'

Gina said, carefully, 'My mother isn't at Chandos House at present. She's staying with cousins. But I don't think she would ask many questions – I think she would leave everything to the family solicitors.' It was impossible to say that her mother would probably be more concerned with knowing the details of her father's will, and with choosing becoming mourning garments. She would almost certainly sell Chandos House and go to live with the prim-and-proper cousins; she had always spent a lot of time with them. Gina had been born in their house, in fact, and had been brought back to Cresacre when she was very tiny.

She came out of these thoughts to hear Mother Superior saying, 'If we were to take up the idea of leaving, the entire convent would have to be part of the lie. I don't think I can ask that of them.'

'Could you tell them the official version – that the journey is to help the imprisoned nuns at Compiègne?' said Dan.

'That would still be lying to them. I'm not sure if I could do that.'

'I could,' said Sister Cecilia, promptly. 'If it meant hiding the secrets, protecting people who need protecting . . .' She glanced involuntarily at Mother Superior. 'We would be leaving old secrets behind, which perhaps is a good thing,' she said.

'And taking the community to France to make a new start,' said Mother Superior, thoughtfully. 'That's true. And God can be served anywhere, of course.'

'But there's Gina,' said Cecilia. 'Do we take her with us?'

'No,' said Dan, at once. 'There's too much danger in that country. For a group of nuns it would be safe, I think. But for a girl from an English manor house—'

Gina said, 'I'm hardly a member of the aristocracy. They're not going to drag me to the nearest lamp-post and hang me from it.'

'Even so.'

'Dan's right,' said Sister Cecilia. 'We can't take you into all that, Gina. But nor can we leave you on your own to cope with all the subterfuge and deceit.'

'I could manage it,' said Gina, although she was not at all sure if she could.

'She wouldn't be on her own,' said Dan. 'I'll stay with her. I'll guide her through it.'

Gina looked at him and felt a little spark of warmth burn up.

'It would be highly irregular,' said Mother Superior. 'Most unusual.'

'This is an irregular and unusual situation,' said Dan. He leaned forward. 'Mother Superior, I'm no traveller. I have no knowledge of the French language. I'd be an encumbrance to you. Chimaera will be very useful – he knows about travelling. But I'd be better staying here and making sure our plan is followed.'

'Gina? What do you think, child?'

'I could cope with it all if Dan were here,' said Gina, and thought: I could cope with anything if Dan were here.

Chimaera said, 'Then if Dan is to remain—'

'Yes?'

Chimaera glanced apologetically at Gina, then said, 'In that cellar, with only the lamplight, it was not possible to see if there were marks of violence. But if Sir John resisted Father Joachim—'

'He did,' said Gina. 'He told me so, just before—'

'Ah. Then it is likely that there are signs. They would raise difficult questions. So I am thinking that Dan could start a small rumour – very subtle – that Sir John had been on the watch for poachers or gypsies. That would explain why he was walking around late at night. And any marks of violence on him would be blamed on a poacher or a gypsy. But it would all be so – what is the word? – so anonymous, that no suspicion would fall on any one person. That,' said Chimaera, firmly, 'would be important.'

'That's an excellent idea,' said Mother Superior, approvingly, and Dan nodded.

'I can do all that,' he said.

'It's a very good idea indeed,' said Cecilia, warmly. 'Mother Superior, shall I talk to the sisters about travelling to France? As bursar it would seem reasonable coming from me, I think. They might suspect there's more to it than helping the nuns at Compiègne – they all know you came here tonight in distress,' she said, looking at Gina and the two men. 'But they would obey our rule of obedience.'

She shivered suddenly, and Mother Superior put out a hand, which Cecilia grasped gratefully. 'So much death,' she said, her eyes suddenly seeming to stare at a distant point. 'So much loss . . . And I have the impression of a darkness ahead of us.'

'None of us ever knows what's ahead of us,' said Mother Superior. She held Cecilia's hand for a moment longer, then, in a practical voice, said, 'Now then, Signor Chimaera, you are the traveller among us. How could such a journey be arranged?'

Chimaera beamed. He said, 'There is a post coach due in two days' time.'

Gina had not expected to see either Dan or Chimaera again that night, but as she was making her way to the room that Sister Agnes had made ready for her, she heard a soft footfall, and turned to see Dan standing beneath one of the wall sconces.

He said, 'You'll be leaving for your cousin's house in a day or two.'

'Yes.' Gina did not say that this was a deeply depressing prospect.

'Shall you return to Chandos House?'

'I don't know. My mother probably won't want to. She'll live with her cousins – she always preferred their company to my father's.'

'You might want to return, though,' he said. He had come to stand in front of her.

'I'm not sure if there would be any reason to,' said Gina.

'How about this,' said Dan, and pulled her into his arms – not roughly but not gently, and not in the smooth, almost-rehearsed way that Chimaera had employed. Gina thought, wildly, he's going to kiss me. And I'm not at all sure I want him to – I don't think I should let myself be kissed by a gardener—

And then his lips came down on hers, and she forgot about him being a gardener and she forgot that any one of the nuns might walk in at any second, and she clung to him and kissed him back.

When, finally, he released her, there was a trace of unusual colour across his cheekbones. Gina said, 'Oh!'

'Yes?'

'Oh, I hadn't thought it could feel like that.'

The now-familiar grin lifted his lips. 'Didn't I get it right?' he said. 'Because if not, we could try again.'

'Oh, yes, it was utterly right.' Gina stared at him with astonished delight, and thought: so that's how I'm supposed to feel!

Why didn't I feel like that with Chimaera, though? She said, 'It was very right indeed.'

'But perhaps we could try again anyway?'

'Oh, yes,' said Gina again, and he pulled her against him a second time. There, again, was the soaring delight and the feeling that something that was very right indeed had happened.

When he released her, his eyes were brilliant, and he smiled down at her. 'You'll come back to Chandos House?'

'Yes. Oh yes, I'll come back. Will you be there?'

'I will. I'll be waiting for you, Gina,' he said.

Gina said, rather awkwardly, 'You don't mind that Chimaera . . . that he was . . . that he and I—'

'I mind very much,' said Dan, and his arms tightened around her. 'But I can accept it for – for what I think it was. A flirtation that got out of hand?' he said. 'Curiosity, even?'

'Both those things,' said Gina, at once.

'He's an unprincipled seducer, of course,' said Dan. 'But I suspect he's not quite as successful as he thinks. The curious thing is that I find I like him. I even trust him.'

Gina said, 'And . . . you really will be waiting until I'm back?'

'I'll wait for as long as it takes,' said Dan.

Lying in the narrow bed made up for her, Gina thought she had been dealt so many surprises that her mind was still reeling. She knew she would soon start to feel deep pain at her father's death. It was like receiving a blow or a cut – you did not immediately feel the pain, only the shock. But when the shock wore off, the pain rushed at you.

But he wasn't alone when he died, she thought. I'll hold on to that knowledge. She would hold on to the knowledge of Dan as well and, despite the tangle of emotions still gripping her, she smiled. She would come back to Cresacre – she would come back as soon as she could – and he would be waiting for her. Did he mean marriage? Would she marry a gardener? Her mother and the prim cousins would certainly want nothing to do with her if she married Dan. I don't care, thought Gina.

The door opened and Sister Cecilia's soft voice said, 'Gina? Are you asleep?'

'No.' Gina sat up in bed. 'Are you all right?'

'I will be, in time.'

'I wish you weren't going away,' said Gina, suddenly, and Sister Cecilia reached for her hand.

'I wish it too. But I can't see any other way.'

'You'll come back, though? Please come back.'

'I'll try. But if I don't—'

'Yes?'

'I would like you to have this.' She pressed into Gina's hand a small silver ring, set with what Gina thought was a black pearl. 'It belonged to a cousin of mine – a cousin whom I loved very dearly. She's long since dead, but I would like to think of you having this and perhaps remembering me.'

Gina stared at her. 'I will remember you, anyway,' she said. 'But I'll keep this for the memory. And I'll think of your cousin.'

'She was a wonderful musician, as I think you could be. A gifted pianist.'

She hesitated, then said, 'Gina – your father. I know his death is an anguish – I understand. But I think he would have taken great comfort in having you with him at the last.'

Gina said, 'You knew him very well.'

'Yes.' A look of pain twisted her face, then she said, 'But now I should go. The Great Silence has begun, and I don't think Mother Superior would see even our present situation as grounds for breaking it.'

But at the door, she turned back. 'Gina – about Dan.'

'Yes?'

'You mustn't care that he's only a gardener.'

'I don't.'

'I don't think he'll stay a gardener,' said Cecilia. 'If he's what you want, don't let go of him.'

She smiled and went out, and Gina lay down again. There had been comfort in Cecilia's words. There was comfort in the small silver ring as well. She would keep it, always.

NINETEEN

When Chimaera had gone down to his supper earlier that evening in the Black Boar, he had not thought that within a few hours he would have committed a murder, or that he would be assisting to conceal another murder, and agreeing to escort ten nuns across the English Channel into France. Ten of them! And actually, France, torn and ravaged by the Terror and the Revolution, with the *sans-culottes* slicing off heads wholesale. Really, it was enough to make a man shudder and beat a hasty retreat.

He did not retreat, though, since that would be the action of a coward, and Chimaera was not a coward, whatever else he might be. A sly voice hissed in his ear that he might not be a coward, but wasn't he a murderer? The dreadful word skittered across his mind, but he pushed it away and concentrated on the practicalities.

'No evidence is to be left in the convent,' Mother Superior said, after Gina had gone to bed, and they were clearing away the coffee cups. 'Nothing that might tell people where we have gone or what happened tonight. Certainly nothing about Father Joachim. Sister Cecilia, you will see to that, perhaps? There may be papers in the sacristy . . . Even ordinary account books shouldn't be left.'

'I will look,' said Cecilia. 'And I'll burn anything I find.'

'Do any of the nuns keep journals? We can't risk any private records being left here. It isn't exactly forbidden to keep a journal,' said Mother Superior, in an aside to Dan and Chimaera. 'Scholarly notes of study or prayer can be very beneficial. But personal diaries are discouraged.'

'Vanity,' said Chimaera, nodding to show he understood.

'Introspection,' put in Dan.

'Either and both.'

'I believe Anne-Marie keeps a journal as part of her novice's training,' said Cecilia. 'I'll make sure she brings it with her, although I shouldn't think there'll be anything damaging in it. I don't think any of the others ever have kept diaries of any kind. I certainly never did, although—'

'Yes?'

'I would like to make a chronicle of our journey as we travel,' she said, thoughtfully. 'For my own reading. That wouldn't contravene the Rule, would it, Mother? Or be a danger?'

'Providing no one else sees it, no. And we'll be in France, and you would be writing in English, anyway.'

Dan stood up. 'You will have to excuse Chimaera and myself for a little while,' he said. 'Because there is Sir John to be dealt with, and I think it must be dealt with now. Before full light.'

'You will make sure that . . . nothing can be found? No trace that might lead to exploration or investigation?'

'We'll make very sure, Mother. Sir John's body will be left in a suitable place on his own land. Later tomorrow I will spread the tale about gypsies or tramps.'

'And the other one? Joachim?'

An abrupt silence closed down on the firelit room. Chimaera had known this was inevitable, but he still felt as if a lump of lead had replaced his stomach.

Dan looked at him, then said, softly, 'I think there is only one thing to do, isn't there?'

Returning to Infanger Cottage with the knowledge of what lay inside and what they would have to do about it was one of the strangest and eeriest experiences Chimaera had ever known.

As they walked through the trees, he thought about Gina. Certainly it would be the act of a villain to drag a young girl into a country in the grip of such terror and turmoil, especially after what had happened to her inside Infanger Cottage. Also, from his own point of view, he was inclined to think he was already heaping quite a fair amount on his plate (ten nuns to escort across a country riven by Revolution, for heaven's sake!), and that the addition of Gina to the party – however sweet and desirable she might be – could be one burden too many.

But he would not part from Gina without some suitable expression of his emotions. He might soliloquize about his deep and abiding love, and his anguish at having to leave her – how it was a torment to be torn from her arms and how she was the love of his life. But trying this out in his mind, it sounded a touch exaggerated, and in fact Chimaera was no longer sure if it was true. Still, it would make a moving scene for his opera – he was starting to think that the opera's story could reflect something of what had been happening here. This was such a strong, emotion-filled story. He would change names and places, of course.

As they neared the cottage, Dan suddenly said, 'Are we mad, do you suppose? I mean – have we entered into a form of madness?'

Chimaera explained that his only experience of madness was on stage.

'People are sometimes required to portray madness there. I have done so myself – I played King Orlando in Handel's *Orlando*, where I had to go mad for the love of Angelica. Every night and twice on matinée days I went mad. The pit cheered me.'

'I can well believe it,' said Dan, politely.

'And when I was in Mozart's *Idomeneo*, it was said of me that the very fabric of the opera house shivered at hearing my tormented aria.'

'That, too, I can believe.'

They had reached the cottage now, and Dan pushed the door open. As they stepped inside, the cottage's darkness enclosed them greedily.

'Like poisoned smoke,' said Dan. 'Let's light those lamps before we venture down to the cellar. It might be approaching dawn, but it's still as dark as the devil's cavern in here.'

The wavering light from the oil lamps, which they had left near the door, sent the shadows scuttling away. Chimaera tried not to notice that they only scuttled as far as the corners, and that they seemed to crouch and coil there.

'The broken-in door might be noticed,' said Dan. 'And it might attract real tramps or gypsies. I'll get Alberic Firkin to put a new lock on it, I think.'

'Should he be asked to brick up the cellar window at the same time?'

They looked at one another. 'Dare we risk that?' said Dan.

'It would mean him going into the cellar – I don't think it could be done from outside.'

'It would be better than risking someone getting in and living there,' pointed out Chimaera. 'How long would it take Alberic?'

'Not very long. It'd be a straightforward matter.'

'Then he would only be in the cottage for as long as it takes. You could arrange to be there with him, perhaps. And you could say that it's to make the place secure because the broken door might mean someone's been getting in,' Chimaera suggested. 'That would strengthen the story about Sir John being killed by tramps or gypsies as well.'

'That's a good idea. Yes, I'll do it. You should be writing stories for the stage as well as performing them,' said Dan, and Chimaera was about to confess his aspirations to Dan, when Dan said, 'Now for the cellar.'

Chimaera would not have been surprised to find that Father Joachim's body had vanished – that the whole thing had been nothing but a nightmare.

It had not, of course. It lay as they had left it, the eyes wild and staring, and empty of all life.

As Dan bent over to take the man's shoulders, Chimaera hesitated. 'We don't have any regrets about what we're going to do to him, do we?' he said.

'Burial in unconsecrated ground? Without the presence of a man of God reciting a few prayers? Is that what's worrying you?'

'It is that I had an Italian Catholic childhood,' said Chimaera, apologetically.

'Chimaera, whether you're Catholic, Protestant, Jewish, pagan or anything else, wherever Father Joachim has gone, he's already there, and anything we do now won't alter that,' said Dan.

'You are right, of course.'

'As for regrets,' said Dan, 'I do have some. But even though this man wasn't sane, I'm remembering what he did to Gina. And that he murdered John Chandos – a decent and honourable man and a fair man to work for.'

'I am being foolish. And perhaps feeling guilty because I was the one who—'

'You acted in self-defence,' said Dan, shortly. 'I saw exactly what happened. I'll stand up in a courtroom and say so if necessary.'

'I hope that won't be necessary.' Chimaera bent down. 'I will take his shoulders,' he said. 'You take his feet.'

Between them they lifted what had been Joachim Bouton and carried him to the torn-open wall. It should not have come as a shock to see again the jagged hole with the shadowy figure of John Chandos beyond, but Chimaera flinched.

'We need to widen the hole a bit,' said Dan, studying it critically. 'We'll never get Chandos out, otherwise, and we'll certainly never get this one in there. But we'll have to work carefully – we'll have to re-use as many of the bricks as we can to rebuild the wall.'

They chiselled out the bricks with extreme care, until they were able to reach in to the body of Sir John Chandos. It was a struggle to lift him out, and Chimaera began to feel as if every muscle in his body was being stretched on a rack, but in the end they managed it.

'He has marks of a blow to the head,' said Chimaera, as they laid John Chandos's body on the cellar floor.

'Yes. And there's blood around his lips. I'd like to clean him up, but I don't think we dare. It would be better if it looks as if he's been attacked.' He laid a hand briefly on John's shoulder. 'Sorry, old boy,' he said. 'But you'll get all the respect due to you soon. I'll be here to make sure of it.' He stood up, and looked at Joachim. 'Now for this one.'

It was more difficult than they had expected to lift Joachim and to push him through the jagged hole and in place inside the alcove.

'He will have to stand upright,' said Chimaera at last, after several unsuccessful attempts to lay the body down. 'It will be a strange entombing.'

'I believe some cultures bury their dead standing up.'

'Sister Cecilia remarked earlier that you are a very unusual gardener. And so you are,' said Chimaera. 'You are constantly surprising me with your knowledge.'

'Never mind knowledge, just get the man in there. Good,' said Dan, presently.

'And now we have to brick up the wall, yes?'

'Yes. Layer by layer, the mortar between each layer to stick the bricks together – you understand?'

'It is not difficult,' said Chimaera, dryly. As he reached for the tub of mortar left by Joachim earlier, the lines of the Lemurrer jabbed spitefully into his mind.

'Brick by careful brick with murderer's hands . . .

I make the layers of death . . .'

Neither of them spoke as they worked, and when they finally finished the macabre task, they were both covered in sweat and their hands were scraped and raw.

'I think it looks all right,' said Dan, lifting the oil lamp and moving its light over the wall's surface with critical attention. 'If anyone does come down here, they aren't likely to notice anything out of place. And there's no reason why anyone would come down here. John Chandos's body will be found on his own land, and it will be assumed he died there. There won't be a search for Joachim – people will think he left with the nuns. There's no reason why anyone would connect anything to this cottage.'

'We should arrange Sir John in a place where he can be found quite soon – and we should do that now,' said Chimaera. 'Before anyone is around. And later it will be up to you, my friend, to spread those tales about poachers and gypsies.' He paused, then said, in a different voice, 'And also to make sure Gina Chandos is safe and well.' He hesitated before starting again. 'You will be better for her than I ever could have been. I should not have—'

'No,' said Dan. 'You should not.'

'I know it. And not often do I admit that. But you will look after her?'

Their eyes met. 'I shall do that,' said Dan. 'You have my word.'

Chimaera had not wanted to return to the Black Boar but, as Dan pointed out, they could not do anything that might link Chimaera to the nuns' disappearance in two days' time.

'You've only got tonight and tomorrow to get through,' he said. 'Stay on, and let it be known you're leaving on that early morning post coach. Oh, and pay your reckoning.'

'Of course,' said Chimaera, shocked that Dan should think he would have done otherwise.

He got himself to bed, and spent much of the next day committing to paper a description of the forest and Infanger Cottage, and the gloomy trees and shrivelled ivy. It would all look very well as a setting for some of the scenes of his opera. Perhaps it could be used in the one where the young heroine was imprisoned. He had still to write this, but he knew how it should look. There was a very talented artist called Bertrando, living in Milan, whom Chimaera might have engaged for the designing of the settings and scenery, had it not been for a small misunderstanding between them regarding Bertrando's wife.

That evening, after supper, he joined the company in the taproom and drank sharp, strong cider in company with some of the locals. He flattered himself that he blended in very well.

Towards the end of the evening, Alberic Firkin came in, looking very pleased with himself, offering drinks to anyone who cared to accept, and calling for some of the Black Boar's cheese and onion pasties for everyone, to help the beer along.

A general murmur of appreciation greeted this, and as the pasties were brought out, Alberic was asked to what they all owed this sudden generosity.

'Come into money, have you, Alberic?' demanded the aged carter.

Alberic said he might have done. 'Matter of fact, I was given a job up at the convent,' he said. 'Broken door on that derelict old cottage between the convent and Chandos House. Mother Superior wanted it putting right as soon as maybe.'

Chimaera immediately donned an air of nonchalance, while listening intently.

'You'd think they wouldn't bother about that old wreck,' observed the Black Boar's landlord. 'Let it fall down, I say.'

'Ah, but they're worried about gypsies,' said Alberic, with an air of triumph. 'Dan – him as gardens up at Chandos House – told me himself. "I'm charged with asking you to fit a good stout lock", that's what he said. "Mother Superior sent me down with the order, and here's a fee for the work." Well,' said Alberic, 'a body ain't going to refuse good money, no matter it comes from a gardener or a duke, that's what I say.'

There was murmured agreement.

'Did you do the work today?' somebody asked.

'I did. Never let it be said that a Firkin neglects a job as he's been paid in advance for. And,' said Alberic, taking a long sup of his ale, 'I did the other job while I was about it.' He wiped the edges of his moustaches fastidiously, and took a bite of his own pasty.

'What other job?'

'Bricking up the old cellar window,' said Alberic, and Chimaera, still covertly listening, was aware of a feeling of relief. It's all right, he thought. The cottage is sealed and safe. Joachim's body won't be found – at least, not until we're all hundreds of miles away.

'They wanted to make sure no gypsies could get in through it,' said Alberic. 'Dan walked down there with me, to point out what was needed – not as I needed it pointing out, for I could see perfectly well with my own eyes. It didn't take me long,' he said, then glanced about him. With a slightly shamefaced air, he said, 'Don't mind admitting among friends that I made sure it didn't take long. Eerie old place, that clearing. I was all right while Dan was there, but he went off to fetch a couple of trowels for the bricking part – I'd left mine in the yard. And after he'd gone—'

'What?'

'It was mighty quiet,' said Alberic. 'But in the quiet was – well, I kept thinking I was hearing things.'

'What kind of things?' demanded the landlord, who did not mind people telling a good yarn in his taproom, but did not want anything that might drive folk away.

'Rustlings and scratchings and tappings inside the cottage,' said Alberic, impressively, and Chimaera stared at him and forgot about being nonchalant and uninterested.

'Tappings?' said several voices.

'Tappings worst of all. Like this they were.' Alberic demonstrated, knocking his knuckles against the brick fireplace. 'Over and over again.' He tapped against the bricks again, and Chimaera repressed a shiver. 'As if someone might be knocking on a wall somewhere. I tell you, it gave me the creeps.'

'What was it?' asked the landlord.

'Never found out. Nor I didn't wait for Dan to come back. I managed to finish the bricking-up with what I'd got – bit of a rushed job between us, but sound enough. Those bricks'll hold for a good hundred years or more. I got myself out of that clearing as fast as a scalded cat. And,' said Alberic, firmly, 'there'll be an ordinary explanation for the sounds, mark my words.'

'A trapped bird, most like,' said the carter.

'Bound to be,' agreed Alberic. 'A trapped bird, fluttering to get out. Or mice, or even rats. Still, whatever was in there, it won't get out now, for that cottage is safe as a fortress. Who's for another cheese and onion pasty?'

TWENTY

The sense of well-being and optimism that Olivia had felt after Phineas's visit seemed set to increase when he phoned next morning, shortly after breakfast. This time Olivia, recognizing the displayed number from the card he had given her, picked up the phone.

'Miss Tulliver? Olivia? It's Phin Fox.'

'Oh . . . good morning.' It was stupid to feel a sudden lurch of pleasure. He could not have read *The Martyrs* already, not unless he had sat up all night with it, and in view of Arabella Tallis's presence, that did not seem likely.

Phineas Fox said, 'I'm calling to reassure you in case you heard about the small disaster at the Black Boar last night.'

This was not what Olivia had been expecting. She said, 'What disaster? I don't know anything about a disaster.'

'It wasn't very much – a bit of a flood, and Arabella and I had to decamp to the school for the night. But I didn't want you to hear a jumbled version and worry about the manuscript being damaged or anything. It's perfectly all right and unscathed and I've got it with me.'

'That's very kind of you to let me know,' said Olivia, pleased at such consideration. She hesitated, then said, 'I daresay you haven't had a chance yet to look at it.'

'I've looked at some of the scenes,' said Phineas. 'And they're very interesting.'

Interesting. That was what people said when they thought something was dreadful, and were trying to be kind. Phineas would not be so two-faced, though.

'And you said something about your uncle drawing on local sources, I think,' he said. 'I'd be interested to know if you've got any more details about that,' he said. 'Any notes he might have made, or any books he might have used, for instance.'

'I've still got most of his books,' said Olivia, and wondered whether to suggest Phineas walk down to the cottage for a cup of coffee so that they could go into this in more detail. They could look along Gustav's bookshelves in case there was anything that might interest him. It would be a very companionable thing to do, just the two of them. She tried to remember if she had any filter coffee. 'There are certainly several that he used to consult,' she said. 'Is there anything in particular?'

'There's an aria he's composed that seems to link up to something I found in the school library here,' he said. 'A book of old memoirs – a kind of published journal – left by one of the nuns from the school's convent era. Late 1790s. The words of your uncle's aria are quoted in it.'

He's talking about Ginevra's song, thought Olivia. Of course he is. She beat down a spiral of apprehension, and said, 'That sounds intriguing.'

'What's really interesting me is that I believe the words are part of a very old ritual,' said Phineas.

'What kind of ritual?'

'It's French – medieval, or possibly even earlier. It was known as the Lemurrer. That translates as immuring.'

'Immuring—?'

'Walling up. I'm afraid that, specifically, it meant walling up alive.'

His words spun Olivia's mind back to that night in the lamplit cellar. Walling up. That's what we did, she thought. I watched. I helped. And as we laid the bricks in place, Gustav was humming Ginevra's song. *Step by measured step the murderers came to me . . .* Murderers. That's what I was, that night. But we didn't wall her up alive, we *didn't*. Those faint sounds I heard later were just old timbers creaking, birds in the eaves. Water hammer.

'It's very rare to find traces of the Lemurrer in this country,' Phin was saying. 'But this chant is almost certainly a fragment of it – which suggests the Lemurrer found its way to Cresacre. That's likely to be of great interest to a number of people.'

'But just finding a couple of verses in an old book—'

'It's not only the book,' he said. 'There's a carving in the church. It's almost an exact copy of an old engraving, and it depicts someone being walled up, with people chanting or singing while they watch. The carving is repeated here in the school as well – in the apartments at the top of the building. Would your uncle have lived in those rooms? When he was headteacher?'

'He did have a set of rooms at the school, of course,' said Olivia. 'And I had a bedroom there as well. So I suppose I've seen both carvings. They wouldn't have meant anything, though. And I never heard my uncle mention them. Are you sure about this?'

'Reasonably sure. I believe people in Cresacre have known about the Lemurrer.' He paused, then said, 'I think it's very likely that not only was it known about, it was actually practised here.'

Olivia felt horror wash over her. If only you knew, she thought, it was most certainly practised here. More than two hundred years ago in this very cottage, and then again just a few years ago. Ginevra and Imogen. But Phineas can't possibly know that. He wants Gustav's research, though, and he said that finding the old ritual would be interesting to people. Does that mean people would want to come here? Pry into things? Into this cottage? Panic welled up.

Phin said, 'Your uncle used what I think was called the victim's chant in *The Martyrs*. But there's a second part – the murderer's chant. It's here in the old journal, if you ever want to see it.'

Olivia said, 'Have you got it there now?'

'Yes.'

'Could you . . . can you read it to me?'

She felt his hesitation, then he said, 'It's very macabre.'

'The chant my uncle used in *The Martyrs* was macabre. But if you read this second part, I might recognize something we could link into his research,' said Olivia.

'All right.' There was the sound of pages being turned, then Phin's voice came again, and the words, read quietly and unemotionally, poured into Olivia's mind, illuminating dark corners – showing up things she had thought safely buried. *Murderer's tread . . . Murderer's brain . . .*

When Phin finally reached the end of the chant, Olivia did not speak, and after a moment, he said, 'I did tell you it was macabre.'

'It is, rather. And I don't recognize anything about it. I do see how it fits with the aria in *The Martyrs*, though.'

'That's why I'm keen to follow all this up,' he said. 'To try to bring your uncle's work and this piece of the past together. Maybe even get to something about the Cresacre legend. I wondered if there might be any of his books I could look at – anything he used for source material?'

'There might be.' Olivia walked over to the bookshelves and scanned the rows of titles. 'Yes – there is something here that he used a good deal. It's about the executions in the French Revolution.'

'What is it?' There was no mistaking the interest – even eagerness – in his voice.

'It's called . . . hold on a minute . . .' She reached up for the book. Dust clung to it, and when she opened it, the scent of age and damp came to her. 'It's called *Curious Legends from the Guillotine.* Would it be of any help?'

'It sounds as if it might,' said Phin.

'I think Gustav found it in an old bookshop. Or maybe it was the local library – one of those shelves they have, selling old books for a few pence.'

'It's remarkable how genuinely useful facts can turn up in forgotten old books – often books that were privately printed, or only had a small print run. I'd like to borrow it, if you wouldn't mind. I'll almost certainly finish reading the opera by tomorrow, so I'll give you a call and arrange to bring it back, and perhaps I could borrow the book at the same time. Will that be all right?'

It would be very far from all right. If Phineas Fox was looking into this old ritual, this Lemurrer, he could not be allowed to enter the cottage again, in case he became interested in the cottage's history. But this book might divert his attention to a different area of research, and when he phoned, Olivia could say she would go along to the Black Boar to collect *The Martyrs* from him there, and that she would take the book about guillotine legends. He might ask her to have a drink or even lunch with him.

She said, 'Yes, do ring me, and we'll see what time would fit.'

It was all friendly and civilized but, as Olivia put down the phone, her stomach was clenching with panic. Phineas could not know – or even suspect – what had happened that night in this cottage. Or could he? What if there had been whispers about Imogen – whispers that Olivia had never known about? And if so, supposing Arabella had heard and remembered them? Since coming here, mightn't she have told Phineas? Olivia had a sudden image of the two of them in bed after making love, falling into what people called pillow talk. She was not really familiar with that; in her experience, men who took you to bed usually collapsed into a snoring stupor afterwards, or got up and got dressed to go home.

But it was suddenly startlingly easy to imagine Phin with Arabella, her hair untidily spread across the pillow, Phin telling her about his work and his research – about the Lemurrer and how it seemed to have found its way to Cresacre. Arabella would seize on it, saying well, now, it was an odd thing and it might only be coincidence, but there had been a few wild rumours about the disappearance of someone who had been in her year at school – rumours that might chime with that old ritual.

Would Phin's interest be caught by that – would he start to see connections? Or would he be so enrapt with his companion, so awash with sexual gratification that he would not be interested? Olivia did not want to think about Phin being awash with sexual gratification, or not as a result of Arabella anyway.

But providing she kept Phin Fox – and any colleagues he might bring to Cresacre – out of this cottage, everything would be perfectly all right. She hoped she was about to do that with the loan of the book about the guillotine legends. But as she went out to the hall, there was a loud rat-a-tat at the front door, causing the panic to come rushing back. It could not be Phineas, though, because he would not have had time to walk down to the cottage. It might be some sneaky council official or surveyor trying to get in, or here to hand over a compulsory purchase order. Olivia was not sure how such things worked, but she was not taking any chances.

She would have ignored the knock, but whoever was out there would have glimpsed movement from the hall, through the little glass pane of the door. So she unlocked the door, but she was prepared to give short shrift to all surveyors and council officials who might be outside.

But it was not a surveyor or a council official. It was Arabella Tallis.

She came into the hall in a flurry of energy, talking as she did so, glowing with pleasure at seeing her old schoolfriend after so long – or was she glowing because she had spent the night in Phin's bed and in his arms?

She seized Olivia's hand in both her own, and said, 'Livvy, I'm so pleased you're in. I hope you don't mind me turning up unannounced. It's great to see you – far too long, isn't it, and people always say they'll keep in touch after school, and they really do mean it, only somehow things get missed and life crowds in. What a nice cottage this is. I've never been here before, and I always wanted to, and the thing is that Phin – you met Phin Fox last night, didn't you? – told me about this wrangle you're having with the local authority and their revolting compulsory purchase order plot.'

'Would you like some coffee?' said Olivia, helpless against this cheerful flood of talk.

'I'd love some. I'm supposed to be seeing the printers later – you wouldn't believe the typos they've got in the draft leaflets for the bicentenary; Hats Madeley had fifty fits. I'm borrowing Phin's car to drive there, but the appointment isn't until eleven, and everyone at the school was immersed in other things, so I thought it would be nice to walk down here on the off-chance that you might be in.'

She followed Olivia into the kitchen, and looked through the windows onto the trees. 'This is a lovely spot, isn't it? You are lucky to live in a forest. I do like forests – I always think you might stumble into Narnia or something, or find the pathway to the enchanter's castle or the end of the rainbow with the pot of gold. On the other hand, you might encounter wolves, of course, and let's face it, Livvy, there are all kinds of wolves in the world, aren't there, and I've met a few in my time – well, I daresay you have as well. I don't mean Phin, of course; he's certainly not a wolf. Is that my coffee? Thanks. Anyway, about this CPO and the planners and plotters . . . Oh, yes, let's go into the study, I love studies.'

She sat in Gustav's old chair – it was annoying to see that she somehow made it look comfortable, which Olivia had never found it to be on account of the seat sagging so badly – and said, 'Now then, I am horrified and appalled about the plotters, because an Englishman's home is his castle, isn't it? – I expect that should be Englishperson. So after Phin shut himself away with his research this morning, I had an idea.'

It did not sound as if Phineas had told Arabella about his phone call to Olivia. Olivia was aware of a small secret jab of pleasure at this.

'I wondered,' said Arabella, 'if this cottage's past might be used to fend off the plotters. Because isn't "Infanger" a corruption of "infangentheof"? Wait a bit, I've got it all here.' She burrowed into her handbag, and produced some printed notes, and her glasses. It had always annoyed Olivia how the donning of spectacles altered Arabella's whole demeanour. She suddenly seemed scholarly and serious.

'I looked it up online early this morning on Phin's laptop,' said Arabella. 'And I found that infangentheof is an ancient law from the Dark Ages. The literal translation is "in-taken-thief", and it permitted the owners of a piece of land the right to mete out justice to miscreants captured within their estates, regardless of where the poor wretches actually lived.'

She looked at Olivia hopefully. Olivia said again, 'Yes?'

'It was an Anglo-Saxon arrangement,' said Arabella, returning to her notes, 'supposedly from the time of Edward the Confessor, but when the Normans came barrelling in, they adopted it for their own nefarious use – I suppose it helped them to keep the rebellious Saxons in their place. The law fell more or less into disuse in the fourteenth century.' She put the notes down, and said, 'Now then, if the Cresacre monks were given the right of infangentheof all those centuries ago – it'd be well before they were booted out by Henry VIII, wouldn't it? – and if that right extended over the land where your cottage stands, and if the cottage's name comes from it, then it might be something you could use against the planners and the plotters.'

'I don't see how.'

Arabella got out of the chair and began to walk round the room, as if she might find fragments of the cottage's past strewn

in corners, or links to its history pushed under a floorboard.
'How old is the cottage?' she said.

'I don't know exactly. Mid-1700s, I think. No, probably a
bit earlier. I don't think it was very large when it was first built.
One or two extra rooms and bits got added over the years.'

'Is it possible it was built on the site of a much older building
– maybe the foundations of that old monastery?'

'And named for the ancient law,' said Olivia, thoughtfully,
and with the words came the memory of Gustav saying
Infanger's cellar was part of the original foundations, and probably even part of the old monastery.

'Yes. And if that's the case,' said Arabella, 'I'll bet that every
preservation society within a hundred miles would rear up and
object to it being bulldozed for a new road. They'd want to
preserve such an old fragment of a lost bit of English law. We
could make the whole thing public, start a protest group – local
TV and local radio and things. People would chain themselves
to railings and take up residence in trees.'

Olivia had no idea how seriously to take any of this, but she
said, 'I'm not sure if I'd want publicity.'

'You could keep in the background,' said Arabella, at once.
'We'd need to be sure of the facts first, of course, but there
might be old land deeds that would help. What I thought is that
we might get someone to take a look at the cottage. A good
builder ought to be able to spot signs of an earlier structure in
the foundations. I've got a definite memory of you once
mentioning a cellar – we all had to write an essay on local
houses or Cresacre's past once, d'you remember? End-of-term
project, I think it was, or a local exhibition, or something like
that. I wrote about Chandos House, which Hats Madeley said
wasn't eligible because nobody knew anything about it, and
Davy said I was venturing into the realms of gothic fiction. But
you wrote about Infanger Cottage because you lived in it.'

'That's years ago,' said Olivia. 'I'd only just come to live
here then. I'm surprised you remember.'

'I do, though, because I thought it was fascinating. You said
there was a cellar and that it was much older than the cottage.
You said there were ancient bricks and a stone arch or
something.'

'There is a cellar, but I never go down there. I haven't done for years. There's never been any reason to. It's a bit spooky, actually.' Alarm bells were starting to sound in Olivia's mind. 'Cellars are always spooky, aren't they?' Arabella sat down on the piano stool. 'But what we could do, we could ask those local builders – Firkin & Co, aren't they called, and I always think it's a vaguely saucy name, although beautifully English rural, of course – we could ask them to take a look at it. I expect they've done odd bits of work on the cottage over the years anyway, so they'll most likely know the place.'

'I really don't think—'

'They wouldn't charge anything,' said Arabella, a bit too quickly for Olivia's liking. 'Not if they thought they were going to get a good bit of publicity out of it.'

'I'm not sure if the cellar's even safe,' began Olivia, then stopped, because Arabella had caught sight of the photograph of Gustav that hung over the piano. 'Gustav Tulliver,' she said, softly. 'I'd forgotten what a striking man he was. It's in the eyes, isn't it? Deep-set. You'd even say they were brooding. Like Heathcliff or somebody. He'd retired by the time I came here, and I don't think I ever even spoke to him, but I used to see him around quite often.'

Olivia managed to say, 'He used to potter around the grounds a bit. Miss Madeley didn't mind, and it did him good. He had heart trouble – angina. It made him look a bit hollow-eyed and sunken-cheeked.'

'I bet he was quite a looker in his younger days,' said Arabella, which Olivia thought was exactly the kind of insincere nonsense she would have expected from Arabella, because Gustav had not been a looker at all, not ever.

'It's nice that you keep this photo of him over his piano. What's the silver chain that's strung across it?'

She was staring at the thin silver chain on which Olivia had threaded the ring with the black stone she had found that night in the cellar. She had never shown it to her uncle, but after he died she had thought he would have liked the small link to Ginevra, whom he had written into his opera. She had always thought of it as a memory of Ginevra herself, as well. Ginevra, who had died here, and who was still here.

Arabella said, in a strange voice, 'There's a silver ring threaded on the chain. With a black pearl set in. Olivia, where on earth did this come from?'

The alarm bells were sounding again, but Olivia said, 'Oh, it's a . . . a family thing. I don't know the story behind it. Why?'

Arabella did not answer the question. She said, 'Can I look at it? I'll be very careful.' Before Olivia could think how to refuse this perfectly normal request, Arabella had reached up to the photograph, unhooked the silver chain, and taken the whole thing across to the window to study it more closely.

Silence closed down, then Arabella turned back into the room. She said, 'This is really odd – did you say the ring is a family thing? An heirloom or something, d'you mean?'

'I don't really know. Why?'

'Because,' said Arabella, slowly, 'I'd be ready to swear it's the very ring we gave that girl who vanished from Cresacre. She was in my year – her name was Imogen Amberton.'

The worn, slightly faded study blurred, and Olivia thought for a moment she might faint. She gripped the arms of her chair so tightly that the wooden edges dug into her palms. The small pain caused the room to steady slightly, and she became aware that Arabella was still speaking.

'D'you remember Imogen, Livvy? I expect you do, because you sang in the choir with her, didn't you – she had a beautiful voice and she was always talking about going on those TV talent shows. Only then she vanished, and there were police enquiries and things, although I don't know if they ever really established what had happened to her. But this . . .' she was still holding the silver chain with the ring between her fingers, 'this is what we gave her for her birthday a couple of days before she disappeared. She was heavily into anything goth and she wanted something really unusual and goth-like for a body piercing she was going to have.'

Olivia managed to say, 'I didn't know that.'

'One of the girls found this in a local antique shop. The man said it had an odd history; something about it having belonged to one of the nuns at the convent – the famous ones who disappeared. We didn't know whether it was true, but we thought Imogen would like the story, so we passed the hat round and bought it for her birthday – her seventeenth. She loved it, and she was going to take it to the jewellers to get the piercing done. I don't know where on her body she was going to have the actual piercing, because you could never tell what Imogen might do. Then two or three days later she was gone.' She looked at the ring closely again. Olivia clenched her fists, praying Arabella would not notice the engraved initial. It was very faint, though – she had only seen it under a direct light.

'You know, I'm sure this is that ring,' Arabella was saying. 'It's so distinctive. And so small – the antique shop said it had probably belonged to a child originally, although how that tied up with the nuns . . . And I know it's all years ago, but I remember it clearly because of Imogen disappearing straight afterwards.' She was still holding the ring, frowning. 'It can't be the same one, though. Because if it is, how on earth could it have got here?'

She looked at Olivia, and there was an expression on her face that Olivia did not like – an expression she did not think she had ever seen on the flighty, frivolous Arabella's face before.

She said, firmly, 'It can't be the same one, of course. Not the exact same one.'

'No, of course it can't.' But the puzzled look was still in Arabella's eyes as she replaced the photo and the ring on its thin chain.

Olivia thought: she's not going to let this go. She'll go away and tell people. Phineas – Harriet Madeley. They'll start asking questions. Phin's already curious about the Lemurrer being linked to Cresacre anyway. Between them, they'll decide to tell the police, and the police will be interested, because no one ever did know what happened to Imogen – the case might still be open. They might get the antique shop to identify the ring.

A chilling realization was starting to creep through her. A realization that a way would have to be found to prevent Arabella from talking about this.

Arabella was saying, 'So what about this idea of the cottage and the infangentheof law thing? What do you think?'

From out of the tumbling panic, Olivia heard herself say, 'I think it's quite a good idea. It's worth exploring.'

'Could we take a look in the cellar ourselves? To see if it

looks worth asking the Firkins to come out. I don't want to push in,' said Arabella, 'but I'd love to help if I could.'

Of course you want to push in, thought Olivia, angrily. You always did. And now you suspect something peculiar's going on, because of finding that ring, so you'll find all the excuses you can to push in very firmly indeed. That's why you'll have to be stopped. Silenced.

She said, 'We could look at the cellar later. You said something about going to the printers this morning, but how about after that?'

'That sounds great. I can come straight back here after I've seen the printers. I'll take the car back up to the school to park, then walk back down, so I'd be here around twelve, I should think.' She reached for her bag, and Olivia saw her glance at the book about guillotine legends lying on the desk.

She said, 'Oh, that's a book I mentioned to Phineas – he's looking for background, or something, and my uncle used it for his own research, so I said Phin could borrow it.'

'I can take it with me now, if you like.'

'Would you? Thanks.'

Arabella picked the book up and flipped through a few pages. 'He'll love it,' she said. 'He delves into the past with such intensity always.' A small, reminiscent smile curved her mouth as she said this, and Olivia hated her all over again.

'In fact at the moment,' said Arabella, 'he might as well have time-travelled back to the French Revolution, or even further back, to when there were all kinds of peculiar medieval practices. He's reading up on all kinds of peculiar customs.' She was not looking at Olivia as she said this, for which Olivia was grateful. 'I'll see you later, Livvy. Thanks for the coffee.'

After she had gone, Olivia sat in the study for a long time, replaying parts of the conversation in her mind. How likely was it that Arabella would tell people about finding and recognizing the silver ring? Phineas had not noticed it and, even if he had, it would not have meant anything to him. Olivia would get rid of the ring, of course, but that would not stop Arabella from telling people . . . She had a sudden terrifying vision of police officers appearing at the cottage. What would they say? 'Miss Tulliver, we have information that you have in your possession a ring belonging to a missing girl from twelve years ago.' 'Miss Tulliver, we want you to come with us to the police station for questioning. And while you're there, our men will be excavating the cellar.'

With the thought, memory looped backwards – back to another dark and deeply buried memory that the old cellar held in its shadowy depths.

TWENTY-ONE

After Imogen Amberton's death all those years ago, Gustav had changed.

He had always been a quiet, reticent man; now he became melancholy. He spent most of his time shut away in his study, but he did not seem to work on his beloved opera. When Olivia asked about it, he said, curtly, that it was finished, and there was nothing more he could do to it. Once or twice he went in quest of a possible staging of it – meeting a small touring opera company or a concert performer who might be interested – but nothing ever came of any of these meetings.

Olivia got the manuscript and the handwritten music score photocopied at the local library, and found addresses of music agents in a reference book there. Gustav composed a very careful letter, which took him several days, and eventually allowed the letter and *The Martyrs* to be sent to several of the agents. There were only rejections, though. 'Not what opera companies are looking for at present,' said one, politely enough. 'Feel we could not justify representing the work,' said another. A third, with what Olivia felt was unnecessary unkindness, said that the work lacked originality, and a fourth actually asked if Mr Tulliver was familiar with Francis Poulenc's *Dialogues des Carmélites*, which was generally regarded as the definitive musical work on this fragment of history. Olivia managed to intercept this letter and burn it before Gustav saw it. He saw the others, though, and he shrugged, and said genius was frequently misunderstood. You had only to look at the great writers and painters and composers to know that. *The Martyrs* would find its place one day, and he, Gustav Tulliver, would find his own place with it.

After a while he began to complain of chest pains. Quite bad, he said, but they would pass. There was some breathlessness as well, and eventually he was persuaded to consult the GP. Angina was diagnosed, and a regime of gentle exercise and various pills – together with the right kind of food – was prescribed. Gustav refused to follow this regime and he threw the pills away on the grounds that doctors knew nothing about him and he was not being told what to do or what to eat by a parcel of quacks.

The closeness that had sprung up between himself and Olivia over Imogen's death vanished. In the months that followed, in a relatively short time, he deteriorated into a querulous, unco-operative middle-aged man, whom life had disappointed, who could not be bothered to find anything of any worth to fill his days, and who would not try to improve his health. At first Olivia thought it was Imogen Amberton's death that had brought this about, but after a time she began to wonder if it might also be *The Martyrs*. Now that it was finished, he seemed to have no goal in his life, and little reason for even living.

And then, one evening, without any warning, he made a statement that shattered Olivia's world into pieces.

They were in the study – it was still Gustav's sanctum, but Olivia was permitted in there after supper so that she could do her homework at the big table, with her uncle in his usual corner by the stove. The theory was that she could ask for his help with her homework. The reality was that he was never able to read anything she showed him on her laptop. The light was always wrong – or the glare of the screen hurt his eyes – or he could not be doing with laptops and fiddly keyboards. One day Olivia was going to insist that proper lights were fitted in this room, and that the stove, with its oily-smelling heat, was torn out and an ordinary fireplace put in its place. Except that she could never do any of that, because they could not risk having work of any kind done to the cottage in case workmen found what was in the cellar.

She had been attempting to untangle the component plot threads of *Bleak House* that evening, and to write an essay about them that would satisfy Miss Madeley's critical eye in English literature, when Gustav spoke.

He said, 'I've made a decision. If I'm going to die—'

'You aren't.' Olivia spoke a bit absently, being absorbed in the complex past of Lady Dedlock. 'Not for ages, anyway. Angina isn't a killer – the doctor said so. Two doctors said so.

You've just got to take your medication and do all the other things they told you.'

'. . . I can't face dying with Imogen Amberton on my conscience,' he said, as if she had not spoken. 'I'm going to confess what happened that night. I'm going to the police about it. I shan't involve you, of course – I shall explain it was an accident, and that I panicked. I shall say very clearly that you weren't there – that you knew nothing about it. They'll be told I pushed her and she fell down the stairs.'

'You can't tell them,' said Olivia, staring at him in horror. 'You mustn't.'

'I can. I will. The guilt – it's eating away at me. That's what these chest pains are. I don't care what name they gave it at the hospital, that's what it is.'

In the dim light, his eyes were dark pits, and his lips were compressed into a thin, bloodless line. Olivia stared at him, and thought: he's mad. He must be mad to be saying all this – to be threatening to tell people about Imogen's death. He's not just melancholy and depressed, he's descended into a dark, quiet madness.

But she said, firmly, 'The chest pains are angina; you had tests – an ECG and that other thing on that machine—'

'Her family never knew what happened to her,' he said, as if speaking to himself.

'She didn't have any family, except that aunt who didn't care about her.'

'And I prevented her from being given a traditional funeral. From being laid properly to rest.'

Olivia abandoned Lady Dedlock and went over to him. 'You're wrong about all this,' she said, gripping his arm. 'And as for a funeral – Imogen wouldn't have cared tuppence about a conventional funeral. She wasn't that kind of person.'

'I can't help that. I can't live with this guilt any longer – I really can't. You'll be safe, though,' he said, with a sudden flare of the consideration he had displayed that night. 'I told you: I won't bring you into it. I can quite easily say I was the one who pushed her accidentally down the stairs, that I panicked because I could see how questionable the whole situation would seem to people – a man of my age and a girl of seventeen in a dark cellar together. And whatever they do to me, you're old enough to live on your own now. You're eighteen next week, and in the eyes of the law that's an adult. There's a bit of money put away. Not a fortune, but enough. And some insurances after I've gone. It all comes to you. Oh, and you'd inherit a seat on the Tulliver Scholarship board, of course. That brings a small fee.'

'But – can't you see that if you tell the police what happened, you won't be able to keep me out of it!' cried Olivia, desperately. 'I live here – I was here when it happened. It was term-time – I wasn't away or on holiday or anything. It's impossible that I wouldn't have known about it.'

'The police will take my word that you didn't know,' he said, maddeningly sure of himself. 'I'm a former headteacher at Cresacre School – a member of the Tulliver Scholarship board. I suppose the word of such a man will be worth something.'

'Oh, for God's sake!' said Olivia in exasperation. 'Can't you see that if you do this, you won't be able to keep me out of it. At best they'll think I helped you cover up her death. At worst they'll think I killed her.'

A sudden silence fell, and Gustav looked at her with an expression she had never seen before. The moment lengthened, and then he looked away.

'My mind's made up,' he said. 'That girl – she haunts me. When I sleep she's in my dreams.' His eyes were inward-looking, and it was as if all the flesh had suddenly fallen away from his bones. 'I can't live with it any longer – knowing her body's in this cottage,' he said. 'I'm going to tell the police what happened – a version of what happened, at any rate. An accident, and I was to blame, that will be the story. I've already told you I'll keep you out of it. But they'll excavate the cellar, and they'll bring her out.'

He went back to the book he was pretending to read, as if that was an end to the matter.

Olivia tried to return to *Bleak House*, but his words had lodged in her mind. *I can't live with it any longer . . .*

Perhaps he shouldn't be allowed to live with it. Because perhaps he knew what had really happened that night.

*   *   *

For the next two nights Gustav sat at his desk, scratching away at his papers, frowning, deleting, tearing up one sheet and consigning it to the stove, and starting a fresh page. He's writing a confession, thought Olivia. Oh God, what do I do? Might the police simply regard him as an eccentric – you heard how people frequently confessed to crimes they could not have committed. But surely not more than two years after the crime.

On the third night, Gustav wrote his signature at the foot of a page, added the date, and shuffled the few papers into a large envelope. Was he intending to post them? No, surely he would not do that. But it was looking as if Olivia would have to move quickly.

It was November, and torrential rainstorms were turning the little woodland around the cottage into a lake of mud. Olivia had to slush her way to and from school in ugly, uncomfortable wellingtons. One or two of the girls made hurtful jokes about them.

The morning after Gustav finished writing his confession, Olivia went up to the school as usual, got through the day's lessons somehow, and plodded splashily home in the despised wellingtons at four o'clock. When she let herself into the cottage, the hall was in darkness, although she could see a line of light under the study door. It would not have occurred to Gustav to get up and switch on any other lights so that Olivia did not have to come into an unfriendly, unlit hall. Nor would it have occurred to him to switch on the cooker or look in the fridge or the freezer to see what they could have for supper.

As she took off her raincoat and hung it up to dry, she had the feeling that Infanger Cottage was sliding down into its dark, menacing mood – the mood that had engulfed it on the night Imogen died, and that had still been there on the following night, when Olivia had thought she had heard Imogen trying to get free. That had been the night she had found the silver ring. She had put it away in the little rosewood jewellery box that had belonged to her mother. She did not remember her mother – she did not remember either of her parents because she had only been two at the time of the car crash that killed them. She did not actually have any jewellery to speak of, but the box was a nice thing to have, and it was useful for storing away small private things.

Small private things . . . A silver ring that might have belonged to a murdered girl from two centuries earlier.

And a recording, on an old-fashioned cassette, of a girl's voice singing in a dark cellar.

Olivia had never destroyed the recording of Imogen and what she thought of as Ginevra's song. Gustav had asked her to do so the day after Imogen's death, and Olivia had said she had burned it in the stove. He had accepted that.

But the cassette had not been burned. Olivia had no idea why she had kept it, but she had. Once or twice she had thought she should get rid of it, but she never had. Now it seemed that some instinct might have been at work, prompting her to secretly keep it.

She washed up the supper things, and waited for her uncle to come out of the study. He always went into the sitting room in the evenings now, sitting there with the whisky bottle, watching television until after the ten o'clock news. Here he came now, shuffling his feet a bit as he usually did nowadays, muttering about the badly lit hall, even though he was the one who insisted on dim bulbs. Olivia waited until she heard the creak of the sitting-room door, and then the faint chink of the whisky bottle.

She went back to the kitchen and took a pack of batteries from a cupboard. Then she went into the study, unplugged the cassette player, thrust it under her sweater, and scooted up the stairs to her bedroom.

Gustav had not used the cassette since he finished *The Martyrs,* and Olivia had no idea if it still worked. As she slotted the batteries in, her heard was racing. Was she really going to do this? And then she thought of the written confession in Gustav's own hand, the envelope containing it lying on his desk, and she thought of what would almost certainly happen if he did tell the police everything, and she knew she was certainly going to do it.

She turned the volume to *Low* and pressed the *Play* switch. There was a faint whirr, and then, very softly, Imogen's voice came into the room.

'*Step by measured step the murderers came to me . . .*'

Olivia pressed *Stop* at once. Her hands were shaking and she

wanted to rip the cassette out and tear it to ribbons. She had
not expected to be in the least affected by hearing Imogen's
voice, but she was very affected indeed.

But if the recording upset her so much when she knew it to
be simply a recording, what would hearing it do to a man in
poor health, a man with heart problems; a man who would
believe, even for a few moments, that he was hearing the singing
of a girl whose dead body was only yards away from him?

She made herself wind the tape back and play the whole
thing from the start. This time it was easier, and she played
the recording twice to make sure there were no flaws. There
were not. Imogen had sung the chant twice over, with a brief
pause in between. Altogether it lasted for about six minutes. Was
that long enough for what she wanted? It would have to be.

It seemed to take forever for the clock to reach ten o'clock,
and for the television news to begin. Olivia pretended to watch
it and made one or two ordinary comments so that her uncle
should not think anything was wrong.

At quarter past ten she yawned, and got up, saying she was
ready for bed.

'I'll take a book up with me,' she said. 'Goodnight.'

Gustav nodded and mumbled goodnight, and Olivia went
out, making sure to leave the door slightly ajar so she could
hear him come out. She collected the cassette player from her
bedroom, and went stealthily back down the stairs. The news
was still going on and the sitting-room door was shut. Good.

She drew back the bolt Gustav had fitted to the door after
Imogen died; it scraped against the metal, and Olivia's heart
leapt in case Gustav heard and came out to see what she was
doing. But he did not. He would listen to the weather forecast
at the end, then he would switch off the lights.

The door came open easily enough, and Olivia stepped
through. She was relieved that there was a reasonable overspill
of light from the hall. Leaving the door open, she made a
cautious way down the stone steps, and crouched at the foot,
waiting and listening. It was cold and she kept looking over
her shoulder to make sure nothing stirred in the dark corners.

The minutes stretched out. Had Gustav fallen asleep in his

chair? This did not happen often, but it had happened once or twice. Olivia felt a stab of annoyance, because it would be like her uncle to spoil things by choosing tonight to fall into a whisky-induced slumber.

She heard the ending music for the TV news, and very faintly a voice announcing the weather forecast. The floorboards creaked as Gustav got up and walked across the room, and then the television was switched off. Olivia's heart was pounding, but her hand was firmly on the *Play* switch. In another moment – less than a moment – he would come along the hall . . . Yes. Here he was now. He was passing the hallstand with the oval mirror – would he see that the cellar door was open? In four steps he would turn onto the stairs to go up to his bedroom. Now? Yes, *now!*

It was astonishing and unnerving how the singing echoed and spun around the cellar. The volume was turned to high, but there was hardly any tinniness from the small speakers, hardly anything to tell that this wasn't a living girl, singing.

And Gustav heard it. Olivia heard him gasp and then call out, 'Who's there? Olivia? Where are you?'

His voice was sharp with fear – was he too afraid to look into the cellar? No, he was there now, outlined in the doorway. Still holding the cassette player, Olivia began to walk stealthily back to the wall – *step by measured step, inch by measured inch* – so that it would seem as if the invisible singer was moving away.

She could still see Gustav. He was turning his head from side to side like a questing animal, trying to see through the thick darkness below.

'Olivia?' he said again.

The tape had reached the second recording, and this time Gustav said, 'Imogen?' His voice sounded odd and ragged, as if he might be forcing the word out, and Olivia saw his right hand come up to the left side of his chest. She inched the volume up to its maximum.

'*Breath by measured breath, my life is being cut off from me . . .*

Heartbeat by measured and precious heartbeat, my life is ending . . .'

Then Gustav gasped and seemed to claw the darkness, as if

for air. A choking, retching noise came from his throat, like somebody trying to be sick, then his knees sagged and he crumpled to the ground.

Olivia did not move. She remained seated on the stone floor, near to the bricked-up alcove, for a very long time. She played Imogen's recording several times. Eventually, very distantly, she heard St Chad's clock chime. Midnight. Only then did she get up and go across to the stone steps and make her way upstairs. It was vaguely annoying that she had to step over Gustav's body to get out to the hall. It was good, though, to discover that he had fallen into the hall itself, rather than onto the head of the steps. It meant Olivia could shut the door of the cellar without having to move him.

Everyone was very kind to her. Dreadfully sad for her to lose her uncle, they said – her only family, hadn't he been? Oh, dear. And how shocking that she had found the body herself – that she had actually come downstairs to make breakfast, thinking it was an ordinary day, and had found his body lying there, stiff and cold.

The doctor who came said there would probably have to be a post mortem, but that he was certain it had been a myocardial infarct.

'Heart attack,' he said, as Olivia looked at him in puzzlement. 'Coronary. He was at risk of it with that unstable angina he had.' He patted her arm and said although there would have to be a post mortem, he thought it unlikely that an actual inquest would be needed, because Gustav had had the angina for some time. The cause of death was clear and simple and there was nothing in the least suspicious about it. It was a bad thing to happen, but Olivia would get through it somehow. Life went on.

Life went on, and exams had to be taken, and finances had to be sorted out, and legalities regarding the transfer of Infanger Cottage's ownership to Olivia needed to be dealt with. There would be a tiny income from an annuity that Gustav had purchased some years ago, and there were a couple of insurance policies, the money from which could be carefully invested.

There would be the Tulliver board as well, of course, and the quarterly fee for attending the managing meetings. Olivia would have to be twenty-one to take up the seat, though – the original trust deed specified that.

Still, there was one good thing; since Olivia had just reached her eighteenth birthday, it meant she could inherit the cottage outright.

After the furore died down, Olivia discovered that, although she did not regret what she had done, she was quite sorry about it. It could not be helped, though. She could not have let Gustav tell people the truth about Imogen's death.

She found that she did not mind living on her own, although she would not want it to be for ever. The problem was that she did not dare try selling the cottage, because it would almost certainly result in Imogen's body being found. Anyone who had watched TV crime programmes knew about forensic science and DNA tests and all those other things, and Olivia knew that Imogen would be identified, even after so many years. So she would have to think of another way to get away from this narrow, tedious life, and out into the world.

After a time it occurred to her that if she could find a way to get *The Martyrs* performed, that could be the way. She could tell people she was doing it as a memorial to her uncle. She found this surprisingly easy to do. After a while she believed it.

TWENTY-TWO

Sitting in the study with the coffee she had made for Arabella cooling, Olivia thought, even at this distance, that she had managed Gustav's murder extremely well. She had not wanted to kill him, of course, and she did not want to kill Arabella now. If you are sane, you do not kill anyone. You do not even contemplate it. Olivia knew this perfectly well. But she also knew it was only the really sane people who could recognize when their safety was imperilled and who could find the resolve to kill. And, in such a circumstance, the act of murder could be permissible.

The act of murder.

She had not been down to the cellar since the night of Gustav's death, but now she collected a torch and walked along the hall. The bolt fitted to the door all those years ago was still in place, of course. She expected to find it had rusted into its moorings, but it had not, or not very much. After two attempts, it slid back, and there was a creak as the old timbers moved slightly. Olivia took a deep breath, and pulled the door open.

A soft, sour breath of age and dirt and darkness gusted out, and Olivia flinched, then pulled the door all the way back, and forced herself to step through. So far, so good. She went cautiously down the steps, holding onto the rail with one hand, shining the torch with the other. There was the brief feeling that the darkness swirled like silt in a pond being disturbed, and for a wild moment she thought hands with impossibly elongated fingers reached out. Then she realized that of course it was only the cobwebs, disturbed by the ingress of light and air, floating forwards in the torch's beam.

The outline of the bricked-up alcove was just about visible, but it did not look peculiar. No one would ever realize what was behind the bricks. But both of them were there. Imogen and Ginevra. Walled up in this grim place. Olivia looked at the alcove for a long moment, and then she looked up at the door at the head of the stone steps – the door that had the heavy bolt on the outside. I can't do this, she thought, in sudden panic. I can't see how to do it, and even if I could, I haven't got the strength – the courage.

You did it before . . . You did it twice before . . .

But that was different! cried Olivia, silently.

And again came the whisper deep within her mind.

It was only different because of the music . . . The music was there when you murdered Imogen to stop her from spoiling the plan about The Martyrs *. . . It was there again on the night you murdered Gustav . . . It could be there again to silence Arabella Tallis . . . Use the music, Olivia . . .*

The music. The Lemurrer. It had been sung on the night Imogen died – Olivia had heard Gustav sing it. And it had been there again when Gustav himself died on hearing Imogen's recording.

Imogen's recording.

Olivia had never destroyed the recording or thrown out the old cassette player; they were both still in the rosewood box in her bedroom. Was it possible that the player still worked? She went back up the stone steps, and foraged in the kitchen drawer for batteries – she made sure always to have several sets of them, because the cottage's wiring was so old it was apt to cut out in thunderstorms. There was a pack of batteries that were the right size, and she took them up to her bedroom, and slotted them into the machine.

And then, on an impulse, she took the player down to the cellar and placed it at the top of the steps. Then she pressed *Play*. Incredibly, the machine still worked. Imogen's voice came into the dim cellar, as clear as it had been all those years ago. As clear as it had been on the night she was murdered, and on that other night, much later, when Gustav was murdered.

Inch by measured inch, the light is being shut out . . . The words were taking hold of her mind again. And now she had the second verse, the verse Phineas Fox had read out, the verse he had said was called the murderer's chant.

'*Step by measured step with murderer's tread . . .*
Inch by measured inch with murderer's brain . . .'

Olivia played the recording twice more, and after the third time she knew she could do what had to be done.

'Brick by careful brick with murderer's hands . . .
I make the layers of death . . .'
The Lemurrer was about walling somebody up. But there
were more ways than one of walling up.

It was a quarter to twelve, so she quickly washed the cellar
dust and cobwebs off her hands, then went to stand at the
sitting-room window. From there she could see the forest path
– she would see Arabella coming towards the cottage.

The minutes ticked agonizingly away. Five past twelve. Ten
past. Olivia's stomach was churning with apprehension. But
Arabella had probably only been delayed at the printers. Or by
traffic. Or she might have had a puncture. But on the other
hand, she might be talking to people about what she had found.

No, it was all right. Here she was now, walking jauntily
through the trees, swinging her shoulder bag as she came.

Olivia went to open the front door, forcing a smile, calling
out a greeting.

'How were the printers?'

'Dire. But I got it sorted out, I think. I left that book up at
the school for Phin. No one was around and I didn't want to
interrupt whatever he was doing, so I left it on the kitchen table
for him with a note.'

'Good.' It was actually very good indeed, because clearly
Arabella had not told anyone she was coming here.

Arabella said, 'Are we ready to plumb the depths of the
ancient cellar? It sounds beautifully gothic, doesn't it?'

'Well, I'm ready,' said Olivia. 'I've found a couple of torches,
so we ought to be able to see quite a lot.'

'Good. I've got a torch on my phone – oh, and it's got quite
a good camera as well. If it looks worth it, we could take photos
to show to the Firkins.'

'Let's take a look ourselves first,' said Olivia. 'Oh – you'd
be better to leave your bag up here, because the steps are quite
steep. There's a bit of a rail, but you'll probably need both
hands to hold on to it.'

It felt strange to be following Arabella down the cellar steps,
almost exactly as – over ten years earlier – she had followed
Imogen. Olivia let Arabella get ahead of her, then remained on
the bottom step, shining the torch around.

She had more than half expected Arabella to squeal with delight at such an eerie place, to clasp her hands in an affected, over-the-top way, to say she could absolutely feel the vibes from the past, and even to start spinning one of her stupid stories about the monks.

But Arabella did none of these things. She stood very quietly at the centre of the cellar, looking about her. Once she shivered, and hunched her shoulders as if against something cold, and dug her hands into her pockets.

'It's a remarkable place,' she said, after a moment. She spoke softly, almost as if she did not want to be overheard. 'And I see what your uncle meant about it being part of the old monastery – that arch going across the ceiling – and those alcoves. I wonder what they were for. Shine the torch on them, can you, Livvy? They're somehow eerie, aren't they? But if this really is a bit of the monastery, I think you'd have a really good weapon to use against the planners, Livvy.'

'Do you?' said Olivia, eagerly. 'Let's do those photos, then.'

'Good idea. My phone's in my bag upstairs—'

This was what Olivia had wanted her to say. Before Arabella could move, she said, 'I'll get it. Stay there, and I'll fetch your bag.'

She had moved back up the stairs before Arabella turned to speak, and she was already through the door and into the hall. She slammed the door shut and slid the bolt across. Only then did she realize she was trembling violently.

Arabella's voice came from beyond the door. 'Livvy? What's happened? Where are you?'

The door shuddered. Arabella must be pushing against it. She had found her way to the top of the steps in the dark much faster than Olivia had expected. It was a good thing that she had acted fast and had bolted the door so quickly.

The door shook again. 'Livvy?' shouted Arabella. 'What's going on? This door's stuck or something. Let me out will you? *Livvy!*' This time she hammered much harder against the door, and Olivia glanced nervously at the bolt. It held, but it was an old bolt, and it might easily snap.

'Will you say something?' shouted Arabella. 'I know you can hear me – you must be able to. Listen, if this is some kind of joke, it's not a very funny one. I hate underground places, and it's pitch black down here. Let me out.'

Olivia forced herself to stay calm. The next move was worked out, but she would have to move fast; once it was realized that Arabella was missing, people would search for her. Phin Fox, of course. Harriet Madeley and probably Dilys Davy. At some point the police would be called in, and they would search the school and the immediate grounds. They would certainly come to the cottage to talk to Olivia. She would display concern, of course; she would say that Arabella had called briefly, but she had not seen her since. But they might well want to search the cottage in case there were any clues. And if they saw the cellar door . . . If they heard Arabella yelling . . . Which meant that the cellar door had to be hidden, and in such a way that sounds from beyond it would be blotted out.

Olivia darted along the hall, to the oak blanket box standing near the front door. The box was only about two feet in height, but it was quite wide – certainly wide enough to go across the bottom of the door – and it was solid and heavy. It was not too heavy to move, though; she had tried it earlier, and it had moved a few inches when pushed hard. She pushed harder now, and managed to shunt it along the tiled floor and into the side hall. Once there, it was easy to push it firmly against the lower part of the door. Arabella was still yelling and hammering on the door, but Olivia tried to shut her ears to the sounds.

Now for the next part. The walls of Gustav's study were lined with books, from floor to ceiling – most of the shelves were fixed to the wall, but under the window were three free-standing units, side by side. Gustav had bought them years ago to house his growing collection of books, and had never bothered to have them bolted onto the wall. They were inexpensive DIY units, and although there had not been time to test their weight, there had been time to take quick measurements. Piled on top of the blanket box, they would completely hide the cellar door.

Mind and body working at top speed, Olivia tumbled the books onto two hearthrugs, and folded the edges over, making a couple of makeshift parcels. Then she carried the first shelf-unit out to the hall and lifted it onto the oak chest. The muscles of her shoulders protested, but that could not be given any attention, and she went back to drag the first hearthrug-parcel of books out.

Arabella was still yelling her head off – Olivia thought she ought to feel shocked at some of the language Arabella was using, but it did not really matter. Soon she would not be able to hear Arabella at all.

Once the first batch of books was in place, she carried the other two units out. It was necessary to fetch the small stepladder to lift the third one on top of the other two, and climbing up with the unit in her hands was awkward. The ladder teetered perilously, at one point almost overbalancing, but in the end she managed it. Adrenaline was coursing through her, and she ran back for the remaining books. She had to climb up and down the stepladder several times, but once all the books were in place, she could barely hear Arabella's yells and hammerings. Anyone coming to the cottage, sitting in the study or the sitting room, would certainly not hear them. And anyone glancing casually at these shelves would simply think that a niche off the hall had been utilized to house bookshelves. Even with the hall light switched on, the side hall was dim and shadowy. Nothing would look odd or out of place.

As for Arabella, she might tear her hands and arms to shreds trying to get out, but even if the bolt snapped, she would never be able to force the door open with the weight of all the books and the oak chest holding it in place.

She would be trapped down there until Olivia had worked out how to silence her in a way that would not risk suspicion falling on this cottage or on Olivia herself.

It was not until she had finished tidying up the study that reaction set in. Olivia realized that she was shaking violently, and that every muscle in her body ached. Her shoulders and arms were spasming with pain from all the carrying and lugging back and forth of furniture.

But the only emotion she felt was a deep, exasperated anger. It was infuriating to have been put in this position – to have been forced to act quickly and even clumsily. But she had not been clumsy; she had, in fact, been swift and clever and resourceful. She had bought herself time to work out how best to deal with Arabella, because it was beyond question that

Arabella must be dealt with, and she must be done soon. She could not just be left down there in the cellar.

Or could she?

Again the thought came to her that there were more ways than one of walling somebody up.

Breakfast at Cresacre at half-term was, it seemed, a casual affair. 'The kitchen staff only come in for an hour or so in the afternoon,' Harriet Madeley had said to Phin and Arabella the previous evening. 'There aren't usually many people here at half-term, though, and we tend to forage for ourselves for breakfast and lunch. So just wander along and help yourselves to whatever you want.'

Arabella's wandering and foraging had unearthed eggs and bread, and Phin scrambled the eggs while Arabella made toast.

'Our first breakfast together,' said Arabella, sitting down at the pine table in the corner of the large kitchen. 'It's not quite how I imagined it.'

'It's not quite how I imagined it, either,' said Phin, rather dryly, and forbore to say that his image of the first morning he would spend with Arabella had included details such as a silk-hung bedroom, a balcony looking out onto somewhere like the Aegean Sea or a Florentine fountain where they would eat a hazily romantic breakfast, following on from a hazily romantic night. A school kitchen did not quite match up to that vision. The Black Boar's chintz and oak-beamed dining room would have been just as good as the silk-hung bedroom, in fact.

Dilys Davy came in as they were finishing the eggs and toast, hunted for wholegrain muesli, helped herself to coffee from the percolator, and sat down to hear Arabella's plans for the day.

It appeared that these included visiting Olivia Tulliver; 'Because I ought to see her, and being friendly might help smooth over any angst about Gustav and his opera. Actually, I've got an idea that might help her solve this compulsory purchase thing. After that, I'll head for the printers.'

Drinking his second cup of coffee, Phin suddenly said, 'Miss Davy—'

'You don't need to be so formal.'

'Dilys, where did the Tulliver Scholarship come from? I mean

– when was it created and who set it up? Where did the money come from?'

'I'm not sure of the precise details,' said Dilys, adding milk to the muesli. 'Harriet might know. But I believe it goes back a good couple of hundred years. Some ancestor of Gustav's set it up – he had an interest in educating people who couldn't afford to educate themselves. Bit of a philanthropist, I think.'

'The scholarship sort of evolved over the years,' said Arabella, eagerly. 'I read it up when I was nominated. I thought I'd better know as much as I could because I was positive I'd fluff the whole thing and be flung summarily out on my ear. There's an exam and an interview. That's the part I wore glasses and pinned up my hair for,' she added in an aside to Phin.

'Why an interview? Wasn't it just on academic prowess?'

'They like to make sure people awarded the scholarship won't squander the opportunity,' said Dilys. 'If they think there's any risk of that, they don't make the offer.'

'Is there some kind of . . . of committee or a managing board?'

'Oh, yes. Some solicitors in Worcester run it these days. I think one or two businessmen or accountants are part of it. And Olivia Tulliver, of course; although what she brings to the table, I can't imagine. But the deed specifies that someone from the family – preferably bearing the actual name – has a seat on the board.'

'Might the solicitor agree to see me, do you think? Just to tell me the broad outlines of the scholarship?'

'He probably wouldn't tell you much – you know what legal gentlemen are – but I could try to fix something up.'

'It's worth trying. Research is full of cul-de-sacs, but you don't know they're cul-de-sacs until you've actually been along them. Thanks, Dilys.'

After Arabella left to visit Olivia, Phin took Sister Cecilia and *The Martyrs* with him to the library. He was going to make copious notes from the memoirs, and then to replace Cecilia on her shelf, but for the moment he wanted to finish Gustav's opera. When he had done all that, he would begin the search for Chimaera. Phin was aware of a twist of excitement at this prospect. He thought the Tulliver Scholarship might provide a starting point for the search. If it had come into existence more than two hundred years ago, its creation could have been before the nuns and Chimaera left Cresacre. Phin thought he could see that long-ago Tulliver involving local landowners and dignitaries in his educational scheme, and it was not such a great leap of imagination to think that Sir John Chandos might have been one of those landowners. If the dates coincided, Chimaera could have been drawn in. He had held what, in those days, would have been regarded as a menial position at Chandos House, but if Cecilia could be believed, he had been an opera performer, musically knowledgeable, and, of course, fluent in Italian. Had the Tulliver plan included music or the learning of languages?

He had already searched for Chimaera online, but he had not been surprised when there was nothing to be found. The internet was rich with myths and legends about monstrous creatures known as The Chimera or The Chimaera, most of them with astonishing qualities and a habit of breathing fire and mating with unlikely partners. But Phin assumed that the Chimaera who had come to Cresacre had latched on to the other meaning of the word for his pseudonym – the elusive, phantom, difficult-to-pin-down dream aspect. The thought just hovered as to whether it might actually be a real name, but he thought it unlikely.

He took a chair in the deep bay window of the library. It was a bit of an effort to return to the world Gustav Tulliver had created, because it was by no means a well-plotted or particularly imaginative world. But as Phin read, he started to realize that, although it was nearly all bad (no, not bad, he thought, but certainly mediocre and dull), it had remarkable flashes of what might almost be called brilliance. Like sudden blinding zigzags of lightning against a dark sky.

Several times he caught himself thinking that it was almost as if someone else had had a hand in this opera. But who? Olivia? But Olivia could only have been quite a young teenager when Gustav was writing this. Someone at the school, then? Phin toyed briefly with the idea of one of the teachers – Harriet Madeley, even? – being involved, but neither Harriet or Dilys Davy had seemed to have much of an opinion of Gustav, or much musical knowledge either, so he dismissed this as well.

It was nearly one o'clock, so Phin wandered along to the kitchen, where he found bread rolls and cold ham for a sandwich, which he ate in solitary splendour at the kitchen table. He was considerably cheered up by a large envelope lying on the kitchen table with his name scribbled on it in Arabella's writing. Inside was the book from Olivia Tulliver – *Curious Legends from the Guillotine*. There was a scribbled note from Arabella as well.

'This is from Olivia – I picked it up when I called on her – I knew you'd want to see it ASAP. Am dashing off to printers now, and then to the Firkins – sorry if that sounds rather rustically rude, and I believe they're actually a very respectable family, churchwardens and Chamber of Commerce and whatnot. But they're arranging the marquee for the gala supper, so I need to make sure the tent poles won't collapse halfway through the pudding, and precipitate the illustrious assembly into the mud, making an Eton mess of the entire thing.

'On the subject of food, I'm looking forward to moussaka tonight . . .' This was followed by a smiley face.

Phin smiled back at the face, contemplated the prospect of the moussaka with pleasure, and took the book back to the library. It would probably be as dry as stale bread and as dull as ditchwater was said to be, and it was unlikely to contain anything of any value. But it would be a welcome relief from *The Martyrs*.

But it was neither dry nor dull, and it contained some very startling information indeed. It had been written by one Dr Ernest Quilt, who announced himself as a Fellow of a notable university (he did not specify which one), and who had apparently applied himself to collecting what he declared, with a touch of alliterative whimsy, might be termed gothic gossip from the guillotine.

In a prologue, he recommended that readers wishing to acquaint themselves with this period of history on a more scholarly level could not do better than consult his own book, *A Study of the French Revolution*, published in 1860. Phin thought Dr Quilt could be allowed this modest plug, and read on.

The first couple of chapters did, in fact, provide general details of the French Revolution and the events and the climate that had led up to it. Then came accounts of people ascending the scaffold with varying degrees of courage. These were vaguely interesting, but none of them seemed to have any connection to Sister Cecilia, or to anything contained in Gustav Tulliver's opera.

Then he turned the page to a chapter headed, 'Defiance and Disharmony', and a name in the first sentence leapt off the page.

Chimaera.

Phin realized he was gripping the book tightly, as if he was afraid it might be wrested from his hands. I've found you, he thought. Or, at worst, I've found something that mentions you, and that might give me a lead to discovering more.

The section covered several pages, and although Dr Quilt's narrative hovered between stilted and florid, his words pulled Phin straight back into Sister Cecilia's world.

'Among the extraordinary acts of courage and heroism – also, sad to relate, of abject terror and selfish cowardice,' wrote Dr Quilt, 'the flamboyant defiance and reckless courage of the Italian gentleman known simply as Chimaera must rank as one of the most extraordinary guillotine scenes of all.

'Imagine, if you will, good reader, the scene. A grim fortress – not the Bastille, infamous to us now for its grisly history – but what was, in many ways, a much worse place. It is The Conciergerie of which I now paint word-pictures – the old palace of the Merovingian rulers. The Conciergerie was noble and impressive, but it was also steeped in cruelty and torture.

'It was in a courtyard within this place that the avid and the ghoulish assembled on a bleak morning, to witness a mass execution – not of brigands or of effete royalists who had fed on the downtrodden masses, but the slaughter of a group of ladies. They were religious ladies who had eschewed the world and all its pomps, and who had taken Christ as their saviour and bridegroom. They had travelled to France, so the story goes, to give support and strength to several French nuns who had been imprisoned and who stood under sentence of death. But they, themselves, had been imprisoned, and were now to be executed in accordance with the savage rule of the land at that time. This was a rule which ruthlessly suppressed the Catholic Church, and forced priests and nuns to swear the oath of allegiance.

'There is a faint, additional layer of the story which I also set down. It is no more than the lightest gossamer thread, but it is told that one of the sisters came to France with a secret purpose – that she was not there to help the French nuns, but to incite Catholics to rise against the new regime. The whisper is that she was a member of an ancient Catholic family that had long been a thorn in the side of the Bourbon House for many decades.

'I have been unable to verify this, but I set it down for the reader's interest and consideration, since there were many strange underground threads and plots at that time, and religion has ever been a source of conspiracy. I do not even know if she existed, that unknown, never-named nun.'

She did exist, thought Phin. Her name was Cecilia. He glanced at the small, leather-bound book, as if nodding towards a close friend.

'It is unclear as to exactly how many nuns were brought out to the guillotine that morning,' wrote Dr Quilt. 'Some reports say it was ten, others insist it was the round dozen, but other sources say it was fewer. It was a small group, though, that is certain. They had been herded into cells – barbarous treatment for such well-meaning souls – but the nun who was suspected of plotting religious incitement had been locked inside the Bonbec Tower, the dread Salle de la Question. The torture room.

'Signor Chimaera, who for reasons I have not been able to uncover had shepherded the ladies into France, seems to have been held in very light captivity. It is fairly obvious that his imprisonment was not intended to be other than transient, and that he was not under sentence of death. I speculate that this was partly because no actual crime could be laid at his door, but more because he was known as a man of the people – as a man of the raffish world of the theatre. He had been one of the motley crew: a troubador, a strolling player, a man who peddled his art and who, while he had known success, would also have known penury and difficulties. These are all things with which the revolutionaries would have had sympathy.'

Phin thought that although the revolutionaries might have had sympathy with this description, Chimaera himself would have been horrified to have been so portrayed.

'Chimaera was permitted to take meals with the turnkeys, and I set out below a description of a night he appears to have spent getting inebriated with them and the events that ensued. The translation is my own – Signor Chimaera wrote in his native Italian. He also wrote sometime after the event, so he had ample time to refine and embellish his tale. I have taken leave to edit some of the earthier phrases the turnkeys seem to have used, and wish to extend my thanks to the Bibliothèque Municipale de Grenoble, who gave kind permission for the fragment to be used. They have a truly splendid collection of letters and memorabilia, largely culled from the libraries of many of France's great historians and chroniclers. Sadly, I could find no other reference to Signor Chimaera.'

Phin thought: I'm about to read Chimaera's own words – or, at least, his words as translated and diluted by Ernest Quilt. How remarkable. He turned the page.

TWENTY-THREE

Chimaera's diary

I was a privileged prisoner in The Conciergerie. I know this because I was told it within days of my being taken there. It wasn't until much later that I found out how widely the treatment of prisoners varied, and how reasonable my own imprisonment actually was.

Kindly treatment (I use the description advisedly) frequently depended on the personal wealth of the individual in The Conciergerie, and on his (or her) willingness to hand out bribes. Sometimes, though, it was simply a matter of the whims of the gaolers themselves – which is what happened in my own case, and which was fortunate for me, since I had little wealth to hand out; in fact I had none at all. Visitors were sometimes allowed in, but that depended on the mood of whichever doorkeeper was on duty.

I was deeply thankful to a merciful god – perhaps the god who looks kindly upon men of the theatre – that even though I was in captivity, the grim blade of the guillotine did not hover over me. It hovered over others, though, and that knowledge was a constant, nagging nightmare. I spent many hours devising a plan to rescue those prisoners with whom I had travelled to France.

My room was unquestionably a cell, but there were far worse cells – I would go so far as to call them dungeons – in that ancient prison-house. I had a stove, a bed, a chair and a desk, and a window overlooking a small courtyard. After only a few hours I realized the window overlooked the privies.

That first night I struck up a cautious friendship with one of the turnkeys – a person by the name of Godefroy. He had heard of me! Here was a piece of good fortune, because I saw at once that this might be very useful in devising a plan, not only for my own freedom, but for the freedom of those others who had come here with me.

I will also admit that I found it gratifying to be recognized in such a way – and in such a place. It was perhaps not surprising, though, because my fame had been widespread.

It transpired that Godefroy, who spoke a smattering of Italian – had worked as a carpenter in the Teatro della Pergola, which was where he had picked up his knowledge of my language. He had seen me there, although I did feel it unfortunate that he had apparently witnessed that last argument with the dastardly Fredo – the encounter which made it necessary for me to skulk out of the theatre, and then out of the country, in fear of my life. However, it turned out that Godefroy had not liked Fredo and had strongly disapproved of his sister, Juliette. He said he was a man who believed in the sanctity of women; that Juliette had been a modern incarnation of the Whore of Babylon, and that clearly I had been tempted by a harlot.

Two nights later he brought a bottle of wine for us to share, and then his fellow turnkey appeared, bearing another bottle of wine, and a dish containing *pot au feu* which he suggested we share. It was nice to have some civilized company, he said; most of the other prisoners were aristos, so bound up with their self-importance that they would not even give you the time of day. At the other end of the scale were the thieves and murderers, who would give you the time of day, but who would slit your throat after doing so in order to steal your last *sou*.

There had been a guillotining that morning, and the man had seized for himself several of the victims' garments – it seems this is a perquisite of the gaolers in this place. He proposed that he and Godefroy examine the spoils to consider which of the garments they could keep. This I found ghoulish in the extreme, but of course I did not say so, and after we had eaten, the two of them began to try on the various clothes, capering around, attempting steps of various elaborate dances, and aping the prancing walk of the aristos.

I was not surprised when, mid-caper, so to speak, the second turnkey, who was still wearing the unfortunate aristo's breeches, suddenly excused himself to visit the privy. I had partaken very lightly indeed of the *pot au feu*, which I suspected to be dubious after the first mouthful, but the turnkey had eaten two large helpings. He made a very hasty way to the privy and, as he did so, a plan began to form in my mind.

The turnkey presently reappeared, in no good order; in fact he looked distinctly unwell, and he had not buttoned up his breeches – which might have been due to the complicated nature of the unfamiliar garment, but might just as easily have been due to his wanting to leave the noisome privy as quickly as he could.

A man who has such an indisposition, and, moreoever, whose breeches are unfastened, is at a considerable disadvantage. As the sufferer continued to struggle with the complicated lacing, I poured him another glass of wine, and said, bracingly, '*Dio mio*, in these garments, you have the air of gentlemen, both of you.' Addressing the unbuttoned one, I said, 'As for you, my friend, I can certainly believe the story that is circulating around the prison of how you succeeded in that seduction. Francine, did you call her? You remember her, I am sure. The word is that you said she was the easiest glove you had ever known – on or off.'

This line, of course, was stolen from William Shakespeare, but I felt it fitted the situation.

At the sound of the name Francine, Godefroy looked up sharply. I had used the name deliberately, of course; not for nothing had I listened to the tales of Godefroy's family.

'A very inventive lady she sounds,' I went on, gaily. 'A room at the top of a house in the Rue de la Huchette was where it all happened, did I hear that correctly? A view towards Notre Dame, and an apothecary's shop on the ground floor – my word, that must have been useful, in light of the rash you discovered the next day.'

(As well as listening to Godefrey's stories about his family, I had also committed to memory the details of where they had lived. His garrulity had turned out to be most useful.)

Godefroy sprang up, as if a red-hot poker had been rammed up his nether regions. 'What?' he shrieked. 'Francine, did you say? And the Rue de la Huchette?'

'Well, yes, I did say that, but—' (Never have I portrayed embarrassed bewilderment so well.)

'You ravished my sister!' yelled Godefroy, and launched himself on the hapless and semi-breechless turnkey.

I had been almost sure the ploy would work. A man who believes his sister – or his wife or daughter – to have been violated, turns like a snarling hellcat on the ravisher. Especially if he is a man who considers women to be vessels of extreme sanctity and believes those who stray are painted whores and harlots.

'I called you my friend!' shrieked Godefroy. 'And all the while . . . you were doing that to my sister . . . Oh, you are a rampant lecher – a flesh-mongering warthog, and you shall pay for what you did! I shall cut off your bull's pizzle and roast it in that very pot on the stove!'

I threw what fuel I could onto the fire, by saying, with anxious helpfulness, 'I am so sorry – I spoke without thinking. But the description I was given was so vivid – such a lively sounding girl. Oh dear. I had no idea she was your sister, Godefroy.'

Godefroy scarcely heard me. He was emitting eldritch shrieks of fury; his eyes glittered wildly in the light from the candles, and his hair stood up around his head like the twisting snakes of a male Medusa. The unbuttoned turnkey had got to his feet, and he was clutching the pilfered breeches around him, but as he backed away he let go of them, and they promptly slid down around his ankles. He tripped backwards, and Godefroy fell on him, seizing his head between his hands, and banging it hard against the stone floor, then grasping the knife that had been used to slice the bread, and brandishing it in a way that suggested he really was about to inflict the gruesome punishment he had threatened moments earlier.

That was when it happened. The turnkey reared up, reaching for Godefroy's throat, and as he did so, the knife Godefroy was wielding slid straight into the man's gullet. Blood poured out, soaking his chest and soaking into Godefroy's clothing as well. For an extraordinary moment the two men stayed motionless, clutching one another in a parody of a lover's embrace, staring into one another's eyes. Then there was a dreadful, choking, bubbling sound, and the turnkey fell back on the floor, his eyes rolled up so that only the whites showed.

Godefroy recoiled, pushing his hands out in front of him as if to push away what had happened.

I said, in a voice of extreme horror, 'What have you done?' And the horror was genuine, for that had been no part of my plan. An argument between the two men, certainly, providing a situation in which I would have had a chance to seize their keys, and to take my opportunity to get out and find my friends.

I bent over the man – careful to avoid the gore that splattered his front and that had dripped onto the floor as well. It was abundantly clear to me, as it would have been to anyone, that he was dead.

As I stood up, Godefroy clutched my arm. He said, 'Help me. If he's found – if I'm found covered with his blood . . .' He broke off, shuddering. His face was pale – it was very nearly green – and for a moment I thought he was about to add to the mess on the floor by being sick.

'They'll execute me,' he said. 'It will be the guillotine – and it will be a bad guillotining, for, believe me, Chimaera, those executioners have their ways.'

I was still staring in horror at the dead turnkey, but at these words, I said, 'What do you mean?'

'The actual blade is weighted,' he said. 'Heavily weighted, so that it falls with great force straight down onto the victim, very fast indeed. But if the lighter weights are substituted, or even removed altogether . . .' A shrug.

'That's surely never done?'

'If they take a dislike to a person, yes, it is,' he said. 'I have seen it.'

'But – do they dislike you?'

'Oh yes.' He nodded, then went on nodding, as if he had forgotten how to stop. 'They jeer at me and make fun of me. I have strict beliefs, you see. I drink very little and I do not carouse or have the women. So I am an oddity. But this one . . .' He indicated the lifeless body at our feet, 'This one is very popular indeed. So, as his murderer, I would be hated and they would turn against me. For me, they would remove the weights altogether, and the blade would fall little by little – a series of jerks – at a snail's pace. And I should be beheaded *slowly*. It's a fate I would not wish on any man. I have seen it done.'

There was a very bad moment when I found myself considering whether I might be suspected of the crime, but Godefroy's garments were covered in blood – and mine were not. And it was not very likely that I, a lone prisoner, would have been able to overcome and kill a gaoler with that gaoler's companion there with him.

So I said, with decision, 'We must hide him. And we must do it so well that the body won't be found, and people will simply think he's gone away of his own accord.'

'How do we hide him, though? Where?' Godefroy looked frantically around the cell, as if expecting to see a convenient place for the hiding of – or the complete disposal of – the body.

I started to say, 'I don't know,' but even as I said it, I could see, through the cell window, the low brick buildings that constituted the privies. Privies, by their very nature, will always have a cesspit somewhere. My mind shuddered – my stomach did, as well – but I said, 'I think there is a way we could do it. You'll need my help, and I'll give it. But in return you must promise to help me.'

He stared at me, then he said, 'You want me to leave the door of your cell unlocked.'

'Yes, I do, but more than that, I want you to take me to the cells holding the ladies who came in here with me.'

He said, 'The nuns? The English sisters?'

'Yes.'

'That would be very dangerous indeed. They're mostly imprisoned in one room, I'm told, except for one of them.'

'Which one?'

'She's called Sister Cecilia. She's being held in a separate cell on her own.'

'Why?'

He moved nearer, glancing over his shoulder, almost in comedic fashion. In a low voice, he said, 'She's not just charged with refusing to take the oath of allegiance. She's a member of a family who have caused incitement. They have an ancient piece of music that was used as part of a brutal old ritual – used by papists against non-papists. You understand my meaning?'

'Oh, yes.'

'She's accused of planning incitement against the Republic. Of travelling here to call together other nuns – monks and priests also. She's a State prisoner, and she's being held in a very secure part of The Conciergerie.'

'Yes. I see. But you know where that is? And the cell of the other sisters?'

'I could most likely find it,' he said, and his eyes went nervously to the prone figure of the other turnkey. 'They're all under sentence of death – they all refused the oath.' He frowned, as if weighing up the situation, then he said, 'I'll do it. If you help me to get rid of . . . to hide the murder, afterwards I'll take you to the death cells.'

'All right,' I said. 'First of all, we'll deal with the dead man. Help me lift him.'

'But what about the clothes?' said Godfrey. 'He's covered with blood and so am I. So are you. That will be noticed.'

'I can put on his clothes,' I said, indicating where the turnkey had left them in a corner of the cell before he donned the garments of the guillotined aristo. 'And you can regain your own.' These were in the other corner. 'There's no blood on those,' I said. 'And we'll take the things you were wearing with us and throw them into the cess pit at the same time.'

'But he'll have to remain in those things he's got on now,' objected Godefroy. 'And they're wet with blood – we'll get smothered in it.' There was a note of panic in his voice.

I looked about me, then seized a blanket from my bed. 'We'll wrap this around him,' I said. 'We'll have to be careful how we hold him, but as long as we only touch the actual blanket and not the bloodstained garments underneath it we should be all right.'

He grudgingly allowed this to be a solution, and we donned the discarded clothes. I had to force myself to put on the dead man's garments, but once I had done so I thought I would pass for a turnkey well enough. We tucked the blanket around the man as tightly as we could, almost making a cloak of it, then we propped him up on his feet, holding him between us, his arms draped around our own shoulders. Then we half-dragged him across the yard below my window. Anyone watching us would have seen merely three gaolers, one of them considerably the worse for drink, wending an erratic way back to their quarters. To add to the picture, I began singing a bawdy song (it was one that the naughty Juliette had taught me, as a matter of fact). I thought this was rather an artistic touch, but I had only got as far as the first chorus when Godefroy told me very sharply to hush, because we did not want to attract attention.

The cesspit was behind the privy block. It had its own small building, and when Godefroy unlatched the door, the stench was appalling. At the centre of the building was what looked like a well with a massive slab of dark stone, or possibly even iron, covering it.

We propped the turnkey against one wall, and addressed ourselves to the task of pushing back the lid. It took considerable strength, and when finally it yielded, the stink that came up was like a blow to the face. I gasped and recoiled, one hand over my mouth, fighting not to be actually sick. Godefroy, unfortunately, was not so stoic, and there were several moments of what I can only describe as wet splatterings, followed by shuddering gasps.

At that point I almost abandoned the entire thing, but I could not think of a better plan and, even after such a long time, I still cannot. Between us, we lifted the turnkey onto the lip of the disgusting cesspit – what people say about dead weight proved true on that night. I muttered a prayer for the poor man, and then I muttered a second prayer that there would be no splash when the body hit what must lie down there.

We tumbled it over the edge, and stepped hastily back.

There was not a splash, but there was the sense of something having been churned up, and the stench was momentarily even worse. But thankfully, Godefroy was not sick a second time, and I managed to throw in the other bloodstained things, and then we dragged the cover back in place.

'Well,' I said, 'I have kept my part of the bargain. Now it is for you to keep your part.' I confess I suffered several qualms, for it was entirely possible that he would simply force me back to my cell and deny everything. But I had judged him a man of honour, and I thought he would honour our arrangement.

And so he did, but it was a skewed honouring.

'The death cell,' he said, not looking at me, 'is on the other side of the palace.'

'I don't care if it takes us the entire night to get to it.'

'It probably wouldn't make any difference if we could fly there within a few moments,' he said. 'Because you're already too late to free them. At daybreak tomorrow they're being guillotined.'

TWENTY-FOUR

Phin, reading this to the end of the page, was aware of an illogical stab of panic. Move quickly, he found himself saying to Chimaera. Run like the Furies to those cells, and get them to safety in time. All of them – romantic little Anne-Marie, and brisk, down-to-earth Agnes. Mother Superior who passed round brandy for seasickness. And Cecilia. Please rescue Cecilia.

He turned the page almost fearfully, not wanting to find that Chimaera, with his eye for dramatic effect, had ended his account there – or that Ernest Quilt had found an incomplete fragment of document, and that this was all there was. He did, though, spare a moment's thought for the scene in which the two turnkeys had tried on victims' clothes and pranced around the cell. It was the scene he had enjoyed in Gustav Tulliver's opera, almost to the letter. Clearly Gustav had read this, and had taken that scene and dropped it into his opera. Phin thought he could not blame him. It was lively and as black humour went it was very good indeed. It was, in fact, one of the better scenes of *The Martyrs*.

He turned the page, and saw with relief that there was more to come.

Chimaera's diary

Walking through the passages and stone rooms of The Conciergerie is an experience that will stay with me for the rest of my life. More – it will *haunt* me for the rest of my life.

I know now that there are many strange tales about The Conciergerie – some inspiring, some tragic, and some downright incredible. But on that night, all I knew and felt were layers of misery. All I saw were dank, dark dungeons in the bowels of that once-glittering royal palace – dungeons which housed hopeless, helpless prisoners and which stank to high heaven.

It felt as if we traversed miles of corridors and stairs and echoing halls for what was left of that night. Sometimes Godefroy's own keys fitted locks, at others he merely nodded to a turnkey and we were allowed through. I was not questioned, and I think that wearing the dead turnkey's clothes allowed me to blend in well. I adopted a surly expression and a shambling walk, which I felt to be in character.

After a while I began to suspect that Godefroy did not know where the death cells were, and that he was simply trying one part of the palace after another. This was not so very surprising; the prison was vast and complex, and turnkeys each had their own individual sections to guard. But Cecilia and the others were to be executed at daybreak, and I began to feel as if a giant invisible clock was ticking away the minutes of their lives while we fumbled around in the shadows. Godefroy refused to ask any of the turnkeys for directions to the death cells for fear of discovery. I did not dare ask them for fear of being unmasked.

And then, just as we were walking along a passage that rippled with greenish light from the river below, we heard loud noises ahead of us. Godefroy stopped, then said, 'I think we've found what we want. If we go to the end of this passageway and a little to the right, we will be at the death cells.'

'How do you know?'

'Listen,' he said. And then I heard it. And, macabrely, it was a sound I had heard many times before – a sound that in the past had filled me with nervous delight and soaring energy, but that now brought only cold dread.

It was the sound of a crowd of people eagerly anticipating entertainment. But it was not the warm, affectionate, benign sounds of men and women awaiting a stage performance. These were shrill female screeches, shrieked jeers and raucous laughter. The *tricoteuses* – the street and market women who unfailingly gathered at the site of executions – were assembled, waiting to witness the latest guillotinings.

We went forward, and came out into a large inner courtyard. A faint light was starting to streak the sky, showing up the rows of rough wooden seats arranged in a semi-circle. People were already seated on them. They were mostly women, many of whom were sharing out items of food, and who were shouting to children (for there were actually children present!) to sit still and watch what happened to traitors and aristos and papists. There were men present as well – not as many, and in the main they were quieter, but somehow surly. They furtively passed bottles of what I assumed was wine to one another. Seeing all that, I felt a surge of such savage hatred I cannot write it down, even after so long.

At the centre of the courtyard was a monstrous shape. Two massive upright posts, surmounted by a crossbeam at the top. Steel within the crossbeam glinted as the sky lightened, indicating a cruelly sharp blade.

The guillotine.

As I started forward, Godefroy said, suddenly, 'We're too late.'

'No, there's still time to get to them—'

But even as I spoke, a bell chimed somewhere deep within the old palace, and massive double doors at the far side of the square were flung wide. Through them marched men in the scarlet and blue uniform of the National Guard of France. They stood along the walls, and then the prisoners were led out. They were all there, and they all walked defiantly. Cecilia was the last; she walked immediately behind the mother superior, and she was so pale her skin looked almost transparent. But her eyes glowed with fervour, and I saw she was determined to maintain a show of bravery to the very end. I wanted to sit down and weep. Then I wanted to sprint across the square and snatch her in my arms and take her – and the others – to peace and safety and comfort. To perfumed baths and silken robes and lavish food and wine . . .

There was a dreadful practised efficiency in the way the guards lined up the nuns. The sky was growing lighter almost by the minute, and the guillotine's shadow fell sharply across them. The bell chimed a single, sonorous note, and the executioner made his entrance – as grandiose an entrance as ever I made myself. He wore the traditional black covering of his face, and he mounted the platform of the guillotine, and stood waiting.

They had placed little Anne-Marie first in the line. The youngest to go first – and perhaps there was a smidgeon of humanity in the action, in that it saved her the torment of watching the others die ahead of her.

I was frantic. I could think of nothing to do to help them, and the knowledge was like a spade in my bowels. Unless—

Unless I could create a diversion that might allow them to break free – to run from the courtyard, back into the palace, and try to hide from their killers. It was not as wild an idea as it might seem: the palace was an absolute maze, through which a person might wander for hours – perhaps even days – undiscovered.

But what diversion could I create? For a dreadful moment my mind was blank, and then it came to me. Of course! I ran forward, zigzagging across the courtyard, and leapt onto the edge of the scaffold itself. There was a stir of astonishment, and the guards made to seize me, but before they could do anything, at the top of my lungs I began to sing the 'Ça Ira', the emblematic anthem of the revolutionaries. I sang the aggressive lyrics the *sans-culottes* had written, and I hurled the words defiantly into the grim square.

Ah! It'll be fine, It'll be fine, It'll be fine
Aristocrats to the lamp-post
Ah! It'll be fine, It'll be fine, It'll be fine
The aristocrats, we'll hang them!

There was a massive cheer, and the crowd leapt to their feet and joined in.

Ah! ça ira, ça ira, ça ira
Les aristocrates à la lanterne!
Ah! ça ira, ça ira, ça ira
Les aristocrates on les pendra!
Si on n' les pend pas
On les rompra
Si on n' les rompt pas
On les brûlera!

As the singing and the cheering reverberated around the square, I bounded across the guillotine's platform, using it like a stage, and from the corner of my eye I saw Cecilia and Mother Superior grasp Anne-Marie's arm and push her back through the still-open door, into the dimness of the palace. Could they get a second one out? Yes – Sister Agnes, dear, capable soul, had been pushed after Anne-Marie.

But the guards had slammed the immense doors shut now, and they had ranged themselves around the nuns, rifles at the ready. Across their heads, Cecilia looked at me very directly. She nodded, and even at that distance her eyes held such gratitude, it is with me to this day.

I was grabbed by two of the guards, and pulled from the guillotine, but it was almost comradely – one even sketched a half-salute to me. I was a man of the people, one of their own, a true revolutionary. I might be chastised, but I was as sure as I could be that I would not be executed.

But then they began to drag the nuns forward. As they did so, one of them – I could not see which one – began to sing. The others at once joined with her, their voices mingling. I recognized what they sang – how could I, an Italian, brought up as a Catholic, not recognize the 'Veni Creator Spiritus' – 'Come Creator Spirit' – the heartbreakingly beautiful ninth-century Latin hymn that invokes the Holy Spirit.

For the second time, the guards were taken by surprise, and I realized that the nuns had seized on my action, and they were creating their own diversion. To give Anne-Marie and Agnes the chance to get away? Yes, for there was certainly no chance now of anyone else fleeing from the courtyard.

The nun who had been standing behind Anne-Marie was seized. It was Sister Gabrielle. She was pushed onto the guillotine's platform, and her head was forced into the wooden section immediately below the monstrous blade. The executioner stepped forward, reaching for the chain that would operate the blade.

The watches fell silent, and through a welter of emotions I looked up and saw with deep thankfulness that the weights – the heavy appendages that would ensure the blade fell swiftly – were in place.

When the executioner released the blade it came down in a dizzying blur. There was the sickening sound of it striking home, and then the soft thud of the severed head dropping into the basket placed directly beneath. The crowd cheered like wild things, and I shuddered and fought down a spasm of nausea.

But the incredible thing – the thing that still causes the hairs to rise on my arms and on the back of my neck, is that the remaining nuns continued the 'Veni'.

I could not see the face of the next one to be pulled forward, but again there was the rapid, blurred descent of the blade, and again came the sickening sound of the head falling. And again the chant continued. But now it was quieter. Now there were fewer voices to sing.

One by one the nuns were pulled forward, and one by one they submitted to the blade. And each time, the voices singing the 'Veni' diminished.

I kept looking towards the doors through which Anne-Marie and Sister Agnes had fled, expecting with every moment to see them dragged out, but the doors stayed shut, and there was no sign of them.

And now there were only two voices ringing out – Mother Superior and Cecilia. I saw the two women embrace – I saw Mother Superior trace the sign of the cross on Cecilia's brow.

Mother Superior ascended the scaffold slowly, waving aside the guards. She was calm and serene and, as she lay down beneath the blade, a lump formed in my throat. And again the blade came down.

Now there was only Cecilia's lone voice ringing out across the courtyard. But as she was pulled forward, a small set of steps was carried out and placed on one side of the platform. The executioner climbed onto the steps, and reached up to the guillotine's mechanism. A murmur of what might have been puzzlement went through the crowd. I stared at the hooded man, trying to understand what he was doing. Was something wrong with the mechanism? Was this another opportunity that might be seized and turned to advantage? And then I saw, with sick horror, that he was adjusting a particular part of the mechanism. He had removed two of the weights. What had Godefroy said happened in that instance? *The blade would fall little by little – a series of jerks – at a snail's pace. A slow beheading . . .*

For the first time I saw Cecilia's resolve falter. She looked at me, and – oh, dear God, if ever I saw entreaty in another human being's eyes—

The executioner had returned to the platform, and Cecilia was thrust down onto the platform, her head pushed into the wooden boards beneath the blade. At any moment the executioner would release the mechanism, and once the blade began its grotesquely slow descent, it could not be stopped.

They say extreme danger lends extraordinary strength. It did so for me, then. I was not being held very firmly, and I jerked myself free and bounded onto the steps. How I did not knock them over I have no idea, but I did not, and as the executioner's hands began to reach for the blade's mechanism, I reached upwards. Grasping the chain operating the weights with both hands, I swung my whole weight on it. In that same instant, the blade's mechanism was released, and the blade came down.

And because my weight had replaced the machine's weights, the blade came down as fast as the blink of an eye – faster than the skip of a heartbeat. I half fell onto the platform, murmuring a prayer of thanksgiving.'

TWENTY-FIVE

t was several moments before Phin could turn the page, but when he did he was relieved to see that Chimaera had added a final piece.

'Looking back, although I did not realize it at the time, that was the moment – that crowded moment on the guillotine platform – when my opera was born properly; not the half-hearted, half-formed idea I had been playing with for some time, but a real story. I saw an imprisoned heroine inside The Conciergerie, and a dashing hero running to her rescue. A band of rebels, colourfully garbed, singing rousing choruses; even scenes in which they scaled the walls of the battlements, and encountered boiling oil poured down over them by the guards trying to repel them.

'The finale must be the heroine and her faithful friends, singing as they walked to their deaths. Their voices would gradually diminish as each one ascended the scaffold. Each time there would be the whoosh of the blade coming down. Finally, the heroine would be left alone and her lone voice would ring out until the blade silenced it for ever.'

Beneath this, Dr Quilt had written, 'A remarkable narrative, as I am sure readers will agree. I found in another account a list of names of prisoners who were freed – in the main they were people who had been identified as supporters of the Revolution, some on the flimsiest of reasons. Among those names was that of Signor Chimaera.

'As to the opera of which he writes so eloquently, I have been unable to find any indication as to whether it was actually ever created. However, my studies do not take me into musical areas.'

The chapter ended there, and Phin put down the book. His mind felt as if it had been wrenched open, and force-filled with information, but two facts stood out very clearly.

Cecilia and the others had died on the guillotine that morning, but at least they had died swiftly and mercifully and bravely. But what had happened to the two who had managed to run from that courtyard? Had they got away? Phin dared to hope they had, because someone had brought Cecilia's journal back to England and back to Cresacre.

Gustav Tulliver had clearly found – and used much of – Chimaera's story for *The Martyrs*. But had he also found Chimaera's actual opera? Phin could easily believe that it was Chimaera's hand – a 'fine Italian hand' in truth – that shone through *The Martyrs* with those erratic flashes of brilliance. But that was to assume the opera had been written. Had Chimaera got any further than the gratifying image of himself as a celebrated composer?

Still, there it was. He had found out what had happened to Cecilia and the nuns, and he knew a bit more about the Lemurrer.

But what about the other players in the story? Sir John Chandos, for instance. And what was it that Olivia Tulliver had been so anxious to hide? 'I could never sell Infanger Cottage,' she had said. 'I would never dare.'

Infanger Cottage. The book about guillotine legends had been there, and it was there that Gustav had written *The Martyrs*. It was there that Phin had seen the letter from Cecilia. Might there be more to be found in that cottage?

It was five o'clock, and almost dark. Phin had no idea where Arabella was, or what was happening about returning to the Black Boar, but he would phone the Black Boar later and find out. His car was parked outside, so clearly Arabella had returned from the visit to the printers.

He replaced *The Martyrs* in its wrapping, and set off down the drive.

Olivia had thought that once she had the bookshelves and the books in place, they would smother all sounds from the cellar. But they did not, not completely. At intervals she could hear Arabella shouting to be let out, and a number of times she heard her banging on the door. The sounds brought back memories of Imogen and those nights immediately after Imogen's death when Olivia had lain awake and believed she could hear her crying and tapping to get out. She could almost hear her voice now.

She sat in the study, her hands pressed over her ears. It was getting dark; shadows huddled in the corners of the room. Switching on lights would chase them away. But lights would let people know she was here. If she had to creep around in darkness for the rest of her life, no one must be allowed inside this cottage . . .

If only Arabella would stop hammering on the cellar door, Olivia would be able to think what to do. If only the memory of Imogen's voice would go away . . .

Then, through the blurred sounds, came a sudden imperative knocking at the front door. Olivia's heart leapt in panic, because she could not allow anyone in here. It would be all right, though; whoever it was would see that the cottage was in darkness and would go away. All she had to do was remain silent and still.

She waited, her heart pounding. Arabella was shouting again – Olivia could hear her, very faintly. Could the sounds be heard outside? No, the cottage was old and solid.

The knocking on the door stopped, and Olivia drew in a sigh of relief. But even as she did so, the phone rang. The answerphone was on, as it always was, and she heard her own message asking the caller please to leave a message. She waited, then heard Phineas Fox's voice.

'Olivia, it's Phin Fox. I seem to have called when you were out, but I wanted to return *The Martyrs*. I'd like to talk to you about it – and about the book with the guillotine legends. Could you give me a call when you get this, please? Thanks.'

This was something that could be dealt with. Olivia would phone at some point and arrange to meet Phin at the Black Boar to collect the manuscript. It would have to be tomorrow, or even the next day, though; she did not dare leave the cottage until she had dealt with Arabella. (How? demanded her mind yet again. How are you going to deal with her?)

Phin Fox had not gone away. Olivia suddenly realized he was walking along the side of the cottage – she could hear his footsteps crunching on the dry old bracken. A shape moved across the study window, and she shrank back in her chair. A face pressed against the glass, and a hand came up, as if trying to see if anyone was in the room. But Phin would not be able to see into the dark room. All Olivia had to do was stay still and quiet and wait for him to go away.

Phin had enjoyed the short walk to Infanger Cottage. It was growing dark, but he took his time, liking the thought that this was where Cecilia and the nuns must have walked on that last night to meet Chimaera, and to wait for the mail coach. After he turned onto the tree-lined forest path that led to the cottage, he expected to see lights ahead, but there were none. Perhaps there was a timeswitch for an outside light, and it had not come on. Or perhaps Olivia was in hiding from the council planners and their threatened compulsory purchase order. It was sad to think of her on her own out here in the dark house, afraid to open the door or answer the phone.

He supposed he should have phoned before coming, but he went up to the door anyway, plied the old-fashioned knocker, and waited. Nothing. Phin stepped back, looking up at the bedroom windows, which were all in darkness, then felt for his phone, and found Olivia's number. It rang three or four times, then went to voicemail, so he left a message asking her to call him.

But as he pocketed the phone, he remembered how nervous she had been of opening the door, so after a moment he went around to the back of the house. If she was in, he might be able to reassure her as to who he was.

The rear of Infanger Cottage was very dark indeed, because the trees grew right up to it. But there was a small paved area, and a door that looked as if it opened onto a kitchen. There was no sign that anyone was inside, though – no lights or sounds of a television or a radio, or of crockery being clattered in the kitchen for an evening meal. No sounds at all . . .

Or were there? They were faint, but it sounded as if someone was shouting for help. Had Olivia been taken ill and been unable to get to a phone? Phin tried the kitchen door, which was locked, then sped around to the front of the house. The door there was locked as well. He looked about him, trying to decide if a 999 call was warranted, then, as the shouting came again, he thought he would get inside and see what was wrong first. He picked

up a large stone from the side of the house, and smashed it
against the larger of the windows, then knocked out the glass
shards, pulling the sleeve of his jacket over his hand to protect
it. Then he climbed through.

The room was in darkness, and it felt as if Infanger Cottage
was listening and waiting. Phin called out.

'Hello? Olivia? It's me – Phin Fox. Is something wrong? Olivia
– are you ill? I heard shouting – someone calling for help.'

There was no response, but Phin had the strong impression
that the cottage was not empty. Was someone watching him?
He began to think he would be better to call 999 after all, but
he went through to the hall, found a light switch, and called
out again. The shouting came again, and, puzzled, and increasingly concerned, Phin went into the study where he had
discussed *The Martyrs* with Olivia – had it only been yesterday?
He switched on the light and looked round. Nothing. There was
something different, though. What was it? He frowned, trying
to recall the layout of the room. There were certainly a great
many books, but there had been more yesterday, hadn't there?
There had been shelves on the window wall, almost the entire
length of the wall itself. Phin had looked along them while
Olivia was making tea, and had noticed that there were a number
of titles on opera and the French Revolution.

He tried the chilly, old-fashioned kitchen next. Again, nothing.
Or was there? Had there been a creak of sound, as if someone
had trodden on old floorboards? Should he go up to the
bedrooms? But the cries were not coming from up there – they
were coming from this level of the cottage. But where? Was it
Olivia who was calling for help? Where on earth was she?

He went back to the hall. The feeling of being watched was
stronger, and he reached for his phone, because clearly there
was something very wrong here, and he would have to call 999
after all. But then the shouting came again, and now it was
definitely nearer. Somewhere in this hall? No, there was a side
hall leading off, and it sounded as if the cries were coming
from there.

Phin went to investigate. The side hall was quite wide, but
it did not seem to lead anywhere. The floor was uneven, as if
this might be part of an older structure, and there was what

looked like an old-fashioned cloaks cupboard halfway along. Phin was about to open this, when his attention was caught by bookshelves at the far end. They were set on top of an oak chest and they almost reached up to the ceiling. It seemed an odd place for bookshelves, and as he stepped closer, he saw that several of the books were familiar – in fact, quite a number of them were familiar from yesterday's visit. Why would Olivia move them out here? And why would you put bookshelves against a wall in a dingy and dark passage unless—

Unless there was something behind them that you wanted to conceal.

Instinct took over and, without stopping to question or analyse what he was doing, Phin began to sweep the books from the shelves. He had only cleared two shelves when he saw what lay behind.

A door. An old door, set back into a stone wall and with a bolt across one side.

The shouting came again – clearer now, and Phin called back.

'Hold on – you're going to be all right. I'm getting to you—'

'Cellar. Locked in.'

It was much louder now, and Phin said, 'Yes, I know. I've found it.'

'Phin?' said the voice, and Phin felt as if he had been punched in the ribs.

'Arabella?'

'Who else?' said Arabella. 'Oh, Phin, she locked me in – Olivia. I don't know why.' Her voice sounded dry and hoarse, and Phin realized with a stab of anguish that she must have been shouting for help for a long time.

He said, 'Hold on, Arabella. I'm nearly with you.'

No longer bothering to move the books with any care, he tumbled them onto the floor, then dragged away the shelves.

'What are you doing?' came Arabella's voice.

'Moving furniture – she's barricaded you in. God knows why. But I'm almost there.'

'Phin, be careful . . . I think she's mad . . .'

Phin was pushing the oak chest out of the way. The door was clear now, and he reached for the bolt. But as he did so a sound came from behind him, and he spun round.

The cupboard door behind him was slowly opening from inside. There was a movement from inside it, then Olivia Tulliver, her hair falling across her eyes, her eyes wild and empty of all sanity, stood there. She pushed the door even wider, so that it spanned three-quarters of the width of the hall, partly blocking the way to the main hall. In one hand she held a large knife with a glinting blade.

Phin looked frantically around him, but he already knew he was in a cul-de-sac. To get out he had to push the cupboard door back into place. And he had to get past Olivia.

In a voice that sent icy prickles across the back of Phin's neck, Olivia said, 'So you've found her. I didn't think you would. I didn't want anyone to find her. Did you know I was watching you?'

Phin just said, 'Yes, I've found her,' and, hoping Olivia did not suddenly attack him, pulled the bolt across and opened the door. Arabella must have been standing immediately behind it, because she almost fell out. She was dishevelled and her face was streaked with dust, but her voice was blessedly normal. Phin pulled her against him. 'Are you all right?'

'Never better,' said Arabella, huskily. There was a fair attempt at a smile. 'But never more pleased to see you.'

In the same unnatural voice, Olivia said, 'Did you find them while you were down there? Or hear them? They still cry to get out – even after so long. I hear them sometimes at night. I hear them tapping and clawing at the wall, as well.'

'I didn't find anything,' said Arabella, rather uncertainly. 'I heard Phin, though – well, I heard someone outside the cellar, so I yelled to be let out. But I didn't know you'd piled all those books and things against the door,' said Arabella. 'Why did you do that? And for goodness' sake, Livvy, put down that bloody knife – you look like Lady Macbeth in the sleep-walking scene.'

For a moment Phin thought this typically Arabella speech might break the strangeness and bring Olivia back to sanity. He thought if there was even a flicker of uncertainty in Olivia's eyes, he would take the chance and rush at her, trusting to luck that – with Arabella's help – he could twist the knife out of her hands. But Arabella was clearly still shaky, and if Phin misjudged it, Olivia would knife him without compunction, then turn her attention to Arabella.

But Olivia said, 'I won't put it down.' In a soft, confiding voice, she said, 'I have to protect myself. One night they crept up the stairs and stood outside my door. I heard them very clearly. So I always have a weapon to hand.'

Arabella said, 'Let's go into the study, and you can explain what this is all about.'

'No,' said Olivia. 'Instead, I'll show you what's down there.' She looked at the cellar door, which was still partly open.

Phin had been stealthily reaching into his jacket for his phone, hoping he could tap out 999 without Olivia realizing, but she moved closer.

'If you're trying to make a phone call, don't,' she said. 'Put the phone down there on the floor.' The knife glinted threateningly, and Phin frowned, then did as requested. Olivia picked the phone up and slid it into the pocket of her jeans.

'Now, both of you down into the cellar,' she said.

'So you can lock us in?' said Phin, angrily.

'Yes, that's right. I'm sorry. I haven't got any choice,' said Olivia.

'But you can't possibly hope no one will find us,' he said.

'Why not? No one ever comes here.'

'What about the purchase order?' put in Arabella. 'The planners?'

'After a few days,' said Olivia, 'you'll both be as near dead as makes no difference, and I can hide your bodies.'

'How? Olivia, hiding bodies isn't so easy.'

'You'd be surprised.' She took a step nearer. 'Didn't you notice the brickwork while you were down there, Arabella? The alcove at the far end, near where the old window was?'

'I didn't notice anything, because it was pitch dark,' said Arabella.

But Phin had guessed Olivia's meaning, and he said, sharply, 'That's absurd. You can't possibly build up a wall.'

'I can. I did it before,' she said. 'I know what to do. And everything's to hand. There are bricks still in the old washhouse. I can get mortar from a DIY shop. I was there when it was done last time – I helped.'

Phin thought: dear God, she really is mad. I'll have to rush her and take the chance; but before he could do anything, Arabella suddenly said, 'All right, Livvy. We'll do what you want. I'll go down first. Phin you follow me.'

She sent him a very direct look, then turned and went back through the cellar door. Phin stared after her, and thought: does she really want me to follow her though, or is she trying to send me a message? Has she got an idea for getting away? But he could not see how, because surely once he and Arabella were both in the cellar, Olivia would slam the door, bolt it, and probably replace the bookshelves to hide the cellar's existence. He was about to lunge forward and trust to luck that he could knock the knife from Olivia's hand, when, from the depths of the old cellar, came the sound of a girl's voice singing. Phin had no idea who it was – it was certainly not Arabella. But the song was unmistakable. It was the Lemurrer.

Olivia gave a shriek of fury. 'You bitch!' she shouted. 'That's Imogen's recording! I didn't mean to leave it down there – I only played it to get strength from it! But I know what it is – I was there when it was recorded!'

The chanting stopped, and there was a curious scrape of sound, as if the tape had jumped or become tangled. The moment seemed to freeze, and Olivia turned her head towards the cellar door again.

It's now or never, thought Phin. Now, while she's off-balance. But even as he moved, the chant started again. And this time it was different. It was fainter, but it was also deeper. It's a man's voice, thought Phin, startled.

'*Step by measured step with murderer's tread . . .*
Inch by measured inch with murderer's brain . . .
Brick by careful brick with murderer's hands . . .
I make the layers of death . . .
Quenching the light . . . stopping the heart . . .
Murderer's hands making the layers of death . . .'

The last few words were only just audible – and they faded like a dying echo. But Olivia was already running towards the cellar door, the knife raised. Phin dodged back to avoid it, then tried to grab her arm from behind.

'That's not the recording,' she shouted, and there was such

terror in her voice that Phin flinched. 'Who is it who's down there? *Who's there?*'

She was at the head of the cellar steps now, and as Phin reached for her arms, he caught a glimpse of a figure walking across the dim cellar below. The Lemurrer words about murderer's hands seemed to whisper on the darkness.

Olivia screamed again, and pitched forward, and Phin snatched at her to save her from falling. It was too late, though. She had already begun to fall, and she went down the steps in a whirling tumble.

As Phin scrambled after her, the dim movement below came again, then melted into the shadows of a far corner. From the other side of the cellar, Arabella said, 'Get your phone from her pocket and call an ambulance, Phin.'

'I think it's too late, though,' said Phin, bending down over the still figure to get the phone. As he tapped out 999, he said, 'I think she's broken her neck.'

Olivia had broken her neck and it was certainly too late.

'Tragic accident by the look of it,' said the police sergeant who had been summoned, and who was taking notes.

'That's exactly what it is,' said Arabella. 'She was a lonely, unhappy person, and I'm very sorry indeed about what happened.'

'What did happen exactly? We'll need to put together statements.'

Phin glanced at Arabella, then said, 'Olivia wanted us to look at the old cellar. Arabella had had an idea that it might have some historic interest – that it might help Olivia to fight a compulsory purchase order.'

'Ah, that'll be the road widening,' he said. 'I've heard about that.'

'We were looking at the cellar,' said Arabella. 'I was down there already, and Phin was up here, and Livvy – Olivia – was going down the steps because I'd found a brick arch that looked medieval, so we were going to photograph it.'

'But she was behaving a bit oddly,' said Phin. 'She thought – she seemed to think someone else was down there.' He quenched the odd half-memory of a figure whisking across the dimness – a figure who had certainly not been Arabella.

'She seemed to think there might be people trapped in the cellar,' said Arabella, carefully. 'But . . .'

She broke off, and Phin said, 'But it seemed to both of us that she was a bit . . . well, unbalanced. Perhaps living out here on her own for so long—'

'Enough to send anyone a bit odd,' said the sergeant, looking about him. 'You said she missed her footing on the stairs?'

'Yes. It was as simple as that. They're very steep steps – as you saw.'

'I did. There'll need to be a post mortem,' he said. 'And, unfortunately, an inquest. You'll most likely be asked to give evidence – is that all right?'

'Perfectly.'

He shut his notebook and prepared to leave. 'Strange old place this, isn't it? Been here a good long time, of course. What're those heaps of books lying around in the hall?'

'No idea. We thought she'd been sorting out books for the charity shop,' said Arabella.

'Her uncle's old books, that'd be,' said the sergeant. 'Sad if that family's ended – there's been a Tulliver here for a very long time; all the way back to the first one who set up the scholarship.'

Phin pounced on this. 'Sergeant, it sounds as if you're a local man. Do you know anything about the Tulliver Scholarship? Its origins, I mean?'

'A bit. Not much. They say some chap who worked for the old Chandos estate started it all. Hauled himself up by his bootstraps, as the saying goes. Married the squire's daughter. Give me a minute and I'll remember his name.' He frowned, and Phin waited.

'Got it!' said the sergeant, triumphantly. 'Dan, that was it. Dan Tulliver.'

Phin said, softly, 'Dan. Of course.'

'Word is that Dan and his lady lived here for a while,' said the sergeant. 'Her family disowned her for marrying a workman. Different times then, of course. Don't know where he got the money for the scholarship. They did a good deal to help children from poorer homes, though. Dan Tulliver's remembered with a lot of respect in this area.'

*   *   *

'I'm glad we agreed to keep the full story quiet,' said Phin, after the sergeant had left, having extracted a promise that they would slam the door of the cottage when they left, and present themselves at the police station on the morrow to sign their statements.

'I'm glad, as well,' said Arabella. 'She certainly intended to put me – and then you – out of the way. But she was clearly mad, and it would have . . . somehow it would have spoiled the scholarship and all it stands for if the truth had become known.'

Phin said, slowly, 'She talked about bricking things up – about hearing something crying and tapping to get out.' He shuddered.

'And she knew about that recording – she said she was there when it was made.' Arabella looked at him. 'Is there something down there, Phin? Something that needs to be – um – uncovered? Because there was that girl who vanished – Imogen. I found a silver ring in this cottage that I think was hers.'

'I think there is something,' said Phin, slowly. 'I think it might go back quite a long way, though.' His mind had gone back to the letter from Sister Cecilia to Alberic Firkin, over two hundred years earlier.

'Sir John wishes unequivocally for privacy for that piece of land,' she had written. And then, 'I must stress that no work of any kind whatseover or wheresoever is to be carried out on Infanger Cottage . . . Nor is it ever to be sold, but is to remain in its present state of ownership . . .'

'Do we report that part of it?' Arabella was saying.

'I don't think we need to,' said Phin, thoughtfully. 'Now that Olivia's dead, I should think the compulsory purchase order will go ahead. Infanger Cottage will be demolished, and any secrets down there will come to light. And I think I'd rather it happened like that – at somebody else's hands – than for us to tell the police what really happened here this afternoon. Because if there is anything down there, it wouldn't automatically be laid at Olivia's door.'

Arabella got out of her chair and came over to put her arms around him. 'You're a very nice person,' she said. 'Might we still be able to have that moussaka, do you suppose?'

'I hope so.' He smiled at her. 'But before I can focus on moussaka, there are a couple of things I need to finish here.'

'Part of the Lemurrer? And connected to Dan Tulliver? That name meant something to you, didn't it?'

'Yes. I'll tell you properly later. Where's that recording?'

'I put it in the kitchen. Out of sight. I found it when I was looking for a way out of the cellar, and I accidentally pressed Play – it was as black as pitch in that cellar, you know. When that singing started, I nearly had a fit, because it was the eeriest thing I'd ever heard. But then I thought if I ramped up the volume, somebody might hear it and realize I was locked in. I'd shouted so much my voice was starting to crack,' she said. 'Don't look like that, Phin – my voice didn't crack and I did get out. You got me out. Knight on white charger and all that.'

Phin took a deep breath, and said, 'I need to listen to that recording again.'

They sat at the kitchen table. Phin played the recording twice.

'It's different,' said Arabella, her elbows on the table, staring at the machine. 'That last time I played it – when I was hoping it would spook Olivia and give you a chance to grab her – there was something else on it. Something I hadn't heard until then. At the time I thought the tape had got tangled or something, and sort of wound back on itself. But right at the end it sounded as if a man was chanting.'

'Yes.'

'The tape's all right, though. And the voice isn't there now, is it?'

'No.' Phin thought he would explain later about the murderer's chant and Cecilia's diary. He did not think he would ever be able to explain how a man's voice had got onto this recording.

He removed the cassette and dropped it in his pocket. He could probably transfer it to an MP3 or something similar, but he already knew he would destroy it.

'You said there were two things?' said Arabella. 'What's the other?'

'I want to plunder Gustav Tulliver's books.' As Arabella looked startled, he said, 'I want to see if he had anything that might have been composed by an Italian opera performer at the end of the eighteenth century.'

'All right. I'll help, shall I? What was the name of this Italian opera performer?'

'Chimaera.'

As they began the search, Phin told himself that Chimaera had almost certainly never written his planned opera. The reality was that Gustav Tulliver had read Ernest Quilt's book and had lifted the scene about the turnkeys trying on victims' clothes. He had read Cecilia's journal in the school library, and lifted the Lemurrer as well. Which meant that expecting to find an opera score from the 1790s by the flamboyant Chimaera was the longest shot in the world.

And then, from the hall where she was kneeling amongst the tumbled books, Arabella said, 'Phin. I've found it.'

And there it was. Battered, faded, dog-eared, edges curling, pages foxed. But with the name of Cesare Chimaera clear on the outside.

Phin was almost afraid to open it. He had the absurd feeling that it might dissolve like cobwebs – that it was little more than chimerical itself. At some vague level of his mind he was deeply grateful to Arabella, who had gone quietly out of the room and left him alone.

Inside the cover, folded into four, cracked and almost splitting with age, but with the words still perfectly clear, was a single sheet, handwritten and adorned with many flourishes. The address at the top was Milan, and the date was 1796.

My very dear Gina and Dan,

I send my felicitations on your marriage – I am, of course, desolate that I did not win your hand for myself, Gina, but I know Dan will make you very happy.

In this package is my opera. When you read the dedication you will understand.

It's to be staged for the first time here in Milan, and it would give me the greatest pleasure if you could travel here and attend the first performance. It will be a glittering occasion, and you would be guests of honour.

Whether you come or not, I want you to know that I am arranging for the proceeds from that performance to be sent to you for the education fund that you want to create.

I was glad to hear that the other parcel I sent reached you safely. On the night before she died, the lady we knew as Sister Cecilia gave her diaries to a young novice called Anne-Marie – one of the two nuns who escaped from The Conciergerie. Anne-Marie later gave the diaries to me, and I knew they rightfully belonged to you, Gina. If you feel they could ever be made public in some form, some-where in the future, I think that would be a very good thing.

Cecilia talked to me during the journey to France – she told me about a great love she had known almost twenty years ago.

'I expected him to repudiate me when I told him I was to have a child,' she said. 'I should have known him better. He arranged it so that the birth would happen in secrecy within the convent, and he arranged that his wife would visit cousins for a long stay, and return to Cresacre with a child. That satisfied her – I would not speak against her, and I will only say she was not a warm-natured or affect-ionate lady. To appear to have given him a child vindicated that for her. Mother Superior and Sister Agnes knew the truth. They never judged or admonished. Perhaps they had known that kind of love in their own lives, in their youth . . . They all lied for me, and they spun the deceit. Everyone kept the secret.'

So there it is, my dearest Gina.
With my best love to you,
Cesare Chimaera

Phin sat looking at this for a very long time, then he opened the opera manuscript. On the first page was a dedication:

'To the memory of Ginevra – the lady who was known to Cresacre Convent and to the world as Sister Cecilia. And for her daughter, Gina Chandos.'

Everyone in Cresacre turned out to attend the funeral of Olivia Tulliver. It was sad that the last of the family had gone, but the name would live on in the scholarship, of course.

Miss Madeley and Miss Davy and all the teachers from the school were present, along with a good number of pupils who had known Olivia. Arabella Tallis was there, of course – a very lively girl she had been in her time. Everyone had liked her, though. She was with a young man who was supposed to have helped with part of the bicentenary work. It was nice to see people from the wider world coming to be part of the celebrations. Everyone was looking forward to the various events.

After the service, somebody was heard to murmur that the local planners had already begun preparations for demolishing Infanger Cottage. A pity to lose such an old piece of Cresacre's past, but the place had been tumbling down for years, of course. It would be good to have that bit of ground properly excavated.

PRESS RELEASE

Cresacre School are delighted to announce that the culmination of their bicentenary celebrations next month will be the performance of a recently discovered opera, written by a famous Italian singer from the eighteenth century, and composed by him as a memorial to the nuns who lived and worked at – and later vanished from – Cresacre Convent.

The opera is a moving and atmospheric work, which details the remarkable story of a local half-French nun who travelled to France at the height of the French Revolution, and lost her life on the guillotine.

The opera will be staged in the school grounds, and it will be a memorable occasion.

The opera is titled *Ginevra*.